P9-CML-276
WEST GEORGIA REGIONAL LIBRARY SYSTEM

STREETS
OF
FIRE

Also by Thomas H. Cook

Flesh and Blood
Sacrificial Ground
Blood Innocents
The Orchids
Tabernacle
Elena

STREETS OF FIRE

Thomas H. Cook

G. P. PUTNAM'S SONS NEW YORK

G. P. Putnam's Sons
Publishers Since 1838
200 Madison Avenue
New York, NY 10016

Published simultaneously in Canada

Library of Congress Cataloging-in-Publication Data

Cook, Thomas H.
Streets of fire / Thomas H. Cook.
p. cm.
I. Title.
PS3553.O55465S77 1989
813'.54—dc19 89-3682 CIP
ISBN 0-399-13490-5

Printed in the United States of America
1 2 3 4 5 6 7 8 9 10

For Robert West and
J. William Broadway
—Southerners—
and
for
Fatima Goldman
—citizen of her own land—

The author would like to thank his students, friends and colleagues at Packer Collegiate Institute for their kindness, stimulation and support.

Birmingham, Alabama
May 1963

One

Ben scribbled into his notebook, balancing the radio mike on his shoulder while he wrote.

"I'm on surveillance," he said irritably, "and King's still talking." He glanced up toward the church. He could see the crowd shifting excitedly as the people stood packed together tightly on its wide cement steps.

"I got to pull you off for a minute," the dispatcher said. "We got a body down in that old football field off Twenty-third Street."

"Twenty-third Street?" Ben asked. "Why don't you let the Langleys handle it?" He kept his pencil poised on the page.

"Nobody knows where they are," the dispatcher told him. "You know what it's like at headquarters."

Ben knew exactly what it was like, and as he looked out toward the crowded cement steps of the Sixteenth Street Baptist Church, they reminded him of the chaos which had overtaken police headquarters as well since the demonstrations had begun. It was a hot May. The jails were already choked with everything from dentists and lawyers to half-blind old women, and every man in the department was on full duty to deal with them. Both uniformed patrolmen and plainclothes detectives slept in their cars or in makeshift dormitories which the department had set up in the hallways and storage rooms of City Hall. Sometimes, as Ben had already complained, the whole place looked more like a skid-row flophouse than a government building.

"You read me, Ben?" the dispatcher asked.

"Yeah, all right," Ben said drearily.

"That old football field off Twenty-third," the dispatcher reminded him.

"I'll get there as soon as I can," Ben said. He clicked off the radio, snapped it back into its cradle and hit the ignition. The engine groaned fitfully in the steamy air, and several of the people who stood crowded together around the old brick church glanced toward him, their brown eyes watching him silently as he pulled away.

It took no more than a few minutes for him to make it all the way across town to the football field. There was almost no traffic, and scarcely anyone on the streets. It was as if all the people who lived in the downtown black district of the city had been drained out of it, so that the whole area now existed only in the ghostly remains of deserted streets and buildings. The sloping wooden porches were empty, along with the weedy yards and plain dirt driveways of the railroad shanties that lined the bumpy, potted streets. Occasionally, an old man would nod to him as he drove past, or a little half-naked child might wave, but it was as if all the rest of them, nearly the whole black population, had been funneled into the few concentrated blocks of the downtown business district. That was where they gathered to block traffic or seize lunch counters or simply march in long dark lines, silently, determinedly, either staring straight ahead or glancing about apprehensively, as if looking for that menacing white tank the Chief had brought in to control the situation.

The football field at Twenty-third Street was as deserted as the surrounding neighborhood. Not even a single uniformed patrolman had been sent on ahead to stand guard over the body, and Ben guessed that someone had simply stumbled onto it and anonymously called in what he'd found, and that everyone but himself, now suddenly appointed as the lone centurion of Bearmatch, had already been far too busy to bother with such a little thing.

He shook his head irritably, then took off his hat and wiped the sweat from his forehead with the sleeve of his jacket. Across the field, the noonday sun struck piercingly toward him, and in its bright glare, he could see only the hazy outline of the goalpost which stood shakily at the opposite end of the field.

For a moment he thought that it might all be a hoax, a prank call, or just some old wino whose imagination had gotten away from him. But as he made his way across the littered ground, his eyes slowly began to focus on what looked like a small dark ball perched motionlessly on the bare red ground beneath the goalpost. As he continued forward, the ball became a tiny fist thrusting out of the dirt, its fingers curled toward the palm as if trying to grab for something which still hung in the air above the ground.

For a little while, he stood casually beside the gray sidepost, listening to the way it creaked and groaned in the summer wind. Bits of paper blew across the empty field, and when one of them came to rest against the small black hand, he nudged it free with the toe of his shoe. Far in the distance, he could hear the sound of sirens, and he knew that things had begun to heat up downtown. But they seemed far away compared to the whisper of the wind through the trees around him, the enveloping heat and the small curled hand that reached toward him from the dust.

Luther arrived a few minutes later, walking briskly up the field, his belly spilling in a doughy mass over his broad black belt.

"What you got, Sergeant?" he asked breathlessly as he stepped into the dusty oval beneath the goalpost.

"Looks like a child," Ben answered.

Luther groaned uncomfortably as he squatted down beside the hand. Instinctively, he reached out to touch the fingers, then drew back. "What do you think, boy or girl?"

"I don't know."

Luther got to his feet. "Well, they're sending a couple of diggers," he said. "They should be here anytime." He pulled a pack of cigarettes from his jacket and offered one to Ben.

Ben took one and lit it.

"Don't guess they's a public john around here," Luther said as he glanced up and down the field.

"I don't think so," Ben said.

Luther's eyes shifted back down to the small black hand. He shook his head wearily. "Bad time for this to happen." He looked at Ben. "They'll try to make a race thing out of it. That's why they sent me down here, to make sure it was just a plain old Bearmatch killing, nothing to do with white folks, trash or otherwise." He blew three large smoke rings into the air, poking a stubby finger through the center of each one as it drifted upward. "Can you do that, Ben?"

Ben shook his head.

Luther smiled. "Trick my daddy taught me." He did it again, then leaned lazily against the unsteady goalpost. "Where were you when you got the call?"

"Surveillance."

"Anybody in particular?"

"King."

Luther looked surprised. "Who put you on him?"

"The Chief."

"He didn't mention it to me," Luther said.

"He just caught me in the lobby this morning," Ben said.

Luther nodded. "Yeah, that's the way he works sometimes," he said, his voice faintly disgruntled. "Once in a while it screws things up down the line."

Ben nodded, and for a moment the two of them stood in silence. Across the field, under the opposite goalpost, an old Negro man watched them cautiously, his ancient face half-hidden beneath a tattered straw hat.

"Place is empty," Luther said, after a moment. "I guess everybody's downtown raising Cain."

"Did it start up yet?" Ben asked.

"Oh, yeah," Luther said. "Same old thing so far. But they say the shit's really going to hit the fan before long." He laughed. "You know, Ben, it's a good time to be working Bearmatch. Hell, the whole place's deserted." His eyes widened. "Down by the tracks, they say even the shothouses are empty." He laughed again. "Can you imagine that, even the whores and gamblers and such as that are out marching."

Ben had never seen the fabled shothouses of Bearmatch, but he had heard of them for years. They seemed to swim in a hazy yellow light to the beat of honky-tonk pianos, and when they were spoken of by people who'd been in them, it was with a kind of distant, dreadful awe, as if life took on a wholly different texture as it moved southward toward the tracks. Down by the tangled iron railyard where the empty freight cars baked in the summer heat, you could hear the steady wail of the blues as it came from the shothouses and honky-tonks of Bearmatch. It was a slow, pulsing rhythm that seemed to sway languidly in the air, and Ben had often heard it during the years he'd worked as a young railroad guard. While searching the cars or patrolling the crisscrossed tracks, he'd glanced more than once toward the huge shantytown that spread out just beyond the high storm fence of the railyard. That was where it came from, the bluesy horns, sudden laughter and occasional gunfire. Others among the guards had sometimes ventured into it, looking for whiskey or a card game or a woman, but Ben had kept his distance in this, as in almost everything else.

Luther gave the tiny hand another peremptory glance. "They kill their kids down here," he said dully. "Sometimes the daddy does it. Sometimes it's the mama." He took another drag on the cigarette, then tossed the butt out into the field. "Just ask anybody who's been on the tour. They'll tell you. It's real different down here. Not the same world we live in at all." He shook his head despairingly. "Course, the Black Cat boys like it. But they's something wrong with those two." He tapped the side of his head with a single, crooked finger. "You know, up here."

Ben dug his toe into the dirt and made a ragged circle. "They should have a crew down here by now," he said impatiently. "It's not right, leaving her in the dirt like this." He stepped away from the body and began pacing about, his eyes locked on the ground.

"What are you doing?" Luther asked after a moment.

"Just looking around," Ben said. He walked a little further out into the field, his eyes still searching the tufts of brownish grass. Up ahead he could see the old man, still leaning against the post, his thin dark arms hugging to it loosely.

"For what?" Luther asked.

Ben shrugged. "Whatever you can find around a body."

Luther laughed. "You're lucky to even have a body. Most of the time they just load it onto a freight car, or take it out of town and dump it in the river." He shrugged. "Either way, it's gone from our jurisdiction. It floats into the next county or rolls into the next state. Then it's their problem."

Ben continued to move outward slowly, his eyes latching onto bottle caps or scraps of paper. When he looked up again, the old man had vanished, and there was nothing but the naked post to block his view of the adjoining street.

Luther lit another cigarette and tossed the match onto the ground. "It's the ones that keep on living that's our problem." He glanced toward the distant buildings of downtown. "They're probably piling into the lunch counter at Woolworth's this very minute." He looked at Ben knowingly. "That's why you're lucky to be on the Bearmatch patrol right now, Ben. I'd rather be anywhere as downtown for the next few days."

Ben eyed the last nondescript bit of paper which littered the ground at his feet, then looked up and saw two patrolmen approach from the opposite side of the field, both of them lugging shovels ponderously through the sweltering air.

"They're going to love this," Luther said. He glanced down at the hand. "Well, least it's fresh. The smell won't kill them."

The two patrolmen began digging only a few minutes later. Slowly, they unearthed the body of a young girl. She was clothed in a flowered dress, white socks and dark-brown buckled shoes. Her eyes, nose and hair were matted with clay, and a single trickle of dried blood ran down from the left side of her mouth.

"Turn her over," Ben said gently, after the body had been placed faceup beside the makeshift grave.

One of the patrolmen bent down and eased the body over, then stood up and stepped away.

Ben knelt down beside the body. The buttons at the back of the dress were missing, and its white collar had flipped open, exposing the dark back. A single shot had been fired into the base of the skull.

"Looks like a twenty-two," Luther said as he stepped over and stared down at the body. He circled slowly around to the other side. "Have to be a twenty-two," he said. "Anything else would have blown the top of her head off." He scratched his chin slowly. "Pull her dress up."

Ben looked up at him sharply. "What?"

"Pull her dress up," Luther repeated matter-of-factly.

Ben did not move.

Luther looked at him oddly. "What's the matter with you?"

Ben snapped to attention. "Nothing," he said quickly. Then he slowly lifted the girl's skirt. She was completely naked underneath it, and her private parts were raw and reddened. Tiny crusts of dried blood clung to barely visible tufts of black hair.

"See what I mean?" Luther asked confidently.

Ben nodded.

Luther's eyes scanned the girl softly. "Pretty little thing," he said quietly. "It's a shame she'll never grow up." He looked at the two patrolmen. "How come you boys didn't bring a stretcher?"

The two young patrolmen glanced awkwardly at each other.

"Ah, never mind," Luther said with a frustrated wave of his hand. "You got blankets in your car. We can load her up in one of them."

The two patrolmen took off immediately, and Luther laughed as he watched them trot off down the field. "They stay dumb for a long time, don't they, Ben?" he asked.

Ben did not answer. He continued to stare at the small girl who lay in the dirt beside him.

Luther's eyes narrowed pointedly as he glanced right and left. "Well, I don't see no burning crosses, do you, Ben?"

Ben looked up. "What?"

"Burning crosses," Luther repeated loudly. "Or anything else that would make this look like some kind of race killing."

Ben shook his head slowly. "No, I don't see anything like that."

Luther drew a small camera from his jacket pocket. "Don't usually do this," he said, "but things being the way they are right now . . ." He waved Ben away from the body. "Stand back," he said. "Let me get a quick shot."

Ben stepped away from the body.

Luther snapped the picture and headed off down the field.

"Wait a second," Ben said.

Luther turned back to him quickly. "Find something?"

"No," Ben told him quietly. Then he took the hem of the girl's skirt and drew it gently back over her slender brown legs.

Two

Missing Persons had never been more than a single metal desk stuck in the back corner of the detective bullpen. Along with a lot of general paperwork, it was Sammy McCorkindale's private beat, and as Ben shifted around the chaos of crowded desks and chairs, he could see McCorkindale's enormous frame in the distance. He was leaning back in a padded swivel chair, his eyes scanning the sports page of the *Birmingham News.*

"How you doing, Ben?" he asked as Ben stepped up to his desk. He smiled. "I'm surprised you're not working the demonstrations, like everybody else."

"I was on surveillance," Ben said, "but they pulled me off of it."

"Why's that?"

"Somebody found a little girl. Dead. Shot in the head."

"Where is she now?"

"The diggers picked her up," Ben said. "I guess she's at the morgue by now."

"Find any identification?"

"Nothing around her," Ben said. "That's why I thought I'd check with you."

McCorkindale ponderously eased himself forward and rooted his elbows on the top of his desk. "Well, run the description by me."

"I'd say between eleven and maybe thirteen years old," Ben said.

McCorkindale took a pencil and paper and began to write it down. "Did you see any distinguishing features?" he asked. "You know—warts, moles?"

Ben shook his head.

"All right, go on," McCorkindale said.

"Dressed in a white, flowered dress, brown shoes, white socks," Ben continued.

"Okay, good," McCorkindale said, his eyes following the pencil as its tip scurried across the page.

"The body was found buried in a football field off Twenty-third."

The flight of the pencil slowed.

"Negro," Ben said.

The pencil stopped. McCorkindale looked up. "You mean you got a little Bearmatch girl here?" he asked.

"That's right."

The pencil dropped to the desk and McCorkindale leaned back in his chair. "How old are you, Ben? Thirty-five? Forty?"

"Thirty-seven."

"And been living in Birmingham all that time?"

Ben nodded.

"Then you ought to know better than to waste your time on something like this," McCorkindale said. "They don't report nobody missing out of Bearmatch." He squinted slightly. "Haven't you ever done that beat before?"

"No."

McCorkindale shook his head. "Well, they got their own way of doing things over there. They don't come to us with things like this. Right or wrong, they just don't do it. If they got somebody missing, they do all the looking their own selves."

"This little girl had to belong to somebody," Ben said.

"I'm not saying she didn't," McCorkindale said. "But it just don't matter, because they don't report nobody missing out of Bearmatch." He shifted slightly in his chair, and the springs groaned painfully under his weight. "How long you been a detective, Ben?"

"Five years."

McCorkindale smiled confidently. "Well, I been sitting at this same desk for a lot longer than that, and they's not ever been a missing person report done for anybody out of Bearmatch. They just don't come to us with stuff like that."

"Well, it's not just a missing person," Ben said, "it's a murder case. Somebody shot this little girl in the back of the head."

McCorkindale smiled slyly. "And the guy that did it, he'll end up with a bullet in his own head, too, or sliced up like a big old piece of pie." He laughed quietly. "Don't worry, Ben, he won't get away with killing no little girl. Not in Bearmatch. Not for a minute.

Because they'll handle it among themselves, and to tell you the truth, they'll get the job done a lot faster than we ever could."

Ben stared at him, unconvinced.

"I mean it," McCorkindale said emphatically. "They'll give the son of a bitch a real fair trial. Probably in some alley somewhere, or in the back of a shothouse. Then they'll cut his goddamn throat and that'll be the end of it."

"All right," Ben said wearily. It seemed useless to argue any further. "But if anything does come in, let me know."

"You'll be the first to hear about it, Ben," McCorkindale assured him. "The very first."

Ben walked back to his own desk, then sat down. Besides McCorkindale, he was entirely alone in the cramped detective bullpen. Several metal cots had been set up to accommodate the increased manpower which had been brought in to deal with the demonstrations. They remained rumpled and unmade, their sheets and blankets spilling over the sides or resting in tangled heaps on the bare mattresses. Outside the dim, unwashed windows, sirens rang continually as one paddy wagon after another made its way down the avenue, then turned abruptly and dove toward the basement of the building. In that dark, concrete cavern, the demonstrators would be hustled out of the sweltering wagons and rushed upstairs to the large holding cells the Chief had set aside for them. It had been going on like this for days, and everyone was exhausted. As the demonstrations had continued, everything had become increasingly on edge. At first there had been some talk of handling King as the police in Albany, Georgia, had, killing him with kindness, "filling up the jails, of course," as Luther himself had put it one day in the detective bullpen, "but doing it politely." It was a way of handling things that quite a few people in the department had rallied behind at first. But as the weeks had passed, the better part of that idea had gotten buried under a steadily darkening cloud of anger and exhaustion. Sit-ins at the segregated lunch counters of major department stores and mass marches through the central business district had turned the city into a riot zone. And now, as Ben let his eyes drift over the bullpen, he could sense that Luther had grown harder, along with almost everybody else, that the whole city had tightened up, that there was no more give anywhere, in anybody. By six in the evening, a few withered detectives would trudge in, slump down on their cots and get whatever sleep they could for the next three or four hours. Then they'd hit the streets again, dirty, smelly, sitting four to a car as they patrolled the colored sections of the city, or kept a round-the-clock surveillance on some designated leader, staring blankly at the darkened windows of his house or motel room while they balanced coffee cups on the shotguns in their laps.

"Well, ain't you the lucky one."

Ben turned and saw Harry Daniels as he made his way through the scarred double doors of the bullpen.

"You mean to say that in the middle of all this shit, there's one cop with nothing to do but sit on his ass?" Daniels added loudly. He turned and called to his partner. "What do you think about this, Charlie?"

Charlie Breedlove strolled up to Ben's desk. "I hear they kicked you onto the Bearmatch beat, Wellman," he said.

Ben nodded.

"Of course, that beat's pretty much the whole city these days," Breedlove added. He smiled mockingly. "So you shouldn't feel like you've been singled out or anything."

"I don't," Ben said.

Daniels took a long slow drink of Coke, then wiped his mouth with his fist. "So what they got you working on, Ben?"

"A little girl somebody found in that football field off Twenty-third Street," Ben said.

Daniels leaned forward and cupped his hand behind his ear. "Found where?"

"Off Twenty-third," Ben repeated. "In a football field."

Daniels straightened himself slowly. "Football field?"

"Yeah."

"Who called it in, one of the Black Cat boys?"

"No," Ben told him. "Front desk said it sounded like an old colored man."

"How old's the girl?"

"I don't know for sure. Twelve, thirteen, something like that."

"Down in Bearmatch, that's old enough to whore," Breedlove said. "You ought to check with Kelly down in the file room. He knows a lot about the whores down there." He laughed. "Matter of fact, the talk is that he had something sweet going on with one of them a few years back." He draped his arm over Daniels' shoulder and gently moved him toward the row of cots on the other side of the room. "Let's get some sleep, partner," he said. "We got a long night ahead of us."

They were asleep almost instantly, and even from his place at the far end of the room, Ben could hear Breedlove snoring loudly as he lay faceup beneath the window.

For a while Ben remained at his desk. He expected to get a call that would put him back on surveillance or send him circling Bearmatch again, idly circling, as he'd done for a few slow rounds after leaving the football field, and which, after a few minutes, had begun to make him feel more like a prison guard than a homicide detective. Within that circle, life might well go on as McCorkindale had described it. But outside the circle, from the fake antebellum mansions to the bleak trailer parks and greasy spoons of the sprawling industrial neighborhoods, Ben could feel a kind of dreadful trembling in the atmosphere, one that was as palpable in the station house as it was along the reeking drag strips of Bessemer and Irondale. He could feel it like a thousand knifepoints in the air, and after a time, it urged him from his chair, and he walked out of the bullpen and headed out into the steamy day.

Three

The phone was ringing urgently as Ben struggled up from sleep. He looked at the clock. He'd come home for a brief nap, but slept for over an hour. He stepped over quickly and answered the phone.

"Ben, this is Captain Starnes," Luther yelped. "Where the hell have you been?"

"I waited around headquarters for a while," Ben explained. "Then I came home for a nap."

"You can nap at the station like everybody else," Luther said irritably. "You missed the Chief's speech."

"What speech?"

"The one he all of a sudden decided to make to the whole goddamn department," Luther snapped. He paused, as if waiting for a response, then continued. "Now you get back down to headquarters right now."

Ben nodded wearily. "All right, Captain."

A few men were still lingering in the briefing room when Ben arrived at the station house. Plainsclothesmen and uniformed patrolmen milled about, along with the top brass who'd come along with the Chief. Clouds of tobacco smoke hung heavily in the air, and the harsh, sporadic clack of police radios could be heard clearly over the murmur of the crowd.

"Get anything on that little girl yet?" Charlie Breedlove said as he walked up to Ben. He was smoking a thick black cigar clenched tightly between his teeth.

Ben shook his head.

"Probably never will," Breedlove said. "It's over and done with."

Ben glanced toward the front of the room. The Chief stood in the distance, chewing his cigar. One of the Langley brothers huddled next to him, listening intently.

"Chief made a real barn-burner," Breedlove told him.

"He knows how to get them going," Ben said.

"Told us we didn't have to take shit from anybody. Now, I agree with that." Breedlove plucked the cigar from his mouth and glanced at the tip. "Lost my fire," he said. "Got a light?"

Ben took out a packet of matches and relighted the cigar.

Breedlove took a deep draw, then blew a tumbling cloud of thick blue smoke into the already stifling air. "You didn't see Harry on the way in, did you?"

"No."

"He disappeared on me," Breedlove said. "It's rough having a partner who's always disappearing on you." He smiled. "They give you a partner yet? I mean, since Gifford left?"

"No."

"So you're just working that Bearmatch thing yourself?"

"Yeah."

Breedlove shrugged. "Well, when all this shit's over, they'll give you a new partner. They just got all they can handle right now."

"I don't mind working alone," Ben said.

"You're a loner type, is that it?" Breedlove asked.

"I guess."

Breedlove's eyes narrowed somewhat, as if he were studying him. "Well, I'm not like that," he said finally. "I like a partner. Speaking of which, I better find the rotten son of a bitch." He nodded quickly, and left the room, his thin, wiry frame disappearing into the pale green corridor like something caught up in a wave.

Ben lingered in the room awhile longer, standing idly to the side as the last of the people filtered out into the hallway. Like all the world around them, they seemed to move in pairs. Partners on patrol went home to their separate wives, coupling up once again. There were times when it had appealed to him, this notion of someone at his side. But each time he'd moved toward it, it had slipped beyond his grasp. A secretary in the Records Department had moved abruptly to Galveston. A bank teller at First Alabama had finally decided to go with what Ben himself imagined to be a better man. Each time he'd taken it well, but each time it had worn him down a little, so that he'd made few attempts in the last few years to be anything but alone. Each night he made his supper, read the paper, then fell asleep on the sofa or in his large orange recliner, his ears tuned to the muffled wail behind the black and white Indian-head test pattern on his television screen. And each morning he awoke needing less and less to make it through the day. It was a life that seemed to suit him, and he no longer felt it necessary to apologize for it, or to look for some way out of it. Even Gifford's wife had finally stopped trying to marry him off to some perfect woman she'd met while squeezing oranges at the A&P. Now it seemed to him that she had been his last hope, and that when she'd finally given up, he'd been able to curl into his aloneness like a bed.

Luther was waiting for him when Ben got back to his desk. He was sitting in his chair, his hair lifting lazily with each pass of the large rotating fan that stood near the back of the room.

"When you left the ballfield, where'd you go, Ben?" he asked immediately.

"Back on surveillance," Ben said.

Luther rose slowly from the chair, then eased himself onto the top of Ben's desk. "You mean King?"

"Yes," Ben said. He pulled the small notebook from his jacket pocket and handed it to Luther.

Luther glanced at it idly. "Anything new?"

Ben shook his head.

Luther pocketed the notebook. "So what did you do then?"

"I came back here," Ben said. "I talked to Sammy."

"About what?"

"That little girl."

Luther looked pleased. "Good. What then?"

"I went home for a rest, and then the phone rang."

"So then you came back to headquarters?"

"Yeah," Ben said.

"Okay," Luther said thoughtfully.

"What's this all about, Captain?" Ben asked. "All these questions, I mean."

Luther looked at Ben as if he were a small child in need of basic instruction. "Well, like I said at the ballfield, this little girl could be a problem for us. If you want to know the truth, she could be a problem in several ways." Luther lifted his hand and shot a finger into the air. "First, they'll be certain people who figure this is some sort of KKK killing or something like that. We have to make sure that it's not." A second finger poked the air. "And we also have to make sure that we're looking into this killing, that we're not just letting it go because the victim is colored." The two fingers curled back into Luther's fist. "See what I mean? We want to cover ourselves in both directions." He smiled quietly. "That's why it's important that you really work this case, Ben," he added. "That's why it looks good that you checked with Sammy. But that's also why it looks bad that you went home and took a nap after being at the ballfield. That makes it look like you don't give a shit one way or the other about this girl." He looked at Ben closely. "You see what I mean, don't you, Ben?"

"Yes."

"It's not like we're checking you out in particular," Luther said. "It's just that things being the way they are, everybody has to be careful."

"I understand," Ben said.

Luther rose slowly, then squeezed Ben's upper arm affectionately. "I knew you would." He stepped away, stopped suddenly, then turned back toward him. His face seemed suddenly strained, and his voice took on a tense and apprehensive tone. "Things are going to be real hard over the next few days, Ben," he said, "and I'll tell you the truth, the closer you stay to this little case, the better off you're going to be." He turned again, and this time pressed forward without stopping, head down, his back slightly hunched, his feet slapping loudly against the checkerboard tile floor.

Four

There was a note on Ben's desk when he got back to the detective bullpen. It was written on a plain square of white paper, and it was from Leon Patterson, one of the medical examiners in the Coroner's Office. It said that he'd finished with case number three-zero-six, which Ben figured was the number he'd assigned to the little girl, and that he'd be in his office at Hillman Hospital until six.

Patterson was already on his way out when Ben met him in the hallway.

"I came over to see about that little girl," Ben said.

Patterson glanced at his watch. "Can it wait till tomorrow, Ben?"

"No."

Patterson looked puzzled. "Why? She kin to somebody important?"

"I don't know who she's kin to, Leon," Ben said. "But I don't want to wait until tomorrow."

Patterson shrugged heavily. "All right, then," he said wearily. "Come back in and I'll show you what I got."

Ben followed Patterson as he walked back down the hallway and into a small room where two stainless steel tables rested beneath a bank of fluorescent lights. An old black man, gray-haired and somewhat stooped, was hosing blood from one of them. It flowed in a broad swath into the drains on either side of the table, then washed down into the two separate buckets beneath them.

"Woman out in Bush Hills," Patterson explained. "Sudden death. Big insurance policy. DA wanted a full autopsy."

"Did you do a full one on the girl?" Ben asked.

Patterson laughed. "Come on, Ben. What for? Anybody could see what happened to her." He walked over to a large metal file cabinet and pulled out a plain manila envelope. "Read it for yourself. It won't take you long. Just about three lines. Death by gunshot wound. You could have figured that out yourself."

"I want a full autopsy," Ben said.

Patterson's eyes widened. "For God's sake, Ben, didn't you see the back of her head?"

"Full autopsy, Leon," Ben told him. "Orders from the top."

Patterson's eyes narrowed. "From the top?" he said unbelievingly.

"I'd like for you to do it now, Leon."

"I've got this woman to do first."

Ben shook his head. "She'll have to get in line."

Leon stared at Ben piercingly. "Who is this girl, anyway?"

"I don't know."

"Bullshit."

"Nobody knows."

"Well, I don't believe that, Ben," Patterson said, "but I'll go along with you anyway." He glanced at his watch. "Just understand that it's going to be a quick cut-and-paste job."

Ben shook his head. "Can't do it, Leon. It's got to be thorough."

"Thorough?"

"That's right," Ben said firmly.

Patterson shrugged. "Okay, I'll call you when I'm finished."

Ben did not move. "I'll stay and watch," he said.

Patterson smiled. "Oh, yeah? You ever seen a full autopsy before, Ben?"

"No."

The smiled broadened. "Well, you're in for a treat," Patterson said. He stepped around him and called to the old man. "Bring me that little girl in the freezer." He looked back at Ben, the smile now large and mocking. "Step right over, Ben. You want a full autopsy? By God, I'll give you one." He walked over to one of the tables, then motioned for Ben. "Well, come on over," he said teasingly. "I want you to have a ringside seat."

Ben stepped over next to Patterson and stood, his hands folded in front of him, while the attendant carefully laid the girl's body onto the bare table. It was naked, and against the bright, blue steel it seemed infinitely dark and pliant. Rigor mortis had already reached its peak, and was now diminishing, so that the legs lay nearly flat on the tabletop, and only a slight arching upward could be seen along the spine.

"Well, let me suit up," Patterson said. He pulled on a white lab coat which had been draped over a stool at the table, then sunk his hands into a pair of transparent rubber gloves. "Beginning to get the idea, Ben?" he asked with a slight laugh.

Ben said nothing.

Patterson looked at the body for a moment, then swept his hand out over it. "Well, as you can see, Sergeant, there is no lethal trauma to the body." He placed his large hands on either side of the girl's face and twisted her head sharply to the left. "Except for this hole right here." He moved his index finger in a circular pattern around the dark, reddish hole. "Now I'll do a scraping if you want one," he said, "but as you can see, we got powder burns all around the wound, which indicates that she was shot at extremely close range, probably no more than a couple of inches." He poked his finger into the hole. "From the size of it, I'd say a twenty-two-caliber slug, maybe a short, maybe a long. I'll have to dig it out to determine that." He looked up at Ben and smiled. "Ready?"

Ben nodded.

"Okay," Patterson said. He took a long, slender scalpel and inserted it into the hole, pressing it deeper and deeper as he twisted it gently. "Pay dirt," he said after a moment. Then he dug a pair of tweezers into the wound, maneuvered it slightly and pulled it out. "There it is," he said, as he lifted it toward Ben's face. "Twenty-two long, wouldn't you say?"

"Yeah."

Patterson grinned teasingly. "Look like it might be the cause of death to you, Ben?"

Ben said nothing.

Patterson dropped the slug into a metal tray and handed it to the attendant. "Bag this and label it," he said. "Case three-zero-six." He looked back at Ben. "Now we can go on to the really good stuff." He took up the scalpel once again, and held it poised above the girl's small body. "You want a nose clamp, Ben?" he asked.

"What?"

"Well, if you ask me, the human body's not much even from the outside," Patterson said, "but on the inside, it's a real mess." He glanced down at the girl. "She's got undigested food, bile, feces." He stopped and looked back up at Ben. "You want a nose clamp?"

Ben shook his head. "No."

Patterson shrugged. "Suit yourself."

By the time Patterson had finished, the body looked as if a hand grenade had exploded beneath it. The chest, stomach and abdomen were slit open and their cavities exposed. Large flaps of skin hung over her sides like pieces of torn cloth, and a continual stream of blood and other fluids trickled down the drainage spouts and into the buckets below.

Patterson peeled the rubber gloves from his hands and dropped them into the wastebasket beside the dissecting table. "Well, we learned two things, Ben, both of which I could have told you without all this." He looked at Ben haughtily. "She was shot in the head. And she was raped."

Ben continued to stare at the ravaged body. The face remained intact, but the skin over the rest of the head had been peeled back, the skull sawed open, and the brain removed. She seemed even more exposed, her body open like a blasted fruit, her small naked buttocks now pressed flat against the cold blue of the tabletop.

"What'd you do with her clothes?" he asked as he glanced back up at Patterson.

"They're in a box in the other room," Patterson said. He stepped over to his desk and put on his jacket. "We'll bury her in them."

"Did you vacuum them?" Ben asked.

Patterson laughed. "You must be kidding, Ben. Till the front office got on it, we were treating her just like any other case." He straightened the knot of his tie. "You want to vacuum them? Go ahead. Just get them back to me by tomorrow morning." He moved to the door and opened it. "Unless you want her buried in a bag." He looked back toward the adjoining room. "I'm finished out here, Davey," he called. "Just put a sheet over it and put it back in the cooler."

The old man appeared at the door, his milky brown eyes staring silently at Patterson.

"I'm going to take a break," Patterson added, "then I'll come back and sew up." He looked back at Ben and politely touched the brim of his hat. "And with that final word, Ben, I'll say goodnight." He smiled thinly, then disappeared behind the door.

Ben continued to stand by the table, and after a moment the attendant walked out of the back room and over to the opposite side of the body.

"You want me to take her now?" he asked.

"I guess," Ben said. He stepped back slightly and watched as the attendant draped a clean white sheet over the body.

"We found her over on Twenty-third Street," Ben said.

The old man did not seem to hear him. He walked to the rear of the table, grasped the handle and began to tug it backward toward the adjoining room.

"What part of town do you live in?" Ben asked as he followed along.

"Thirty-second Street," the attendant said dully.

"That's not too far from where we found her," Ben said. "You know that old ballfield around there?"

"Yes, sir."

"That's where she was. Buried under a goalpost."

The old man said nothing. He continued to tug the table slowly forward, maneuvering carefully toward the open door behind him.

"What's your name?" Ben asked him.

"They calls me Davey."

Ben grasped the edge of the table, stopped its movement, then pulled the sheet back to reveal the girl's face.

"You ever seen this little girl, Davey?"

The old man gave the small face a quick glance. "Naw, sir."

"Maybe playing in the park, something like that? Maybe just walking along the sidewalk?"

"I ain't never seen her," the man said. He drew his eyes from the girl's face and gave a tentative pull on the table.

Ben held it firmly in place. "Who runs things over in Bearmatch?" he asked.

The attendant kept his eyes downcast. "The Black Cat boys," he said quietly.

"I don't mean them," Ben said. "I mean your own people."

The old man said nothing.

"Lots of things go on in Bearmatch," Ben said. "Somebody has control of it."

The attendant shook his head. "It ain't my business," he said softly. He waited a moment, then gave another tug on the table.

Ben released it, then followed it into the adjoining room. He leaned against the wall and watched as the old man opened the freezer door and pushed the table inside. When he turned back around, he seemed surprised to find Ben still lingering in the room.

"You ask the Black Cat boys what you wants to know," he said. "You one of they own."

Ben smiled quietly. "You trust them, Davey? You trust the Black Cat boys?"

The old man said nothing, but he looked at Ben knowingly.

"I don't either," Ben said. "That's why I want to talk to somebody else about this girl." He paused, letting it sink in. "Give me a name, Davey. Just one name."

The ancient brown eyes squeezed together slowly as he turned it over in his mind.

"They're going to bury that little girl tomorrow," Ben added. "I think her mama ought to be there."

The old man's face lifted slightly, as if with sudden pride. "Roy Jolly," he said.

Five

Night had begun to come down over the city by the time Ben left the chill, white corridors of Hillman Hospital. The sirens which had filled the air all day were now silent, and as he walked to his car in the pinkish-blue light, he could almost imagine that the worst was over. But he knew that it wasn't, and the evening quiet only reminded him of the sort he remembered from the war, when, after a day-long assault, Japanese and Americans would retire to their encampments and wait nervously for dawn. He knew that that was more or less what was happening now, and when he pulled into the cavernous basement of the station house, he was not at all surprised to find ragged lines of state troopers oiling their rifles, checking their cartridge bags, or edgily adjusting the plexiglass shields of their helmets.

He nodded to a few of them as he walked toward the cement stairs that led to the first floor, but he didn't stop to talk. The unventilated basement always smelled faintly sour, but now the odor was even denser, and Ben realized it came from the overheated tires of the paddy wagons, rubber which had melted slightly, as if from hurtling back and forth down streets of fire.

It was better upstairs, where the large rotating fans whirred continually, and Ben took a deep, refreshing breath as he walked into the detective bullpen and sat down at his desk.

"Anything come in, Sammy?" he called to McCorkindale in the back corner of the room.

McCorkindale glanced toward him, then shook his head vigorously.

"Captain Starnes around?"

"Just stepped out to take a leak," McCorkindale said dully.

Luther walked back into the office a few minutes later, still pulling casually at the zipper of his trousers.

"Heard you sort of strongarmed the guy in the Coroner's Office," he said as he strolled up to Ben's desk.

"A little."

"Good, good," Luther said happily. He took a chair from another desk and sat down. "Well, what'd you find out?"

Ben took out the original report and handed it to him. "That's all Patterson had from his first look at her," he said, "but he didn't learn much more after a full autopsy."

Luther glanced briefly at the report. "The rape looks good though," he said. "If it was a race thing, some kind of KKK killing, something like that, there wouldn't have been a rape." He slid the report back onto Ben's desk. "Good job, Ben," he said. He reached over and squeezed his shoulder. "I think that's about all we need."

Ben leaned forward slightly. "For what?

"To close the case," Luther said matter-of-factly.

"I just started on it."

"And you already got as far as you're ever going to get," Luther told him. He smiled. "It's a Bearmatch thing, Ben. If you'd ever worked that part of town before, you'd know what I mean."

Ben's eyes drifted down toward the report, then back up toward Luther.

"I have a lead," he said.

Luther looked at him doubtfully. "A lead? What kind of a lead?"

"A name. Somebody who knows a lot about what goes on in Bearmatch."

"What name?"

"A Mr. Jolly," Ben said. "Roy Jolly."

Luther's face broke into a broad grin. "Mr. Jolly?" he said with a chuckle, "You mean old Roy-Joy? That's your contact?"

Ben nodded slowly.

"You know who Roy-Joy is, Ben?" Luther asked. "He's the biggest pimp in Bearmatch, maybe the biggest in Birmingham, maybe even the biggest in the whole goddamn world." He stopped, then looked at Ben coolly. "Who gave you his name?"

For an instant, Ben started to identify the old attendant. Then, suddenly, something stopped him as fully and abruptly as if a hand had shot up to cover his mouth.

"It was just something I heard on the street," he said with a slight shrug. "Nobody in particular."

Luther placed his hands palms down on Ben's desk and leaned into them. "If you want to know about things in Bearmatch, you ought to ask the Langley boys. They been working it for the last two years."

"I'll do that," Ben said.

Luther straightened himself. "Look, Ben," he said quietly, "if you want to work this case a little more, go ahead. It just makes the department look better if you do. But you've still got to cover King until all this shit is over." He glanced at his watch. "He's scheduled to make a speech at the First Pilgrim Baptist Church tonight at eight o'clock. Be there."

Ben nodded quickly. "All right."

"And as far as this little girl goes, talk to the Langley brothers," Luther said insistently. "They should be chowing down at Smith's Cafe right about now."

"Okay," Ben said.

Luther started to leave the room.

Ben touched the sleeve of his coat to stop him. "That picture you took of the little girl," he said. "You got it with you?"

"Yeah," Luther said. He patted his coat pockets. "Here it is," he said as he handed Ben the photograph.

Ben lifted the picture slightly in order to bring it into a better light. It was a small, square Polaroid, shot in a grainy black and white, but he could see the girl's face quite plainly as it looked up toward him from the grayish dusty ground. It had the same look the dead always had. No matter how big or how small, how much or how little had been done to them, they always looked as if they'd never had a chance.

Black Cat 13 sat obliviously at rest in an emergency parking zone in the alleyway behind Smith's Cafe. It was gray with black side stripes, and a large black cat, yellow-eyed and with its silver claws exposed in an outstretched paw, had been hand-painted on the hood. The number 13 had been scrawled in white across its side, and a dab of red hung like bloody drool from its snarling mouth.

Tod and Teddy Langley sat in the far left corner of the cafe, each of them finishing up what looked like the usual blueplate special:

hamburger steak, mashed potatoes and a faded mixture of green peas and tiny cubes of carrot.

Teddy sat up slightly as Ben approached.

"Well, hello, Ben," he said. He smiled thinly. "I hear they put you on King."

Ben pulled one of the chairs from beneath the table and sat down. "Yeah," he said. "How are things in Bearmatch?"

Teddy laughed. "Couldn't be better, now that we're filling up the jails." He pulled a bottle of Coke over to the side of the table, opened a package of salted peanuts and poured them into the bottle. A hissing brownish fizz boiled up almost to the rim of the bottle, then settled back slowly.

"Well, not all of them," Tod said quietly. He took the last crust of biscuit into his mouth and chewed it slowly. "Not all of them, right, Teddy?"

"That's right," Teddy said. He took a long pull on the bottle. "So what's the story, Ben? What's King's next move?"

Ben let his eyes wander aimlessly about the diner, from the front, where the cafe's menu was written on a chalkboard in the front window, to the rear wall where two photographs hung from either side of a Coca-Cola clock, one of Governor Wallace, and the other of Vice-President Johnson. "I don't know," he said.

"Breedlove and Daniels are watching King, too," Teddy said matter-of-factly, as if demonstrating how much he already knew. "And there are probably a few more in undercover."

Tod laughed. "Undercover?" he screeched. "How you get undercover with them—paint your face black?"

Ben smiled limply. "So what are you boys doing instead of Bearmatch, loading the paddy wagons like everybody else?"

"Hell, no," Tod said excitedly. "We got a special—"

"Shut up, Tod," Teddy said. His eyes shot over to Ben. "Never seen you in Smith's before," he said.

"I don't come here very much."

"So why are you here now?"

Ben shrugged casually. "I saw your car outside, and I thought—"

Teddy leaned toward him. "Word is, they's an informant in the department," he said. "Somebody who's working for the other side."

"I thought you might help me with this case I'm working on," Ben continued without hesitation.

Teddy's eyes squeezed together. "What case is that?"

"Something that broke this morning," Ben told him. He took the photograph from his coat pocket and laid it down on the table. "A little girl. Somebody shot her in the head and buried her in that old ballfield off Twenty-third Street."

Teddy leaned back slowly, his eyes casually lingering on the picture. "She from Bearmatch?"

"I guess so," Ben told him. "But the front office still wants a full investigation."

"Why's that?"

"So the murder can't be made to look like a racial thing," Ben said.

"They're worried about that, huh?" Tod asked.

"A little."

Teddy shook his head resentfully. "Then we've already lost, Ben."

"It's what the Chief wants," Ben said.

"That's how it looks," Teddy said emphatically, "but that's not how it is." He smiled helplessly. "Don't you see, Ben? Don't you see how it really is?"

Ben said nothing.

"Even the Chief is having to pay attention to them," Teddy explained. "We're having to be worried about what they think." He looked at his brother angrily. "When the fuck did we ever have to do that before?" He shifted his eyes back over to Ben. "You know what a mongrel is?" he asked. "You ever see an old mongrel dog?"

Ben didn't answer.

"That's what they want to turn us into," Teddy said darkly. "A race of mongrels."

Tod's eyes shot over to Ben. "That's right," he said emphatically. "That's what they want."

Teddy paid no attention to him. He kept his eyes on Ben. "They don't really give a shit about eating with us, or going to school with us, or anything else like that. They just want to ruin us, ruin our race, so they can take over everything." He shook his head wearily, painfully. "And they're doing it, too. They're already making us do what they want. And before long, we'll just be like a bunch of mongrel dogs." He picked up the picture, held it a few inches from Ben's face and slowly ripped it in two. "I am loyal to my race, Ben," he said darkly, "before everything." He released the photograph, and its torn parts fluttered back down onto the table.

Ben stared at him silently for a moment, then gathered up the two halves of the photograph and returned them to his coat pocket. "I'm just doing my job, Teddy," he said quietly.

"Well, you'll have to do it without me," Teddy said.

From somewhere deep within him, Ben felt a sudden, inexplicable surge. "I intend to," he said.

He drove home slowly, turning north, so that he could move along the central boulevards of the city. The streets were almost entirely deserted. The restaurants and cafeterias were tightly closed, and some had already taken the added precaution of boarding up their windows. Even the brilliant chandeliers of the Tutweiler Hotel appeared somehow dim and exhausted in the fully fallen darkness. The streetlamps swung ponderously in the heavy summer air, and the light that swept down from them seemed to fall to earth in thick blue drops. Uniformed policemen patrolled the empty sidewalks two abreast, their holsters already unsnapped, their fingers playing at the handles of their revolvers. In front of Pizitz, black sanitation men were gathering together stacks of broken placards and tossing them into the grinding steel jaws of the compactors, and a little further down, only a few blocks from the park, another crew was hosing waves of accumulated litter into the cement gutters.

The park itself was green and lush, and Ben knew that within only a few hours it would be shimmering brightly in the early morning dew. Far in the distance, he could see the outline of its empty playground. The swings were moving languidly in the air, and under the tall gray lantern, the slide took on a ghostly silver.

To the left, and barely visible through a wall of trees, he could make out the high wire fence of the softball field, and it instantly reminded him of the goalpost off Twenty-third Street. He made a hard left at the end of the park and headed out toward the distant perimeters of Bearmatch.

There were no streetlamps in the ballfield, and so, when he reached it, he could see only a spot of dry ground beneath the covering darkness. No line of benches, no mound of freshly turned earth, no goalpost. Only a wall of impenetrable black which seemed to rise at the very edge of the broken, weedy sidewalk and then extend outward forever. For a while he sat in his car and smoked a cigarette while he stared out into the dark field. From time to time, people would casually approach the car, moving steadily down the sidewalk until they were close enough to notice that the man behind the wheel was white. Then they'd suddenly freeze, as if they'd just stumbled upon a rattlesnake in the brush, eye him cautiously for an instant, then hurry away toward the other side of the street. It happened first one time, then another and another, until Ben grew tired of seeing it, hit the ignition and drove away.

Six

On his way to work the next morning, Ben parked at almost the same spot on Twenty-third Street where he'd stopped the night before. But by seven o'clock, when he finally pulled over to the curb, the streets were already busy. Small knots of people strolled briskly up and down the sidewalks and across the ballfield. Children sped past on their rusting bicycles, and the traffic along the street and the adjoining avenues was quick and noisy. It was as if the whole neighborhood had been resurrected with the morning light, and now, when people approached his car, they didn't hesitate or step aside, but simply continued forward without so much as a break in stride. The bright sunlight seemed to serve them as a kind of shield against the dangers which inevitably returned with the night, and under its brief protection, they strode openly to the bus stops, talking quietly as they walked.

For a while Ben sat behind the wheel and watched, just as he had the night before. But this time, he knew that he had only a few minutes to linger at the edge of the ballfield before the inevitable voice from the radio ordered him to headquarters. By now the detectives on the morning shift would be trudging up the cement stairs to receive what they had lately come to call their "combat orders," assignments which shifted by the minute, but which generally had to do with handling the crowds, paperwork and jailhouse overflow caused by the demonstrations. It was as if everything else had stopped, all the burglaries, assaults and domestic quarrels, and that now there was only this single, dreadful preoccupation with the streets, a great black pit into which everything else, the whole varied texture of daily life, had fallen.

And yet, as Ben continued to sit in his car, his eyes slowly moving from one corner to the next, he could see that much of the general flow of life continued. Bearmatch went on with its routine, and from behind the wheel, he could sit quietly and take in its pace, its odors, the broad tone of its common life. He could see how the maids in their white uniforms gathered in little knots at the bus stops, how the laborers in their gray worksuits or shirtless beneath their tattered bib-overalls moved like a slow, silent army toward the railroad yards and sweltering steel mills. He could hear the morning shift-horns as they sounded loudly through the alleyways and over the sloping shanties, and he remembered that in his youth, they had sounded over his house too. He could smell the bacon grease, redeye gravy and warm half-risen biscuits, and for an instant they seemed to come from his mother's kitchen, and he could recall how, in the morning, after breakfast, his own father and mother had moved out onto the street like the people who now flowed around him, taking him first to school, and then trudging on down the avenue to board the old electrical trolleys that crisscrossed the city on a grid of wire and steel.

For a long time, his parents had been mostly ghosts to him, his father brought down by a slow disease, his mother simply dead for a reason no one at Hillman Hospital had ever bothered to explain. In the summer, as he remembered now, they'd sometimes fallen asleep in their swing while he remained inside, listening to the radio. Later he would find them slouched to one side, the old man's face buried in his wife's large, fallen breasts, the old woman's head dropping so far down toward her husband's that it looked half-severed, and both of them snoring wheezily while the lightning bugs twinkled in the humid air. But now they suddenly returned to him as more than bodies floating silently in a little wrought-iron swing, and for a moment he found himself wondering about what their lives had really been, what they had thought about as they sat together, listening to the crickets and katydids, the slicing sound the traffic made after a fierce summer rain, the tinkling bells of the trolleys, what they would think about even now if they were alive, what they would think about the uproar in the city, about the nameless little girl beneath the goalpost, what they, knowing about all this, would tell him he should do.

The clack of the radio sounded suddenly, and after it, the dispatcher's voice. "Headquarters calling Car 17."

Ben picked up the microphone. "Car 17."

"That you, Ben?"

"Yeah. What's the matter?"

"Nothing much," the dispatcher said. "Patterson, at the Coroner's Office, he wants you to give him a call when you get a chance."

"Is he at Hillman?"

"I guess so."

"I'm not too far away," Ben said. "I'll drive over. Everything okay at headquarters?"

"About the same."

"I'll come over as soon as I leave Hillman," Ben said.

He snapped the radio back into its cradle, then paused a moment, staring out once again into the field. Perhaps a hundred yards away, he could see groups of children gathering under the goalpost. They looked as if they were dressed in their Sunday best, the girls in clean white dresses, the boys in dark trousers and plain white shirts. For a moment, Ben thought it might be some kind of memorial service for the murdered girl, some strange Bearmatch rite which no outsiders knew about. Then, suddenly, a tall young man in a dark blue suit stepped from their midst and shouted something. Instantly a smattering of placards shot into the air. They were made of white poster-paper tacked to spindly wooden slats, and they were the sort Ben had seen a great many of since the demonstrations had begun. The thick, black lettering conveyed the same protests and demands, and as the children filed silently off the littered field, two abreast, holding hands, smiling with what seemed to him an odd and unknowable happiness, Ben wondered if, under different circumstances, the murdered girl might have been among them, her hand in someone else's, her buckled shoes skipping lightly across the parched ground, her face emboldened with the same bright smile.

Patterson was going through a stack of files in the outer office when Ben arrived.

"Well, they got to you pretty fast," he said.

"What do you have?" Ben asked.

"I wish I had more, to tell you the truth," Patterson told him. "You find out who the girl was yet?"

"No."

"Well, I probably can't help you much with that," Patterson said. "But I did find something you might want to see." He smiled slyly. "Especially since the front office is so hot for the Coroner's Office to work this case." He pushed himself back from the desk slightly and opened the top drawer. "I vacuumed her dress, and while I was doing that, I found something." He drew a plastic bag from the desk drawer and handed it to Ben. "It was in one of her pockets. I'm surprised you guys didn't find it when you dug her up."

Ben lifted the bag up to the light. He could see a metal ring. The plated imitation gold was already turning green. Its setting contained a large, purple oval of cut glass.

"Not exactly a priceless piece, is it?" Patterson said softly. "But what with her being from Bearmatch, it probably meant something to her."

Ben continued to look at the ring. "Where'd you find it?"

"It was tucked inside one of her pockets," Patterson said. He shrugged. "It's just a piece of old costume jewelry, but the little girl probably thought it was worth a lot."

Ben turned the bag slowly before his eyes. "Then why wasn't she wearing it?" he asked. Then he looked at Patterson. "Where is she?"

"Still in the freezer," Patterson said. "We're not burying her until late this afternoon."

"I'd like to see her again."

"She didn't come back to life overnight," Patterson said. "We can't do that for her."

Ben turned abruptly and walked into the adjoining room. The girl was still in Compartment 7. He opened the door, pulled out the carriage and drew back the sheet.

"What are you doing?" Patterson asked as he stepped up beside him.

Ben did not answer. He took the ring out of the bag, lifted one of the girl's hands from the carriage and inserted the ring onto her little finger. It was too large to hold it. He tried the index finger, the middle finger and finally the thumb. The ring was far too large to fit any of them.

"She wasn't wearing it because it wasn't hers," he said as he dropped the ring back into the bag.

Patterson nodded. "Boyfriend's, maybe?" he asked hesitantly.

Ben looked at him. "I don't know. She could have worn it on a chain around her neck. She could have picked it up on the street." He walked over to the small metal desk at the rear of the room and looked at the ring under the desk lamp, turning it slowly in his fingertips. "No name," he said, almost to himself. "No initials." He dropped it back into the plastic bag and handed it to Patterson. "Send it over to be dusted," he told him, "and tell them to let me know what they find."

"Okay," Patterson said with a slight edge of sarcasm. "Whatever they want in the front office, that's what we do."

Ben did not seem to hear him. "Where's her dress?"

Patterson pointed toward a plain cardboard box which rested beneath a long wooden table. "Over there."

Ben walked over to the box, took out the dress and spread it across the table. "Which pocket did you find it in?"

Patterson pointed to a single shallow breast pocket. "Right there."

Ben gazed steadily at the dress. In addition to the one on the right front of the dress, it had two side pockets, and he inserted his hands into each of them. "They're a lot deeper," he said.

Patterson looked at him oddly. "So what?"

"Well, I was just thinking," Ben said. "If I were a little girl who wanted to keep from losing my ring, I'd put it in one of my side pockets." He looked at Patterson pointedly. "Wouldn't you, Leon?"

Patterson glanced down at the dress, then back up to Ben. "Yeah, I would." he said. He shrugged. "Unless I was careless."

Ben picked up the dress by the shoulders and turned it slowly in the light. It was badly soiled from the burial, and there were bloodstains on the skirt.

"Those bloodstains," Ben said. "Where'd they come from?"

"The rape," Patterson replied authoritatively. "Where else would they come from?"

Ben twisted the dress around so that Patterson could see the back of it. "How come there's no blood on her collar?" he asked. "She was shot in the back of the head. Head wounds are usually pretty bloody."

Patterson stared silently at the white, ruffled collar for a moment, then looked at Ben. "I can't answer that, Ben," he said at last, "I really don't know."

"I do," Ben said. He glanced back over toward the body. The small dark hand dangled from the metal carriage, casting a tiny shadow across the polished tile floor. "She was naked when somebody shot her," he said. He lifted his right hand, fingers spread, and held it suspended in the air at about four feet from the floor. "She was naked, and she was standing about this high, Leon," he continued softly. "And somebody a whole lot bigger came up behind her and put a gun a few inches from the back of her head and pulled the trigger."

Something very dark silently passed over Patterson's face. "Let me know if I can help you any more on this one, Ben," he said finally. Then he turned very quickly and walked away.

Seven

During the night, police barricades had been set up at the entrance of the underground garage at headquarters, and several uniformed patrolmen now stood determinedly behind them, nightsticks already drawn, and with their eyes squinting menacingly as Ben pulled to a halt.

"Looks like you boys are getting ready for a rough day," Ben said as one of the patrolmen approached his car.

"We've been told to expect anything," the patrolman replied. "Do you have business here?"

Ben took out his identification.

"Fine, Sergeant," the patrolman said instantly. "I'm sorry I didn't recognize you." He looked over at the line of patrolmen who stood silently behind the barricade. "Open up," he called loudly. "Sergeant Wellman passing through."

The other patrolmen pulled back one of the long sawhorse barricades and Ben drove past them, nosing his car downward into the garage. On either side, men were lined up in marching formation, their commanders taking them through the paces of a military drill. At the southern corner of the garage, metal tables had been set up like a subterranean field headquarters, complete with telephones, typewriters, and, at the far end of the table, a cardboard box filled with an assortment of what looked like civilian handguns: thirty-eights, forty-fives, a few puny twenty-twos, and snuggled among them like a nest of sleeping vipers, a .357 Magnum, a P.38, and a few other high-powered pistols.

Sammy McCorkindale sat behind the box, routinely cataloging the serial numbers of one pistol at a time.

Ben picked up an old German Luger, shifted it slowly from one hand to the other, then threw open the cartridge clip. It was fully loaded. He shoved the clip back into position, then laid it down on the table in front of McCorkindale.

"What the hell is this all about?" he asked.

McCorkindale looked up slowly. "What does it look like?"

"It looks like a lot a firepower," Ben said. "But what are you doing with it?"

McCorkindale returned to his ledger. "Chief wants all confiscated weapons to be put in working order," he said casually.

"Why?"

"Case we need them, I guess," McCorkindale said.

"Need them for what?"

"To arm the deputies."

"What deputies?"

"The ones the Chief's going to swear in if we need them."

"You mean civilian deputies?"

"That's right," McCorkindale said idly. He pulled a forty-five automatic from the box and began to write down its serial number.

Ben glanced to the left. A group of civilian office workers was busily unloading wooden crates filled with tear-gas canisters from a police van with Mississippi license plates and a large Confederate flag festooned across its rear double doors.

"Looks to me like they're expecting the shit to hit the fan," McCorkindale said. He looked up from the ledger and grinned. "They're even going to put my fat ass on the line."

Ben drew his eyes back over to McCorkindale. "How long's it been since you fired a gun, Sammy?"

"You mean my service revolver? You mean in the line of duty? I ain't never fired it, Ben."

Ben shook his head irritably, then picked up the Magnum. "You think these so-called deputies will know how to use a thing like this?"

McCorkindale smiled cagily. "Well, I figure if things really get out of hand, they'll learn pretty quick," he said. "And I figure that's what the boys in the front office are thinking, too."

Ben placed the Magnum back down on the table. "They'll shoot their own toes off, or they'll shoot each other, or they'll shoot one of us, Sammy, and that's what's going to happen." He looked down at the Magnum, then back up at McCorkindale. "You just don't hand somebody a gun like that and then tell them to go on out and make up the rest."

"I'm not saying I agree with it," McCorkindale said, almost in a whine, "but we can't just let the whole town go up in smoke."

Ben's eyes drifted over to the right, past a line of cement columns to where the Chief's white tank rested near the garage entrance. Black Cat 13 was parked only a few feet away, and next to it, one of the bright red station wagons the Fire Department used to whisk the Chief from one blaze to another across the city.

"I mean, I'm just an ordinary dogface in the department, Ben," McCorkindale continued. "They don't come to me for the big decisions."

Ben returned his eyes to McCorkindale. He smiled softly. "Sometimes I wish they did, Sammy," he said quietly. "Sometimes I sure do wish they did."

Upstairs on the first floor, Ben found the lobby crowded with what looked like a completely new contingent of Alabama highway patrolmen. They wore flat-gray uniforms, Sam Browne holsters and the sort of rounded black hats that Gifford, Ben's former partner, had called "Wyatt Earps." Ben didn't recognize any of them, and after a moment he realized that they must have been brought in from the distant rural counties which surrounded Birmingham. They had the look of country boys who were uneasy in the city, and who had spent most of their lives pulling over the occasional teenage speed-demon on some unpaved backwoods road. It was the sort of half-frightened, half-baffled look that he remembered from the war when a batch of reinforcements would suddenly show up, fresh-faced boys who'd been trained for thirty days, then handed an M-1, shipped to the Pacific, spewed out onto a rocky island and told to kick the hell out of a dug-in, battle-hardened army of suicidal Japanese.

For a moment, Ben simply stood to the side and watched them, trying to figure out what use they could possibly be on the streets of Birmingham, or why they had suddenly appeared in such large numbers, unless it was to make the very idea of resistance to them unthinkable.

He was still considering it all when Luther walked up and leaned against the wall beside him.

"King's scheduled for a speech at the Sixteenth Baptist Church late this afternoon," he said matter-of-factly. "I want you to be there."

Ben nodded.

"And before that, I want you to follow along with the march down Fourth Avenue," Luther added. "It starts in about an hour, and we're hoping there won't be any trouble, but we want all hands on deck anyway." He hurriedly handed Ben a white slip of paper. "This tells you where to be and when to be there. Now as far as King's speech is concerned, I want you to take down everything he says. If he so much as burps, I want it in your notebook, you understand?"

"Yes, Captain," Ben said.

"And make sure you're armed, Ben," Luther went on breathlessly. "In the next few days, we don't want any of our people hurt. And remember what the Chief said yesterday. Keep control of yourself, but don't take any shit." He took a deep breath. "Got that?"

"Yeah."

"Good."

Ben pointed to the crowd of patrolmen. "What are they here for?"

"Relief," Luther said. "For the time being, they'll be taking over some of our more routine duties. Traffic control, that sort of thing."

"McCorkindale said something about civilian deputies," Ben said.

"That's just a contingency," Luther told him. "In a situation like this, you can't be caught without a plan."

"McCorkindale's downstairs getting ready to distribute handguns."

Luther looked at him sternly. "You got a problem with that?"

Ben said nothing.

"This is not a department for little girls," Luther added coldly. "You feeling like a little girl, Ben?"

"No."

"I'm glad to hear it," Luther said. "Now you just go on about your business, and leave policy to the people who know how to make it. Do you read me, Sergeant?"

"Yes, Captain."

"Good," Luther said. "Now get on with your assignments."

Ben walked back to the detective bullpen immediately. At his desk, he found a note from Leon Patterson telling him that he planned to have the girl buried in Gracehill Cemetery at around six in the evening. For a moment he tried to think if there was any reason to delay the burial, decided that there was none, crumpled the note in his fist and tossed it into the wastebasket beside his desk.

"Giving up on something, Ben?" Breedlove asked as he sat down at his own desk only a few feet from Ben.

"They're going to be burying that little girl this afternoon," Ben said.

"You got something on that case?"

Ben shook his head. "Nothing much. A few things that seem a little funny."

Breedlove leaned toward him slightly. "Like what?"

"Well, Patterson found a ring in her pocket, but it didn't fit her. There was blood on her skirt, but none on her collar. She wasn't wearing any panties."

Breedlove laughed. "These Bearmatch girls, they don't always wear panties."

Ben's eyes shot over to him. "She was about twelve years old, Charlie," he said.

"So what?"

Ben turned away and idly glanced at the slip of paper Luther had handed him.

"How about the Langleys," Breedlove said. "Did you talk to them?"

Ben continued to stare at the paper. "Yeah."

"They know anything about it?"

Ben shook his head.

"Then I guess you better just fold it up and drop it in the shitter," Breedlove said, "because if the Black Cat boys don't know, nobody knows." He stood up. "Well, I got to go pick up Harry. We're going to have a little talk with that Coggins kid."

"Who?"

"The little shit that's organizing the school kids for the march today," Breedlove said. He pulled out his service revolver, threw open the chamber and checked that it was fully loaded. "You want to come along?"

"No."

"Could be fun," Breedlove said with a narrow, mocking smile.

Ben shook his head. "I'm just supposed to follow along with the line of march," he said.

Breedlove shrugged. "Hell, Ben, these days that amounts to a goddamn desk job." He slipped the pistol back into his holster. "Sure you don't want to come along with me and Harry?"

"Not today," Ben said.

Breedlove shrugged. "Suit yourself," he said, "But hell, anything's better than sitting around here."

Ben leaned back in his chair and watched as Breedlove quickly checked inside the cartridge pouch that hung at his side, then walked briskly out of the bullpen.

With Breedlove gone, Ben was now entirely alone in the large, desk-littered room. All the other detectives had already gone to take up their positions. By now, as Ben knew, many of them were laboriously mounting the stairs to the roofs of the squat brick buildings that fronted Fourth Avenue, while others were hunkering down behind the windows just below, their telescopic rifles cradled in their sweating arms. Still others were simply standing on the corners in their rumpled brown suits, staring nervously left and right, searching for that one face that did not go with all the others, the wilder, meaner, more desperate face of one who was armed as they were armed, and just as willing to meet them on the common ground of sudden and annihilating violence. For a moment he saw them as the comrades they still were, men with bills to pay, children to feed, men in cheap Robert Hall suits, who smoked five-cent cigars and drank their iced tea out of old jelly jars, men in the midst of engulfing circumstances who suddenly seemed almost as fully helpless as the dead.

Eight

Scores of police cars had lined the streets off Fourth Avenue by the time Ben arrived. The black-and-whites of the Birmingham police mingled with the gray-and-blacks from the Highway Patrol and an assortment of vehicles from the Jefferson County Sheriff's Department. On the closest side streets, paddy wagons and school buses were parked one after another for almost as far as he could see, all of them manned by troopers with automatic carbines and double-barreled shotguns. They stood tensely along the otherwise deserted sidewalks, smoking cigarettes and staring off toward the avenue as if looking for the first dark whirl of a tornado.

On the avenue itself, police blockades had been set up near the entrance to Sixteenth Street, and uniformed patrolmen stood behind them, their legs spread wide apart, their lead-tipped leather truncheons already in their hands. There was no traffic, not a single civilian car, and the sidewalks on either side of the street were entirely deserted. Only a few yards away, Ben could see the Chief dashing here and there, shouting commands, deploying his troops, and generally overseeing the entire operation. His short, stocky frame darted in and out of the sunlight, and wherever he went, his men stiffened suddenly, as if coming to attention. Luther followed close behind him, along with an assortment of officials from the front office, all of them under the solitary protection, or so it seemed to Ben, of Teddy Langley.

"So you finally made it down here, Ben," Charlie Breedlove said as he stepped up beside him.

"No need to hurry," Ben said casually.

"None at all," Breedlove said. He pulled a pack of Lucky Strikes from his pocket and lit one. "You've not been on riot detail before, have you?"

Ben shook his head.

"Why is that, Ben?"

"I guess they needed somebody to keep watch on other things," Ben said.

"Probably didn't think they needed you before now," Breedlove said. "But you know how it is. Things build up. Things get hotter and hotter. It's been doing that now for a long time."

Ben nodded.

"So today they figure to put a stop to it once and for all."

Ben looked at him. "You think they can?"

Breedlove shrugged. "Who knows. They got King back with them." He shook his head. "They should never have let him out of jail."

Ben glanced back toward the avenue. The dark-gray pavement seemed to bake sullenly under the morning sun. At the far end of the street, up a slight incline, he could see eight or ten motorcycle patrolmen take up their positions several yards beyond the barricades.

Breedlove glanced at his watch. "They should be coming over the hill anytime. Harry radioed in that they left the church about fifteen minutes ago." He winked gaily. "Singing their little song, you know." He spat onto the street. "But it could be a little different today. Today they just might get themselves 'overcome' a little."

A few yards a way, the Chief darted back into the street, his short, fat legs pumping fiercely across the steaming pavement.

"You know what I think about the Chief?" Breedlove said as he watched him. "I think he's loving every minute of this." He laughed. "You know, one of those New York-type reporters came up to him this morning at City Hall, says he wants to ask the Chief a question or two about the situation here." He laughed lightly. "And you know what the Chief said? He said, 'First, I don't talk to no New York reporters, but I'll tell you one thing. They's three things wrong with this country: Communism, Socialism and Journalism.' " He shook his head happily, relishing the tale. "And he was loving it, loving every minute of it."

Harry Daniels stepped up beside Breedlove, his eyes fixed on the wide gray boulevard.

"Well, you made it over here pretty fast," Breedlove said to him.

Daniels peered down toward the end of the avenue. "They're just over the hill," he said. "It's all kids, nothing but kids."

Breedlove looked at him wonderingly. "Nothing but kids?"

"That's right," Daniels said. He pulled a small pamphlet from his coat pocket. "They were handing these things out in all the nigger schools yesterday."

Breedlove took it from his hands and glared at it. It was a call for the schoolchildren to join the march to City Hall.

"Don't that beat all," Breedlove said as he handed the pamphlet to Ben.

Ben glanced at it casually, then handed it back.

"These people," Daniels said disgustedly. "I tell you, Charlie, they don't care what they do. They figured we were ready for them this time, and so they decided that they'd just send the kids after us." He leaned forward slightly and looked at Ben. "I bet you there's not one of them over eighteen years old, and most of them are a lot younger than that. I'm talking about school kids, fourth- and fifth- and six-graders, and such as that."

Breedlove's mouth curled downward. "Shit."

Daniels shook his head. "King's one smart nigger. They wouldn't have a brain without him."

"Yeah," Breedlove said grimly, "they wouldn't have a thing without him." He tossed his cigarette angrily into the street. "But I'll tell you one goddamn thing, Harry. Kid or no kid, I'm going to handle them the same." He curled his hand into a fist. "I going to give back double whatever I get." He glanced at Ben. "What about you, Ben?"

"I'll do what the Chief said," Ben told him. "I'll protect myself."

Breedlove's eyes squeezed together slowly. "That's what we all have to do," he said, "Protect ourselves." He glanced toward Daniels and smiled. "Right, Harry?"

Daniels nodded determinedly. "Absolutely."

For a moment the three of them stood silently together, staring up the avenue and along the small grocery stores, poolhalls and flophouses that lined it on either side. The Chief was now moving toward them with Luther and Teddy Langley racing breathlessly beside him.

He stopped only a few feet away and motioned for a group of troopers to form themselves into a line across the avenue.

"We're going to stop them right here," he shouted. "Now line up! Line up! I want you all to stand shoulder to shoulder!"

The troopers moved out into the street and formed a straight gray line across it. When they had formed their ranks, the Chief paced back and forth in front of them.

"Now I want you to know that the people of Birmingham are proud to have you here today," he said loudly. "And ever-body in this city owes a debt to Colonel Lingo for bringing you in to help with this ridiculous situation." He smiled gratefully for a moment, then the smile disappeared suddenly, as if a hard wind had blown it from his face. "Now I want to make something clear to you gentlemen." He pointed to the ground and raked the tip of his shoe across the pavement. "This is like the Alamo, gentlemen, and this is the line we are drawing in the dust." He paused, and dug his fists into his sides. "And don't you let one Nigra pass it. Not one solitary Nigra." He pulled a small green notebook from his jacket pocket. Ben recognized it instantly as the one he'd turned in to Luther. "You know what King said to his people at the church?" he asked. He flipped through the notebook and began to read: " 'They know how to handle violence, but they don't know how to handle nonviolence. It confuses them. They don't know how to deal with it.' " He closed the notebook and stared angrily at the troopers. "Well, bullshit, gentlemen. We know how to handle violence, all right. And by God we know how to handle violence that just *looks* like nonviolence." He pointed to the left where a group of reporters stood clustered together beneath the tattered green awning of a barbecue parlor. "Now these marches and demonstrations, they may look like nonviolence to people who don't know any better," he cried, "but we know what it really is, and we know how to handle it." He returned the notebook to his jacket. "Do your duty as God gives you the wisdom to see your duty. And do it with pride, gentlemen, pride in your city, your state, your governor and your God." He paused a moment, eyeing each man in the line. "Are there any questions?"

Some of the troopers shifted uneasily on their feet, but no one spoke.

"Very well, then," the Chief said. He clicked his heels together, saluted them, and then rushed off toward the cooler shades of Kelly Ingram Park.

Luther and Teddy Langley remained at the Chief's side, and from across the street Ben could seem them nodding vigorously as he spoke to them, waving his arms right and left, deploying his men up and down the length of the park and sending squads of others out along the steaming brick side streets and parking lots.

"Old Dynamite Teddy," Daniels said. "He's always sucking up to the Chief." He looked at Breedlove. "You know they almost got him for some schoolhouse bombings in Tennessee."

Breedlove smiled. "Teddy? Is that a fact?"

"Actually locked him up one time for about an hour or two."

"Whereabouts?" Breedlove asked.

"Right here in Birmingham."

"When was that, Harry?"

"Back when Big Jim was governor."

Breedlove scratched his chin. "You reckon he's been doing stuff like that around here lately?"

"If the Chief wants him to," Daniels said without hesitation. "He'll do anything the Chief says, that's for sure."

Ben's eyes drifted over toward the park. Several squads of troopers were marching double-time across the southern end of the park, their feet kicking up a low, grayish-brown dust. Beyond them he could see a convoy of school buses as it nosed its way up the length of the far end of the park. The Chief's white tank headed the procession, as if clearing away enemy positions.

Suddenly the Chief was in the street again, yelling through an electric megaphone. "Get ready now, gentlemen," he cried. *"Here they come!"*

Almost at that instant a line of marchers crested the hill at the end of the avenue and then proceeded slowly down the street. Their placards flapped loudly in the summer wind, snapping in the air like distant gunshots.

"Take up your positions," the Chief shouted.

Another line of troopers moved in front of the first, while others marched forward in ragged flanks, their once-straight lines now breaking awkwardly around police cars, trees, telephone poles, until their ranks finally dissolved entirely into a jaggedly moving chaos of gray uniforms and gently waving nightsticks.

"You there, up ahead!" the Chief screamed. "You will not be permitted to continue this march."

The single line of marchers continued forward at their same languid pace, flowing slowly, like a dark syrup, over the hill and down the avenue.

"I repeat," the Chief yelled. "You will not be permitted to continue this march. You will not be permitted to reach City Hall." His voice, high and metallic, echoed from the surrounding buildings and rebounded into the shadowy park. "You will not be permitted to continue this march. Do you understand? Turn around. Turn back."

But the marchers continued forward, some silently, some singing and clapping their hands. The breeze billowed out their skirts and blouses and rippled through the torn cloth awnings which stretched out toward the avenue.

"Halt!" the Chief screamed now at the top of his voice.

But the marchers moved onward, their long dark line lengthening steadily as one pair after another crested the gently rounded hill.

"Jesus Christ," Luther breathed softly as he stepped up behind Ben. "What are we going to do about this?"

"We've all got our orders," Breedlove replied crisply.

Daniels nodded. "That's right. Let's go."

Ben felt himself swept forward with them as they moved in between the two lines of troopers. He could now see the faces of the first marchers, two young women in light-blue skirts and white blouses, their eyes staring straight ahead, their faces utterly expressionless.

The Chief retreated before them, now silent, sullen, walking backward slowly as he motioned the troopers forward.

Then he abruptly wheeled around. "You are under arrest," he shouted as he stepped briskly out of their line of march and strode angrily back into the park, where he stopped, let the megaphone drop from his hand, folded his arms over his chest and waited.

The first line of troopers stiffened as the first wave of marchers approached it. Some of them began slapping their nightsticks into their hands, while others shifted uneasily from one foot to the next, as if preparing themselves to receive a burst of violent wind.

Ben stood near the middle of the street, while Breedlove and Daniels took up positions at the far end of the line. Luther lingered near Ben for a moment, then moved to the left where he stood beside T. G. Hollis, his thumbs in his belt, his eyes fixed on the line of march.

At the instant the first marchers reached the line, the troopers stepped forward, took them one by one by the arms and began rushing them double-time toward the paddy wagons and school buses which crowded the side streets and stretched out along the edges of the park. A great roar rose from the line of march as more and more of them were pushed and pulled forward, the troopers tugging wildly at their arms or shoving them along with the ends of their nightsticks.

Ben stepped forward and looked helplessly toward the hill. The last of the marchers had crested it, and behind them there was nothing but the flat gray of the street. He could feel a terrible relief sweep over him at the knowledge that it would soon be over, and he allowed himself to relax a little, simply to stand and watch as the last of the demonstrators were hustled into the waiting vans and school buses. To his right, he could see Breedlove and Daniels as they pushed and pulled at a skinny young girl. A few yards beyond them, Teddy Langley was shoving a tall, lanky boy, poking his nightstick into his kidneys to move him along.

Ben flinched away, stepped back slightly and watched as the last of the line was broken by the troopers and hauled roughly across the park. He could hear the tumult in the distance as the marchers were tossed into the paddy wagons or shoved, half-stumbling, through the rubber-lined doors of the school buses. The air around him filled with the grinding engines of the vans and buses as they began to pull away, weaving slowly left and right, as if trying to throw off an intolerable burden. Everywhere, the troopers were laughing and joking as they gathered together in small gray knots. The Chief strode proudly among them, shaking their hands or slapping them affectionately on the back. In the background, the sounds of the engines and their accompanying sirens died away, and a sudden quietness drifted down over the park and the avenue, one that was broken only by the occasional clatter of a police radio or some muffled shout which seemed to come from far away.

"Well, looks like we did it," Breedlove said as he trudged across the street toward him.

Daniels walked along at his side, both men smiling broadly.

Breedlove's eyes shot up toward the hill. "Kids or no kids, we kicked their ass."

Daniels laughed happily. "Maybe we outsmarted them, Ben. What do you think?"

Ben did not answer. Instead, he turned back toward the deserted hill and casually lit a cigarette. The smoke billowed up before him in a thick white cloud. He raised his hand and batted at it, clearing away the air. The white haze tore apart instantly, and as it did so, he saw two figures move slowly over the hill, very young, holding hands, and behind them two more a little older, and behind them, two more, perhaps the same age, and then two more and two more and two more.

He snapped the cigarette from his mouth and dropped it on the street. He could hear the general talk and laughter of the troopers die away slowly, as one by one their attention was drawn toward the hill.

"Form ranks!" the Chief shouted.

Daniels and Breedlove whirled around.

Breedlove's mouth dropped open. "What?"

"They're trying it again," Daniels said, his eyes now fixed on the line of march.

Once again, the troopers formed themselves into two straight lines across the avenue.

The Chief marched out in front of them, lifted his megaphone, then stopped and slowly lowered it. He turned back toward the troopers and grinned. "Forget it," he said. "They don't know English, anyway."

The second wave hit only a few minutes later, and the troopers pulled and shoved them across the park and down the side streets. The sounds of near and distant sirens mingled with the shouts of the troopers, the singing of the marchers, the heavy wheeze of the engines as they started up again, pulled away, then returned again and again for yet another load.

For a time Ben simply stood, frozen in place, and watched the swirling tumult around him. Sirens now wailed continually, and beneath them, like the murmur of a drum, the steady beat of the troopers' boots as one line after another rushed forward into the unending stream of children.

Then, suddenly, Luther was in his face, screaming wildly. "What the hell are you doing!" His flabby jaws shook with rage and frustration. "Get going, goddammit!" Then he raced away, almost falling over a small boy before he stopped himself, took the boy's shoulder in his large beefy hand and pushed him into the park.

Ben moved toward the thinning ranks of troopers, his eyes desperately scanning the line of marchers. He saw a tall, slender boy of about nine years old, walked over to him, dug his fingers into the soft flesh of his shoulder and tugged him toward the park.

The boy moved forward without protest, clapping his hands and singing as he walked, his eyes straight ahead. At the school bus he turned, glanced at Ben, as if to record his face, then walked up the short steps and headed toward the rear of the bus.

Ben returned immediately to the line of march, took another child, this time a teenage girl, and began walking her toward the bus.

All around them, the troopers were driving other demonstrators forward at a breakneck pace, pushing and shoving, until they often fell together, demonstrators and exhausted troopers lying in a tangled mass in the swirling dust of the park. The noise of the melee built steadily as the arrests continued, so that the orders of the commanders could barely be heard above the sirens, the engines, the cries of the demonstrators and troopers.

A third wave followed the second by only a few minutes, and the troopers formed ranks again, sweat now streaming down their faces, their uniforms wet beneath their arms and down their backs. The cries of the children rocked through the air, high and wailing, as the troopers stumbled forward, falling upon the demonstrators with a steadily building fury.

Ben seized a teenage boy in one hand and a teenage girl in the other and led them briskly through the park. He could feel his shirt wet against his back and chest, and the dust which now tumbled in thick, suffocating clouds burned his eyes and choked his throat. He could feel his fingers growing numb at their tips, and his legs now seemed to drag behind him like heavy weights rather than propel him forward. But still he trudged back and forth from the line of march to the buses, back and forth from the street to the paddy wagons, and after a time he seemed to be moving will-lessly, as if his body were no longer a part of him, but something different, distant and estranged, so that it required nothing to perform the incessantly repeated actions which it had learned during the long pull of the afternoon, learned as the sun mounted toward noon then fell toward evening. And hour followed hour as he took them, large and small, hostile or compliant, took them with whatever force their resistance required, tugged them along or pushed them forcefully, stood in the sweltering air until he knew they were securely in the buses or paddy wagons, and then returned, again and again, until at last there were no more, and he walked out into the torn and battle-weary park, into the still blue air of the evening, and pressed his back against a tree and let his legs give way beneath him, so that he slumped down onto the ground and let his face drop slowly into his open hands.

Nine

"You look like hell," Patterson said grimly as Ben walked into the Coroner's Office. He eyed him closely. "I heard it was real bad today."

Ben nodded. "Bad enough."

Patterson shook his head despairingly. "You were in it?"

"Yeah," Ben said weakly. Just beyond the entrance to the freezer room, he could see the old man sweeping a jagged line of grit and sawdust toward a large metal garbage can.

"We're in a world of trouble these days, Ben," Patterson said, "and nobody knows how to get out of it."

The old man bent forward, placed a rusty dustpan in front of the sweepings, then whisked them in.

"The Chief knows exactly where he is in all this," Patterson added, his eyes watching Ben intently. "But others, they have some problems."

The old man winced with pain as he slowly straightened himself. He rubbed his back with a flat open hand. His eyes moved over to Ben, then darted away.

"I hear there's a lot of unhappy people in the department," Patterson said. "And not just in the ranks. People in the front office." He looked at Ben quizzically. "Any truth in that, Ben?"

Ben turned to him. "I don't know."

Patterson shook his head. "My God, Ben, you look like the best part of you got flushed down the drain."

"Did you bury that girl yet?" Ben asked.

"No."

"When are you planning to do that?"

Patterson looked at the clock on the opposite wall. "Kelly should be here in about an hour."

"Kelly?"

"Kelly Ryan. You know, from the Property Department," Patterson said matter-of-factly. "He does all the colored burials."

Ben placed a small paper bag on Patterson's desk. "I bought this little dress," he said. "It's not much. Just a little blue thing." He shrugged. "Hers looked too dirty to be buried in."

Patterson's face softened almost imperceptibly. "I'll put her in it for you." He reached for the bag and stood up. "I'll be back in a second."

Ben lingered idly in the room outside the morgue. The dissecting tables were all empty, and their polished stainless-steel surfaces took on an icy coldness beneath the hard fluorescent lights. For a moment he thought about the dead woman from Red Mountain, the one whose insurance policy had hung like a bounty above her head. He had no doubt that her body was now nestled in the white satin lining of an expensive mahogany casket, that it was in a room decked with flowers and hung with thick red drapes, that somewhere in the background an organ was playing sonorously while the mourners filed by silently or whispered their farewells.

"All done," Patterson said a few minutes later as he walked back into the outer office. "Would you like to see her?"

Ben shook his head.

"Well, I can tell you that she looks real nice," Patterson said as he strolled back over to his desk. "Real nice." He pulled out the top drawer and lifted a small plastic bag from it. "By the way, I got this back about an hour ago."

It was the ring which had been found on the girl's body, and Ben could see the cheap glass stone shining pinkish purple in the light.

"What'd they find?" he asked.

"One set of fingerprints," Patterson said. "I'm having them traced every way I can."

Ben walked over to the desk and took the bag from Patterson's fingers. "Just one set?"

"That's right?"

"And they weren't the girl's?"

"No," Patterson said. "No trace of hers at all." He pulled a manila folder from the same drawer. "These are the prints."

Ben took them out and held them under the lamp on Patterson's desk. "The ring—was it wiped?"

"Not that I could tell."

"So the girl never touched the ring?"

"That would be my conclusion," Patterson told him. "And as far as the prints go, it looks like you were right."

Ben looked at him. "About what?"

"Well, I remember yesterday, how you said that someone a whole lot bigger than the girl came up behind her and put that little pistol upside her head and shot her."

"What about it?"

"Well, just that if the guy that owned this ring was the one that did it," Patterson said, "well, then you were right. Chances are he was a whole lot bigger than the girl." He smiled. "Probably a whole lot bigger than you or me, too."

"How do you know?"

"By the prints," Patterson said. "It works like a dog's paw. Big hand, big man. At least most of the time." He glanced down at the prints. "And these were real big. Maybe the biggest I've ever seen."

Ben continued to look at the prints. Wide gray whorls spiraled upward from the black negative and finally formed a rounded nub at the apex of each finger.

"He's not exactly a giant," Patterson said, "but I wouldn't want to bet my house that I could beat him arm-wrestling." His eyes darkened. "And I guess that's why she was torn up so. You know, in her privates."

Ben returned the prints to the envelope.

"And we found this, too," Patterson added. He handed him a rectangular microscope slide. "Some kind of sticky stuff was on the ring. I'm having it tested tomorrow."

Ben took the slide carefully between his thumb and index finger. He could make out a granular yellowish powder which had been smeared across the glass. "What do you think it is, Leon?" he asked.

Patterson shrugged. "I don't know. Could be something like pine pollen. There's plenty of that around in the summer." He smiled. "It could be that yellow stuff that sticks to your fingers after you eat a bag of Korn Kurls." He shrugged again, this time more helplessly. "In other words, it could be just about anything."

Ben handed back the slide. "Well, let me know what you find out." He looked into the adjoining room. He could see the plain wooden box where the girl now lay, the little blue dress covering the thick black stitching which he knew ran in an upside-down Y formation from her throat to head to her abdomen.

"What do you want to name her, Ben?" Patterson asked suddenly.

"Name her?"

"For the record, I mean," Patterson said. "Unless you want me to just use a number. Plenty of times that's what I do."

"No," Ben said. "A name."

Patterson sat down at his desk, picked up a pencil and held it poised an inch or so above a sheet of white paper. "Well, what'll it be? Give me a name."

Ben looked at him wonderingly. "Me?"

"Why not," Patterson said offhandedly. "Hell, Ben, you're as close to being her daddy as anybody else right now."

For a moment he allowed a list of names to flow featurelessly through his mind. He thought of movie-star names, then those of the colored singers he'd heard of. Nothing seemed to fit the way he wanted it to, but he finally called her "Martha," after his own mother.

"Okay," Patterson said, as he wrote it down. "And what about a last name?"

He glanced back toward the small wooden box, then returned his eyes to Patterson. "Give her mine," he said.

A large middle-aged white man walked into Patterson's office a few minutes later. He was followed by two young blacks, both of whom were dressed in the uniforms of the city jail.

"I've come to pick up a body," the white man said. He squinted hard at Ben and Patterson. "Who do I see about that?"

"Me," Patterson said immediately. "Where's Kelly?"

"Kelly who?"

"Kelly Ryan from the Property Department," Patterson told him. "He usually does the colored burying."

The man shrugged. "I don't know nothing about that," he said. "I work with the Highway Department. I just got a call to pick up a couple of hands from the jail and then come on over here for a body."

"You know where the cemetery is?"

"They got a place dug for it in Gracehill," the man said.

"They give you a plot number?" Patterson asked.

The man shook his head. "They didn't say nothing but come over to Hillman and pick up a body."

"Okay," Patterson said wearily. He led the three men into the freezer room and stood beside the coffin. "This is it."

"A kid?" the white man asked.

"That's right," Patterson told him. "And it's a murder, too, so I want you to remember where you put her. Find a tree or a stump or something and remember where it is. I'll get a plot number later."

Ben stepped up beside the two young men. "I'll go, too," he said.

The white man nodded quickly. "Well, with the four of us, we can do it the right way," he said, "one shoulder at each corner, just like they'd do it in church."

The four of them took their positions, one at each corner of the coffin, and lifted it up onto their shoulders.

As he headed out toward the parking lot, Ben could feel the body shift slightly as they juggled the coffin awkwardly, and he could imagine the girl's face jerking left and right inside, as if looking for a way out of the darkness.

A dusty, mud-spattered pickup truck sat waiting for them in the parking lot, its battered front fenders sloping wearily toward the ground. The white man took down the tailgate with one hand while continuing to balance his corner of the coffin precariously on his shoulder.

"Okay, just set it down real slow," he said, after he'd undone the gate. Then he turned cautiously and eased the coffin down onto the bed of the truck.

"All right, let's just shove it in now," he said. "But soft-like. We got a little child here."

When the coffin was in place, the two black youths hauled themselves into the back of the truck and sat silently on either side of it, their hands resting motionlessly on the top of the coffin.

Ben and the other man crawled into the cab of the truck.

"Name's Thompson," the man said as he started the engine. "Lamar Thompson."

"Ben Wellman."

Thompson eased the truck forward, moving slowly toward the avenue and then out into it.

"You some kind of preacher or something?" he asked when he brought the truck to a halt at the first traffic signal.

"No," Ben said, "I'm with the Police Department."

Thompson smiled. "I figured you might be coming along to say a few words over the body. I thought maybe the state provided something like that."

"No."

"Want me to do it then?" Thompson asked immediately.

"If you want to," Ben said indifferently.

"You got any idea what this child was?"

"She was a Negro," Ben told him.

"I figured that," Thompson said. "They don't bury white people in Gracehill. But what about her religion?"

"I don't know anything about that."

"Well, I'm a Primitive Baptist, myself," Thompson said. "You know, an old foot-washing Baptist, what you might say." He smiled softly. "With us, it don't matter what this child was, because in the end, she was, what you might say, a child of God." He pulled a red handkerchief from his back pocket and wiped his neck vigorously. "So what I mean is, well, I could say a few simple things over her, if that's all right with you."

"It's all right with me," Ben said. He kept his eyes straight ahead, peering out into the deepening night as the truck moved shakily alongside Kelly Ingram Park and then on ahead into the Negro district. To his right, a string of poolhalls stretched out for nearly a block. A soft green light glowed behind their painted windows, and he could imagine the people inside, lined up along the wall in small wooden chairs or bunched over the tables, their bright, gleaming eyes following the flight of the balls.

"How long you been a policeman?" Thompson asked after a while.

Ben drew in a deep breath. "Long time."

"I've worked with the Highway Department for a long time, too," Thompson said cheerfully. "It's rough in the summer. You spread that steaming black tar all over everything. It steams right up in your face. You blow your nose when you get home from work, it looks like you're blowing coal soot out of your head."

Ben nodded slowly, but said nothing. He could hear the jukeboxes humming noisily in the night air, loud, pulsing, rhythmic, as if they were being played to warn off an approaching danger.

"I used to think about doing something else," Thompson went on, "but by the time I got to thinking real serious about that, I was near to forty, with three kids and a big car payment." He hit the brake suddenly to avoid a small dog, and the coffin slid forward and bumped loudly against the cab of the truck. "Sorry, sorry," Thompson said quickly. "Didn't want to hit that dog, though."

The truck moved steadily down Fourth Avenue, then out beyond it, to where more and more vacant lots lined the increasingly bumpy and untended streets.

"They ought to get a crew out here," Thompson said. He peered to the right. "There it is," he said.

Gracehill Cemetery rested on a small, rounded hill near the far southwest corner of the city. Small unpaved roads snaked windingly among the small gray stones, slowly curling upward toward the crest of the hill. All along the gently sloping banks, tombstones jutted out of the ground in broken clusters, their bases covered by the unmown grass. The mounds of dirt which stretched out from them were decorated by clumps of plastic flowers rooted in dirt-filled tin cans and quart jars. Here and there a plywood cross leaned unsteadily toward the earth, or a plain brown stone lifted from it, jagged, nameless, accompanied by a small one at the foot of the mound.

"It's supposed to be right around here," Thompson said matter-of-factly. He craned his neck out the window, his eyes searching through the ever-deepening brush.

The grave had been dug in a slender trench between two others, and when Thompson finally spotted it, he wheeled the truck over, then backed it in, as if preparing to dump the coffin like a load of sand.

"Okay," he said as he turned off the engine.

Ben got out and walked to the back of the truck. The two youths had already lowered the tailgate and pushed the coffin to the edge of it. They now stood above it, their eyes lifted up over the hill, toward the distant twinkling lights of the city.

"Okay, now," Thompson said. "We'll just lower it down real slow. Don't drop her."

Within a few minutes, the coffin was in the ground, and Thompson walked to the head of the grave and bowed his head. The two young men bowed theirs as well, while Ben slumped back on a large stone and sank his hands in his pockets.

"Dearest and most gracious God," Thompson began, "we commend to your care the soul of your servant . . ." He stopped and glanced up at Ben. "What's this child's name?" he asked.

"Martha Wellman," Ben told him.

Thompson lowered his head again. "We commend to your care

the soul of your servant, Martha Wellman." He folded his hands together gracefully. "We know that she was your child, that her soul was saved long before it was even clothed in flesh. For the grace of Jesus Christ is a gift which cannot be refused."

Ben's eyes drifted over to the two black youths. They stood on either side of the grave, their heads bowed reverently, their lips pressed tightly together. Behind them, the nightbound city glittered silently. Ben's eyes drifted down toward the grave, then back up again. The city lay utterly quiet in the darkness, a grid of streets lit by what seemed in the distance a thousand tiny fires. He wondered how many streets the girl had come to know, which ones she had liked, feared, the last one she'd walked down before she died.

King had not yet begun to speak when Ben arrived once again at the Sixteenth Baptist Church, but the crowds were already singing and clapping as they filled the streets which fronted the church.

Ben got out of his car and stood beside it, leaning on the hood, his pen and notebook already in his hand. From his position he could see a group of black leaders standing on the small porch at the side of the church. They were talking quietly and fanning themselves with paper fans from A. G. Gaston's Funeral Home. Just beyond them, Breedlove and Daniels were squatting together in front of a bush, and even from several yards away, Ben could see that they had both taken out their own pens and notebooks.

Just as the day before, the crowd suddenly grew quiet, and then King's voice rang out.

"Today was D-Day in Birmingham," he cried, his voice already at that high pitch which it had achieved the day before. "But there will be many more D-Days in Birmingham. There will be Double D-Days in Birmingham until we have won our freedom."

Daniels was writing furiously in his notebook, when Ben looked up, but Breedlove had vanished. For a moment he looked for him, a pale white face in a sea of black, but it was as if he had disintegrated where he squatted, dissolved into the warm evening air.

"The eyes of the nation are on Birmingham," King intoned, and the crowd cheered wildly. "The eyes of the world are on Birmingham." The cheers grew louder and more ecstatic. "The eyes of God are on Birmingham." A wave of trembling jubilation lifted the crowd inside the church, then swept out over the people surrounding it, passing back and forth over them again and again like the flow of wildly eddying waters.

Ben's pen scurried across the page, the point burrowing into the white paper, scarring it as he wrote.

"So don't get tired," King cried.

"No!" the crowd screamed in return.

"Don't get bitter."

"No!"

King's deep, sonorous laughter settled over the crowd. Then, suddenly, his voice rose out of it like a lick of fire.

"Are you tired?" he shouted.

"No!"

"Are you bitter?"

"No!"

"Then go out and go out and go out again," King cried. "And let justice flow down from the mountainside."

"Yes!"

"Let justice flow down from Red Mountain."

"Yes, Lord!"

"Let justice rise like the mighty waters."

"Amen! Amen!"

"Until it is high in the streets of the city."

"Yes! Yes!"

"O Lord, let justice flow down upon Birmingham like a mighty stream."

The furious cheers of the people seemed to be even greater than the day before, and as Ben brought his pen to rest and glanced around him, he realized that they had reached such a deafening pitch that they now drowned out everything, as if their thunderous roar came like an immense and shuddering wave from the deep core of the earth.

Ten

Kelly Ryan was slumped behind the single gun-metal gray desk of the Property Room, and he did not move as Ben approached him. His small green eyes peered expressionlessly forward, and his lips remained tightly closed. He wore a plain blue shirt, open at the collar, and with the sleeves rolled up above the elbow, so that he looked more like a farmhand than a policeman.

"I wasn't sure you'd still be here," Ben said as he stepped up to the desk.

Ryan nodded slowly. "They had me on special duty."

"Doing what?"

Ryan said nothing, but his thin lips jerked down slightly.

"Doing what, Kelly?" Ben repeated.

"All those girls they brought in today," Ryan said. "They're doing VD checks on them."

Ben felt the air grow cold around him.

Ryan looked at him pointedly. "Were you in the park?"

"Yes."

"Must have been really something down there today."

"It was," Ben said. "Where were you?"

"They kept me right here most of the time," Ryan said. He smiled thinly. "They had me running back and forth from the cells, bringing the girls upstairs." He drew in a long, weary breath. "Is there something you want from Property?" he asked.

Ben's eyes surveyed the rows of metal shelving which lined the walls behind Ryan's desk. They were almost entirely empty.

"Looks like they cleaned you out," he said.

"Just the guns," Ryan told him.

"Yeah, I know. I saw McCorkindale signing them out." Ben

paused. "We buried a little girl in Gracehill this evening," he said. "They sent a man over from the Highway Department. Patterson was surprised it wasn't you."

"Well, that's because I do all the colored cemeteries."

Ben leaned forward slightly. "Why's that, Kelly?"

Ryan looked at him evenly. "You never struck me as the nosy type, Ben."

Ben shrugged. "I was just wondering," he said.

"Wondering about what, exactly?"

Ben did not answer.

"Wondering why I get all the nigger work?" Kelly asked. There was a bitter edge in his voice. "Is that what you were wondering?"

"I guess."

Ryan sat back in his chair and folded his arms over his chest. "Well, what have you heard?"

"Nothing," Ben said lamely.

"I don't believe that."

"Well, I know that you used to work Bearmatch."

Ryan said nothing.

"That little girl we buried," Ben added. "We found her in that old ballfield off Twenty-third Street."

Ryan remained silent, but Ben could see something stirring behind his eyes.

"And I thought you might be able to help me."

Ryan turned away sharply. "I haven't worked Bearmatch in two years. If you want to know something, go ask the Langleys. It's strictly their beat now."

"I talked to them," Ben said. "They weren't much help."

Ryan said nothing. He kept his eyes averted slightly.

Ben continued to stand over him, staring down. He could feel an odd tumult building in Ryan's mind, and for a moment he simply stood by silently and let it grow.

"Bearmatch was my first assignment," Ryan said as he turned slowly toward Ben, his voice almost wistful as he continued, "I was fresh as a daisy." He started to go on, then stopped himself and drew his eyes quickly to the left, as if he were looking for a way out. "I feel old now," he added finally. "I don't know why." He said nothing else.

Again, Ben waited, allowing the silence to lengthen slowly. When it seemed stretched to the limit, he broke it.

"You want to have a drink with me?" he asked.

Ryan's eyes flashed toward him. "I haven't had a drink with a cop since they took me off Bearmatch," he said.

Ben smiled quietly. "Want to have one now?"

Ryan looked at him suspiciously. "Why?"

"A little girl," Ben told him softly. "A little colored girl."

It was a small, honky-tonk bar, nestled among the raw metal clutter of two steel mills. Outside, the air quivered with the roar of the blast furnaces, but inside there was only the jukebox and the low murmur of the factory workers who lined the bar itself or gathered in loose clusters around tiny wooden tables.

Ben guided Ryan to a booth in the far back corner, ordered two beers, then offered him a cigarette.

Ryan took it immediately. "This is a real night out with the boys for me," he said with a mocking laugh.

Ben lit the cigarette and Ryan inhaled deeply.

"I hope there's nobody working undercover in this place," he said as he let the smoke filter slowly out of his mouth. "You don't want to be seen with me."

Ben lit his own cigarette and eased himself back into the padded seat. "Why's that?"

Ryan smiled sardonically and took another drag on the cigarette. "I worked Bearmatch before the Langleys took it over. You might say I handed it over to them." He started to continue, but the barman stepped up with the beers, and he stopped until he had deposited them on the table and returned to the bar. Then he lifted his glass. "Here's to the Chief."

They drank together for a moment, then Ryan set his half-empty glass down on the table and looked at Ben squarely.

"What exactly do you want to know?" he asked.

"Like I said before, I'm working a case," Ben told him, "A murder. Little girl without a name. In Bearmatch."

Ryan lifted his glass again, his eyes peering steadily over the rim. "You said you talked to the Langleys?"

"That's right."

"What'd they say?"

"That they don't bother with nigger murders."

Kelly laughed derisively. "No shit." He took a quick gulp from the glass then returned it to the table. "Those two are wolves. There's no telling for sure what they've been doing over in Bearmatch.

Nobody keeps an eye on them." He leaned forward slightly, his hand squeezing the handle of the mug. "But everybody says they've really been kicking ass lately. Busting places up, harassing everybody. Sometimes they make five or six arrests a day over there."

"Who are they arresting?"

"Anybody they want to," Ryan said. "From bootleggers to jay-walkers, I guess." He took a quick sip. "You know what I think? I think the Langleys feed on Bearmatch." He laughed bitterly. "After me, I guess the Chief figured he needed guys like them for that particular beat." He took another drink, then rolled the nearly empty glass rhythmically in his hands.

A jukebox started up at the front of the bar, and the growling voice of Ernest Tubb swept over the room with "I'm Walking the Floor Over You."

For a while, Ryan listened to the lyrics, his eyes fixed on a flashing Pabst Blue Ribbon sign near the center of the bar.

"I lost my head," he said at last, his voice almost in a whisper. "I forgot where I was." He finished the beer, then signaled for another. The barman brought it over immediately. Ryan took a quick sip, then fastened his eyes on Ben, as if trying to read something written on his soul.

"Like I said before," he began finally, "it was the first thing they gave me. I was fresh to the work. They gave me Bearmatch, and I took it serious. I walked the beat, Ben, walked it like a real cop, you know?" He laughed. "There ain't an old lady in Bearmatch I didn't help across the street." He laughed again, a thin, high laugh, tense and edgy. "Anyway, I come across this young girl one day." He shook his head. "Her name was Memora." His eyes brightened somewhat. "They have wonderful names, the colored people. Her baby sister was named Neopolitana. After that ice cream, I guess, the one with strips of strawberry and chocolate and vanilla." He shrugged halfheartedly. "Anyway, I'd run across her just about every day. She'd be tending this little patch of flowers in the front yard. I'd say hello, and she'd say hello. Before long I started taking a rest in front of her house. We'd talk and talk." He shook his head wearily. "She was the most beautiful thing in the world and I . . ." He stopped, and his eyes dropped back down toward the glass. "And I got quite a feeling for her." He looked up quickly. "You know what I mean?"

Ben nodded.

Ryan smiled mournfully. "You don't know nothing until you know a person. You may have an idea about something, but until you get to know somebody, you don't know what you feel about anything." Once again he fell silent, his eyes studying Ben's face. "You know what I'm saying?"

"Yes."

Ryan scratched his chin slowly. "I'm not one bit ashamed of what I felt for that girl. That's what they can't stand down at City Hall. That's what the Chief can't stand. That I have never done anything since then to apologize for it or to say I was wrong. That's why they keep me on with the department. They're waiting for me to break down and cry over it and say what a fool I was." His eyes hardened. "I'll die first," he said determinedly. "And they can bury me in Gracehill where they've made me bury so many others." His face grew red suddenly and a trembling swept over it. His eyes widened wildly, then closed slowly as he drew in a long, lean breath. "You good for another beer?"

"Yeah," Ben said. He signaled the barman for another round and sat silently until he deposited them on the table.

Ryan took a long draw and wiped his mouth quickly. "I have a little problem with drink. Did you know that?"

"No."

Ryan gave him a slow, curious look. "You married?"

"No?"

"Never have been?"

Ben shook his head.

Ryan smiled. "Like me."

"I guess," Ben said. He took a sip from his glass. For an instant he saw his little wooden frame house, saw it empty without him, unenlivened by any presence other than his own. "This girl, the one you liked," he said finally. "What happened to her?"

Ryan emptied the glass. "She went up North," he said. Then he lifted the glass slightly. "And I guess you might say I went a little bit to this."

For a time Ben watched as Ryan sat quietly, staring into the empty glass. His face had the kind of grief he'd seen in pictures of Jesus in the Garden, silent, inexpressibly mournful, waiting for something even worse than what had come before.

"This other girl," he said at last, "the one we found in the old ballfield. I'm not getting very far with it."

Ryan's eyes lifted toward him slowly. "What do you have on it?"

"A few things, nothing much," Ben told him. "What I really need is a name, some way to trace her." He took out the picture and brought the two sides together on the table in front of Ryan. "That's her."

Ryan stared expressionlessly at the photograph.

"Somebody in Bearmatch must know who she is," Ben said insistently. "Somebody must know everything that goes on there." He looked at Ryan pointedly. "You know a man named Roy Jolly?"

Ryan glanced up immediately. "Everybody who's ever known anything about Bearmatch knows about Roy Jolly."

"Where can I find him?" Ben asked.

Ryan said nothing.

"Help me," Ben said.

"Telling you where to find Roy Jolly may not be the best way to help you."

"Right now it's the only way you can."

Ryan thought about it for a moment, then nodded slowly. "Over on Twenty-first Street there's a little yellow house. It looks like all the others, except it's yellow. That's where you'll find Roy Jolly."

Ben swept the photograph back into his pocket. "Thanks, Kelly."

They finished their drinks silently, then walked outside together. The orange glow of the furnaces could be seen through the rusty storm fence across the way, and above it a single enormous smokestack belched a thick tumbling smoke into the sulfuric night air.

"Get in," Ben said as he stepped over to his car.

Ryan remained some distance away, standing idly in the middle of the street. "No, thanks," he said softly. "I'll walk. I don't live too far from here."

A sudden piercing whistle shook the air around them.

"Late shift coming in," Ryan said. Then he hunched his shoulders slightly, sunk his hands deep into his pockets and disappeared into the thick, humid darkness.

Eleven

The windows of the little yellow house on Twenty-first Street were glowing brightly when Ben pulled up at some distance down the street from it. He could see a steady stream of figures moving in silhouette behind the thin red windowshades, and even from several yards away, he could make out the soft tinkle of muffled piano music. A continual flow of lightly murmuring voices came from the small open windows, and as he sat behind the wheel, staring at the house, he could sense the dark, guarded happiness that seemed to energize the air around it. It was a Negro shothouse buried deep within the folds of a dense Negro district, and for the first time in his life Ben suddenly felt the odd allure he remembered from his youth when he'd worked in the nearby railyards until late in the night, and then, before going home, stood behind the rusty fence that cordoned off the Negro district and peered out longingly toward the beguiling lights of Bearmatch. At the time, he could not fathom the look he saw in the eyes of the other men who sometimes watched beside him, or even begin to understand the strange and fearful stirring he felt in himself. But now, as he listened to the music and the voices, it all came back to him, and he felt his hand grasp the door, then his feet drop to the ground, felt himself moving toward the house with a strange, beguiling urgency.

Several cars were parked in the adjoining driveway, while others lined the street in both directions. Most of them were empty, but a few contained a varying assortment of men and women in their front and rear seats. The people inside fell silent as he passed them, and he knew that they were staring at him with a mixture of fear and resentment.

People continued to filter in and out of the house as he approached it through the covering darkness. Others lounged idly on the small front porch, and as he drew steadily closer, he could hear them talking and laughing, but he still could not make out any details. A single lone figure stood silently at the end of the front walkway, glancing left and right down the street, his body bathed in the bluish glare of a streetlamp not far away. His body tightened as Ben emerged suddenly from out of the shadows, still walking slowly but with a steady, determined gait. For a moment the young man stood completely still, his eyes staring straight at Ben as he chewed his lower lip nervously. Then he glanced back toward the house, nodded quickly and raced away.

Instantly the voices on the front porch fell silent.

Ben turned up the walkway. From behind, he could hear several of the cars start their engines and pull away, some peeling loudly as they dashed from the curb.

When he reached the first small step of the front porch, he stopped and looked silently at the people who still remained in place. He could see a tall slender woman in a bright red dress, and another, larger woman beside her. A tall, heavyset man stood behind them, his enormous arms draped loosely over their shoulders.

"You sure you in the right place?" the man asked finally.

"I think so," Ben said.

The man pushed his way between the two women, strode to the middle of the porch and glared down toward Ben, his enormous frame blocking the light from the front windows and throwing Ben once again into deep shadow.

"What you want, mister?" he asked in a hard, demanding voice. "A little jelly-roll?"

"What?"

"A little poontang, maybe?" the man added. He glanced at the women. "A little chocolate poontang?"

The women laughed as the man returned his eyes to Ben.

"So what you want, huh?"

Ben moved his hand inside his coat, reaching for his police identification.

"Hold it right there now," the man said instantly.

Ben's hand froze in place, then lowered slowly to his side.

"You wouldn't happen to be toting a piece, would you now?" the man asked.

Ben nodded.

The man's eyes widened. "That's not nice. That's not friendly. How come you toting a piece?"

"It's just my service revolver," Ben told him, hoping that would explain it.

The man looked at him oddly. "Service revolver? You in the service? How come you ain't wearing no uniform?"

"Police Department," Ben said.

The man took a step toward him, his eyes darting about nervously. "You with them Black Cat boys?"

"No."

"Well, what you want then?"

"I'm looking for Roy Jolly."

The man looked surprised. "You is? How come you looking for Mr. Jolly?"

"I want to talk to him about something."

The man smiled, his large white teeth glowing yellow in the kerosene lamp which rested on the rail beside him. "You sure them Black Cat boys didn't send you?"

"I'm sure."

The smile disappeared. "Well, you ain't too smart coming over here all by yourself, looking for Mr. Jolly."

"Is he here?"

The man took the lamp from the rail of the porch and held it up to Ben's face. "I don't know you," he said, "and I bet Mr. Jolly don't know you neither." He lowered the lamp toward Ben's chest. "Open your coat."

Ben drew back the sides of his jacket, and in a single, smooth motion, the man quickly reached beneath his arm and snapped out the pistol. "Nasty little thing," he said as he tossed it over Ben's shoulder.

It plomped softly into the dry grass, and at the very edge of his vision Ben could see it glinting dully in the lamplight.

"I'm not here to cause anybody any trouble," he said.

The man continued to stare at Ben suspiciously. "What you want then?"

"A little girl was murdered a few days ago," Ben said.

"So what?"

"A little colored girl."

The man stared at Ben expressionlessly.

"So I was hoping Mr. Jolly might be able to help me find out who did it."

The man said nothing. He placed the lamp back on the railing and stepped forward slightly. A purple stud-pin winked from his shirt. Two enormous fingers adjusted it unnecessarily, then crawled up to straighten a light-blue silk tie.

"We found her body over in that old ballfield not far from here," Ben added.

The man cocked his head slightly, as if to listen to the chorus of crickets and katydids that filled the air around them.

"Just a little girl," Ben said. "About twelve years old, something like that."

In a movement that was blindingly swift, the man suddenly swatted at a moth that had swept up from the lantern. "Got it," he hissed. His hand squeezed together, then opened, and one of the women stepped up and wiped the crushed moth from it with a white handkerchief.

Ben could feel his skin tightening around him. "Somebody shot her," he said. He pointed to the back of his head. "Right here."

The man grinned lethally. "You scared, mister? You look scared." He turned to the women and laughed. "Don't he look scared to you?"

"He gone die of it pretty soon," one of the women said jokingly.

Ben nodded quickly and offered her a thin, nervous smile. "Yes, ma'am, I think I might," he told her.

For a moment the man regarded him closely. Then his belly shook with a small laugh and he stepped back toward the front door of the house. "I'll check with Mr. Jolly," he said almost playfully. "Come on in."

The people inside stopped talking immediately as Ben followed him slowly through the whole narrow length of the house. The front room was almost entirely filled by a large pool table, but in the second the walls were lined with pinball machines. An odd assortment of chairs and settees were scattered about in the center of the room, along with a few makeshift card tables. Men and women sat drinking from paper cups or playing at the pinball machines whose bells and whistles echoed throughout the smoke-filled house. Their eyes followed him intently as he continued through the house, elbowing his way left and right through the steadily thickening crowd. At the rear of the house, a large bar had been set up, its top covered with a dull speckled formica top, and behind it a man in a dark-blue shirt dispensed bonded whiskey by the bottle, and clear white lightning by the cup. A large sheet of plywood had been spread out near the center of the room, and people danced languidly on it while an old woman in a flowered dress and pillbox hat played honky-tonk tunes on an baby-blue upright piano.

The man stopped abruptly at the door of the last room of the house and tapped lightly at its heavy metal.

"Yeah?" someone said in a husky voice.

"It's Gaylord, Mr. Jolly," the man said. "I got a fellow wants to talk to you 'bout that little girl they found."

When there was no answer, Gaylord gently opened the door, then stepped aside and let Ben pass into the room.

Roy Jolly looked enormously old as he sat behind a plain wooden desk in an unlighted corner of the room. His hair shot out from the top of his head like thin silver wires, and his watery yellow eyes stared out from a face that looked as if it had been carved from a dark, crumbling wood. His breath broke from him in shallow gasps, and his voice sounded as if it came from somewhere deep beneath a pool of water.

"Go on back to the front," he snapped at Gaylord, who instantly left the room, closing the door tightly behind him.

His eyes shifted over to Ben, as his hand waved over the stacks of money which were piled on his desk. "Set down," he commanded.

Ben took a seat opposite the desk. In the corner of his eye, he could see another man in the room, tall, his body half hidden in shadow, but with just enough of it visible that Ben could make out the stock of the shotgun he cradled in his arms.

Jolly leaned back in his chair and drew in a loud, wheezing breath. "Gaylord say you come 'bout that dead gal?"

"Yes."

Jolly took a white meerschaum pipe from a rack of twenty or thirty of them and shakily filled the bowl with tobacco, his palsied hand scattering dark-brown fibers across the length of his desk. "What fur?" he asked after he had lit it.

"I'm with the police."

Jolly's eyes rolled upward toward a ceiling which, Ben noticed, had been carpeted with a dark-blue shag. "That don't mean shit to me," he said. "Even them Black Cat boys is with the police, and they 'bout sorry as you can git." He blew two columns of smoke into the air, one from each corner of his mouth. "How come you mess with me?"

"I didn't come to make trouble," Ben told him.

Jolly didn't seem to hear him. He reached for a pair of gold-rimmed glasses, the lenses a solid, impenetrable black, and put them on slowly. "Police ain't nothing but trouble," he said. Then he laughed to himself. "Like most everything else." The two black lenses settled on Ben like the twin barrels of a shotgun. "Old man, he deserve his peace, don't you think?"

"Yes."

"How come you disturbing mine, then?"

"I'm just trying to find out something about a murdered girl."

"What's a murdered little colored gal to you?" Mr. Jolly demanded harshly.

"A case," Ben said.

"We had gals dead from murder before," Jolly went on. "How come ain't nobody seen you then?"

"I've never been assigned to Bearmatch."

Jolly's lips parted slowly, revealing an array of golden teeth. "So it ain't been your problem before?"

"You might say that," Ben told him.

The old man shifted uncomfortably in his seat, wincing with pain as he did so. "That's the way it is. Uh huh. If it ain't your trouble, don't mess with it." He pushed himself to the left, revealing a sharp, leathery profile. "Now we had murdered gals over here before," he said. "We always find out who done it. When we do, don't nobody see them guys no more." He allowed the pipe to droop from the side of his mouth like a curled white tongue. "That's the way it is over here."

"Do you know who killed the girl we found in the ballfield?" Ben asked directly.

"Naw," Jolly said. "I ain't looked into it that good."

"Do you know who she is?"

"Naw," Jolly said. Then he grinned menacingly. "You looking for something free, Mr. White Policeman? Seem like you looking for something free."

"What do you mean?"

"You think it done for free?"

"What?"

"Us finding out who done it."

Ben stared at him, puzzled.

"You want to find something out for free?" Jolly asked again. He stuck out his hand, palm up, gnarled fingers raised toward the ceiling. "You got something for Mr. Jolly?"

"No," Ben told him.

Jolly drew his hand back and laughed. "Where you from, Mr. White Policeman? You from Beulah Land?" His eyes dropped toward the stacks of money. "You see all these niggers in the streets? Huh? You see them?"

Ben said nothing.

The old man's dark, rasping laughter broke across the room. "They make me sick. They set next to Mr. Whiteman, they think they're in Heaven; they think they're in Beulah Land, setting there with God hisself." He turned away as if to spit on the floor, then looked back at Ben. "But they're still broke. They ain't got a dime. You know why? 'Cause they ain't yet figured out that don't nobody do nothing for free." He laughed again, a hard, thick laugh that ended in a slight, trembling cough which he willfully brought under his control. "They talk about dirty money. These newfangled preachers they done brought in here, they talk about dirty money. But money is the cleanest thing in the world. Clearest, too. It don't bullshit you. It tell you right to your face what you worth." He allowed another burst of laughter to escape him for a moment, then sucked it back in. "Now 'bout this gal," he said. "Maybe I know a little. What you got I want, Mr. Whiteman?"

"Nothing," Ben said without hesitation.

"Nothing?" Jolly asked. He leaned forward slightly. "You can buy anything, did you know that? You can buy gals. You can buy cars." He grinned thinly. "Hell, you can even buy yourself a whole new way of thinking. But if you can't buy nothing, you ain't nothing."

Ben stood up immediately, his contempt washing over him like a hot wave.

Jolly's eyes followed him. "I ask you one more time," he said. "You got anything I want?"

"No," Ben said curtly.

Jolly looked at him as if he were something filthy which had washed into his life. "Now ain't that a funny thing?" he said mockingly. "A white man—all growed up—and he don't have one thing a nigger wants." He shook his head in disgust. "That's pitiful, ain't it?"

Ben walked out quickly, leaving the door open behind him. He could hear the old man laughing to himself, and the laughter seemed to snap at him like the end of a long, black whip.

It took him only a few minutes to reach his small house, and once there, he poured himself a whiskey and sat out in the little iron swing on his front porch. It was a quiet neighborhood, filled mostly with workers from the iron and rubber plants, too tired to make a fuss, as his father used to say. To the right, he could see the illuminated spire of the Methodist Church, and beyond it Vulcan's torch lifted high over the brow of Red Mountain. He had grown up practically beneath its shadow, but its once majestic power now seemed shrunken and besieged. It creaked like the old iron swing, grew rusty, fell apart.

He took the small notebook from his shirt pocket and went over King's speech, but this time there didn't seem to be anything in it that the Chief could use, and so he simply checked his notes for spelling and legibility and put them back into his pocket.

He leaned back deeply and let his legs thrust out, pumping the swing softly to stir the air. Far in the distance he could hear the shift-horns call from the foundries and mills and power plants that surrounded his small neighborhood like a jagged metal wall. It was the shift they called the Dawn Patrol, and he could remember the many years his father had worked it, trudging out into the deep night and not returning until almost noon. He had thought that by choosing the police, he had chosen a different life, but it struck him now that he, too, had joined the Dawn Patrol.

He took out the torn photograph of the little girl, brought the severed halves slowly together and stared at the small face. Her eyes were closed, her cheeks slightly puffed, as if she'd died with a mouthful of candy. The quiet, unresisting look on her face betrayed nothing of what she must have suffered, but he found something disturbing in it nonetheless. He had seen the dead look surprised. He had seem them look frightened. He had even seen them staring up, almost radiantly, as if in the final instant they had grasped some impossible hope. But the face of the little girl looked helpless, vacant, resigned, as if this last assault had not been much different from the first one.

"Up late," Mr. Jeffries said as he paused at Ben's walkway.

Ben quickly tucked the photograph back in his shirt pocket and smiled softly. "I reckon so."

"Guess you boys have your hands full these days," Mr. Jeffries added. He hesitated a moment, then moved shakily up the walkway and sat down on one of Ben's front steps.

"Pretty much," Ben said.

The old man drew the straw bowler from his head and wiped the sweat from his forehead. "I got to get up to pee. And after that, I can't get back to sleep." He fanned himself gently with the hat and drew in a deep, appreciative breath. "I do love a summer night," he said. "Peaceful, for all the trouble."

"Yes," Ben said.

Mr. Jeffries eyed him closely. "You didn't get hurt in all this trouble we had today, did you?"

Ben shook his head. "No," he said.

"Nor hurt nobody, I hope."

"I don't think so," Ben told him. Then he suddenly thought of the photograph, the broken will he saw on the little girl's face, and with a deep, unsettling shock, he realized that he could not be sure.

Twelve

Sammy McCorkindale was standing outside the detective bullpen when Ben arrived the next morning. He smiled brightly as Ben approached.

"Well, the joke's on me, Ben," he said. He shook his head with slight embarrassment. "You know that little girl you found in that ballfield?"

Ben nodded.

"You know how I said nobody'd report her missing?"

"Yeah."

The grin broadened. "Well, I reckon the joke's on me."

"Somebody's asked about her?"

"As I live and breathe, Ben," McCorkindale said with a hint of genuine wonder in his voice. "First time I ever heard of such a thing coming out of Bearmatch."

"Who was it?" Ben asked quickly. "Who asked about her? Did you get a name?"

"Better than that," McCorkindale said. "I got the thing itself. She's sitting by your desk this very minute."

Ben pushed through the doors instantly and saw a slender, well-dressed black woman sitting in the chair beside his desk. She wore a dark-red, short-sleeved blouse and long, loose-fitting skirt that fell all the way to her ankles. Her hands were folded primly in her lap, and her eyes stared straight ahead.

"Good morning, ma'am," he said to her as he stepped up to his desk. "I'm Detective Wellman."

She started to rise, but he stopped her.

"No, no," he said, "sit down." He pulled his chair from beneath his desk and sat down. "I understand you're interested in a missing person."

She stared at him steadily, her lips tightly pursed.

"Could you tell me a little bit about that?" Ben prodded.

"Everybody warned me not to come down here," the woman said evenly.

"Why is that?" Ben asked politely.

"They said it was useless, and that it might be dangerous," the woman told him. Her voice was crisp and precise, despite the Southern accent, and there was a kind of flame which seemed to burn continually behind her eyes.

"Are you from Birmingham, ma'am?" Ben asked.

"Not always. My family came from New Orleans."

"Been here long?"

"Since I was fourteen," the woman said. "Why?"

Ben suddenly realized that his questions might seem threatening rather than casual, a way to break the ice. He shrugged, almost playfully. "Just wondered," he said.

The woman's face suddenly grew more agitated, as if something were coming to a violent boil in her mind. "It's my niece," she said finally.

Ben smiled quietly and took out a sheet of notepaper. "And she's been missing?"

"Yes."

"Since when?"

"She's been gone for two days."

"About how old is she?"

"She's twelve."

Ben felt a slight tremor in his fingers. "Would you happen to remember what she was wearing the last time you saw her?"

"Just a plain white dress."

"How about shoes?"

"Brown shoes."

"Lace-ups?"

"Buckle."

"Any socks?"

"White socks."

Ben wrote it down, then looked up. "And her name?"

"Doreen," the woman said. "Doreen Ballinger."

He knew that the two halves of her picture were in his jacket pocket, but for a moment he could not bring himself to take them out. "Would you say she's about four and a half feet tall?"

"Something like that, I guess."

"With her hair tied behind her in a little bun?"

The woman's face stiffened suddenly. "Yes," she said softly. Then she leaned forward very slightly. "How come you knew that?"

Ben did not answer. He dropped his eyes to the paper. "May I have your name, ma'am?"

"Esther Ballinger," the woman said immediately. "How come you knew about my niece's hair?"

"And could I have your address, Miss Ballinger?"

Her whole body grew rigid. "Tell me what you know about Doreen," she demanded.

Ben said nothing.

She shot out of her chair and glared down at him. "I'm not some dull-eyed, grinning nigger that you can sweet-talk and be polite to and then send on her way," she said fiercely. "Now I want to know what's happened to Doreen."

Ben nodded slowly. "Sit down, Miss Ballinger."

She did not move.

"Please," Ben said, almost in a whisper.

For a moment she continued to look at him resentfully. Then she eased herself back down into her chair.

Ben took out the torn photograph and handed it to her. "Is this your niece?" he asked.

For a while she didn't answer, but only stared silently at the photograph, her eyes growing suddenly very dark and still.

"Yes," she said finally. Her eyes lifted toward Ben's, and for an instant they struck him as intensely beautiful. "What happened to her?"

"Somebody shot her, Miss Ballinger," Ben said.

Something seemed to collapse behind her eyes, the walls of a tiny burrow, which she instantly shored up again.

"Do you know who did it?" she asked resolutely.

"No."

"Are you trying to find out?"

Ben could hear the accusation in her voice, and it was like an arrow going through him.

"Yes, I am," he said determinedly. "I most certainly am trying to find out, Miss Ballinger."

He couldn't tell whether or not she believed him, so he simply went on according to the formula of such investigations, went on as he would in any other case.

"When was the last time you saw Doreen?" he asked.

"Sunday morning."

"Where was she?"

"She was in her room—getting ready for work."

"Work? What kind of work?"

"She baby-sits for this family over in Mountain Brook," Esther told him. "A rich white family. She goes over there every weekend."

"Saturday and Sunday, both?"

"Yes."

"What's the family's name?"

"Davenport. Mr. and Mrs. Horace Davenport. My mother worked for them all her life."

"And the address?"

"2407 Carlton Avenue."

"How did she go to work? By bus, something like that?"

"They have her picked up," Esther said. "They have her brought home. It's the usual thing. And they give her toting privileges."

Ben looked up from the paper. "Toting privileges?"

Esther shrugged. "It's an old custom among the rich white people," she said. "You bring a little tote bag to work with you, and they drop a few things in it before you leave. Soap. Maybe some flour, a few hamburger patties. Anything that's around that they want to give you."

Ben watched for a moment as Esther's eyes drifted back down toward the photograph. Something of her previous energy seemed to drain into it, and when she looked up, she seemed older than herself, older than him, older than the world.

"Did she ever bring home a ring?" Ben asked.

She looked at him oddly. "A ring? What kind of ring?"

"Sort of a cheap ring, with a big purple piece of glass in it."

She shook her head. "No."

"Did you ever see her with something like that?"

"No. Why?"

"We found one in her dress," Ben said. "Large heavy thing. Way too big for Doreen."

"I never saw her with anything like that," Esther said. She glanced down at the photograph. "You got any tape?"

"I think so," Ben said. He fumbled through the top drawer of his desk until he found it. "Here."

She took the tape and carefully mended the photograph. Then she turned away from it for a moment and fixed her eyes on the windows at the far end of the room.

"Where is she now?" she asked.

"She's been buried, Miss Ballinger," Ben said. "The state does that if no one claims a body."

"Where?"

"Gracehill."

Esther's eyes closed slowly. "It's not very nice up there," she said.

"We didn't have anything else to do," Ben said quickly. "You can have her moved if you want to."

Esther shook her head determinedly. "No." Her lips curled down bitterly. "Let her rest."

"Would you want to see the grave, then?"

She did not hesitate in her reply. "Yes, I would."

Ben got to his feet. "I'll take you."

They were halfway out of the building before Luther came rushing up to them, his huge face wild and agitated as if still shaking from the storm the day before.

"They've all gathering over at First Pilgrim," he said breathlessly. "Get over there right away."

Ben nodded toward Esther. "This is that little girl's aunt," he said to Luther. "I'm taking her to see where they buried her."

Luther seemed barely to notice the woman. He kept his eyes on Ben. "That can wait," he said. "Get on over to that rally right away."

"Yes, Captain," Ben said.

He moved forward quickly, tugging Esther gently along with him until they were both standing in the garage beside his car.

"Get in," Ben said when Esther stopped at the door.

She looked at him questioningly. "I thought you had to go somewhere else."

Ben opened the passenger door, then stepped back to let her in. "I'll get there in time," he said.

A line of thunderclouds had begun to advance along the northern horizon by the time Ben pulled the car to a stop near the grave. A small cooling breeze rippled through the dense waves of kudzu that swept down along the sloping hill or spiraled upward into the surrounding pines.

"We buried her last night," Ben said as he escorted Esther to the edge of the grave.

"Who did?" Esther asked.

"Well, I was here," Ben said, "and there were a few others. A preacher said a few words over her."

Esther said nothing. She gazed down at the little mound of red-clay earth, then shook her head gently.

"I'm sorry we couldn't find you before we had to bury her," Ben added quietly.

Esther remained silent.

"And her other relatives," Ben added.

"There's just me and her grandfather," Esther told him. "My brother—Doreen's father—ran off when she was three years old. Her mother died last year." She looked at Ben. "That's why I moved in with them. My father's too old now to see after a little girl." She took a deep breath and looked out toward the horizon. "I was going to take her someplace with me one of these times. New York, maybe. Someplace like that. But I just couldn't get up the money." Her eyes fell back toward the grave, and she smiled bitterly. "You can't save up much on toting privileges."

Ben nodded silently and watched as Esther bent forward, took a handful of dirt and sprinkled it over the grave.

"I'll bring some flowers up here tomorrow," she said.

"I don't guess you'd have any idea about who might have done this," Ben asked cautiously.

Esther shook her head. "No, I don't."

Again, Ben fell silent while he watched Esther closely. If she were grieving for her niece, it was the oddest grief he'd ever seen, cold, stony, the sort he'd seen in the army when things had been bad for so long that only the hard nub of feeling remained, along with a hatred so raw it seemed to bite into every nerve.

"Did you ever see anybody hanging around Doreen?" he asked finally.

Esther looked at him. "Hanging around?"

"Like he might be interested in her," Ben added hesitantly, "A man, I mean."

Esther's lips parted slowly, but she said nothing.

"Like somebody who might want to force himself on her," Ben said.

Esther turned away from him instantly and faced the line of stormclouds that was now billowing darkly over the city. "Somebody raped her? Is that what you're trying to say?"

"Yes, ma'am."

He saw her shoulders lift suddenly, tremble very slightly, then fall again.

"I'm awfully sorry to have to tell you this," he said.

She kept her back to him and said nothing.

"It could have been a very big man," Ben added. "So big it would be noticeable. Did you ever happen to see anybody like that hanging around your house or following you on the street?"

"No."

"White or black, it's all the same to me," Ben said, because he knew he had to.

She turned slowly and faced him. "Do you think I believe that?" she asked hotly.

Ben stared at her evenly. "I'm not an animal," he said, this time with a measure of his own tingling resentment. "I didn't kill your niece. I didn't hurt her." He could hear his voice shaking almost inaudibly beneath his breath. "And I'm trying real hard to find out who did." His anger was like a hot wind in his face, fierce, enveloping, moving toward explosion. "And maybe I'd like a little help from you," he added in a voice that seemed to break suddenly at the very edge of rage, "But I'll go on, Miss Ballinger. I'll go on whether I get it or not." He turned abruptly, strode back to his car and got in.

For a moment, he tried to regain control of himself. Through the dusty film of the windshield, he could see Esther as she continued to stand at the edge of the grave, her arms now folded around her waist, hugging tightly, as if trying to protect an unborn child. He could imagine what she felt, but he realized that he could not grasp it in its entirety, that a certain portion of her grief would always lie beyond the farthest reach of his sympathy, that something in the darkness of her skin was lost to the pallor of his own, so that he could hope for little more than her distant, grudging aid. He knew that if it came, it would be apprehensive and suspicious, but it was no less than he could ask for, and no more than he deserved.

Thirteen

Ben was still waiting patiently in the car when Esther finally returned to it, a long dry reed nestled in her hand.

"I'll take you home if you want me to," he said.

Esther nodded. "Maybe you ought to talk to my daddy," she said. "He might have seen something the day Doreen didn't come back home."

Ben nodded slowly. "When was that?"

"She should have come Sunday," Esther told him. "Late in the afternoon. I was still at work."

"Where do you work, Miss Ballinger?"

"At a little restaurant on Fourth Avenue," Esther said. "Smiley's Barbecue. I'm a short-order cook." She shrugged. "I been doing it for a long time."

"What time do you get to work?"

"About five-thirty," Esther said. "We have a breakfast crowd."

"And your father. What does he do?"

Esther shook her head. "Nothing."

Ben glanced back toward the grave. The air was darkening all around it as the wall of stormclouds drew closer to the city. "Would he talk to me?" he asked.

"I don't know. Maybe."

Ben turned back toward her. "And the neighbors. Can you get them to talk to me?"

Esther shook her head wearily. "You picked a real bad time to start poking around Bearmatch," she said.

"I didn't pick it," Ben said. He looked at her pointedly. "Maybe we could go someplace and have a cup of coffee."

She gazed at him wonderingly. "What?"

"Just sit down and talk about Doreen," Ben explained. "You might remember something."

Esther continued to stare at him, half-puzzled, half-amazed. "You want the two of us to go someplace and have a cup of coffee?"

"That's right."

"In Birmingham?"

It was only then that the impossibility of such a thing occurred to him.

"How about that fancy restaurant in the Tutweiler?" Esther said, almost derisively. "Or maybe just the lunch counter at Pizitz's."

"At my house, then," Ben said suddenly, to stop her from going on. "We could have a cup of coffee at my house."

The look of wonder was still in her face.

"It's not that far from here," Ben added firmly. "We could be there in a few minutes."

She seemed to consider it a moment, to take his offer almost as a challenge. Her eyes moved over him as if he were some oddity that had suddenly and unexpectedly appeared in a wholly familiar world. "All right," she said finally, "but after that, you'll come over to mine, and maybe talk to my daddy."

It was more than he'd expected from her, and he took it immediately.

"All right," he said quickly as he started up the car.

They arrived at Ben's house only a few minutes later. Esther got out of the car slowly and stared about as if looking for snipers in the trees.

"Right this way," Ben said. He swept his hand out over the small cement walkway. "Watch your step, though, some of the slabs are jutting up. Sometimes I nearly trip, myself."

Esther made her way gingerly up the walkway, then stood stiffly while Ben opened the door.

"Forgive the look of this place," he said as he led her inside. "It's a bachelor's mess, you know."

For a moment the two of them stood awkwardly in the front room. Ben could see a strange uneasiness gather slowly in Esther's face.

"You want coffee?" he asked quickly. "Or maybe a glass of iced tea?"

A quick nervous laugh broke from her. "Iced tea? All right. I'll have a glass of iced tea."

It was made from a brown powder and it looked like muddy water, but she drank it quickly when he brought it, then set the nearly empty glass down on the small table in front of the sofa.

"Guess I was thirsty," she said tensely.

"The heat'll do that," Ben said.

She smiled at him. "You know I never been in a regular white person's house. That's strange. I mean, I been in rich white houses, but never one like this, a regular house."

"My daddy was a steel worker," Ben said. "He left me this little place." He shrugged. "Otherwise I guess I'd just live in one of those furnished rooms they have downtown." He glanced about the room. "As you can see, I'm not too fancy."

"Got a TV," Esther said. "All the white people got TVs?"

Ben took a sip from his own glass of tea. "I don't guess so," he said lamely.

For a moment, neither of them spoke, and as the silence lengthened, Ben could feel Esther's growing discomfort at being in his house.

"Listen," he said quickly. "About Doreen. When did you say the Davenports had her picked up?"

"She went there every Saturday and Sunday at around ten in the morning," Esther told him. "I'm always at work by then, but I know that's when she leaves."

"Is your daddy usually there?"

"Yes."

"And you spend time with her on the weekend?"

"Yes."

"Did she seem okay when she came back on Saturday?"

"She seemed the same," Esther said. "That night she went over and heard Dr. King."

"Who did she go with?"

For a moment she hesitated to answer. "With me," she said finally. "We walked over to the church together. Does that change anything?"

"No," Ben said. "Did you come back home together?"

"No," Esther said. "She was with a group of her friends from school. I walked back home and went to bed. The next morning I went to work. When I got back, my daddy said that Doreen hadn't come back from the Davenports'."

"And that was late Sunday afternoon?"

"Yes."

"Did you call the Davenports?"

"Yes, I did."

"What did they say?"

"Mr. Davenport wasn't there," Esther told him. "But his wife said that he'd taken her home himself."

"And we're still talking about Sunday afternoon?"

Esther nodded. "I asked all around Bearmatch. I didn't go to work on Monday. I kept trying to find her. I thought she might have stayed with a friend, something like that. I went over to her school and asked around. I tried my best. I even asked one of the men who was organizing the kids for the march."

"Which man?"

"Leroy Coggins," Esther said. "I think he must be in jail now. Just about everybody on the march is in jail."

Ben was about to ask another question when someone knocked at the door. He stood up and opened it. Mr. Jeffries was standing quietly behind the screen.

"I saw you was home," he said. "I thought you might be up for a game of checkers."

"Not right now," Ben said.

Mr. Jeffries' eyes peered to the right, then widened as he caught sight of Doreen.

"Oh," he said with surprise. "I didn't realize you had somebody with you." He leaned toward the screen and lowered his voice conspiratorily. "Is she a prisoner?"

"No," Ben told him. "She's helping me with a case."

Mr. Jeffries looked at him, amazed, but said nothing.

"Maybe later tonight," Ben said. "That game of checkers."

Mr. Jeffries backed away slowly, edging himself toward the end of the porch. "No, no," he said, his eyes leaping back toward Esther, then settling once again on Ben. "That's all right. Don't trouble yourself. I'm sorry to interrupt." He turned quickly and made his way down the walkway, his thin, spindly legs scissoring rapidly toward his house across the street.

"Now, about that girl," Ben said as he returned to his seat.

"I shouldn't stay here," Esther said nervously.

Ben looked up at her. "Why not?"

"All the reasons you already know."

"This is police business," Ben told her.

"That doesn't matter," Esther said. "Some things go beyond that. Some things go a long way beyond that."

Ben looked at her determinedly. "This is my house. I own it. I pay the taxes on it. Whoever I ask in can stay as long I say so, Miss Ballinger, and there is nothing in the world beyond that."

"Yes, there is," Esther said.

"What?"

"Me. What I want. And I don't want to stay here."

"All right," Ben said wearily. He pulled himself heavily to his feet. "Where do you want to go?"

"Home," Esther said, but without conviction or affection, as if Bearmatch were nothing more than a little patch of earth where she'd been set down and kept in place by the force of an immense and unrelievable gravity.

Esther's house looked like almost all the others in Bearmatch. Its unpainted wood had turned dark gray, and large patches of rust spread out across its tin roof. The front porch slumped downward toward the unseeded front yard, and two of the three wooden steps that led up to it had broken years before and never been replaced. Flaps of torn screen hung from its sideposts, and several slats were missing from the splintery rail that ran along its edges. A large Double Cola thermometer had been nailed to the front door, and as Ben stepped up to it, he noticed that its thin red line stopped at the number ninety-two.

"My daddy goes off during the day," Esther said as she opened the door. "He comes home when it suits him." She swung the door open and stepped away. "Come on in."

The floor creaked loudly as Ben stepped inside the house. For a moment its bleakness overwhelmed him. There was a shaky rocking chair in one corner and a small sofa in the other, its springs entirely visible beneath the worn upholstery. A stack of unpainted apple crates leaned uneasily from the far wall, and just in front of it, two sawhorses supported a single sheet of plywood.

"That's the dining table," Esther said. "In case you're wondering."

Ben looked at her. "I figured it was."

"I'm not crying over it," Esther told him. "I'm just pointing it out."

Ben glanced about. "Where do you want me to sit?"

Esther nodded toward the sofa. "Right there," she said. "I'll put the coffeepot on."

Ben eased himself down onto the sofa and waited. Outside the front window, the air was graying steadily, and the cool breeze that wafted through it seemed already heavy with the coming rain. From time to time, he could hear the casual talk of various people as they passed by the house, but they seemed very far away. Only the front room was near at hand, and he let his eyes drift around it like a languidly weaving smoke. There was a small portrait of Jesus on the Cross on one wall, and an enormous calendar advertising The Alabama Bank and Trust Company on the other. In between, there was only the blank wooden wall, its uneven slats rising unsteadily toward a huge square beam. An enormous old coal stove sat in the center of the room on a base of tightly placed red bricks. Its black funnel rose like a crooked finger to the roof and then passed on through a circular hole in the sheeted tin. Thick gobs of whitish caulking sealed the space between the flue and the roof, and some of it had cracked with the heat, peeling away in slender strips which now fluttered slightly in the summer breeze.

The adjoining room looked much the same, and Ben could see its bare walls clearly from his place on the sofa. An iron bed rested against the far wall, flanked on either side by two overturned apple crates. A small plastic ashtray sat on top of one of the crates, a kerosene lamp on the other. The wall behind it was bare, except for a magazine page which had been taped to it, a blurry color poster of a Negro singer, complete with ruffled shirt and light-blue tuxedo, his hands wrapped passionately around a microphone as he crooned into it.

"That's Doreen's room," Esther said as she handed Ben a cup of coffee. "You want to see it?"

"Yes."

He followed her into the room and allowed his eyes to sweep it. Despite its bare essentials, it was undoubtedly the room of a young girl. A small metal shelf held a few old dolls, a game of Chinese Checkers and a tiny plastic record player.

"She liked Smokey Robinson," Esther said as she nodded toward the poster. "She liked them all. Elvis. Little Richard. I think she wrote them letters." She shook her head. "From the way she acted, you'd of thought she could hear them."

Ben's eyes snapped over to her. "What?"

"Oh my," Esther said softly. "You couldn't have known, could you? Doreen was deaf. She was born that way. She never heard a thing in her whole life."

Suddenly he saw her face again, oddly gray on the dark ground, and more isolated at the moment of her death than it would ever be possible for him to imagine.

"I just didn't think about anybody not knowing that about Doreen," Esther explained.

Ben walked over to a small cigar box which rested on a scarred wooden stool beside her bed. "What's in here?"

"Open it."

It was filled with costume jewelry, strings of plastic pearls, snap beads, a few rhinestone necklaces and a single ivory cameo.

"This was her mother's," Esther said as she picked up the cameo. "My sister gave it to her before she died." She returned it to the box. "You said something about a ring."

"A large one was found in the pocket of her dress," Ben said. "But it didn't look like any of this, and it was way too big for Doreen." He closed the lid. "It was way too big for almost anybody." He walked to the small square window that looked out onto the muddy alleyway behind the house. A skinny yellow dog, its rib cage clearly visible beneath its hide, was hungrily sniffing its way down the shallow ditch that ran beside it. Not far ahead of it, the rusty frame of an old car, its tires torn off, its windows shattered, rested in a weedy lot. A large spotted cat watched the dog anxiously from the car's dented hood, then leaped into the brush and disappeared.

"She was almost too old for toys," Esther said as her eyes moved over the little metal shelf.

Ben continued to stare out the window. Rows of dilapidated shacks lined the unpaved roads, and the mounting clouds seemed to draw a dark curtain over them, as if to shield them from his eyes.

Fourteen

The first thunder could be heard rolling in from the north by the time Ben made it back to headquarters. Dozens of squad cars surrounded the area, and police barricades seemed to sprout up at every corner. Lines of young Negroes were being funneled into the underground garage, while still others were being moved to the large parking lot which spread out, flat and gray, behind City Hall.

Ben parked across the street, then walked up the stairs and into the building. He could see Luther sitting nervously in the Chief's outer office. He looked as if he had been summoned to his own execution, and Ben hurried up the stairs to the detective bullpen before he could be spotted.

Even before he walked through the double doors of the bullpen, he could hear loud voices coming from the room. The loudest one belonged to Breedlove, and when he walked into the room, he was not surprised to find Daniels standing alongside him. A tall slender Negro stood quietly between them, his eyes glaring straight ahead while they screamed at him.

"You're going to keep these fucking kids out of this!" Breedlove yelled.

The young man did not move. His eyes remained calm, his face utterly expressionless.

"Did you hear me!" Breedlove demanded.

"We have a constitutional right to demonstrate," the young man said coolly.

"You don't have shit!" Breedlove shouted. He stepped in front of the man and shoved him backward, pressing him against the wall. "You hear me, Coggins? Huh? You hear me, Leroy?"

"The constitutional rights of the United States apply to the children of the United States," Coggins intoned.

"Bullshit!" Breedlove shouted. "Bullshit on your fucking rights."

Daniels laughed slightly, then stepped forward, pressing his face near Coggins. "You know what kind of shit these kids could get caught up in if you keep using them, Leroy?"

"They are demonstrating for their constitutional rights," Coggins said. "Sacrifices must be made."

"You want them dead, Leroy?" Daniels asked. "You want them shot down in the streets?"

"They'll be blood and hair all over the place if this keeps up!" Breedlove screamed.

Coggins closed his eyes wearily. "I came up here to discuss having the children you have gathered in the parking lot—probably more than a hundred of them—to discuss bringing them inside before it begins to rain."

"Yeah, well we don't want to talk about that, Leroy," Breedlove said. He grabbed him by the collar and jerked him forward. "We want to talk about the fact that these kids shouldn't be doing what they're doing in the first place."

"Thunderstorms are predicted," Coggins said quietly.

"Who gives a shit?" Daniels asked with a laugh.

"Yeah," Breedlove said. "You know what this whole thing is, Leroy? It's a passing fad." He grinned maliciously. "Like the hula hoop. It'll be gone in no time, and everything will be back just the way it was."

Breedlove and Daniels laughed together for a moment, then stopped suddenly.

"Stop putting them kids in the streets, Leroy," Breedlove said icily. "Everybody's had enough of that shit."

Coggins eyes slid over toward Breedlove. "Were VD tests conducted on the girls who were arrested yesterday?"

Breedlove and Daniels exchanged cheerful glances.

"Well, what if they were?" Breedlove asked.

Coggins eyes narrowed mockingly. "Did you do that, Mr. Breedlove? Did you check those little girls out?"

Breedlove's hand flew up and struck Coggins hard on the side of the face. Coggins' head snapped to the left, and Breedlove hit him again, this time with his fist.

"Charlie, stop it!" Daniels cried.

Breedlove drew back his fist. His face was trembling wildly as he held Coggins by the throat, his fingers digging into his neck.

"You better stop me, Harry," he cried. "You better stop me before I kill this nigger shit!"

"Ease off now," Daniels said, almost soothingly. "Ease off, Charlie."

Ben moved forward quickly and gripped Breedlove's shoulder. "Let go, Charlie," he said.

Breedlove turned toward him and smiled thinly. "You just saved this nigger's life, Ben," he said. He pulled his hand from Coggins' throat. "You ought to get some sort of award."

Coggins gasped loudly and massaged his throat. "You can't get away with this shit!" he said angrily.

Breedlove glared at him. "You ain't took over everything yet, Leroy," he said grimly.

Daniels swept his arm over Breedlove's shoulder and tugged him away. "Let's go have a drink, Charlie," he said. He looked at Ben and winked. "You don't mind cleaning this nigger up, do you, Ben?"

Ben stared silently at Coggins until Daniels and Breedlove were safely out the door.

"You going to 'clean me up' now?" Coggins asked sarcastically after they had disappeared.

"I'm going to try to keep you alive," Ben told him. "But you're not making it very easy for me."

"I'm ready to die," Coggins said. "There's not one person in all these jails that's not ready to die."

"That may be so," Ben said. "But does it have to be today?"

Coggins turned away slightly and wiped a line of sweat from his lip. His hand was trembling. "I just came up here about those kids they have out in the parking lot. That's all I came up here for, and I got into this shit."

Ben said nothing.

"It's going to rain like hell," Coggins went on, "and those kids shouldn't be left out in it like a herd of cows or something."

Ben eased himself back down on the desk behind him and folded his arms over his chest.

"They used to be able to treat us that way," Coggins added angrily, "but no more, goddammit!" He sucked in a deep, shaky breath, and let it out in a loud burst. "No, sir," he proclaimed loudly, regaining his resolve, "I'm not afraid to die."

"Then you're a fool," Ben said.

Coggins' eyes shot over to him. "Don't you believe there's anything worth dying for?"

"Quite a few things, I guess," Ben said. "But what's that got to do with fear?"

Coggins eyes squeezed together. "You trying to make a fool out of me?"

"I admire you," Ben heard himself say with a sudden surprise.

Coggins laughed bitterly. "Yeah, I bet you do."

Ben pulled the photograph of Doreen Ballinger from his pocket and held it up in front of Coggins. "You ever seen this little girl?" he asked.

Coggins looked closely at the photograph. "She's dead."

"Murdered," Ben said. "Shot in the head. Buried in that little ballfield over on Twenty-third Street."

Coggins smiled cagily. "And you're trying to pin it on me," he said, as if everything had now suddenly come clear to him.

Ben let it pass. "Do you know her?"

"No."

"Have you ever seen her?"

Coggins glanced back at the photograph. "She looks familiar. A lot of people do."

"Her aunt said she saw her in a group of young girls that was hanging around you on Saturday afternoon," Ben said.

"Whereabouts?"

"Outside the Sixteenth Street Baptist Church."

"Oh, yeah," Coggins said. "I remember that. A few of them came up and asked some questions about the Thursday march." Again, he looked at the picture. "She could have been there, but I don't recognize her in particular."

"Are you from Bearmatch, Mr. Coggins?" Ben asked.

"No, I'm from Ensley," Coggins said. He looked at Ben knowingly. "I know what you're thinking, just another one of those rich niggers trying to get the poor ones stirred up."

"Doreen was from Bearmatch," Ben said. "She was deaf. Her father ran off when she was three. Her mother died last year. Did your father run off, Mr. Coggins?"

"My father is a doctor," Coggins said.

Ben continued to hold Doreen's picture in front of him. "You're right, a lot of people look familiar. But they don't live the same."

"I can't help how I was born."

"Doreen couldn't either," Ben said as he pocketed the photograph. "Who can?" He was about to say more, routinely ask Coggins to report anything he might learn about the girl, but suddenly Luther burst into the room.

"You're goddamn lucky they canceled that speech at First Pilgrim," he shouted to Ben from across the room. "Because I get the feeling you never made it over there."

Ben said nothing, and Luther's eyes slid over to Coggins.

"What are you doing up here, Leroy?" he asked.

Coggins' body stiffened, as if he were coming to attention. "I came to formally request that the children that have been gathered together in the parking lot be brought inside."

"What for?"

"Because it's about to rain," Coggins said.

"It's already raining," Luther said. "Request denied."

Leon Patterson walked into the detective bullpen a few minutes after Coggins had been escorted back down to his cell. He smiled brightly as he came up to Ben's desk.

"Got something for you," he said excitedly. He dropped the ring onto the desk. "Remember that yellowish powder we found on that thing? It's not pollen, after all. It's just plain old chalk dust."

"From a school?" Ben asked.

Patterson laughed. "Not quite, unless school's changed a whole lot since my day." He glanced down at the ring. "It's chalk dust like from a pool hall, that stuff you use to cue the ball. It was all over that guy's ring." He looked at Ben and smiled. "Maybe you ought to start looking for a pool hustler."

Ben picked up the ring and twirled it slowly between his fingers.

Leon pulled a chair up beside Ben's desk and sat down. "I figure this was the guy's lucky ring, the one he wore when he played. What do you think about that theory?"

Ben said nothing.

"There was so much of that shit on the ring, he must have worn it every time he played. We're talking about a very heavy residue here, very heavy, and it doesn't look like he ever bothered to wash it off, or shine up the ring or anything like that."

Ben continued to look at the ring. It winked bright-dark, bright-dark as he turned it slowly in the light.

"Like it was maybe a sacred object or something," Patterson went on. "What do you think about that?"

Ben placed the ring on the desk, then turned toward him. "Any idea where it was made?"

"Best guess, Cracker Jacks," Leon said. "Or some circus sideshow where you get a cheap prize if this asshole can guess your weight." He shook his head. "That ring never saw the inside of a real honest-to-God jewelry store, I can tell you that."

Ben was about to make the guess that the ring could have been bought at one of the two or three costume jewelry stores that squatted between the barbecue stands, curling parlors and poolhalls of Fourth Avenue when Luther once again dashed into the room. He scanned the empty desks, then marched over to Ben.

"I got nobody else to give this to," he said.

"What is it?" Ben asked.

"I want you to get over to Kelly Ryan's place," Luther said hastily. "It looks like the poor bastard killed himself last night."

Kelly Ryan's little house looked a good deal like his own, and as Ben pushed himself through the rain toward the front door, he could not help but remember the night before, the way Kelly had seemed to disappear into the night, his shoulders hunched, his back to the world.

A uniformed patrolman was stationed at the front door. He nodded as Ben came up onto the porch.

"He's in the bedroom, Sergeant," he said quietly as he opened the door.

Ben stepped into the front room and realized that it had been a long time, perhaps years, since anyone but Kelly had been in the house. It had Kelly's rumpled clutter, his barely controlled drinking, even his odd, distinctive odor, a sweet rubberish musk that had been joked about in the department for years. There was no other smell in the front room, or the little den, or finally the bedroom where he hung motionlessly from a large oak beam.

He had thrown a rope over the beam, knotted it around his neck, climbed up on a small kitchen chair, handcuffed himself with a pair of Police Department issue, and then kicked it from beneath his feet. His face was now a purple-blue and his tongue hung from the side of his mouth like a piece of unchewed meat.

Ben suddenly felt a great wave of weariness pass over him. He slumped down on the bed, folded his hands in his lap and stared toward the single open window of the bedroom. Outside, the rain poured down in dense gray curtains, slapping mercilessly at the little mimosa tree that grew beside the house. He was not sure how long he sat there, but only that when he finally heard a voice in the outer room, it took him a moment to recognize it.

"Well, this sure puts the cherry on top," someone said.

Ben glanced toward the door and saw Daniels and Breedlove standing inside it.

"Is there any doubt it's a suicide?" Breedlove asked as he stepped into the room.

Ben got to his feet. "None that I can see."

The two men circled the dangling body slowly.

"At least he didn't mess himself," Breedlove said. "These twisters usually do." He pulled off his hat and slapped it against his coat. A spray of droplets leaped from it and spilled on to the floor. "A real toad-stringer we got going out there."

Daniels lingered at the entrance to the room, his body half-hidden behind the flowering curtain that hung across the doorway. He pointed to Ryan's wrists. "Pretty cut up."

Breedlove shrugged. "Probably changed his mind at the last minute. Strangling gives you time to reconsider." He gave the body a sudden small push. "No more morning roll calls, Kelly," he said.

"Why don't you just leave him alone," Ben said as politely as he could.

Breedlove looked at him oddly but said nothing.

Daniels stepped from behind the curtain, then shrank behind it once again. "Well, it seems to me he's beyond caring about what anybody does," he said to Ben. Then he glanced at Breedlove. "Seem that way to you, Charlie?"

Breedlove glanced toward his partner. "Yeah," he said. "Way beyond." His eyes darted back to the body, following its line upward from the feet.

Daniels bent down slightly and peered out the single bedroom window. "Imagine seeing this every morning," he said. "Nothing but barbed wire and blast furnaces. No wonder he got tired of it."

"Nobody trusted him," Breedlove said matter-of-factly. "Not after the business with that girl in Bearmatch." His eyes shot over to Ben. "He ever tell you about that?"

"No."

"Fell in love with a girl over there," Breedlove said with a slight laugh.

"Yeah, he had a problem with that all right," Daniels said. He laughed lightly. "But you know, I sort of liked old Kelly. He could come up with the craziest ideas."

Breedlove smiled. "Like what, Harry?"

Daniels thought for a moment. "Well, one night about four months back, he got about three sheets in the wind at this bar downtown. I wasn't with him, I just happened to run into him there. He started crying in his cups about some nigger that had disappeared. He claimed he knew for an absolute fact that the Langleys had killed this old boy and buried him in a chert pit in Irondale." He laughed mockingly. "I said to Kelly, I said, 'Kelly, if the Langleys killed a nigger, they wouldn't even bother to bury the son of a bitch. They'd hang him from a streetlight in Bearmatch."

"That's the truth, too," Breedlove said as the two of them laughed together.

Ben turned away abruptly and walked to the door. "You fellows can handle it from here," he said.

"Yeah," Breedlove said as the laughter trailed off. "It's a job for the coroner, anyway."

For a moment Ben paused and looked back into the room, leaning his shoulder against the unpainted doorjamb. Breedlove and Daniels were casually going through the drawers of Ryan's dresser, as if he might have left a note for them nestled among his underclothes. The body, itself, continued to hang motionlessly above the unswept wooden floor, and thinking back to the night before, Ben tried to imagine if there might have been something he could have said or done to save him.

"Goddamn," Daniels said as he pulled out the bottom drawer of the dresser. "You'd think he'd of folded something once in a while. Look at this mess."

Breedlove glanced quickly toward Ben, then back at Daniels. Then he laughed loudly as he waved his hand dismissively. "Aw, that's just the way you get," he said, "when you lose your best girl."

Fifteen

The heavy rain had slowed traffic considerably, so it was already early afternoon before Ben made the graceful turn down the circular driveway of the Davenport house. It was a large colonial mansion, complete with tall white columns and a rounded portico. Even in the rain the dark-blue façade appeared grand and inviolate.

The great oak door opened almost immediately, and the woman who stood behind it looked surprised to see Ben standing on her front porch. She was small, with a pale, angular face, and her gray hair was gathered in a small bun which sat at almost the exact top of her head.

"May I help you?" she asked.

Ben showed her his badge.

"My goodness," the woman said softly. "I am Mrs. Davenport. Has something happened?"

"May I come in?" Ben asked.

"Of course," the woman said. She stepped out of the door and allowed him to pass into the foyer. "Please now, what is it?" she asked urgently.

"You have a little Negro girl who works for you, I believe?" Ben said.

"Yes," the woman said.

"Doreen Ballinger," Ben said.

"Little Doreen, yes," Mrs. Davenport said. "Has something happened to her?"

"Yes."

The woman's right hand lifted to her throat. "What?"

"She's dead, Mrs. Davenport," Ben told her.

The hand curled gently around her throat. "Hit-and-run?"

"She was murdered," Ben said.

The hand dropped softly to her side. "May I sit down?"

Ben nodded.

The woman's hand swept to the left toward a large sitting room. "In here, please," she said.

Ben followed her into the room and watched as she took a seat on a large floral sofa.

"Such a pretty little girl," Mrs. Davenport said. "So sweet." She looked up at Ben. "Please, sit down."

Ben took a seat at the other end of the sofa. "How long had Doreen been working for you?"

"Almost a year," Mrs. Davenport said. She thought for a moment. "Yes, almost exactly a year. It was last spring when she came to us."

"When did you see her last?"

"She was here on Sunday," Mrs. Davenport said. "She attends to my daughter on Saturdays and Sundays." She picked a gold frame from the table and handed it to Ben. There was a picture of a small child standing happily beneath the green curtain of a weeping willow. "That's Shannon," she said. "She'll be so upset to lose Doreen."

Ben handed her back the picture.

Mrs. Davenport gazed lovingly at the photograph. "She's actually my adopted daughter," she said.

Ben shifted slightly in his seat. "About Doreen," he said. "You said you last saw her on Sunday afternoon?"

"Well, no," Mrs. Davenport said. "Doreen was certainly here on Sunday afternoon, but I was not."

"Was she here alone?"

"Goodness, no," Mrs. Davenport said. "My husband was here attending to some business. He's in Atlanta right now, but I'm sure he'd be pleased to talk to you when he gets back."

"When would that be?"

"The day after tomorrow."

Ben took out his notebook and wrote it down. "Was anyone else in the house on Sunday?"

Mrs. Davenport considered for a moment. "Well, Molly, our maid, was off, but Jacob was here."

"Jacob?"

"Jacob, our driver," Mrs. Davenport said. "He always went and got Doreen, and, of course, took her home when she was through."

"Did he do that on Sunday?" Ben asked.

"I suppose."

"Is he around?"

Mrs. Davenport's face grew cold. "No, he is not," she said crisply.

"When will he be back?"

Mrs. Davenport's back arched upward. "He is no longer in our service."

"Why not?"

"A question of loyalty," Mrs. Davenport said. "Jacob had been with this family for over forty years, then one day he suddenly decided that we weren't good enough for him anymore." She laughed. "Can you imagine? Since he was just a boy my husband's father, and then, later, my husband, had provided him with everything he needed, a place to live, money, everything." She shook her head. "The passion of the moment, what can you do about it? Especially with Negroes."

"He quit?" Ben asked.

"He decided to join the other side."

Ben looked at her, puzzled.

"The Negro side," Mrs. Davenport explained. "The demonstrators."

Ben nodded.

"Well, if you know anything about the Davenports," Mrs. Davenport added, "you know that you are either with them or against them."

"So he was fired?" Ben asked, trying to pin it down.

"Well, I prefer to think that he abandoned us," Mrs. Davenport said. "We had made it clear that we would not tolerate anyone in our service having anything to do with all this business in the streets and lunch counters and that sort of thing." She waited for Ben to respond, and when he didn't she added, "It's not as if we hadn't made it clear."

Ben took out his notebook. "What does he look like?"

"Sort of gray around the temples."

"Big? Small?"

"A large man. Tall. I'd say a little over six feet."

"You wouldn't happen to have a picture of him, would you?"

Mrs. Davenport chuckled. "Of course not. What would I be doing with a picture of Jacob?"

"Do you have any idea where he went?"

"Not the slightest."

"Maybe to family," Ben suggested. "Does he have any family in Birmingham?"

"I have no idea," Mrs. Davenport said.

"Sister?" Ben asked insistently. "Brother? Anything like that?"

"I never mingled in Jacob's life," Mrs. Davenport said resolutely.

"All right," Ben said exasperatedly. "What's his full name?"

"Jacob, like I said."

"I mean his last name," Ben said.

Mrs. Davenport looked at him with amusement. "Now isn't that funny?" she said.

"What?"

She laughed lightly. "I don't know if he had one."

The unpaved alleys of Bearmatch had been turned into muddy trenches by late afternoon, so Ben finally pulled the car over to the side and slogged toward Esther's house on foot.

The door opened only slightly when he knocked.

"Who there?" someone asked.

"Mr. Ballinger?" Ben asked.

"Who that?"

Ben could see a single cloudy eye staring through the crack in the door. "I'm looking for Esther," he said. "Are you Mr. Ballinger?"

"You looking for Esther? How come?"

"It's about Doreen," Ben said.

"She dead," the man said. "Somebody done kilt her."

"I know," Ben said. He pulled out his badge. "I'm trying to find out who did it."

The door opened slightly. "Little gal never hurt nobody," the man said resentfully. "Didn't deserve to git kilt."

"May I come in, Mr. Ballinger?" Ben asked.

The door opened wider and the old man stepped into the light. "Esther ain't here," he said. "She gone to work."

"I know," Ben told him. "I wanted to talk to you."

Mr. Ballinger looked at him suspiciously. "What fer?"

"Just ask you a few things."

The old man continued to stare at him apprehensively.

"I'd be much obliged if you'd let me in out of this rain," Ben said.

The old man retreated back into the room, leaving the door open. Ben followed him inside.

"Set down, then," the old man said.

Ben waited for Mr. Ballinger to lower himself into the rocking chair, then sat down on the sofa opposite him.

"Esther told me that you noticed Doreen never made it home on Sunday afternoon," Ben said.

The old man nodded. "That's right."

"You didn't see her at all on Sunday night?"

"Naw, sir. But Esther seen her on Saturday. They went down to the church together."

"When was the last time you actually saw Doreen?" Ben asked.

Mr. Ballinger took a can of snuff from his shirt pocket and opened it slowly. "Well, now, that musta been on . . . lemme see . . . that musta been on . . ." He took two fingers, dug them into the snuff, then brought them to his mouth. "I ain't too good at figuring back." He thought a moment longer. "Saturday afternoon, I guess. I was still sleeping when she left on Sunday."

Ben took out his notebook. "Well, I know that she went—"

Mr. Ballinger leaned forward suddenly and held out the tin. "Want a dip?"

"No, thank you," Ben said.

Mr. Ballinger smiled. "Young folks don't much like snuff no more," he said. His eyes drifted over to Doreen's room. A large tin bucket sat at the base of her bed, gathering a stream of droplets that fell from the ceiling. "I promised her I'd fix that leak in her room," he said quietly. "Now, I guess it don't matter."

"The man who used to take Doreen to work and then bring her home," Ben said. "Do you remember him?"

"Why sure," Mr. Ballinger said. He started to go on, then suddenly stopped, his eyes squinting slightly as he concentrated on Ben's face. "I seen you before," he said. "You was at the ballfield. You the one that come to look after Doreen."

It came together instantly. "And you're the one who found her," Ben said. "Who called the police. You're the one who was watching us from across the field."

Mr. Ballinger's eyes seemed to grow inexpressibly weary. "I seen that little hand from a long way off," he said. "But I knowned it was Doreen. My heart knowed it." He shook his head. "She a good little girl. When she didn't come home that night, I knowed it was something wrong." He picked an empty Buffalo Rock bottle from off the floor beside his chair and spit into it. "I looked all over just the same. But that wadn't enough for Esther. She stubborn, that gal. She say she gone down to the police, and that's what she done."

Ben glanced down at his notes. "The man who drove Doreen back and forth from her job—did you get to know him?"

"I talk to him a few times," Mr. Ballinger said. "Name of Gilroy, Jacob Gilroy. He got a sister down on Nineteenth Street."

"Where on Nineteenth Street?" Ben asked immediately.

The old man shrugged. "Little house there on the corner of First Avenue. Look like a cave or something, all them vines growing on the porch."

Ben wrote it down quickly, then glanced back up at Mr. Ballinger. "I talked to Mrs. Davenport today," he said. "Gilroy doesn't drive for them anymore."

"That's right?" Mr. Ballinger asked without surprise. "I thought something wrong."

"What do you mean?"

"Well, that last Sunday," Mr. Ballinger said, "I waited and I waited, but I never did see her." He blinked rapidly. "I seen the car, though. It passed right by the house."

"This house?"

"That's right," Mr. Ballinger said. "Went right by, but they wasn't no little Doreen in it."

"Did you see anyone?"

"Just a white gentleman," the old man said.

"Mr. Davenport?"

Mr. Ballinger shrugged. "Don't know 'bout that. I never seen Mr. Davenport." He shook his head. "He live a long way from here."

Sixteen

The house was not hard to find, and from Mr. Ballinger's description, Ben instantly recognized it. Dense clusters of poke salad grew along the porch, their pink stalks surrounding it like a rail. Vines spiraled upward toward the roof, then nosed over it, while thick waves of kudzu tumbled over the edge in an impenetrable green flood. A dark oval had been hacked out of the vine, and through it, Ben could make out the brown rectangle of the front door.

He knocked once and waited. There was no sound but the rain as it slapped against the leaves or drummed on the tin roof overhead.

He knocked again, this time a bit louder, rapping his knuckles against the wooden frame of the screen. Still there was nothing but the rain which swept across the sodden porch or streamed off the roof in slender white threads.

A low moan came from the house after he knocked a third time, and the door opened slowly to reveal a large man, slightly bowed, with gray hair and large brown eyes.

"Yes, sir, what can I do for you?" the man asked blearily, his eyes blinking painfully in the grayish light.

Ben took out his identification. "I'm looking for Jacob Gilroy."

The man's head bobbed slightly to the left as he stared at Ben. He labored to hold it upright. "What you want him for?" he asked weakly.

"It's about Doreen Ballinger," Ben said.

The man's eyes lowered drowsily. "That little deaf girl?"

"Yes."

The man retreated back into the house. "I'm Jacob," he said. "You can come on in, I guess."

Ben followed him into the house and stood near the center of the room as the old man lowered himself uneasily into a small blue chair. "I hope you be gone before my sister come back. She mad at me enough already. She mad at me for having to stay with her." He leaned to the side, picked up a bottle of whiskey and took a long pull. "But I can't help it. I ain't got no other place to go."

Ben took out the picture of Doreen and showed it to him.

"Yes, sir, that's her," the old man said. "That's surely her."

"How well did you know her?" Ben asked.

"I knowed Doreen a little," Gilroy said. Another line of whiskey spilled from one corner of his mouth, then washed over his belly. "Something happen to her?"

"She's been murdered," Ben told him.

Gilroy stared at him nervously. "Didn't know her that good," he said quickly, "but she was real sweet, far as I could tell."

Ben took out his notebook. "I understand you used to work for the Davenport family."

Gilroy's eyes squeezed together. "Forty years, I done it," he said as if it were a badge of honor. "Forty years I work for them." He shifted uneasily in his chair. "I ain't got nothing against them. Not a thing. Wouldn't do them no harm at all."

Ben returned the picture to his pocket.

"I done everything for them," Gilroy protested. "Everything they said. I done their driving, done their errands, done ever-thing they said."

"And Doreen worked for them, too," Ben said.

"She a nice little girl," Gilroy blurted immediately. "She real nice. I ain't got nothing against her."

"Did you spend much time with her?"

"She tend to Miss Shannon," Gilroy said. "They up in Miss Shannon's room a whole lot."

"So you didn't see her very often?"

"No, sir, I didn't," Gilroy said. He took another drink from the bottle, then burrowed it deep between his legs. "I take a drink once in a while, but it don't do nobody no harm."

"Did you pick Doreen up on Saturday and Sunday morning?" Ben asked.

"That was my job, so I done it," Gilroy said. His head drooped forward slowly, bobbed softly, then lifted again. "You be gone before my sister come back," he said. "She mad at me for quitting."

"Why did you quit?" Ben asked immediately.

Gilroy shook his head despairingly. "Just a stupid thing, like my sister say, just a stupid thing." He looked at Ben plaintively. "It happen so fast, I don't know what hit." He shook his head. "Fast as anything, that's the way it goes," he went on, beginning to ramble, his voice slurred. "Like he say, 'Hey, now, ain't that the way it is?' And you got to say, 'Yes sir, that's the way, sir, just like you said, sir.' " The light in his eyes swam in and out rhythmically. "Got to say, 'Yes, sir, you right, sir.' "

Ben could see the stupor coming on him, and he raced forward to find out what he could before the old man was gone entirely.

"Did you take Doreen home Sunday afternoon?" he asked.

Gilroy shook his head. "I was gone by then." He looked up slightly, his large eyes now deeply hooded by dark lids. "I was gone way 'fore supper."

"Was Mr. Davenport there when you left?" Ben asked.

Gilroy nodded shakily.

"Anyone else?"

"Just him, just ole Massa," Gilroy said. He smiled grimly. "He say, 'Jacob, what you think 'bout all this what's going on downtown?' I say, 'Well, I guess they's something to it.' " Gilroy's voice deepened mournfully. "And he look at me like I ain't nothing, and he say, 'Pack up, Jacob. I ain't having no agitators in this house.' "

"So you were fired?" Ben asked.

" 'Cause I said they was something to it," Gilroy told him. His eyes drifted toward the small window to his right. "My sister, she say I crazy for saying anything. She say I lose my job over nothing." He nodded clumsily, his head shifting heavily to the left. "I can't say she wrong."

"What do you know about Doreen?" Ben asked.

Gilroy shrugged. "I come and get her. I take her home." He gazed at Ben helplessly. "She deaf, like I said. Ain't much talking to her." He glanced down at the bottle. His fingers tightened around its neck. "I ain't saying what these folks is doing is a good thing," he protested. "I just say they's something to it." He gazed at Ben pleadingly. "I ain't never marched or nothing. I just say they's maybe something to it, that's all."

"Did you see anyone else in the house on Sunday?" Ben asked.

"Just ole Massa," Gilroy told him. "The Missus, she gone someplace. She not around when he ask me." He brought the bottle up slowly and took another drink.

"Do you think he took Doreen home?"

Gilroy dropped the bottle to his side suddenly, and some of the liquor sloshed up out of the bottle and onto his fist. Gilroy licked it off quickly, then lifted his eyes slowly toward Ben. "They think it's me that done it?" he asked.

Ben said nothing.

"They think it's me, don't they?" Gilroy repeated earnestly. A sudden steely terror infused his eyes. "They think somehow I kilt that little girl."

"No," Ben told him. "I don't think so."

The old man's eyes grew wild in panic. "They send the Black Cat boys, that's what," he cried. "They send the Black Cat boys for ole Jacob."

Ben lifted his hand toward him. "No," he said emphatically.

Tears welled up in the old man's eyes, then ran down his face. "That's what they do when they got you," he cried. His whole face was trembling violently, "They gone send the Twins for ole Jacob." The bottle slid from his hand and crashed onto the floor. A wave of whiskey swept out over the broken glass, then disappeared between the cracks in the floor.

Ben stepped toward him quickly. "Nobody's sending the Twins anywhere," he said insistently.

The old man stared at him in wide-eyed disbelief. "They gone whip ole Jacob, that's what," he wailed. "Maybe gone shoot him in the head."

"No," Ben repeated.

The old man's body slid out of the chair. "Naw, naw, naw," he moaned.

"Get up," Ben said desperately.

Gilroy slumped forward at his feet. "Naw, naw, naw," he begged.

"Stop it."

The old man's body curled inward, as his lean brown arms wrapped around Ben's legs. "Don't let them shoot ole Jacob," he whimpered just before he passed out.

Ben marched directly into Luther's office and closed the door behind him.

"I want to ask you something, Captain," he said.

Luther looked up from an enormous gray ledger. "Ask me something?" he said. He swept his large pink hand out over the book. "You see this, Ben?" he said. "This is the Police Department Budget. Now I look at what we got, and I think about all the extra shit we've been having to do since all these demonstrations started, and I ask myself a question. I say, 'Luther, how the hell you going to pay for all this?' "

Ben stared at him resolutely. "I want to know what the Langleys have been doing in Bearmatch."

Luther's face stiffened. "What are you talking about?"

"I was questioning this old man about the murder," Ben said. "He was drunk, I admit it, but he got to thinking about the Langleys, about how they might just come and get him, and it just about tore him up."

Luther leaned back slightly. Sheets of rain continued to sweep against the large window at his back. "You think a scared old colored boy is worth my time, Ben?"

Ben stared at him evenly.

Luther folded his arms over his chest. "The Langleys? That's what's bothering you? Well, the only thing I know for sure about those two boys is that one of them is a whole lot smarter than the other one." He glared at Ben hotly. "Now get on out of here," he said as he returned to the ledger.

Ben did not move, and after a moment Luther's eyes snapped back toward him.

"Did you hear me, Ben?" he demanded.

"I never saw a person more scared than that old man," Ben said.

Luther smiled thinly. "They're a little rough, the Langleys," he said. "Everybody knows that. They've put the squeeze on a few things."

Ben said nothing.

"But you got to be a little rough to work Bearmatch," Luther added. "If you don't beat it, it'll beat you. Look what happened to Kelly Ryan."

"Can they just do anything?" Ben asked. "Don't they answer to anybody?"

Luther looked at him squarely. "And what are you saying they've done, Ben?"

Ben did not answer.

"Are you saying they had something to do with killing that little girl?"

Ben said nothing.

"Huh?" Luther demanded. "Is that what you're saying?" He did not wait for an answer before rushing on. "Do you have one little tiny piece of evidence that connects the Langleys to that girl's murder?"

Ben shook his head helplessly. "No."

Luther went back to the ledger. "Well, if you ever do, let me know."

Ben walked over to his desk and leaned into it. "I want to see your face when you tell me that," he said.

Luther looked up. His voice was absolutely resolute when he spoke. "If you ever find anything on the Langleys, let me know."

Ben nodded quickly and turned back toward the door.

Luther took a deep, weary breath. "Look, Ben, after this business with Kelly, the department figured Bearmatch needed a certain kind of people to keep an eye on it."

"Like the Langleys."

"That's right."

"Who decided that?"

Luther laughed. "Who do you think?"

"The Chief?"

"He hires the police," Luther said, as if he were explaining the facts of life to a child. "He hires the firemen. He is the Commissioner of Public Safety."

"So they answer to him," Ben said.

"Everybody but Jesus answers to the Chief," Luther said. There was a troubled weariness in his voice. "And that's the way it is." He drew himself heavily out of his chair and turned toward the window, pressing his face near the glass. Not far beyond him, lines of Negro children could be seen standing, soaked and chilled, in the steadily sheeting rain.

"Can't they be brought inside?" Ben asked as he joined Luther at the window.

"No," Luther said sharply. "No room." His eyes drifted to the right where, at the entrance to the lot, Teddy Langley could be seen standing in a black rainslick, a double-barreled shotgun pointed toward the sky. "But I won't say I think it's right," he whispered. "Nobody can ever get me to say I think it's right."

Seventeen

The rain had finally subsided by early evening and the warm orange glow of a radiant summer sunset drifted down on the city. Ben sat at his desk, rethinking the slender threads of the case while he twisted the large purple ring in his fingers. In his mind, he could see Doreen as clearly as if she stood before him, bright and smiling in her clean white dress. But who had brought her to Bearmatch? How had she gotten home from Mountain Brook? And if it was Davenport who had taken her, why had he not brought her all the way home, as his driver always had? Why had she been let out? And where? Had someone seen her, perhaps for the first time, as she made her way home that afternoon, some gray figure watching her from one of the dark windows of the scores of shanties she must have passed on the way?

It was already night when the phone rang on Ben's desk. It was Patterson, and he sounded very tired.

"Well, I've put everybody through the ringer, Ben," he said. "I checked that fingerprint on the ring three ways from Sunday, and it's absolutely clean as far as I can figure out." He drew in a long, exhausted breath and continued. "Which means that whoever had that ring had never been arrested or been in the armed forces or worked for a liquor company or done anything that would have required him to be fingerprinted."

"All right," Ben said.

"A big zero," Patterson added. "Sorry."

"Thanks, Leon," Ben told him.

He hung up the phone and looked once again at the ring, then walked down to his car and headed home.

The streets were still slick with the long day's rain, and the whole city seemed somehow refreshed, renewed, as if it had been washed clean of its accumulated grime. Huge pools of water lay placidly under the streetlamps of Kelly Ingram Park, and the shallow gullies which lined Fourth Avenue were empty of the scattered cans and bits of paper and cigarette butts which usually lined it from downtown to the outer reaches of the Negro district.

He stopped at a traffic signal, and suddenly Kelly Ryan's face came into his mind. He saw the popped swollen eyes again and the thick, distended tongue, and it made him dread the thought of going home. For a moment he tried to think of some alternative, but nothing came to mind but redneck bars, which he didn't like, or drive-in movies where, shoved in among carloads of necking teenagers, he'd feel like some kind of pathetic middle-aged bachelor leering hungrily at young love. There were always the sizzling all-night cafes of Bessemer, where the Dawn Patrol gathered for scrambled eggs and bacon, but even his little house cradled among the factories seemed more appealing than such bleak and lonely haunts, and for an instant he gave up the search and headed toward it. Then he thought of Esther, of the way she had sat quietly in his front room, and he made a hard right at the next corner and headed out toward Bearmatch.

She was in the tiny front yard when Ben pulled up in front of the house and she looked at him curiously as he got out of the car and walked toward her.

"Evening," Ben said quietly.

Esther nodded. "My daddy told me that you came by today," she said. "I just got home from work myself."

Ben smiled softly. "Me, too." He looked down at the green cuttings which she held in her hand. "Planting something?"

"A rosebush," Esther said. "For Doreen, I guess." She hoed slowly at the unbroken earth, easily turning the wet ground. "Sort of like she's buried here."

Ben kept his eyes on the cuttings. "I like roses," he said. "I have a few bushes in my backyard. Red. What color will those be?"

"Red," Esther said. She continued to dig at the ground, inching the blade deeper and deeper with each stroke.

"My daddy planted them," Ben told her, "the red roses in the backyard. Most of the time you think it's the woman. But I'm not sure flowers meant much to her."

Esther leaned the hoe against the wobbly, chicken-wire fence that bordered the yard. "I don't know if Doreen liked them," she said. Then she took the small spade that had been lying on the fencepost beside her and knelt down. "Could have been, she did," she said as she began to shape the small hole. "Could have been, she didn't."

Ben eased himself down beside her. "Need some help?" he asked almost lightly.

Suddenly the spade stopped, and Esther looked at him insistently. "Why are you here?"

"What?"

"Did you come to tell me something?"

"Nothing in particular," Ben said.

"Just to talk, something like that?"

"I guess," Ben said. He stood up immediately. "I didn't mean to bother you."

For a moment, Esther lingered on the ground, then she rose slowly and faced him. "You just can't come over here like this," she said. "It worries people. It gets them to thinking."

"Thinking what?"

"About what you're up to."

Something in him seemed to break a little. "Nobody has to be afraid of me, Esther." he said.

"They think I'm letting you know things," Esther told him. "About the demonstrations and all. They believe you're over here spying on us. They don't believe you're trying to find out about Doreen. Nobody believes that."

Ben looked at her pointedly. "Do you?"

She did not answer.

"Do you, Esther?"

She shook her head. "I don't know."

He started to take her shoulders in his hands, but stopped himself. He felt a deep longing sweep over him, dense, demanding, barely controllable. "I don't mean any harm," he said helplessly.

"It can't look right, though," Esther said. "It just can't look right."

Ben could feel his longing giving way grudgingly, as if it were being driven from him like a hungry animal from the fire.

"I won't come again," he said, "unless it's about Doreen." He nodded gently. "Good night, ma'am."

He started to turn, but she reached out quickly and touched his arm.

"Wait."

He turned toward her.

"What do you think about all this?" she asked bluntly.

"All what?"

"All this trouble we're having," Esther said. "All this business in the streets."

"I'm sorry about it."

"But us, the Negroes," Esther asked insistently. "What do you, yourself, think about us?"

He realized suddenly that he had never been asked, and for a moment he couldn't find an answer. But he remembered how as a little boy he'd first noticed that the Negroes always took seats in the back of the trolley. He'd once asked his mother about it, and she'd only said, " 'Cause they like it." But his father shot back, "No, they don't. Nobody'd like having to do that." Having to do that? It was the first and last exchange he'd ever heard about the matter, and yet in all the years that followed, he'd never glanced toward the back of a trolley to see the dark faces staring toward him without thinking of what his father said.

Now he looked at Esther. "Well, I think that people ought to have a chance to do something, or be something, that makes sense to them," he said. "I think everybody ought to have that chance." He could feel the hard, insistent quality of the belief rising in him. "Nobody should have to give them that in the first place. But if it comes down to it, they should just up and take it."

She watched him with an odd intensity. "Good night, then," she said.

He drove directly home and slumped down in the little swing on his front porch. The long day's rain had cooled the air and filled it with an aromatic lushness. He could smell the rich sweetness of the flowers which grew across the street in Mr. Jeffries' yard.

He pressed his feet to the floor and pushed himself back, then swung forward. The wind hit him lightly, ruffling his hair, and he thought of Ryan again, not dead, but living as he should have lived, with that girl he'd met and come to love, living far away, no matter how far, in the place he should have taken her, north toward the huge anonymous cities, or west into the islands of the Pacific, but somewhere far away from the little house in which he died. He could see the house in his mind, but it was the smell of it that lingered in his memory. Ryan's smell, and only Ryan's smell. How long, he wondered, did someone have to live alone before he sank his own isolated smell into everything around him? How long did it have to go on, such loneliness, before someone said, "Enough."

He felt a sudden wrenching agitation cut through him like a strand of barbed wire, and his hand jerked up and took the purple ring from his shirt pocket. He lifted it slowly and let the gray light of the streetlamp sweep over it. It winked dully, like a dead eye, but he held on to it anyway, as if, in all the world, it was all he had.

Eighteen

Stacks of mattresses lined the walls of the lobby when Ben got back to headquarters the next morning, and Luther was busily directing a couple of highway patrolmen in how to carry them.

"Over your goddamn shoulders," he said irritably. He heaved one onto his own shoulder. "Like this."

Each of the patrolmen began wrestling awkwardly with a mattress.

Luther shook his head helplessly as he walked over to Ben. "Shit for brains," he said. "Where does Lingo find these assholes?" He glanced back over to the two men. They had finally managed to hoist the mattresses to their shoulders. "Now take them down to the cells and throw them in with the female prisoners. The bucks can sleep on the fucking springs."

The two men lumbered toward the stairs, one of them giggling mindlessly.

Luther turned to Ben. "By the way, I didn't have time to ask you last night. What'd you find over at Kelly's?"

"Just the body."

"No sign of foul play?"

Ben shook his head. "Not that I could see. Daniels and Breedlove were going over the place when I left."

Luther shrugged. "Well, they had nothing better to do. The rain had put a damper on the demonstrations. At least for a while." He glanced toward the front door where bright shafts of warm sunlight could be seen cascading through the glass. "Not like today. Today we're going to get it."

"That guy Coggins," Ben said. "The one Breedlove was after yesterday. Is he still in custody?"

"I'd keep that agitating bastard in jail for twenty years, if it was me," Luther snapped. "The idea of putting little kids in jail. It makes me sick."

"Is he still around?" Ben repeated.

Luther looked at him as if he were a naive little boy. "Well, nobody's trying to get out, Ben. Shit, that's the whole idea, fill up the jails." He shook his head. "We got them in Mountain Brook, Irondale, Bessemer. We're hauling by the truckload all over Jefferson County." He sighed loudly. "When's it going to end?"

"Coggins," Ben said. "I want to talk to him."

"All right," Luther told him, "He's in one of cells with the rest of the male prisoners. Ask McCorkindale. He's supposed to be keeping track of people." He glanced nervously at the stairs. "Let me go check on those two monkeys," he said irritably. "They could end up trying to stuff those mattresses down the goddamn toilet." Then he rushed away.

Ben found McCorkindale straddling a metal chair at the entrance to the cellblock.

"Howdy, Ben," he said. "They got me watching the niggers." He frowned unhappily. "They'll probably have me doing a lot of this shit now that Kelly's gone."

Ben looked down the hallway to the lines of cells. Scores of black hands could be seen clutching loosely to the bars.

"Looks like you're full up," he said.

McCorkindale lifted a small box of chocolate candy toward him. "Want one?"

"No, thanks," Ben said.

McCorkindale popped one into his mouth and chewed it slowly. "Nothing to do down here but feed your face."

"I'm looking for one of the prisoners," Ben told him.

"Take your pick, son," McCorkindale said. "They all look alike."

"Leroy Coggins."

McCorkindale smiled. "Oh, one of the big boys. Got a mean mouth on him, too."

"Captain Starnes said you might know where he was."

McCorkindale scratched his chin. "They brought him down yesterday afternoon," he said thoughtfully. "He was bitching about something upstairs." He peered off down the hall. "I believe he's in that far-left cell. You know what he looks like?"

"Yeah."

"Well, go check that far-left cell," McCorkindale said. "I think that's where I put him."

Ben made his way slowly toward the cell McCorkindale had indicated. A murmur rose slowly among the prisoners as he passed them, and, as if in response to some silent cue, some of them began to sing and clap their hands. On either side, the individual cells were packed tightly. Young black men sat Indian-style on the bare springs of the metal bunks or stood, shoulder to shoulder, on the cramped cement floor. The cool which had swept over the city with the rain had not penetrated to the cellblock, and the suffocating smell of hundreds of sweaty crowded bodies thickened the air.

"You a lawyer?" someone called desperately as Ben continued toward the rear of the cellblock. "You gone git me out of here?"

In response, a chorus of boos and low moans swept the cellblock.

"You staying like the rest of us, chickenshit," someone cried, and a series of cheers and catcalls broke from the stifling cells.

At the last cell, Ben stopped and looked in. Scores of young men and teenage boys milled about, and near the center of the cell one of them was urinating into the single toilet.

"Looking for somebody, Preacherman?" someone asked suddenly.

Ben glanced to the right and stared into a face that poked toward him from behind the bars.

"Leroy Coggins," Ben said.

The man studied him a moment, then called toward the back of the cell. "Hey, Leroy. Preacherman's here to see you."

The crowd shifted about and a space opened up, as it seemed, between two dark furrows. At the end of it, Ben could see Coggins standing idly, his back to the rear wall.

"What do you want?" Coggins asked.

"To talk to you."

"About what?"

"That girl."

"Ooo wee," someone cried in a high, mocking voice. "Leroy, you got a girl?"

Coggins smiled. "Not one that would have anything to do with you," he said.

The crowd laughed.

"That dead girl," Ben said.

"She'd sure have to be dead to have anything to do with Leroy," the same voice shouted, and once again the crowd laughed.

Ben smiled, his eyes fixed on Coggins. "How about it, Mr. Coggins?" he said.

Coggins hesitated a moment, then pried himself from the wall and ambled leisurely to the front of the cell.

"I've already told you everything I know," he said.

"I know," Ben told him. He glanced down the hallway. "Sammy," he called, "come here a minute."

McCorkindale lumbered down to them. "What can I do for you, Ben?"

"Open up," Ben told him. "I want to take Mr. Coggins out for a minute."

McCorkindale opened the cell immediately, but Coggins did not step out of it.

"What's the matter?" McCorkindale said tauntingly. "Scaredy-cat?"

Coggins straightened himself quickly and strode boldly out of the cell. "Not of anything you crackers can dish out," he snapped at McCorkindale.

McCorkindale's face reddened instantly. "You better watch yourself, boy," he blurted.

Ben stepped between them and took Coggins lightly by the arm.

"This way," he said as he tugged him forward quickly and led him up the stairs. He did not speak to him again until they were back in the detective bullpen.

"You got to want to die to talk to people like you do," Ben said, almost lightly, as he sat down behind his desk.

Coggins remained standing, his face grim. "Maybe a part of me wants to do just that," he said.

Ben looked at him seriously. "Well, let the other part take over for a while," he said, "because we both know you've got work to do."

Coggins face softened suddenly, but he did not move.

Ben nodded toward the empty chair which rested beside his desk. "I'd be much obliged if you'd take a seat."

Coggins studied Ben's face a moment longer, then he slowly sat down.

Ben took the purple ring from his jacket pocket and handed it to Coggins. "The fellow that killed that little girl—this might be his ring." He shrugged. "I don't know that for sure, but right now it's all I've got to go on."

Coggins looked at the ring. "Well, you don't have much, do you?"

"No."

Coggins laid the ring on the top of the desk. "I've never seen it. Where would I have seen it?"

"I'm not expecting you to recognize it," Ben said.

Coggins leaned forward slightly. "Well, what exactly are you expecting, then?"

"That ring had chalk dust all over it," Ben told him. "The kind you use on a pool cue."

"So?"

"It's the kind of ring you see down in some of those shops on Fourth Avenue."

"Maybe," Coggins said. "Up until recently I hadn't spent much time down there. I'm from Ensley, remember?"

"I was thinking it might belong to a Negro."

"Well, you certainly wouldn't want it to belong to a white man."

Ben let it pass. "And that this Negro just might hang around some of the poolhalls down on Fourth Avenue."

Coggins smiled. "You're a regular Sherlock Holmes," he said.

Ben let that pass too. "The thing is," he said, "the people who hang out on Fourth Avenue aren't in much of a mood to talk to someone from the Police Department."

"Well, maybe if you had some Negro policemen in Birmingham, you wouldn't have that problem," Coggins said.

"I can't deny that, Mr. Coggins," Ben said. "I really can't. But right now I've got a little girl, and I've got to find out who killed her." He looked at Coggins determinedly. "I got to find that out right now, not a few months or maybe even years from now, when things may be different."

Coggins eyes returned to the ring. "What do you want from me?"

"I want you to come with me down to Fourth Avenue," Ben said. "I want to go in some of those poolhalls, bring this ring with me, ask a few questions."

Coggins looked up slowly. "I'm not sure I can do that."

"Why not?"

"Because of the way it would look," Coggins said. "I mean, working with you. The way it would look to my people."

"You think maybe I might have the same problem with mine?" Ben asked pointedly.

Coggins smiled but said nothing.

"He's still out there," Ben said, "whoever it was who killed Doreen Ballinger." He shrugged. "That wouldn't be all that much to think about," he added, "if more little girls weren't out there, too."

Coggins did not speak immediately, but from the look in his eyes, Ben knew that he had won.

Nineteen

Ranks of fireman in boots, helmets and rubber slicks were lined up in the basement as Ben and Coggins made their way to the car. The Chief paced up and down before them, his voice echoing through the concrete chamber. "You all pledged to serve the City of Birmingham when you came to the department," he cried. "And you are going to be asked to render that service, no matter what."

Several of the firemen glanced at each other apprehensively, but the rest stared expressionlessly at the Chief.

"We are all part of the same city," the Chief went on, his hand sweeping out into the gray air of the garage, "and we've all sworn an oath to protect it."

"What's this all about?" Coggins whispered as Ben ushered him around a concrete column.

Ben shrugged lightly and continued moving steadily forward, one hand gently held to Coggins' arm, until they reached the car.

"He's a dinosaur, that old man," Coggins said as he glanced back at the Chief.

"Get in," Ben said.

Coggins pulled himself into the car, his eyes still directed toward the Chief and the lines of fireman who stood in formation before him. "He's like a bug trying to hold back the ocean," he said.

"Think so?" Ben said idly.

"Just like a little bug, trying to protect its hole against the tide," Coggins added. Then he looked at Ben and smiled, almost tauntingly. "You don't believe that, do you?"

Ben said nothing. He grasped the wheel and jerked it to the right, sending the car in a wide arc through the garage.

Coggins returned his eyes to the ranks of firemen and the stocky little man who paraded back and forth in front of them. "No sense of history," he said, almost to himself. "No idea at all of how they'll be remembered when all this is over."

Ben kept his eyes straight ahead as he guided the car past knots of city police and highway patrolmen until it nosed up the embankment to the street.

Breedlove stood at the top of the hill, his hat pulled down over his eyes. When the car stopped, he strolled over and leaned in, his arms resting on the open window.

"Looks like it's going to be a pretty day," he said to Ben. Then his eyes shifted over to Coggins. "What do you think, Leroy? Reckon we might bust some ass today?"

Coggins sat rigidly in place. A line of sweat formed on his upper lip.

"What do you think, Leroy?' Breedlove repeated in a thin, threatening voice, "Think maybe some of us crackers might bust a few burrheads before the sun goes down?"

Coggins did not move. He kept his eyes straight ahead, but as Ben glanced over toward him, he noticed that his knees were trembling.

Breedlove glanced at Ben. "Where you taking this boy?"

"Just going for a ride," Ben said.

Breedlove laughed. "Bullshit."

"I'm checking a lead," Ben told him.

Breedlove smiled as he stepped away from the car. "Well, you guys have a great time, you hear? But if you get a chance, come on down to the park. It's going to be real lively down there this afternoon." He stepped back from the car and tipped his hat. "Have a safe and happy day."

Coggins let out a quick, nervous breath as Ben pulled into the street. "I'm tired of being scared," he said angrily, his teeth tightly clinched. "I'm just tired of it."

Ben eased the car on down the street. Lines of helmeted highway patrolmen stood at intervals all along the avenue, their pump shotguns held casually in their arms. To the right the Chief's white tank could be seen wedged in between two brightly polished fire trucks, and a few feet away Black Cat 13 seemed to be sunning itself lazily in the bright morning light. Teddy Langley sat behind the wheel, his eyes silently following Ben's car as he muttered into his police radio.

"You know them?" Coggins asked. "You know the Langleys?"

"A little."

Coggins' eyes bore down on Ben. "You could be taking me to them, for all I know. This whole thing could be a setup."

Ben slammed on the brakes and the car skidded to a squealing halt in the middle of the street. "Get out!" he said hotly.

Coggins stared at him, thunderstruck.

"Get out!" Ben repeated sharply. "If you think I'm taking you off to be whipped or killed or something, then get the hell out of this car right now!"

Coggins did not move.

"Just open the goddamn door," Ben told him.

Coggins smiled nervously. "And be shot for trying to run away or something."

Ben whipped his pistol from his shoulder holster and handed it to Coggins. "Take this with you." He thrust it toward Coggins' face. "Take it. Or do you think I have another one, some little sawed-off job in my back pocket?"

Coggins pressed his back against the door. "I'd have to be crazy to take that thing."

"Take the fucking gun," Ben demanded. "Throw the chamber open. Make sure it's loaded."

Coggins shook his head. "No way, man. They see me with a gun, I'm dead."

Ben let the pistol drop from his hand. It fell into Coggins' lap and he shuddered to the right, as if it were a rattlesnake. "Get that thing away from me!" he cried.

"As long as we're out together," Ben said, "you're going to keep the gun. Then maybe after a while, you might get the idea that I'm not setting you up for anything." For a moment he glared at Coggins angrily. "If I wanted you dead, I'd do it myself," he said finally. Then he kicked the accelerator angrily and the car jerked forward, twisting wildly as it roared toward Fourth Avenue.

The morning heat had already begun to build on the street by the time Ben pulled the car over to the side and stopped. All of Fourth Avenue swept out before him. It was a wide boulevard which made up the main street of the Negro section of downtown. The sweet smell of curling parlors and barbecued meat hung in the air, and as Ben stepped out of the car, he could see the racks of discount clothing which had been brought out onto the sidewalks and which now fluttered lazily in the slow, heavy breeze.

"They'll bring all that stuff back inside when the marchers come," Coggins said, as if he were divulging a trade secret. "That's how you know when it's beginning." He smiled at Ben. "Have the cops figured that out yet?"

Ben did not answer. He continued to stare down the street. It was crowded with early morning pedestrians, and he found that his eyes were already sorting out the large from the small, concentrating on men with big hands.

"What do we do now?" Coggins asked after a moment.

Ben pointed to a small jewelry store across the street. "We'll start there," he said.

Coggins nodded toward the pistol, which still rested in his lap. "What do I do with this?"

"Put it in your belt, then cover it with your shirt," Ben told him casually.

"But I can't just—" Coggins began.

Ben stared at him fiercely. "You get out of this car without that gun, and I'll kill you myself."

"But, I can't—can't—"

Before he could finish, Ben stepped out of the car and headed toward the store. He was peering into its front window when Coggins came up beside him.

"This is the sort of place that has that kind of ring," Ben said quietly. He pointed to a shoe box filled with gaudy costume jewelry. "See there. It could have been bought from any place on Fourth Avenue." He walked to the door and opened it. "Come on," he said.

Coggins followed behind as Ben made his way into the store.

It was a cramped space, little more than a narrow hallway bordered on either side by two large glass display cases. A large woman sat on a stool between the cases. She seemed to pull back slightly as the two men entered, and her hands crawled into the large purse that rested on her lap.

"What can I do for you gentlemans?" she asked suspiciously.

Ben stepped back slightly and nodded toward Coggins.

Coggins took the cue and walked in front of him. "How you doing, sister?" he asked with a bright smile.

The woman smiled at him with everything but her eyes.

Coggins sunk his hands in his pocket and shifted nervously for a moment before leaning awkwardly onto one of the display cases.

"Careful there," the woman warned sternly. "They ain't built that good."

Coggins straightened himself immediately. He jerked his hands out of his pockets and folded his arms over his chest. "Actually, my uh, my friend and I are looking for something."

The woman's eyes narrowed suspiciously. "I don't sell nothing but jewelry," she said.

Coggins laughed tensely. "Oh, well, that's okay. It's about jewelry."

"And I don't takes no hot stuff, neither."

"Hot stuff?" Coggins asked. "We haven't stolen anything, sister."

The woman's hand moved within the carpetbag. "What you want, boy?" she asked menacingly.

"It's about a ring," Ben said.

Her eyes shifted over to him.

"We think it might have been bought in one of the stores around here," Coggins put in quickly, as if trying to regain the high ground. "Maybe even from you."

"Something wrong with this here ring?" the woman asked bluntly.

"Not with the ring, no," Coggins told her. "But maybe the guy who bought it."

The woman watched him impatiently. "What's this here ring look like?"

Ben moved to take the ring out of his breast pocket, saw the woman's hand move again, then stopped. "It's right here," he said. Then he slowly took it out and handed it to her.

The woman took the ring in her one free hand and looked at it closely. "Ain't nothing special," she said. She lifted it slightly and turned it in the light. "Ain't real. Just cheap stuff."

"Have you ever seen one like it?" Coggins asked authoritatively.

The woman handed it back to Ben. "Seen a million of them. Ain't nothing special about it. Just a big old ugly ring like any poot-ass could wear." She grinned cheerfully. "I probably sold plenty of them myself."

Ben turned the ring slowly in his fingers. "I guess so."

"All the stores around here, they mostly sell stuff like that," the woman added. She drew her hand out of the carpetbag and seemed to relax slightly. "You wanted to, you could even get earrings to match."

"Earrings?" Ben asked.

"Why sure," the woman said. "Bracelets, too. Even a necklace if you wants one."

Coggins' eyes shot over to Ben, then returned to the woman. "You mean that's a woman's ring?" he asked.

The woman nodded. "Course it is," she said with a small appreciative laugh. "Ain't you got no sense, honey?"

"But it's so big," Ben said.

She snapped the ring from his hand and turned it over. "See here, it's been sawed into so it could fit a bigger finger." She gave it back to Ben. "But it's a woman's ring, all right. Couldn't be nothing else." She laughed. "Ain't no man would wear something like that. Least not one that's got good sense."

Twenty

An enormous bright-red fire engine roared down the avenue as Ben and Coggins walked back out onto the sidewalk. Several firemen clung to its right side, the wind slapping wildly at their black rubber jackets. They leaned outward slightly as the engine careened around the far corner of Kelly Ingram Park, then came to a halt, half-hidden behind a wall of large elm trees.

"I wonder if the Chief gave them a talk this morning, too," Coggins said with a small laugh. He turned to Ben. "What do we do now?"

"Hit some other places," Ben told him.

"Why?" Coggins asked, "We know that ring could have been bought anywhere."

Ben did not answer. He kept his eyes on the park. Lines of highway patrolmen were assembling barricades at the downtown corner of the park. Just behind them, several firemen were unspooling yards of flat black waterhose while small groups of pedestrians looked on wonderingly.

"You don't think the killer could be a woman, do you?" Coggins asked.

For an instant Ben saw Doreen's ravaged body, the caked blood which was smeared across her thighs. "No," he said.

"But can you really be sure about that?" Coggins asked. "I mean, you know, it's possible that—"

"There was semen in her," Ben told him abruptly.

Coggins' face froze. "Semen? You mean that little girl was raped?"

"Yes."

"You didn't tell me that."

Ben looked at him. "It was after she was dead. Somebody killed her, then raped her." He shook his head. "And whoever it was, you can be sure it wasn't a woman."

Coggins' eyes drifted away from him and out toward the street. For a moment, all his attention seemed to center on a hand-lettered sign in the window across the way: BETSY'S IRONING TREATMENT—BEST IN BIRMINGHAM. "All right," he said finally, "what next?"

"The poolhalls," Ben told him. "And after them, nothing."

There were only two poolhalls on the avenue, and the first was only a block away. Ben and Coggins made their way steadily through the shifting crowds, walking shoulder to shoulder, despite the odd looks of the people they passed along the street. Coggins walked stiffly, as if trying to control a slowly building fear. His eyes darted left and right, but his face remained rigidly in place, and as he walked along beside him, Ben noticed that parallel lines of perspiration had gathered on his forehead.

"Where is this poolhall?" Coggins asked shakily as they stopped for a traffic signal at the end of the block.

"Just a block ahead," Ben told him.

Coggins' hands dipped into his pockets, then came out again. He bounced slightly on the balls of his feet.

"What's the matter?" Ben asked.

Coggins' eyes shot over to him. "Nothing."

"You look a little jumpy," Ben said.

"This neighborhood," Coggins admitted, "I'm not used to it." He nodded toward the lines of Negroes that gathered across the street, idly waiting for the light to change. "I don't know any of these people." He laughed nervously. "I'm a law student at Columbia, for Christ's sake. I've lived my whole life in Ensley."

Ben said nothing.

"I'm a middle-class Negro, goddammit," Coggins added vehemently, "I don't belong down here." A nervous laugh broke from him, thin and edged with self-mockery. "My mother never shopped on Fourth Avenue." He glared at Ben helplessly. "She goes to New York to shop. She shops in Bloomingdale's, for God's sake." His eyes snapped forward as the light changed and the milling crowd of Negroes swept toward him like a high black tide. "I'll do my best," he whispered quickly as he stepped off the curb, "but you really picked the wrong guy for this deal."

Ben continued to walk beside him as the thickening crowds swarmed around them. Coggins looked as if he'd been gathered into the tentacles of some strange dark beast, but he moved boldly forward anyway, his head held almost artificially high, as if he were trying to give off an attitude of complete control.

"There it is," Ben said as they neared the first poolhall.

Coggins nodded apprehensively but maintained his stride. He did not stop until he reached the door. Then he pressed his back to the front wall.

"Okay," he asked, "what now?"

"We go in," Ben told him.

"And do what, exactly?"

"Ask a few questions."

"And what if the people inside don't feel like answering them?"

"Then we'll leave," Ben said with a shrug. "What else can we do?"

The simplicity of the answer seemed to ease Coggins' nervousness a bit. He drew in a slow deep breath, as if preparing for a long dive into dangerous waters.

"All right," he said finally. "Let's go."

A smoky gray light engulfed them as they stepped into the poolhall. Inside, two rows of about twenty tables stretched the length of the room, each resting beneath its own shaded fluorescent light. A jukebox ground out Little Richard's latest number, and the men who were waiting to shoot rocked to its beat while they stood back from the table and watched their opponent's moves. An ancient Coca-Cola machine was wedged in between two cigarette machines at the back of the hall, and the side walls were covered with advertisements and pinup girl calendars.

For an instant everything went on as usual, but then it stopped abruptly. The low murmur of conversation dropped into an eerie silence, and even the men who had begun to calculate their shots froze in place and stared at Ben and Coggins as the two of them continued to stand at the front of the room, their bodies backlighted by the still open door.

Coggins shifted nervously, then offered a toothy grin. "How y'all doing?" he bawled cheerfully.

No one spoke.

Again Coggins shifted from one foot to the next. "Listen, I want to talk to you fellows about something."

Silence.

"You guys may have heard about this little girl who got killed over in Bearmatch," Coggins continued. "The fact is, I'm trying to find out who did it, you know?"

Several of the men sat back on the edges of the tables and stared mutely at Coggins.

Coggins nodded toward Ben. "This fellow, here, he's helping me out a little. He's from the Justice Department. He works with Robert Kennedy."

The men did not seem impressed.

"He's been sent down from Washington, you know," Coggins went on wildly. "We figure some . . . some cracker killed that little girl, and we aim to find out who it was." He turned swiftly and snapped the ring out of Ben's jacket pocket. "You see this?" he asked as he lifted it to the crowd.

All eyes turned toward the ring, but no one spoke.

"This ring just might have belonged to the guy who killed that little girl," Coggins explained shakily. "Yeah, that's right. And the thing is, it had chalk dust all over it. You know, like you use here on your pool cues."

A loud, husky voice came from somewhere in the back of the room. "What color?"

Coggins' eyes searched the room. "What was that?"

"What color was the chalk dust?" the voice answered.

"Yellow," Ben said.

Suddenly a small man in a floppy gray hat and bright-red bow tie stepped out of the crowd. "We don't use yellow in this poolhall," he said. He picked a small cube of chalk from the table beside him and tossed it to Ben.

"We use blue chalk here," the man said. "That's all we've ever used." He glanced around at the other men and smiled. "Ain't that right?"

"That's right," someone said.

"Uh huh."

"Yeah."

"That's right, Larry."

The man walked over to Coggins. "Ain't I seen you before?" he asked.

"I don't think so," Coggins told him.

"When all them kids was marching down the street," Larry said. "Didn't I see you with one of them little walkie-talkies, sort of in charge of things?"

"Well, maybe," Coggins said slowly. "I was monitoring the demonstration?"

"Say what?"

"Keeping tabs on things," Coggins added. "Watching out for the kids."

Larry laughed. "Yeah, I thought I seen you." He offered his hand. "Larry Sugarman. I own this place."

Coggins grasped Sugarman's hand and shook it vigorously. "Pleased to meet you, Mr. Sugarman."

Sugarman's eyes slid over to Ben. "Robert Kennedy, huh?"

Ben said nothing.

Sugarman thrust out his hand. "Well, good luck to you, sir."

Ben shook his hand.

Sugarman stepped back, smiling. "And as far as that yellow chalk's concerned, they got that over at Better Days Pool Hall. You might ought to check in over there."

"We will," Coggins assured him enthusiastically. "We sure will, Mr. Sugarman." He glanced back toward the other men. "And thank you, gentlemen," he said hurriedly. "Sorry for the interruption."

Back on the street, Coggins drew in a deep, relaxing breath. "Well, that wasn't so bad, was it?" he asked.

Ben glanced back toward the downtown corner of the avenue. Several fire trucks had joined the first one at the edge of the park, and the Chief's white tank was stationed in front of them, almost like a mascot. Lines of firemen had taken up positions along the avenue and at various places within the park. Long strands of firehose snaked out behind them like thick black tails.

Coggins slapped his hands together happily. "Well, want to hit the next one?"

"Yeah," Ben said quickly. He glanced down the hill to where the Highway Patrol was massing.

Twenty-one

Ben and Coggins moved down Fourth Avenue toward the Better Days Pool Hall through steadily thinning crowds. On both sides of the street, people were hurrying off the avenue and onto the side streets. Shopkeepers had begun removing goods from their display windows, and by the time the two men reached Better Days, almost all of them were empty.

When they stopped outside the door of the poolhall, Coggins turned to face the street, his eyes sweeping it north and south. "I'd say we have about twenty minutes before it starts," he said confidently.

"You don't know for sure?" Ben asked.

Coggins shook his head. "This is a civilian demonstration, not a military operation. You can't time things that well." He glanced up at the sign above the poolhall. It was written in thick red letters, and on either side of BETTER DAYS someone had drawn crisscrossed pool cues. "Nice," he said as he looked back at Ben. He smiled mockingly. "I mean, what's law school compared to a classy place like this?"

Inside, the atmosphere was decidedly different from the poolhall down the street. There was the same smoky air, the same jukebox, soda and cigarette machines, even the same speckled linoleum over the cement floor, but the tone was darker, grimmer, and Ben recognized it immediately as being similar to the sort of white redneck bar where he'd seen violence erupt like a broken sore, spewing blood on all four walls.

Coggins appeared to see no difference at all, and as he stepped forward toward the first line of tables, he offered the men who were standing at them the same innocent grin. "How y'all doing, fellows?" he asked cheerfully.

One of them lifted his cue slowly and massaged the tip. "What you want, dickhead?" he asked in a voice as flat as steel.

Coggins' smile vanished.

The man continued to finger the tip of the cue. His eyes squeezed together slowly as they moved back and forth from Ben to Coggins. "This is a nigger pool hall," he said when they finally settled on Ben.

"Well, now, we . . . uh . . . we," Coggins sputtered.

The man's eyes shifted over to Coggins. "I said a nigger poolhall," the man said menacingly, "and you don't look black to me, Tomboy."

Coggins offered a high nervous laugh. He glanced down at his arm and rubbed it smoothly. "My skin looks as black as yours," he said.

The man shook his head. "No, it don't," he said. He looked around at the other men. Some of them began to move forward slowly, slapping their cue sticks in their hands. "No, you look like a cracker to me, boy," he said. He smiled coldly. "Don't this boy look like a cracker to you?" he called to the other men.

A thin, edgy laughter rippled through the room.

The man's eyes remained fixed on Coggins. "What's your name, boy?" he asked.

"Leroy Coggins," Coggins said tensely.

The man took a small, barely perceptible step toward him, and the group behind him seemed to move forward at his signal.

Ben glanced to the left and saw a tall, thin man circle over toward the wall, then stand stonily in front of the room's only rear exit.

"I'm here about a little girl," Coggins said quickly.

The man laughed as he took another small step. "You want a little dark meat, that it, cracker?"

Laughter broke through the room again, and as it faded away, a large man stepped through the front door, closed it behind him, and then stood, his arms folded over his chest, and stared lethally at Ben and Coggins.

Now there was no way out, and Ben felt his body tense suddenly, as if preparing for the worst.

"She was murdered," Coggins said desperately, his voice all but breaking over the last word. "We found her body over in Bearmatch."

The man's eyes seemed to draw together. "We? Who's we, Leroy?"

"The police," Coggins blurted before he could stop himself.

A low murmur swept around them.

"Police," the man bawled. He glanced back at the other men. "You hear that? This boy's with the police."

"No, I'm not!" Coggins cried. "I'm not with the police."

The man took another small step, his hand crawling slowly toward the back pocket of his trousers. "Who the white cracker, Leroy?" he asked mockingly.

Coggins looked imploringly at Ben, but he said nothing.

"Who the white cracker, Leroy?" the man repeated.

Coggins stared at him, terrified, but he did not answer.

"What's the matter, nigger, you deaf?" the man asked. He took another step, and the men behind him surged forward. "*Who this white cracker?*" the man screamed suddenly.

Coggins stepped back slightly, but the man was on him, a knife glinting in the light from the tables.

Instantly, Coggins' hand snapped the pistol from his belt and pressed it hard under the man's chin. "Drop that knife!" he screamed, his hand trembling almost uncontrollably, his finger squeezing down on the trigger. "Drop it, motherfucker!"

The man at the front door lunged forward, and Ben turned and punched him hard in the stomach, then pulled him up by his collar and slammed him against the wall.

"Now don't move!" Coggins squealed. He dug the barrel of the pistol deep beneath the other man's chin. "You tell them not to move, motherfucker," he shouted.

The man lifted his arms slowly, then let them drop, and as he did so, the others moved back slightly.

Coggins glanced back and saw Ben pressing the man against the wall. He looked at him imploringly.

Desperately, Ben tried to come up with a next move. Then, suddenly, a deep sonorous voice broke over him from the rear of the room.

"Now what you boys gone do?"

Ben's eyes searched the room until they settled on a huge figure which stood in a small doorway on the right side of the room.

"You remember me?" the figure said.

Ben squinted into the thick gray light, trying to bring him into focus.

"Gaylord," the man said. Then he stepped forward into a shaft of light and Ben saw the little purple stud-pin wink brightly in the shadowy darkness.

Gaylord walked to the front of the room. For a moment he looked very grim. Then a smile swept over his face. "What you gone do?" he asked Ben. "Strangle poor ole Jackie to death?"

Ben released his grip somewhat, and Jackie broke away, gasping.

Gaylord continued to watch Ben closely. "You sure do end up in the most ridiculous places," he said. "You still checking on that girl?"

"Yes."

Gaylord stared at him expressionlessly. "Why don't you tell your buddy to let Albert go."

Ben nodded to Coggins.

Coggins looked at him wonderingly. "You sure?"

"Let him go," Ben said.

Coggins pulled the pistol from the man's chin, and Albert stumbled backward against one of the tables.

"Now we all can talk like nice folks," Gaylord said lightly. "Why don't you come on back to my office."

The men at the tables parted immediately as Gaylord walked through them. Ben and Coggins followed along behind him until they were in a small cluttered office at the back of the hall.

Gaylord closed the door, then took a seat behind a plain metal desk. "You shouldn't pull something like this again," he said. "You could get yourself hurt real bad." He glanced at the pistol, which was still dangling from Coggins' hand. "Why don't you put that away, boy," he said.

Coggins glanced at the pistol, as if surprised to find it still in his hand. He quickly tucked it into his belt.

"Now that's a lot more friendly," Gaylord said cheerily. He looked at Ben. "What'd Mr. Jolly tell you?"

"Nothing," Ben said. "He wanted money."

Gaylord laughed. "He got more than he could spend in two more lifetimes, but he still want more." He leaned back slightly, and the springs in his chair squeaked painfully under his shifting weight. "He own this poolhall," he said, "but I runs it for him." He looked at Coggins. "Who you, boy? You don't look like you from Bearmatch."

"Ensley," Coggins said in a whisper.

A sly smile slithered onto Gaylord's lips. "Ensley? You a long way from home, son."

Coggins said nothing.

"You gone be the first nigger policeman, or what?"

Coggins pulled himself to his full height. "I don't think the man who killed that little girl should go unpunished," he declared.

Gaylord didn't buy it. "That right? Well, lemme see, what if I done it? How you gone punish me?"

Coggins did not answer.

Gaylord stared at him smugly. "You got a big mouth for such a little ole pecker, boy." He turned back to Ben. "Now you and me, maybe we can talk," he said.

Ben took out the ring and handed it to him. "Doreen had this in her pocket when we found her."

Gaylord studied the ring. "Doreen? That the little girl?"

"Yes."

"Doreen Ballinger?"

"That's right."

Gaylord nodded and handed Ben back the ring. "She deaf, right?"

"Yes."

Gaylord shook his head. "That's not right, kill a little deaf girl."

"No, it's not," Coggins said loudly.

Gaylord ignored him. "I seen that ring before," he said evenly.

Ben leaned forward instantly. "Where?"

"I know the guy that used to wear it," Gaylord said casually. "He made like it was something real nice, like it was a diamond or something."

Ben reached for his notebook and opened it. "Who?"

"Don't know his real name," Gaylord said, "but I recognize the ring. Ugly, cheap ole thing." He smiled. "You looking for a big man," he said. "Even bigger than ole Gaylord."

"I know," Ben told him.

"He big," Gaylord added, "but he harmless. He wouldn't hurt a fly."

"But you don't know his name?" Ben asked.

"It's like I said before," Gaylord told him. "He ain't got no regular name. But everybody call him Bluto, 'cause he so big and such."

"Where does he live?"

"Well, I hear tell he ain't got no house."

"He must live somewhere."

Gaylord laughed. "Way I hear it, he live in a pipe."

"Pipe?"

"One of them big old pipes around the rubber plant."

"A storm drain?" Ben asked unbelievingly.

"That's right."

"When did you see him last?" Ben asked.

Gaylord's eyes rolled toward the ceiling. "He was in here late Sunday. He come in most everyday."

"And plays pool?"

"That's right?"

"Where does he work?"

Gaylord laughed. "Aw, he don't work. He do a few little errands over in Bearmatch. Little of this, little of that. But he don't have no regular job."

"Well, where does he get the money to play so much pool?"

Gaylord looked as if it had never occurred to him.

"He has to get it from somewhere," Ben said insistently.

"Guess so," Gaylord said.

"How about friends, relatives?"

"Ain't got none, far as I know."

"Then he must have a job."

"Naw," Gaylord said with certainty. "He couldn't have no regular job."

"How do you know?"

" 'Cause he ain't got enough sense for a regular job," Gaylord said.

"What do you mean?"

"He like a child," Gaylord repeated. "You know, in his head."

"Retarded?" Coggins blurted suddenly. "You mean, mentally retarded?"

Gaylord looked at him. "Yeah, like that. He like a little bitty child. Ain't a speck of meanness in him."

Twenty·two

The avenue was almost entirely deserted when Ben and Coggins walked back out onto the sidewalk. It was as if a great wind had blown everything away, the wooden stalls packed high with socks and T-shirts, the racks of cheap dresses and shiny ready-made suits, even the old men who often sat in front of the barbecue stands, whittling idly with their pocket knives. Only the grit of the gutter remained, bits of paper, cigarette packages, bottle caps, all of which looked like little more than the residue of a vanished population.

"I screwed up," Coggins said as he and Ben walked back down toward the car.

"You did the only thing you could do."

"I believe in nonviolence," Coggins said. "I really do. I believe in persuading people, in moving their consciences."

Ben shrugged. "Well, sometimes maybe you just have time to stop them."

There were no other cars on the avenue, and when Ben and Coggins got to theirs, they found Breedlove and Daniels lounging on the hood.

"They were about to tow this old wreck," Daniels said, "but Breedlove told them it belonged to one of Birmingham's ace detectives."

Breedlove laughed. "That's right. Besides, I figured you'd be back before the action started." He looked at Coggins. "You too, Leroy. I didn't figure you'd want to miss this."

Ben opened the passenger door. "Get in," he said to Coggins.

"Where you going, Ben?" Breedlove asked as he slid off the hood. "Aren't you supposed to help with the arrests?"

Ben closed the door then walked over to the driver's side. "Nobody's said a thing to me about that," he said, "so I'm just going to continue what I was doing."

Daniels stepped up beside him. "Still working on that little girl?"

Ben nodded as he opened the door and pulled himself inside.

"I hear her mama filed a Missing Person."

"Her aunt," Ben told him.

"A nigger woman," Breedlove said. "That's what McCorkindale told me."

Ben stared at him coolly. "That's right. What about it?"

Daniels stepped back slightly and flashed Breedlove an icy smile. "Hey, Charlie, I think Ben's getting a little testy in his old age."

Breedlove leaned in from the other side. "King's giving another speech tonight, Ben," he said teasingly. "I heard you missed the last one."

Ben said nothing, and Breedlove was still studying his face with an odd, indecipherable intensity when he hit the ignition and pulled away.

The first wave of marchers crested the hill as Ben drove slowly up it. He guided the car over to the far right and stopped.

"You taking me back to jail?" Coggins asked.

"You want me to?"

Coggins smiled tentatively. "It seems a little safer."

"I'm going to check out the rubber plant," Ben told him. "See if I can find this Bluto character, the one Gaylord was talking about." He glanced over at Coggins. "You want to come?"

"Yes, I do," Coggins said. He pulled the pistol from his belt and handed it to Ben. "But this time you keep the gun."

For a few minutes they sat together in silence while the long line of Negroes filed past the car. Down below, the first sirens had begun to wail, and Ben could hear the engine of the Chief's tank as it started to grind loudly at the far end of the park.

Coggins watched the demonstrators for a while, nodding to a few as they passed. Then he turned to Ben. "It's strange, what you did," he said, "the way you just pulled over and stopped when you saw the people coming over the hill. Why'd you do that?"

Ben shrugged. "I don't know. It's what country people do." He looked at Coggins. "You ever lived in the country?"

"No."

"I haven't either," Ben said. "But once, when I was visiting a cousin, we were heading down the road in his old truck when we met a funeral procession. My cousin pulled over and stopped and waited for it to pass on by."

"Why?" Coggins asked.

"I don't know," Ben said. "I guess out of respect."

"For the dead, you mean?"

"Yeah," Ben told him. He watched as the last few stragglers moved haltingly forward at the end of the first wave. They were mostly older people, gray and unsteady. One of them was an old woman who pushed an aluminum walker before her. When she'd finally gotten by, Ben started the car and moved quickly to the far edge of the park, then made a hard right just as the second wave of marchers began to stride, clapping and singing down the avenue.

The Alabama Rubber Plant occupied a huge sheet-metal warehouse in the southern corner of the city. A guard was posted at the gate, and Ben waited quietly until he ambled over to the car.

"How ya'll," the man said with a grin as he leaned into the window.

Ben took out his badge. "I understand you've got a few storm drains around the plant."

The man nodded. "They's a big old one right down yonder," he said as he pointed to the northern corner of the lot. "But don't nobody use it no more."

"Is that right?" Ben asked.

The man's face suddenly registered something. "I mean the plant, it don't use it. But they's a nigger fellow that lives in it sometimes, I think. Nice fellow." The guard lifted his hand to his head and twirled his index finger. "A little loose in the head, you understand, but nice."

"A big man," Ben said. "People call him Bluto."

"That's right," the guard said. He looked at Ben pointedly. "Is he in trouble?"

"I just need to talk to him about something," Ben said. "Have you seen him lately?"

The guard shook his head. "Naw, I ain't seen him," he said. "Not for a couple days."

"When did you see him last?"

The guard shrugged. "I don't know. Last weekend maybe. I don't go poking around over there much. Sometimes Bluto'll come by here and talk awhile. It ain't no secret that he sleeps in that drain in the summertime."

"Well, I need to drive out there and see if he's around," Ben said.

"Go right ahead," the guard told him as he stepped away from the car.

A long tail of dust wagged behind the car as Ben drove through the back lot of the factory and out to the storm fence which bordered it. Near the far right corner he could see a small gully open up in the flat earth, and he pulled the car to the edge of it and stopped.

As he walked the crest of the gully, Ben could see the rounded cement border of the drain. It was packed in loose earth and gravel, and as he half-walked half-skidded down the side of the ravine, scores of small stones swept down in front of him and leaped into a chain of small puddles which still remained after the rain.

Coggins remained at the top of the gully, staring down apprehensively.

"You don't have to come," Ben told him.

"No, no," Coggins said immediately. "I've gone this far." He skidded down the side of the ravine, his arms thrust out for balance, and joined Ben in the narrow gully.

Up ahead, the storm drain could be seen clearly. It was a circular cement pipe which protruded only a few inches from the embankment. A large white sheet, muddied at the bottom, covered the entrance like the flap of a tent. An assortment of tin cans and paper wrappers lay strewn about the floor of the gully, and just to the right, only a few feet from the drain's rounded entrance, there was a dark mound of what looked to be human excrement.

"Oh, God," Coggins breathed.

Ben moved forward slowly and Coggins, after a moment's hesitation, came along beside him.

The sheet billowed out lazily as Ben and Coggins continued to move toward it, but it revealed nothing but a quick glimpse of piled clothing and a stack of rain-soaked magazines.

Once at the entrance, Ben swept back the sheet. A wave of foul odor burst from the drain. It was thick and sickly sweet, and Ben recognized it immediately. He fanned the air and a swarm of flies lifted from the pile of clothing, hung a moment in the sickening air, then swept down again, buzzing loudly.

Ben crawled inside the pipe and jerked at the clothing. First one article gave way, then another, until he finally found a hand, blackened, the skin split open and quivering with hundreds of maggots. A small, slender ribbon weaved in and out of the dark swollen fingers, white with tiny red hearts.

For a moment he simply stared at it, as if it were some holy object, then he returned to the pile, digging furiously through the clothing, flinging tattered shirts and soiled trousers right and left until he found the face. It was large, and staring upward with enormous faded eyes. It had a look he had seen before, only more so. Not just surprise, amazement.

"He's in here," he said finally, as he glanced back toward the entrance to the drain.

Coggins peered in. "Bluto?"

"Yes," Ben said.

Coggins did not move. "You want me to come in there? I mean, you need me for anything?"

"No, not in here," Ben said. He pulled a card from his jacket and wrote down a number. "Go call this number," he said as he tossed it to Coggins. "It's the Coroner's Office. Tell Leon Patterson to get out here as soon as he can."

He could hear Coggins' footsteps rushing up the side of the embankment as he turned back to the twisted clothes and the face that stared up at him from their tangled ruin. The eyes had dried, and a crusty film now covered them, but they still offered up the strange animal woundedness of something damaged to the core. For a little while he stared at the eyes as if there was something in them that could tell him what had happened. Then he returned to the hand, and the small ribbon that wound itself delicately through its fingers like a sad unraveled bow.

A half hour later the ambulance from Hillman Hospital arrived to pick up the body. Leon Patterson finally showed up almost an hour after it had left. The heat had been building steadily since early morning, and now a hard bright light swept down upon the ravine. For a long time after the ambulance had departed, there had been no sound but the incessant buzzing of the flies.

"I want this done right," Ben told Patterson as the two of them stood in the gulley a few feet from the drain. "I don't want a lot of rookies throwing things all around."

"I understand," Patterson said.

"I want everything bagged and catalogued," Ben added. "I mean everything." He nodded toward Coggins while he stared at Patterson pointedly. "We'll all work together. You got any problem with that, Leon?"

Patterson shook his head. "Nope." He grabbed the sheet and pulled it back. "Let's get started."

Inside the drain, the heat was stifling. The sweet smell of putrescent flesh seemed to sink into everything, the piled clothes and candy wrappers, the sodden magazines, even the old junk television which rested on a stack of bricks a few yards away from the body.

Patterson worked methodically, his gloved hands picking relentlessly through the clothing, folding it into neat stacks, then bagging each article in its turn. Beneath the clothing, the body lay on its back, entirely naked. Its right hand still clung loosely to the handle of a twenty-two-caliber pistol. A single sheet was stretched beneath it. There were bloodstains near the top and around the middle.

"Turn him over," Patterson said unemphatically, once the body was exposed.

From crouching positions inside the drain, Ben and Leroy rolled the body over onto its side, then let it tip, facedown, onto the sheet.

"You got fixed lividity on the back," Patterson said routinely. He looked at Ben. "You don't have it anywhere else. And that pretty much means this boy died right here. Nobody moved him, turned him over or anything like that. He died right here in this drain."

"When?" Ben asked.

"Hard to say," Patterson said with a shrug. "The heat throws things off. But I'd say sometime on Sunday night." He pointed to the side of the head. "And there's the cause of death right there."

Ben glanced down and saw a small hole about a quarter of an inch above the entrance to the ear.

"Shot in the head," Patterson said, "just like that little girl." He picked up the small plastic bag that held the pistol. "Probably with this little twenty-two." He glanced down at the the body, his eyes moving from the wound, down to the shoulder, then along the arm to the outstretched hand. "From the angle, I'd say he could have done it to himself." He looked at Ben. "Murder-suicide," he said. "Neat as a pin."

"So he raped the girl," Ben said.

"We can make sure the semen in her body and this boy's blood type are the same," Patterson said, "but I'd guess that the blood at the top of the sheet is this boy's, and that the blood in the middle of the sheet belongs to the girl."

"But even before that, he'd already killed her," Ben went on.

Patterson nodded.

"Then he buried her in that ballfield," Ben continued. "Came back here and shot himself."

"That's my guess," Patterson told him.

Ben glanced about the ravine, then looked at Patterson. "Where's the shovel?"

"What?"

Coggins smiled. "Where's the shovel?" he repeated.

"The one he buried her with," Ben said. "We didn't find it anywhere around the girl's body. And we haven't found it around here."

"He could have tossed it anywhere," Patterson said.

"Why would he?"

"To get rid of evidence, of course," Patterson said.

"But he kept the gun he killed her with," Ben said, "And he kept a ribbon from her hair." He looked at Patterson doubtfully. "Does that make any sense to you, Leon?"

Patterson's face darkened. "No." His whole body seemed to shift into a higher gear. "I'll get all the lab stuff done as quickly as I can, Ben," he said. "It'll take a few hours. Will you be home tonight?"

"Yes."

"I'll call you the minute I have anything," Leon assured him as he gathered the bundles of clothing into his arms and headed quickly toward his car.

After he'd gone, Ben walked back into the storm drain. It was almost entirely empty now, except for the battered television with its cracked screen, and a few fluttery bits of string and paper. Blood had soaked through the sheet and left wide rust-colored stains in the cement, but aside from them, the drain looked as if no human being had ever lived or died in it.

"It's not right, that ole boy having to live out here," someone said suddenly.

Ben turned toward the entrance to the drain, half-expecting to see Leroy crouched down and staring into it. But it was the watchman, his stooped body backlighted by the hard noon sun, his dark-blue eyes peering into the drain.

"How well did you know him?" Ben asked immediately.

The watchman shrugged. "Well as you could, him being the way he was."

"Did you ever see anybody else out here?"

The watchman shook his head. "He was always alone. But it didn't seem to bother him all that much."

"Ever talk to him?"

"Sometimes. So he killed himself, huh?"

Ben duck-walked his way out of the drain and stood beside the watchman.

"Maybe," he said. "Or maybe he was murdered."

The watchman looked surprised. "That right? I'd never of thought anybody'd want to hurt that boy. He was just like a little kid, you know." He smiled gently. "I mean, he didn't know that there was anything wrong with him. With his head, I mean. He was just sort of happy-go-lucky." He looked back toward the drain. "Thought he was all growed up," he said, "just like you and me." He laughed silently. "Wasn't afraid of nothing. Went out all the time. Claimed he was a policeman."

"Policeman?" Ben asked.

"Oh, yeah," the watchman said. "He had a little toy badge and a little toy pistol. Claimed he's been deputized."

"We found the badge," Ben said. "The pistol, though—you said it was a toy."

"Yeah, a toy," the watchman said, "like a little cap pistol." The watchman smiled sadly. "He used to run around shooting it at things. Tin cans and such like that. You know, like a kid. Sometimes he'd stick it right up to his own head and shoot it off. 'I'm dead,' he'd say. 'I'm dead.' Then he'd fall right over on the ground." He glanced back toward the empty drain and shook his head ruefully. "We're gonna miss that ole boy around the plant," he said. "An outfit always needs something funny hanging around."

Twenty-three

Fourth Avenue looked as if it had been hit by a gigantic thunderstorm as Ben drove Coggins back down toward Police Headquarters. Small oily streams flowed slowly down the gutters, pushing swirling clumps of debris along with them, and in the park across the street, long thin trenches had been dug into the earth and now rippled with pools of muddy water.

"They can clean up all they want," Coggins said confidently, "but a demonstration leaves more behind than litter." His eyes shifted over toward the deserted park. Far in the distance a single fire engine winked bright red in the afternoon sunlight.

"They can spray the streets forever," Coggins added. "They can try to make them nice and clean. But by the time it's all over here, everybody in the world is going to know just how dirty Birmingham really is."

Ben said nothing. He kept his eyes on the street ahead. A scattering of uniformed patrolmen was pulling down police barricades while a small contingent of the Highway Patrol watched lazily from a few yards away. One of their commanders stood in front of them, very tall and erect. His uniform was perfectly pressed, and his high black boots had been shined to a gleaming finish. He stepped out into the middle of the street, his eyes narrowing in concentration as Ben's car approached.

Ben brought the car to a halt, and the commander stepped over to him.

"This area is under heavy security right now," he said. He glanced at Coggins, then back at Ben. "Do you have some business being around here?"

"I'm on my way to Police Headquarters," Ben told him. He took out his badge.

The commander glanced at the badge, but did not seem impressed. "What are you doing with this man here?" he asked as he nodded toward Coggins. "Is he under arrest or something?"

"No," Ben said. He glanced at the small black nameplate which had been pinned to the commander's uniform: Halsey.

"Well, we've had some trouble here today," the commander said, "and so we're keeping a close eye on things."

Ben nodded slowly. "Looks like it," he said. His eyes drifted to the right of Halsey's body. He could see what looked to him like an unmarked police car, dark green and very dusty, with nearly treadless blackwall tires, parked at the edge of the park. Two men sat in the backseat, and as their faces moved in and out of the shadowy gray which engulfed the inside of the car, he could tell that one of them was Teddy Langley.

"So my suggestion to you, Sergeant Wellman," the commander said, "is to get this man back to headquarters as soon as possible."

"Yeah," Ben said dully, his eyes still on the unmarked car.

Tod Langley suddenly emerged from behind one of the trees in the park, walked to the driver's side of the dark-green car and got in.

"It's dangerous to be in this area right now," the commander concluded.

Ben did not answer. Instead he continued to watch as the car pulled out slowly and headed down the avenue. In the small square of light between the commander's broad body and the end of Ben's line of vision, Ben could see Teddy Langley's eyes catch sight of him, then widen slightly as he peered at him through the dusty rear window of the car.

"So be on your way," the commander said authoritatively as he stepped away from the car, "and be alert to what's going on around you."

"Okay, thanks," Ben said as he pressed slowly down on the accelerator. In his rearview mirror, he could see the other car as it sped quickly up the still wet street. Its tires threw up a glistening fan of droplets which fell like a silver curtain through the bright air.

"Well, I can't say I'm exactly glad to be back," Coggins said as Ben closed the cell door.

"You boys have a high old time, did you?" McCorkindale asked with a laugh.

Ben continued to stare at Coggins. "I'll let you know what I find out," he told him.

An odd, appreciative smile spread across Coggins' face. "Thanks," he said. He wrapped his fingers around the bars of the cell. "And of course you'll know where to find me."

McCorkindale smiled slyly as he walked down the cellblock. "You two look like you're getting real close," he said.

"You're going to be getting in some stuff from the Coroner's Office," Ben told him. "Keep a real close eye on it."

McCorkindale looked interested. "What kind of stuff?"

"Evidence. From a homicide. A gun, at least. It's being dusted now. The rest will be going to the lab. You probably won't see that for weeks."

At the end of the hall, McCorkindale dropped himself heavily into his swivel chair. "Well, I got your afternoon assignment," he said. "Captain Starnes gave it to me."

"What is it?"

"Peace in the valley, Ben," McCorkindale said. "A real plum. You're supposed to represent the department at Kelly Ryan's funeral this afternoon." He tore a piece of paper from a steno pad and handed it to Ben. "He didn't have no relatives. So they're burying him fast. Here's all the details."

Ben glanced at the paper, then shoved it into his jacket pocket.

McCorkindale smiled happily. "I swear, Ben, you are getting the sweet treatment these days." He shook his head wonderingly. "Why, if it weren't for me, I think you'd get all the cushy jobs."

Ben smiled thinly, then stepped away.

"One more thing," McCorkindale said quickly. "Captain wants to see you. He's in his office."

"Okay," Ben said. He turned, then walked back down the corridor to Luther's office.

Luther was hunched over his desk, his large hands wrapped around a ham and cheese sandwich.

"Just grabbing a quick bite between crises," he said as Ben stepped into his office. He took a gulp of coffee, then wiped his mouth with the side of his hand. "Listen, I heard you got something on that little girl thing."

"Yeah."

"What is it?"

"Well, we traced the ring we found on her to a colored man that used to live in one of those storm drains over at the rubber factory."

"Used to live?"

"He's dead," Ben said. "Shot."

"With what?"

"A twenty-two."

"Same one used on the little girl?" Luther asked.

"Probably," Ben said. "We found the pistol in the storm drain. It was still in the guy's hand. We're checking to make sure it killed both of them."

Luther nodded thoughtfully. "So it's a murder-suicide, you think?"

"Could be," Ben said. "People called this guy Bluto. He hung around a poolhall on Fourth Avenue. He was mentally retarded." He decided to keep his doubts about Bluto's death to himself for the moment.

"Good," Luther said. "Good job, Ben." He took another quick bite from the sandwich. "Well, I guess everything's pretty much wrapped up, then."

Ben nodded noncommittally. "We're checking the guy's blood to see if it matches the semen we found in the little girl."

Luther seemed no longer interested in the details. "Sounds like it's all over, Ben," he said, waving his hand dismissively. "Listen, did McCorkindale talk to you about the funeral?"

"Yeah."

"It's not the greatest assignment," Luther added, "but I figured you were the one to do it. Kelly wasn't exactly the most popular officer on the force."

Ben said nothing.

"You don't mind sort of being the department's representative, do you?" Luther asked.

"No," Ben said.

"Good," Luther said. He smiled. "You know how it is, when a cop goes down, there needs to be a little blue in the boneyard." He laughed. "No matter who he was."

Kelly Ryan was buried at three o'clock in the afternoon in a small cemetery not far from his house. A single hearse delivered the body, and no one came with it but an old preacher who'd long ago been designated Police Chaplain and who usually showed up at cop funerals when no private minister was indicated.

"Did you know Mr. Ryan very well?" the preacher asked as he stepped over to the grave.

"No."

"I didn't either," the preacher said. "I just got a call from the Chief's office. They just said they needed me over here at the cemetery." He looked at Ben intently. "I don't suppose there are any relatives?"

"Not that I know of," Ben said. He shrugged. "I'm just here to represent the department, I guess."

The preacher nodded slowly as his eyes fell toward the coffin. "I guess he was a good cop."

Ben thought of Kelly alone behind the battered metal desk of the Property Room or standing by the rows of plain brown file cabinets that lined the walls of the Records Department, of Kelly trudging up the steps with one young girl on either side, taking them to their VD examinations, of Kelly in the bar, soaking up one drink after another: "I haven't had a drink with a cop since I left Bearmatch," he'd said, his eyes lolling left and right as if almost unable to look a fellow officer in the eye.

"Yeah," Ben said, "I guess he was."

"Young man?"

"Yeah."

The preacher shook his head sorrowfully. "Terrible for a man to die young. Of course, it happens. The heart is a tricky thing."

"What?"

"The heart," the preacher explained. "Sometimes it just gets you, young or not."

"Heart attack, you mean?" Ben asked.

The preacher nodded. "That's the way they say he died. Nobody told you that?"

Ben shook his head. He could see Ryan's body swinging beneath the lamp, the overturned chair, the black, swollen tongue and round, protruding eyes.

"No, nobody told me," he said.

The preacher smiled politely, then stepped to the head of the grave. A mound of reddish earth stretched out before him, naked as a corpse.

"Okay to begin?" he asked Ben.

Ben nodded.

The preacher bowed his head slowly and began to speak, but Ben could hardly hear him over the roar of the diesel trucks that swept loudly up and down the street, groaning under the weight of so much iron and steel. He glanced away from the grave and down the long avenue that led up to it. At the end of it, he could see the high storm fence of the rubber plant, and he realized that if his vision could rise above the line of trees which blocked it, he would be able to see the cold round eye of the storm drain, and then, sweeping to the right, the gray, unpainted goalpost that had briefly marked the grave of Doreen Ballinger. In his mind, they seemed to form a triangle, these three bleak, impoverished graves, but as he continued to consider it, he realized that it was one which was made up of little more than lines drawn over a vast and empty space.

The bar where Kelly had taken Ben the night he died was only a few blocks from the cemetery, and as he sat in the same booth through the evening, Ben tried to imagine the way Kelly had had to live during the long years before he'd finally decided to end it. In his mind, he could see his body hanging grimly at the end of the rope, circling slowly in the small breeze that swept through the bedroom, turning, turning, as if sleeplessly in search of some impossible deliverance. "The thing is, I loved her," he'd said over the night's final drink, with his eyes already hooded, his words vaguely slurred. For that, he'd paid a heavy price, living more alone than even Ben could now imagine, alone in a tiny, dilapidated house set down among a raw assortment of clanging factories, without family or friends, mocked by the people he worked with. Death would at last seem lovely after such a life.

Ben took a sip of whiskey and glanced toward the front of the bar. The early evening air had turned bluish-pink, and just over the roof of the rubber plant, he could see the residue of sunset, a spray of purple which rose like a light mist above the city. It might have looked beautiful, setting over a beautiful city, but it looked only dreamy and out of place above the cinderblock and tin-roofed factories which surrounded him. He turned his eyes from the window and glanced about the bar. A few factory workers crouched in a booth a few feet away, while a couple of others leaned against the bar, sipping slowly at their beers while they made idle conversation with the bartender. He wondered if Kelly had known any of the men who trudged into the bar after their shifts, had ever had a single decent talk with even one of them. He could not know for sure, but it struck him that he probably hadn't. For what would be the use, after all, since the one great experience of his life could not be talked about with any of them. And so Kelly had chosen not to deceive anyone, but to take the isolation instead, the silence, the absolute apartness, and to live with that as long as he could, and when he couldn't anymore, to go out like a man, asking no one's pity, apologizing to no one, but simply going out of life in the way he had lived it, utterly and unbreachably alone.

It was almost midnight by the time Ben turned into his own gravel driveway. Across the street, the light in Mr. Jeffries' window was burning brightly, and it was easy for him to imagine the old man tossing sleeplessly on his bed or ambling shakily toward the bathroom. His own father had been like that in the last days, pointlessly moving from one room to the next, dazed, unreachably confused, only half-aware of who or where he was. Ben had gotten up many times in the early morning hours to find him stranded in the hallway, glancing about hopelessly, like a child lost in an unfamiliar city. He had finally died in this state of helpless bafflement. It was as if his mind had simply fallen away, like a body over a ledge, and Ben could still remember their last meal together, the old man mumbling incoherently while he stared expressionlessly at his food. He kept his eyes on Mr. Jeffries' lighted window for a moment longer, as if by watching from a distance, he could somehow help him if he fell, or guide him back to his bed and safely tuck him in as he had his father so many times before.

Suddenly the light went off, and Ben turned up the narrow walkway toward his house, then trudged up the short wooden stairs, unlocked the front door and stepped inside.

He felt the pistol barrel at his ear before he could reach the light switch beside the door, and the very shock of the cold round steel against his head froze him instantly.

"Don't move," someone said in a tense, trembling voice.

It was a man's voice, but that was all that Ben could tell.

"Don't move," the man repeated sternly.

Ben stood motionlessly in the darkness, his right hand still lifted slightly toward the light, his fingers stretched toward it, but halted in midair, stiff, wooden, a puppet's brittle hand.

"Just take one step forward," the man said.

Ben could feel the barrel as it pressed more deeply into the soft flesh behind his ear.

"Real slow, now," the man said. "Just one step."

Ben took a single step, then stopped immediately. He could feel his eyes burning with an odd fierceness, as if trying to sear away the covering darkness.

"Keep your hands where they are," the man told him. "Now take one more step."

Ben did as he was told.

"Get on your knees," the voice commanded.

"What?"

"Get on your goddamn knees!"

Ben slowly lowered himself to the floor.

"Now kiss the street," the voice said with a sudden, bitter harshness.

Ben instantly tipped forward, spreading out onto his stomach.

"Now spread them," the voice demanded in a tone that now seemed less harsh, even slightly muffled, as if a handkerchief had been placed over it and pressed down. "Spread your arms over your head."

Ben flattened himself facedown across the hard wooden floor, then drew his hands up and over his head, as if he were reaching for something just beyond the limits of his grasp. For an instant he lay motionlessly in the darkness, then he felt the man kick at his heels.

"Spread your legs!"

Ben did as he was told.

"Shit," the man said softly.

Ben felt a hand reach down, quickly unsnap his holster and jerk his pistol from it.

"That's better," the man said.

Ben said nothing, and for a time he simply lay flat against the floor. Then, suddenly, he felt the man's body as it pressed its full weight onto his back.

"You ain't moving now," the man said mockingly.

"Guess not," Ben said weakly.

The man laughed. "The thing is, you got a problem," he said menacingly. "What you might call a nigger problem. Know what I mean?"

Ben did not answer.

The barrel of the pistol bit into his flesh.

"You hear me, mister?" the man demanded.

"Yeah."

"I said you got yourself a real bad nigger problem."

Ben remained silent, waiting, until he felt the barrel pressing into him again. "What problem is that?" he blurted.

"That little nigger girl," the man replied immediately. "The dead one."

"What about her?" Ben asked weakly.

"What do you know about her?"

"Nothing," Ben told him.

He felt a fist strike him on the back of the head.

"Don't fuck with me," the voice hissed. "What do you know about that girl?"

Ben did not answer, and the fist struck him again.

"Don't fuck with me," the man repeated. "You do, you're one dead nigger-lover."

"I don't know anything," Ben said quietly. He could feel a haze moving down on him, descending like a curtain through the pain. "I don't know anything," he repeated dully.

Once again the fist struck him, and he felt his head jerk to the left with the force of the blow.

"Where was she?" the man demanded, his voice now oddly changed, tense urgent.

"What?" Ben asked puzzled.

"Where was she?" the man repeated, his voice almost frantic.

"I don't know what you're talking about."

For a moment the man said nothing, and in the darkness, Ben could almost hear his mind ticking desperately.

"You hate niggers?" the man asked finally.

Ben did not answer. He could feel a raw pain shooting up and down his back. Then a large hand grabbed the back of his head and pushed forward, shoving his face into the floor.

"You hate niggers?" the voice demanded.

Ben said nothing.

The barrel dug into his flesh.

"Tell me you hate niggers," the voice said. "Tell me right now."

Ben remained silent.

"Right now," the voice said sharply. "Or you're dead."

Ben said nothing. He could feel the man's fingers as they tugged at his hair, hear his shallow, angry breath, feel the weight of his body as it pressed down upon his back.

"Tell me you hate niggers," the voice said. "Tell me that, right now."

Ben did not speak. He could feel the barrel of the pistol as it circled around the back of his head, then pressed into his ear.

"I'm gonna blow your fucking brains out," the man said.

Ben heard the pistol cock. He glanced up and saw a small yellowish light flow toward him from the front window. Mr. Jeffries had turned his light on again. He took in a long breath, very deep, then tightly closed his eyes.

"Bye bye," the man repeated mockingly.

Ben waited, his hands clenched, his eyes shut tight, his mouth now suddenly so dry, his thirst so extreme that it felt unquenchable.

For a moment there was only silence, and during those few seconds, Ben regretted that it was night, rather than morning, that there was no sunlight to penetrate his closed eyes, no birds for him to hear, no reassuring traffic or street chatter, but only this flat, absolute silence in a dark which was broken only by a sickly yellowish light.

Suddenly the weight lifted, and Ben realized that the body was no longer on him. Still, he did not move, did not open his eyes, did not reach for an impossible hope.

"Move, just once, and you're dead," the man said, almost wearily, as if the exertion of his attack had all but taken the final measure of his strength.

In an instant, he was gone, moving quickly down the long corridor to the kitchen, then out the back door and into the thick black night.

Ben could hear his feet as they padded swiftly away, then the soft beat of the screen door as it closed behind him. It was only then that he pulled himself up and walked slowly back to the kitchen. He closed the door and locked it, then turned on the small light in the backyard. At the far edge of the yard, he could see the rusty wire fence that bordered it. It was still weaving slightly from where the man had climbed over it, and Ben could see his own service revolver hanging awkwardly from one of its unsteady metal posts, its barrel carefully nosed upward toward the still thickly clouded sky.

Luther looked astonished when he opened the door and saw Ben staring at him evenly.

"Good God, Ben," he yelped, "You got any idea what time it is?"

"I need to see you, Captain," Ben said bluntly.

Luther's eyes narrowed. "This better be important," he said. "I got a sick wife, and that knocking probably woke her up for the night."

"It's important," Ben told him.

Luther stepped out onto the porch, carefully closing the door behind him. He wore a pair of bulky light-blue pajamas, and the shirt billowed out slightly as he walked down the steps, then out into the yard, his bare feet nearly covered by the wet, dewy grass.

"All right, what is it?"

"I got jumped tonight," Ben said.

"Jumped?"

"In my own house," Ben added significantly.

Luther chuckled. "Well, shit, Ben, a cop can run up on a burglar just like anybody else."

"This wasn't a burglar."

Luther eyed him carefully. "How do you know?"

"He was waiting for me."

"Waiting for you?"

"That's right."

"What time was this?"

"A little past midnight."

Luther seemed to reconsider things. "Well, go ahead," he said gruffly. "What happened?"

"The guy jumped me as I came in."

"You don't look that bummed up," Luther said casually. "Did he rob you?"

"No," Ben said. "He wasn't interested in that."

"What do you mean?"

"He was interested in the girl."

"What girl?"

"That colored girl we found in the ballfield."

Luther's face tightened. "The guy that jumped you was interested in that?" he asked unbelievingly.

"That's right."

"What'd he want to know?"

"Everything. Whatever I'd found out about her."

"What'd he ask exactly?" Luther demanded with a sudden heightened concentration.

"He wanted to know where she was."

"You mean her body?"

"Where she was before she died," Ben said. "At least that's what I think he meant." He shrugged. "Or maybe he just wanted to know where we found her." He shook his head. "I don't know for sure."

"Did he want to know who killed her?"

"I guess he wanted to know everything," Ben said. "But he didn't ask about that."

"What'd you tell him?"

"That I hadn't found out very much."

"Could it have been some crazy relative?" Luther asked. "Was the guy colored?"

"No."

Luther shook his head despairingly. "This is bad, Ben. This is real bad."

"It's worse," Ben said bluntly.

Luther's eyes flashed toward him.

"He was a cop," Ben said.

Luther laughed nervously. "A cop?"

"Yes."

"You must be nuts, Ben."

"There's no doubt about it, Captain," Ben said resolutely.

"And just how do you know that?" Luther demanded.

"By the way he handled me," Ben said. "He went right by the numbers. You get the guy on his knees, then on his belly. He even kicked my feet apart."

"Anybody could do that," Luther said doubtfully.

"When he forgot to pat me down before I hit the floor, he noticed that he'd done things in the wrong order."

"That could be military training," Luther said dismissively. "Or any other police department."

"He left my pistol hanging on the fence outside."

"So?"

"Why do you think he did that, Captain?"

"Who knows?" Luther replied with a shrug.

"It's the first thing I thought about," Ben told him.

"Why?"

"Because a cop in our own department would know that we have to buy our own weapons, that if he'd taken it with him, then I'd have had to replace it out of my own pocket."

Luther's face slackened visibly, but he said nothing.

For a moment the two of them stood silently beneath the heavy limbs of the large oak in Luther's yard.

"So what do you really think, Ben?" Luther asked finally.

"That somebody in this department is scared."

"Because of the girl."

"Maybe the way we're looking into it. The way we're being serious about it."

"But all you've got's that Bluto fellow."

"Maybe we're missing something."

"What?"

"I don't know."

"So what do want to do about it?"

"What do you mean?"

"You want off the case?"

"No," Ben said immediately, offended by the question. "Why would I want that?"

"In case it all has something to do with a brother officer in the department," Luther said. "I mean, we could turn the whole thing over to the State Police."

Ben laughed. "Lingo's men?"

"They may not all be like what we're used to seeing lately," Luther told him. "At least you wouldn't be looking into things that could involve people you know."

Ben shook his head. "No, I want to stay on it."

"Okay," Luther said quietly. His eyes drifted upward toward the tangled overhanging limbs. "Things are too complex for me these days, Ben," he said unhappily. "Too mixed up for a simple mind." He looked at Ben determinedly. "Just remember. I'm right behind you."

Ben nodded quickly, turned away, and walked back to his car. From behind the wheel he could see Luther's large figure as it stood facing him darkly from beneath the tree's gently sloping limbs, and as he watched from behind the dusty windshield, he could sense that the old pattern of the world had shifted suddenly into a more dangerous and complicated weave, and he realized that he could no longer tell for sure whether Luther's last remark was meant to comfort or to threaten him.

Twenty-four

When Ben arrived downtown early the next morning, the blocks around police headquarters were already teeming with firemen in full duty gear. They wore black slicks, rubber boots and hard hats, and as they huddled together in small groups beside their gleaming red trucks, they reminded Ben of the swarms of crows that had plagued his grandfather's cornfields—nervous, squawky, their heads continually jerking left and right, always ready to leap into the air at the slightest sound.

Teddy Langley and Sammy McCorkindale stood at the entrance to the building, both of them staring expressionlessly in the general direction of Fourth Avenue.

"What's all this, now?" Ben asked as he walked up to them.

"Just more bullshit," Langley said bitterly.

McCorkindale laughed. "What do you want to do, Teddy, mow them all down with machine guns?"

Langley looked at Ben pointedly. "Maybe just one would do. What do you think, Ben?"

McCorkindale shook his head. "You beginning to sound like a racist, Teddy," he said. He smiled jokingly. "I think you're turning mean in your old age."

Langley frowned irritably, hunched his shoulders and stalked off down the stairs toward his car.

"Everybody's wearing down, Ben," McCorkindale said as he watched Langley walk away. He glanced toward Ben. "How you doing?"

"Well as anybody else, I guess," Ben said.

"Still working that dead girl?"

"Yeah."

"Let me know if you need a partner," McCorkindale said tiredly as he started down the stairs. "I'm getting tired of the riot detail. It's too much work for an old fat boy."

Ben turned and headed into the building.

T. G. Hollis met him just outside the bullpen. "You got a call a few minutes ago," he said. "Somebody connected to that case you're working."

"Who?"

"A guy named Davenport," Hollis told him. "He said he could see you this morning. I left everything on your desk."

Ben smiled. "Thanks, T.G."

"Oh, I'm a good note-taker," Hollis said with a laugh. Then he slapped the handle of his nightstick. "But I'm even better at busting heads."

Horace Davenport nodded amiably as his secretary led Ben into his office.

"Good morning, Mr. Wellman," he said. He looked at his secretary. "That's fine, Helen. Just close the door on the way out, please."

The secretary did as she was told, and after she'd left, Davenport's hand swept out toward an empty chair opposite his desk.

"Please, sit down," he said.

Ben took a seat.

"I didn't hear about Doreen until I returned from Atlanta last night," Davenport said as he lowered himself into the chair behind his desk. "I can't tell you how shocked I was."

"I'm trying to find out where she was the day she died," Ben said immediately. "I understand she worked at your house all day that Sunday."

"Yes, she did."

"Did you take her home on Sunday afternoon?"

"Yes, I did," Davenport said. "We'd had some trouble with our driver. I think my wife mentioned that?"

"Yes."

"Well, of course I couldn't let Doreen go home by bus," Davenport said. "I wouldn't have felt right about that."

"So you took her?"

"Yes."

"What time was that?"

"I suppose we left the house at around five in the evening,"

Davenport told him. "I was in quite a hurry. I had to be back at the house for a meeting by six."

"And you took her straight home?"

"I drove her myself."

"Did you stop anywhere?"

"No."

"And you took her all the way?"

"You mean, right to her door?"

"Yes."

"Well, now that you mention it, I didn't take her all the way home."

"We're trying to trace her movements," Ben explained. "At least for the twenty-four hours before she was killed."

"I understand perfectly," Davenport said. "And I hope you know that I want to be as helpful as I can."

Ben smiled thinly. "So where did you let her out?"

Davenport's eyes drifted toward the ceiling. "Well, it was in her own neighborhood."

"Bearmatch?"

"Well, not just Bearmatch," Davenport said, "but her own little neighborhood."

"Where exactly was that?"

"I think it was around that little park they have there, that little ballfield."

"Where we found her body?"

"Is that where you found it?"

Ben nodded.

Davenport leaned forward. "Are you saying that Doreen never got home that Sunday evening?"

"No, she didn't," Ben said.

Davenport shook his head mournfully. "How awful."

"Mr. Gilroy usually took her right to her door," Ben said.

"Who?"

"Your driver."

"Oh, yes," Davenport said. "Of course. Well, that's true. He was always told to take her right home. I guess that's what I should have done."

"Why did you let Doreen out of the car?" Ben asked.

"She wanted out," Davenport said.

"Why?"

"She saw some other colored children," Davenport said. "She wanted to go play with them." He shrugged. "It being summer, night doesn't come down till late. She wanted to play awhile. A little girl like her, who'd been in the house all day, of course she wanted to scuffle around a little with some other kids."

"So you let her out."

"That's right," Davenport said. "That's what she wanted."

"How did you know that that's what she wanted?"

"What was that?"

"Well, she couldn't have told you."

"Oh no, that's true," Davenport said. "But she had a way of making people know things. She'd use signs, you know. She'd point to things. She was a very smart little girl."

"And so she pointed to . . . what?"

"Another little girl," Davenport said. "One that looked to be about Doreen's age."

"Where was this other girl?"

"On the other side of the field," Davenport said. "She was swinging under a tree."

"Alone?"

"I guess so," Davenport said. "I didn't see any other kids around her.

"Did you get the idea that Doreen knew this little girl?" Ben asked.

"Yes, I did," Davenport told him. "She seemed very excited about going to play with her."

Ben nodded quickly. "So you just let her out then?"

"That's right."

"If you saw this little girl again, would you be able to identify her?"

"I'm not sure," Davenport said. "She was quite a distance from me."

"Do you remember what she was wearing?"

Davenport thought a moment. "Something green," he said finally. "But that's all I can say for sure. She was swinging, and her legs were together. I couldn't even tell if she were wearing a skirt or pants."

Ben nodded. "Did Doreen go directly into the field when you let her out?"

"Yes."

"She didn't go down the street or head in another direction?"

"No, she went right out to the field, toward that other little girl."

"And that's when you drove away?"

"She was trotting off toward that other girl," Davenport said. He shook his head. "Poor little thing." His eyes lowered slightly. "That was the last I saw of her."

"Did you stop anywhere else before you let Doreen out?"

"No."

"Just the ballfield?"

"That's all."

"While you were stopped, did you notice anyone hanging around?"

"No."

"I was thinking of a large man."

"You mean, you already have an idea of who might have done this?"

"Maybe."

"Colored man?"

"Yes," Ben said. "But he's already dead."

Davenport looked at Ben quizzically. "Dead?"

"Yes," Ben told him.

"Am I to take it that this death was not of natural causes?"

"It could have been a suicide," Ben said. "Or a murder."

Davenport's mind appeared to be running through a serious of quick calculations. "Well, that would tie it up nicely, wouldn't it?" he said after a moment.

"Tie what up?"

"The case."

"I guess it would," Ben said. He looked at Davenport closely. "Your driver has a drinking problem."

"Like his daddy before him," Davenport said tiredly.

"Is there any reason to think that he might have hurt Doreen?"

"Why would he?"

"To get even."

"With her?"

"With you."

"What for?"

"Well, you fired him the day you took Doreen home."

"That's true," Davenport said, "but that was over something else entirely. It had nothing to do with Doreen. I mean, if Jacob were harboring some resentment over being let go, he'd try to hurt me, wouldn't he? Or Shannon, maybe. Or my wife."

"I guess so," Ben said. "I'm just trying out all the possibilities."

"I understand."

"So you left your house at around five, is that right?"

"Yes."

"And about what time would you say you let Doreen out by the ballpark."

"Probably about ten minutes later," Davenport said. "It doesn't take long to get to Bearmatch from here."

"You're pretty sure about that?"

"As sure as I can be," Davenport said. He looked at Ben pointedly. "You're working the case very hard, aren't you?" he asked.

Ben did not answer.

"Isn't that a little bit unusual?"

"Maybe a little bit," Ben replied dully.

"Of course, things are changing," Davenport added. "People have to be ready for change. They have to make room for it."

Ben said nothing.

"Are you the only one working this case?" Davenport asked after a moment.

Ben nodded.

"Everybody else's pretty busy, I guess."

"Yeah, they are," Ben said quietly.

Davenport smiled limply, then glanced at his watch. "Is there anything else I can do for you?"

"I guess not," Ben admitted.

Davenport stood up immediately and offered Ben his hand. "Well, it was nice meeting you," he said.

Ben shook his hand politely. "Thanks for your time."

"Let me know if you need anything else," Davenport said as he walked Ben to the door.

"I will," Ben said.

"We'll miss Doreen," Davenport said softly. "Especially Shannon." He shook his head. "It's a tragedy when something like this happens."

Ben stepped out into the foyer of Davenport's office. "Yes, it is."

Davenport shook his head sadly. "Poor little Doreen. She sure was a sweet little girl."

. . .

The Coroner's Office had the results of its work by early in the afternoon, and Ben went over to Hillman Hospital to pick them up.

Patterson was working at one of the tables when he came into the dissecting room.

"Fellow comes into Hillman with a little touch of pneumonia," he said, "and twelve hours later he's dead as a doornail." He looked up at Ben and winked. "You know what that means? Full autopsy."

"You said you'd finished with that man we found in the storm drain?"

"Yeah," Patterson said. He pressed the blade down near the man's throat. "Report's on my desk." He made a large vertical incision down the chest. "Everything checks out."

Ben walked to the desk and picked up the envelope.

"His blood type matches the semen we found in the girl's body," Patterson said from across the room. He glanced over toward him. "I guess we've got our man."

Ben tucked the report under his arm. "Thanks, Leon," he said as he stepped away from the desk.

"The gun's there, too," Patterson said quickly. "You might as well take it over to Property."

"What'd the lab have to say about it?"

"It's the same gun for both of them," Patterson told him. "The little girl and this Bluto character." He moved the knife steadily downward and to the right. "From the angle on the man, I'd say it was definitely self-inflicted." His eyes shifted over to Ben. "You got a lot of powder burns, too. A nice little gray circle right about the hole in his head." He looked at Ben. "Maybe the guilt got to him, what do you think?"

"Maybe," Ben said. He glanced about the desk. "Where's the gun?"

"I put it in a plastic bag," Patterson told him. "It's in the left-hand corner of my desk."

Ben pulled open the drawer and took it out. "Thanks again, Leon," he said. He started toward the door.

"One more thing, Ben," Leon said.

Ben stopped instantly and turned toward Patterson.

"I got a call late last night," Patterson said. "From the State Pathology Unit down at the University in Tuscaloosa."

"What'd they want?"

"The man said he was checking to find out how long a man's race could be determined after he'd been buried," Patterson said. "You wouldn't have thought he'd have needed to call Birmingham to find that out, would you?"

"No."

"It struck me as a funny question," Leon said. "Especially the way things are around here these days."

Ben said nothing.

"Anyway, I told him that it depended on a lot of things. Whether the man had been embalmed, how long he'd been buried and in what kind of ground, whether he'd been exposed to the weather, to animals, whether it was summer or winter, the state of decomposition, soil chemistry, details like that. You know, important."

Ben nodded.

Patterson brought his scalpel to a halt and looked directly at Ben. "But after I was finished, I sort of got to wondering about it all, and so when I got to work this morning, I called down to the university, and it was just like I thought."

"What?"

"They don't have anything called the Pathology Unit down there, Ben," Leon said with a sudden ominousness. "They don't have anything that even sounds like that."

Ben looked at Patterson intently. "What do you think, Leon?"

Patterson's voice turned solemn. "If I had to make a guess, I'd say that maybe somebody's got a colored guy they want to get rid of," he said.

Twenty-five

The firemen had disappeared by the time Ben got back to headquarters. The outside of the building was completely surrounded by a grim cordon of highway patrolmen, but the inside was almost wholly deserted.

Only the jails remained choked with people. Hundreds of demonstrators were still crammed together in the tiny, sweltering cells. Ben expected to find Coggins among them, but as he walked down the corridor, he saw him standing quietly in front of McCorkindale's desk.

"I'm out for now," Coggins said to him. He shifted his eyes over to McCorkindale and glared at him. "But I'll be back."

McCorkindale grinned. "Sure you will, boy. I can't hardly wait."

Ben touched Coggins' shoulders. "Come with me a second," he said. "I want to ask you something."

Coggins glanced at his watch. "Okay, but let's make it fast. They need me back over at the church. That's why they bailed me out."

Ben walked him out of the building. At the top of the steps, Coggins waved to a waiting car. Several men waved back.

"They're here to make sure I get from the steps to the car," Coggins said to Ben.

"I want you to keep an eye on everybody, Leroy." Ben said. "Just like those guys are keeping an eye on you."

Coggins looked at him darkly. "Can you be more specific?"

Ben shook his head. "Somebody called the Coroner's Office with a strange question. He wanted to know how long you could tell if a man was a Negro after he'd been buried."

Coggins shivered. "Oh, God."

"I don't know what it means," Ben warned, "but just keep a close watch. And tell everybody else to do the same."

Coggins nodded, his eyes oddly quiet. "Do you think they're after me?"

"It could be anybody."

"I meant it, you know—what I said," Coggins told him. "I'm ready to die. I really am."

Ben smiled. "I know," he said. "Just try not to, that's all."

McCorkindale was flipping through the newspaper when Ben returned to his desk.

"Here's that gun I was telling you about," Ben told him as he set it down on McCorkindale's desk.

McCorkindale gave it a quick glance. "Okay, I'll log it in after a while," he said. He looked up at Ben. "You know, I think that Coggins boy really likes you."

Ben glanced about the empty room. "Where is everybody?"

"Over at the park," McCorkindale said, his eyes returning to the newspaper. "They're expecting a lot of trouble this afternoon."

"More than usual?"

"I guess so," McCorkindale said absently. "Word is, the Chief's come up with some new idea on how to handle things."

"What new idea?"

McCorkindale shrugged. "Beats me," he said. "But I guess we'll all know soon enough."

"Yeah," Ben said dully as he turned away.

He walked back to his desk in the detective bullpen and sat down to consider his next move. He thought of Doreen, Coggins, the city's long fury, and suddenly he felt more locked within its grip than he ever had before. It was as if the fingers of some invisible fist were tightening around his throat. He could sense its presence as animals sensed an approaching storm and then either retreated into their burrows to wait it out, or dug their feet into the ground, tightened every muscle and slowly turned their faces toward the wind.

The streets off Fourth Avenue were as deserted as the ones around Police Headquarters. As Ben got out of his car, he could see only desolate, empty alleyways and tightly closed shops. The avenue itself did not look much different. At the northern end of Kelly Ingram Park, a long line of fire engines stretched like a wide swipe of bright red paint across the motionless trees and deserted buildings. Contingents of fireman huddled in small knots beside the engines. Not far away, thin gray lines of highway patrolmen crisscrossed the avenue or blocked off its adjoining streets. Files of municipal police paced back and forth between the lines, moving nervously from one position to another.

Ben turned away from them and headed south, up the rounded hill that rose gradually, then dropped off toward the central Negro district.

The Better Days Pool Hall was near the top of the hill, and Ben was sweating heavily in the summer heat by the time he reached it.

The few games that were going on as Ben came through the door stopped instantly.

"I'm looking for Gaylord," Ben said instantly. He pulled out his badge. "This is a friendly visit."

The men looked at him doubtfully.

"Last one wasn't too goddamn friendly," someone said from the back.

Ben turned in the direction of the voice and recognized the man he'd slammed against the wall only the day before.

"I'm hoping this one will be," he said to him.

The man stepped forward, half his face illuminated by the naked bulb that hung over the pool table beside him. A raised tan scar ran along the side of his face, curling upward from the edge of his jaw to the side of his ear.

"You slammed me good, boss," the man said. "You not too smart to come back here."

"I'm not looking for you," Ben told him resolutely.

"Gaylord, like you say."

"That's right."

"What for?"

"That's for me to tell him," Ben said bluntly.

The man leaned against the table, and the slant of light now cut in a yellow diagonal across his dark face. "We heard about Bluto," he said. "We heard maybe you done it."

Ben said nothing.

"Maybe we set you on him," the man added. "Told you where he was. Then you killed him. That how it was?"

"He was dead when I found him," Ben said. "He'd been dead for several days."

The man squinted as he stared evenly at Ben. " 'Round here, we ain't no house niggers. Not like them that's in the streets. Always singing and shouting for Jesus."

"Was Bluto like that?"

"House nigger, you mean?"

"Yeah."

The man laughed. "Bluto wadn't hardly nothing at all." He shook his head. "Shit, that boy didn't have the sense of a fieldhand."

"It doesn't take much sense to kill a little girl," Ben said bluntly.

Again, the man laughed. "Kill a child? Bluto? You crazy, boss." He waved his hand. "Why, Bluto, he . . ."

The door of the back room swung open suddenly, and Gaylord's massive frame stepped out of it, immediately filling up the dark space, the pool tables shrinking to miniature before him.

"Who ask you?" he demanded harshly of the other man.

The other man stiffened.

Gaylord thumped his enormous chest. "The man come looking for me, you sends him to me. He don't need none of your shine before we talks."

The man nodded quickly, then slinked out of the light and disappeared into the far corner of the room.

Gaylord's eyes flashed over to Ben. "You be some kind of crazy coming back down here this afternoon."

"I needed to talk to you."

"Gone be all hell breaking loose before long," Gaylord said.

"Looks that way."

"Better get your saying said and then be gone from here."

"Fine with me."

Gaylord waved him toward the back room. "Come on, then," he said quickly. "I wants to be out of here before the trouble starts."

Ben followed him quickly into the back room and took a seat opposite Gaylord's small wooden desk.

"I just need to know as much as I can about Bluto," he said.

"Nothing much to know," Gaylord said. He placed his hands behind his head and leaned back in chair. "He come in here sometime."

"Just to play pool?" Ben asked.

"That's right," Gaylord said.

"Did he have any friends around here?" Ben asked. "People he hung around with?"

Gaylord shook his head. "Not that I ever seen."

"And as far as you know he didn't do any work?"

"Once in a while I let him rack the balls," Gaylord said. "I paid him a little for that. Sometimes he do an errand or two for somebody. Deliver something down the street."

"Who'd he do that sort of thing for?"

"Anybody that asked him," Gaylord said. "I guess they paid him whatever they wanted to. But like I say before, he didn't have a regular job, far as I know."

Ben shifted to a different direction. "Was he ever rough, violent?"

Gaylord looked at Ben wonderingly. "Bluto? Violent? Naw, he ain't like that. He ain't got the sense to be rough."

"Did you every see him act mean to anybody?"

Gaylord shook his head. "Nah, he ain't like that." He chuckled. "He think he a cop, you know. He always trying to act big, like he a cop. He say he deputized. He had a little badge to prove it."

"Police badge?"

"Yeah, look like."

"Did he carry it with him?"

"All the time."

"When was the last time you saw it?"

"When I seen Bluto the last time, I guess," Gaylord said. He thought a moment. "Yeah, he had it on. Pinned to his shirt, like always."

"Did he say who deputized him?" Ben asked immediately.

"One of the Langleys, I guess it was," Gaylord said. "Probably that silly one. Tod. Nobody else would do a fool thing like that."

"Did you ever see Bluto with the Langleys?"

Gaylord nodded. "Once in a while. They liked to play with him. Kid him, you know?" He frowned. "They liked to watch him act a fool. They tell him he a regular policeman. They tell him they gone find a woman for him, so's he can git married, so they can be lots of new little Blutos for the police force."

"When was the last time you saw them together?" Ben asked immediately.

Gaylord thought for a moment. "Been awhile, I reckon."

"Try to remember exactly," Ben said insistently.

"Mor'n a week," Gaylord said. "Maybe mor'n two weeks."

"Where did you see them?"

"Right here," Gaylord said. "Right here in the poolhall."

"What were they doing in here?"

"Jes' hanging around," Gaylord said with a shrug. "Sometimes I think they must love the colored folks, the way they hangs around them." He laughed. "Naw, they looking for something bad, something they can bust up, card game or something like that."

"Did they talk to Bluto?" Ben asked.

Gaylord shook his head. "Not that I remember," he said, "and I usually watches them boys real close. They give me a bad feeling when they come 'round. Like a chill in my bones."

Ben allowed his eyes to roam the cluttered back room silently. Scores of old license plates had been nailed to the walls, one of them going back to 1921. There were pinup-girl calendars mingled with aging photos of black athletes: Joe Louis, Jesse Owens, Jackie Robinson.

Gaylord watched Ben silently, until their eyes met once again. Then he leaned forward slowly. "You better be going now," he said. "The boys up front liable to say something."

"Say what?" Ben asked.

"Say maybe ole Gaylord's a little too close with a white policeman."

"Are you afraid of that?"

Gaylord smiled nervously. " 'Bout the only thing I is afraid of, you want to know the truth." He stood up immediately. "Les' go, now. This place ain't gone be too good for you to be at in a few minutes."

Ben did not move. "The little girl," he said. "She was raped. Could Bluto have done something like that?"

Gaylord shrugged. "I don't know. Maybe he could. He was always pulling at hisself, you know what I mean?"

Ben nodded.

"Right out in the open," Gaylord added. "Pulling at hisself. I'd say to him, I'd say, 'Stop that, Bluto. You out in the open. You want to do that, you go on home.' " He shook his head sadly. "But he'd just smile that big ole smile of his and keep on pulling, like he couldn't figure out why everybody wadn't doing it all the time."

Gaylord walked to the door of his office and opened it. "Don't come back here no more," he said quietly. "It ain't good for nobody."

Ben stepped out into the poolhall. It was empty now, all the players gone.

"Look at that, now," Gaylord said disgustedly. " 'Nuther one them demonstrations coming down Fourth Avenue. All they do is ruin business." He shook his head. "I can't figure it out, why these colored folk wants to be mixed up with the white people." He looked at Ben wonderingly. "It just don't make no sense to me. You know why? 'Cause white people, they don't ever look like they're having any fun."

Twenty-six

Ben headed across the street toward his car. At the end of the avenue, he could see the firemen darting frantically around their engines. Some were busily unspooling yards of thick hosing, while others rushed to uncap the few hydrants which dotted the streets around the park. For a moment he stood in the middle of the avenue and stared at them wonderingly. Then suddenly he heard voices in the distance behind him, turned and saw the first demonstrators come over the hill. The few stragglers who were still on the avenue rushed down the side streets, and for a moment Ben stood alone, his body frozen between the unmoving lines of firemen and police and the dark, slowly rising wave that continued to flow smoothly over the hill.

He glanced down the avenue. Luther was peering at him, his hand cupped over his eyes to protect them from the harsh afternoon light. Only a few feet away Breedlove and Daniels stood together, staring at him too, and for an instant, Ben had the sensation that everyone's attention was focused intensely upon him, the firemen and police who stood motionlessly in the summer air, his fellow detectives, Breedlove and Daniels on one corner, the Langleys on the other, even McCorkindale, perched on top of one of the fire trucks that blocked the end of the avenue like a blood-drenched wall.

Finally, Luther's voice broke the air, as his short, stubby arm motioned to Ben frantically.

"Get out the way!" he shouted. "Get on down here!"

Ben did not move.

"Get on down here!" Luther called wildly, his voice barely audible in the distance.

Ben stared at him without moving, his mind hurling through a thousand calculations.

"Ben!" Luther screamed. "Hurry up! Get on down here with us!"

Ben stood in place. He could hear the engines of the school buses as they started up, then the sirens after them, and from behind, the chorus of gently singing voices that swept toward him from what seemed like an entirely different world.

"Get on down here, now!" Luther shouted. "Hurry up! You're in the way!"

But still he could not move. He saw the long gray lines of the patrolmen grow taut, saw their polished black boots wink in the bright summer air. Then the atmosphere filled with the glint of scores of camera lenses as a small army of reporters turned them toward the hill. They seemed to fire at him silently, in white flashes, and he felt that he was trapped on some bizarre and unforgiving front, a man between the lines. He knew that Luther was still calling to him, but he could hear only the steady drum of the marchers as they continued to flow by the hundreds over the gently curving hill. Their singing swayed in the air, slow and rhythmic, and as their line of march moved steadily toward the tensely waiting squads of firemen and police, he felt himself suddenly and inescapably lost in the middle of it, floating helplessly, as if the earth had turned to air beneath his feet. In the distance, he could see Coggins clapping and singing as he headed down the hill, but he seemed less a person in his own right now than simply part of the dark line which continued to roll toward him. He turned away, glancing down the hill once more. He could see Luther staring at him motionlessly, no longer calling to him or waving him forward, but simply peering at him speechlessly, as if unable to take him in. For an instant he felt his body move down the hill toward Luther, then stop, turn around, and move in the opposite direction, toward the marchers. He'd only gone a few paces before he stopped again, and remained stopped, as if waiting for yet another signal. When it came, he spun around quickly and rushed down one of the side streets, his legs pumping more and more rapidly until they finally brought him to his waiting car.

The sound of sirens was still ringing in the air when Ben pulled up to the small wooden guardhouse at the factory gate.

The guard walked slowly over to the driver's side and leaned in. "Sounds like all hell's breaking loose downtown," he said.

"Yeah," Ben said dully. "Listen, I wanted to ask you a few questions about Bluto."

"Okay," the guard said. "Want to set in the car or is it getting too hot for you?"

"It's too hot," Ben said as he opened the door and stepped out.

"I got a little patch of shade over here," the guard said. He pointed to a small rectangle of shadow which stretched out from the guardhouse.

Ben followed the guard over to the wall of the guardhouse, and the two of them leaned idly against it. A large truck turned into the drive, and the guard walked out to it, spoke to the driver, then waved it through.

"When was the last time you saw Bluto?" Ben asked him when he returned to the guardhouse.

"That would have been on Sunday afternoon, I think," the guard said. He watched the truck as it made its way to the enormous warehouse a few hundred yards away.

"He was killed that night," Ben said. "Probably between eight and one or two in the morning, the coroner says."

The guard's eyes snapped over to him. "Is that so?"

"Do you remember about when it was you saw him?"

The guard thought for a moment. "Well, I saw him a few times on Sunday. I've got a twelve-hour shift on the weekend."

"When does it begin?"

"Noon."

"So you were here until around midnight."

"Until exactly midnight," the guard said. "I don't try to beat the company. I'm not like that." He looked back toward the truck, his eyes focused on the large cloud of dust that tumbled up from behind it. "We've been having some things disappear off the lot," he explained. "I got to keep my eyes open."

Ben nodded quickly. "And during that twelve-hour shift, you said you saw Bluto several times?"

"Yes, sir, I did."

"Could you tell me when that was, exactly?"

The guard thought a moment. "Well, I walk the grounds when I first get here," he said. "I have me a cup of coffee, then I walk all over the place, you know, to check things out."

"And you saw Bluto then?"

"Yeah," the guard answered. "He was sitting up on that little ditch, the one above the pipe." He shook his head. "He was sort of curled up, you know. Had his knees crunched up against hisself."

"Did he say anything?"

"Said, 'Howdy, boss.' That's all."

"He didn't say anything else?" Ben asked insistently. "It doesn't matter what it was. Just anything at all."

The guard tugged at the brim of his cap. "Said, 'Looks to be pretty, don't it?' " He smiled. "The weather, that's what he was meaning. He always had something to say about the weather. I don't think he knew about much of anything besides rain and shine, you know?"

"Did he say anything else?"

"I just kept walking," the guard said, "and that was it."

"When did you see him the next time?"

"Well, that must have been around six, I guess," the guard said. "That's when I go looking around again."

"Where was Bluto then?"

"In the pipe," the guard said. "I heard him carrying on down there. So I sort of peeped over the edge of that little gully and took a look."

"What was he doing?"

"Sanging, that's all," the guard said. "He loved to sang, that old boy."

"And he was in the pipe?"

"Sitting in there by hisself, that's right," the guard told him, "just a-sanging away."

"Did you speak to him?"

"No."

"Did he say anything?"

"I don't figure he saw me," the guard said. "I just took a quick little peep at him. I didn't say nothing." He shrugged. "It was real hot that day, even after it got late, and so I wasn't in no hurry to stand out there by them pipes and have a talk with Bluto."

Ben took out his handkerchief and wiped his neck and face. "No, of course not," he said. "But you saw him again, right?"

"Yeah, I did," the guard said. "Now this was later. 'Bout nine at night. He come wandering right through the front gate, big as you please. It 'bout knocked my eyes out."

"What do you mean?"

"Well, he never come through the front gate before," the guard said. "He ain't allowed to do that."

"How does he get in?"

"They's a place cut in the fence," the guard explained matter-of-factly.

"Where?"

"Right near the pipe," the guard said. "That's how Bluto always comes and goes. He don't use the front gate. It ain't allowed."

"Except this last time," Ben said.

"That's right," the guard said. "This last time he just come right up. Says, 'Well, boss, I'm going to town. Got to get back pretty soon, though.' Says, 'I'm a-getting married.' "

"Married?"

"Plain as day, that's what he says."

"Had he ever said anything like that before?"

"Not to me, he hadn't."

"Did you ever see him with a woman?"

"Bluto? No, I never seen him with much of anybody," the guard said. "Matter of fact, I asked who the girl was. He said he didn't know yet. So I said, 'Well, where is she?' And Bluto, he just said, 'She's coming later,' and that was the last of it. He went right out the gate."

"And what time did you say this was?"

"I'd put it right at nine o'clock."

"Did you see him come back?"

"Yeah, I did," the guard said. "It was only about an hour later."

"Around ten?"

" 'Bout then," the guard said. He smiled. "And, my God, did that ole boy look happy."

"He came through the main gate?"

"No, he didn't," the guard said. "I figure he caught the way I looked at him when he done that before." He shook his head. "No, he didn't use the gate no more. I guess he must have come back through the fence."

"Where did you see him?"

"When I made my final rounds," the guard said, "I always say goodnight to him before I go home. That's what I went over to the pipe for."

"Was he in the pipe?"

"He was sort of cleaning it up," the guard said. "Straightening things out. He was sanging, too."

"Did he say anything?"

"Said, 'Hey, boss, what you think about my new TV?' " the guard told Ben with a chuckle. "Somebody'd probably wanted that ole thing toted off, so they fooled him into thinking it'd work without no electricity or anything like that."

"And that's the last you saw of him?"

"That was it."

"Did you see anyone else around?" Ben asked. "I mean, a girl maybe?"

The guard laughed. "A girl? What would a girl be doing around Bluto?"

"The one he was talking about marrying," Ben explained.

The guard waved his hand. "Oh, that was just Bluto's way of saying things. He didn't have no sense when it come to talking to people."

Ben straightened himself slowly. "That hole in the fence," he said. "The one he used. Where is that?"

"Right close to the pipe," the guard said. "You want to go look at it?"

"Yeah."

The guard turned and pointed to the southeastern corner of the lot. "Right out there," he said. "You can't miss it if you walk along the fence."

"Thanks," Ben said as he stepped out of the shade of the guardhouse and headed out across the flat dirt field.

It took him only a few minutes to pass beyond the still littered drainpipe and find the hole in the fence. It looked as if it had been made long ago with a pair of industrial wire-cutters. The tips of the severed fence were rusted over, and the hole had been widened over the years as Bluto's large body had passed in and out of it. The ground around it was smooth and grassless, and a narrow footpath could be seen as it snaked from the opening back to the ditch and its exposed drainpipe. Ben allowed his eyes to move up and down the path. He could not imagine Doreen having ever walked down it. He leaned against the fence, then he pulled himself up again and walked along the trail to the edge of the ditch. He could see the drainpipe below him, and as he stood, staring into its dull gray eye, he tried to put the events in some kind of chronological order. Bluto had left the plant through the front gate at around nine. By then he'd come up with the idea of a wife. At ten, he was cleaning his place, as if in preparation for her arrival. A few hours later, both he and Doreen Ballinger were dead.

Ben lowered himself onto the stony ground, his eyes still staring into the cement cave of the drain. He tried to imagine what must have gone on there at some time between nine and midnight only a few days before. "She's coming later," Bluto had told the guard, and it seemed to Ben that this meant that he had expected someone to arrive of her own free will, a woman for whom he had cleaned what amounted to his house, trucked home a battered television, and for whom he had seemed to feel in his own childish way an unparalleled delight. "She's coming later," Ben repeated in his mind. But had he expected her to come by herself, or be delivered to him by someone else and placed into his hands, like a prize?

Twenty-seven

The few people who were seated inside Smiley's Cafe turned instantly toward Ben as he stepped through the door. They seemed frozen in place, stunned into a strange and utterly motionless silence.

"I'm looking for Esther Ballinger," Ben said quietly as he closed the torn screen door behind him.

"She's out back," said the small man behind the counter. He wiped his hands on the soiled apron which hung from his neck. "What you want with her, boss?"

"It's police business," Ben said. "About her niece."

The man glanced questioningly at the others as if unsure of what to do next. "Well, I guess you ought to see her then," he said finally, his eyes darting away from Ben's. "Just go on round back. She out there throwing away the garbage."

Ben turned and walked out immediately, then headed around the corner of the building to the alley which ran behind it. He could see Esther at a large wooden bin. She was breaking down a large assortment of cardboard boxes, then tossing them into the bin.

"Afternoon, ma'am," Ben said politely as he stepped up to her.

Esther looked up from her work but did not speak. She continued to tear at the boxes, pulling at the locking flaps until they were flat. She wore a light-blue blouse, and a line of perspiration swept in an arc across her chest. Her hair was pulled back and knotted, and in the bright summer light she looked suddenly much younger than in the past few days. Only the expression in her face aged her, the weariness in her eyes.

"I'm still working on your case," Ben said to her, "and I've found out a few things."

Esther wiped her forehead with her arm, then began breaking down another box. "Go ahead, then," she said, almost absently, as if there were greater things to consider now, her niece's death reduced in her mind to a small incident in a larger history.

"Well, I may have found out who raped Doreen," Ben said. "It was a colored man. A guy named Bluto. Ever heard of him?"

"No," Esther replied crisply.

"He's dead."

Esther suddenly began to rip more violently at the box in her hands, tearing at its cardboard flaps.

"Shot," Ben said. "Might have done it to himself."

Esther nodded curtly and tossed a large piece of cardboard into the wooden bin at the back wall of the cafe. "Is that the end of it, then?"

"I don't think so," Ben told her.

"Why not?"

"Well, there's something that keeps bothering me," Ben said matter-of-factly.

"What?"

"I can't figure out how Doreen got to his place," Ben said. He picked up one of the boxes, tore apart one of the flaps and broke it down. "So I'd like to just ask you just a few more questions." He threw the box into the bin. "Is that all right with you?"

"Go ahead," Esther said, her eyes turning from him oddly, as if she did not want him to see what was in them.

"Did Doreen ever give you the idea that somebody was watching her or keeping track of her in any way?"

Esther shook her head. "I think she could have let me know if somebody was scaring her."

Ben pulled out a picture of Bluto. "Have you ever seen this man?"

Esther stared expressionlessly at the photograph. "Is that him?"

"Well, this was taken at the morgue," Ben said, "so it doesn't look quite right. But, yes, it's him."

"The man who raped Doreen?"

"Maybe."

Esther's eyes shot away from the picture. "I don't recognize him."

"You never saw him hanging around your house or neighborhood, or anything like that?"

"No," Esther said crisply.

"He was real big," Ben went on. "Did Doreen ever indicate that she knew or had seen a big man?"

"No."

Ben returned the photograph to his pocket. "You know the rubber plant not far from Bearmatch?"

"Yes."

"Did Doreen ever mention going over there?"

"No."

"Do you think she might have hung around that place?" Ben asked. "Maybe with other kids?"

Esther looked at Ben, puzzled. "No. Why would she?"

"That's where the guy lived."

"Around the rubber plant?"

"Inside the fence," Ben said. "In a storm drain."

Esther's eyes glistened. "Is that where . . . ?"

"It looks that way," Ben told her. "But I still can't figure out how she got over there."

"Maybe he took her there," Esther said.

"I thought about that," Ben said, "But Mr. Davenport says that he let her out at around five in the afternoon. He says that she wanted to play with another little girl she saw in the ballfield. You got any idea who that little girl might have been?"

Esther thought for a moment. She seemed to move back toward him from some distant place she'd occupied during the few preceding minutes. "There's a little girl named Ramona. She lives over near the ballfield. I've seen Doreen play with her."

"You know the address?" Ben asked immediately.

"It's that light-blue house at the far end, the downtown corner."

"Twenty-second and First," Ben said.

"That's right," Esther told him. "That corner."

Ben threw the last box into the bin. From the corner of his eye he could see several dark faces staring at him from behind the dusty window at the back of the cafe.

"They're all watching us," he said to Esther.

"Course they are," Esther said edgily. "What do you expect?"

"Do they know about your niece?"

"Just that she's dead," Esther told him. "The rest of it, that's nobody's business."

"I'm going to find out who did it, Miss Ballinger," Ben said.

"I thought you already had."

It was only then that it struck Ben how little he thought he knew, how much more there was to know. He shook his head slowly. "I don't think so," he said quietly, in a voice that seemed aimed at no one but himself.

It was almost evening before he glanced in his rearview mirror and saw a few weary stragglers as they trudged across the bare, unseeded ground toward the downtown corner of the old ballfield. All through the late afternoon hours, Ben had remained in his car, carefully eyeing each passerby who approached the small light-blue house. With each passing second, the air had seemed to grow heavier, and as he sat in his car and listened to the steady blare of sirens, he could sense that something had surely gone wrong on Fourth Avenue or beneath the swaying elms of Kelly Ingram Park. He could see it in the drawn angry faces of the people who glared at him as they slogged up the street in their sopping wet clothes and tangled hair. Their pants and skirts were ripped and caked with dirt, as if they'd been rolled in a muddy field, but Ben did not get out of his car to find out what had happened to them until, toward evening, he saw a tall, slender woman pass through the rusty gate of the light-blue house. A young girl clung to her hand, and she only appeared to grip it more tightly as Ben stepped out of his car and moved toward them.

"Afternoon, ma'am," he said as he took off his hat.

The woman's eyes stared at him fearfully. She did not speak.

"I'm looking into something that happened to one of your neighbors," Ben added softly, "Doreen Ballinger."

The woman continued to watch him suspiciously. "What's that got to do with me?"

"Well, I'm told that Doreen sometimes played in this old ballfield with a little girl named Ramona Davies," Ben said. He glanced down at the little girl, then back up at the woman. "Is this Ramona?"

The mother instinctively drew the little girl up against her waist. "What you want with her?"

"Just to talk to her," Ben said. "About Doreen. It's possible that your little girl was the last person to see her alive."

"You with the po-lice?"

"Yes, ma'am," Ben said.

"They sprayed us today," the woman snapped bitterly. "And sicked them dogs on us."

"I didn't know that," Ben said.

"They wasn't no call fer 'em to do it," the woman said fiercely. "We was peaceful, all of us."

Ben nodded gently. "Yes, ma'am."

"And they just done it out of meanness," the woman added sharply. "Just pure ole meanness."

Ben's eyes fell toward the girl. He smiled quietly, but she only stared at him expressionlessly, her small fingers tightening around her mother's hand.

"You wasn't there, was you?" the woman asked.

Ben looked at her. "No, ma'am."

"How come?"

"I guess you might say I'm trying to stay out of it," Ben told her. "I just want to figure out who killed Doreen Ballinger."

The woman's eyes seemed to search his face. "Well," she said after a moment, "I guess I could let you talk to Ramona."

"I'd appreciate it," Ben said.

The woman looked at her daughter. "You stay in the front yard with the man, here," she said. "I'll go fix supper."

The girl did not let go of her mother's fingers.

"It's all right, Ramona," the woman assured her. "I'll be right inside here." She tugged her fingers free of the little girl's grasp. "You holler if you need anything," she added as she headed up the walkway toward the house.

The little girl's eyes shifted over to Ben.

"Hi," Ben said softly.

"Hey."

Ben sat down on the grass just inside the fence. "I know you probably want to go play," he said. "I won't keep you too long."

The girl shifted nervously on her feet.

"I hear you played with Doreen from time to time," Ben said.

Ramona nodded.

"Did you play with her last Sunday afternoon?"

The little girl stared at him blankly.

"I'll bet you go to church on Sunday night, don't you?" Ben asked.

"Yes, sir."

"Just before you went last time, did you see Doreen?"

"Yes, sir."

"Where'd you see her?"

Ramona pointed to the field. "Over there, behind them trees."

Ben looked in the direction she indicated. There were three large trees in the far corner of the field, a rope swing had been hung from one of them, and it swayed very slowly in the early evening breeze.

"I was swinging," Ramona said. "That's when she come up."

"About what time was that, you got any idea?"

The little girl shrugged gently.

"Was it close to suppertime?"

"Right before."

"So that would have been around five, something like that?" Ben asked.

"Right before supper," Ramona repeated. "My mama come to call me."

"Was Doreen with you when your mama called?"

"No, sir."

"Where was she?"

"She done left for home."

"How long did she play with you?"

"Not long."

"An hour, something like that?"

"She come across the field," Ramona said, this time pointing to the right, toward the opposite end of the ballfield.

"She came from that direction?" Ben asked.

"Yes, sir," Ramona said. "I seen the light flashing, and I looked, and then I seen Doreen."

"Flashing? A light?"

"From the police car."

"You saw a police car?"

"Yes, sir. It done stopped somebody."

"Another car?"

"Yes, sir."

"What did the police car look like?"

"It was the Black Cat car."

"Why was it stopped?"

"They was writing a ticket to somebody."

"They'd stopped a car?"

"Yes, sir, they had," Ramona said. "And they was over leaning in the window, writing him a ticket."

"Both of them?"

"They calls them the Black Cat boys," Ramona said, "them two brothers. Ever-body in Bearmatch knows who they is."

Ben leaned toward her slightly. "What about the other car? Do you remember what kind it was?"

"No, sir."

"What'd it look like?"

Ramona shook her head. "Just black, or blue or something like that."

"And that's when you saw Doreen?"

"Yes, sir."

"Where was she?"

"She was walking across the field right toward me."

"Was she alone?"

"She was by herself, yes, sir," Ramona told him. "She didn't have nobody with her." She smiled tentatively. "She looked real happy. She was sniggering to herself. She always sniggering. She can't talk, you know."

Ben nodded.

"But she sure do snigger a lot," Ramona added with a smile.

"And so she came across the field, and you two played for about an hour, is that right?" Ben asked.

"Played till she left."

"Which direction did she go in when she left?"

"Right toward her house," Ramona said, once again pointing toward the opposite end of the field. "Right down that way."

Ben nodded slowly. "Now this may seem like a funny question, but do you know where the rubber plant is?"

"Yes, sir," the little girl answered immediately. "My daddy work there."

"It's over there, isn't it?" Ben asked as he pointed in the opposite direction. "Are you sure Doreen didn't walk toward the plant?"

"Oh, no, sir," Ramona said loudly. "She walk toward her house." Again, she pointed in the direction opposite to the plant. "That way, just like always."

Ben smiled quietly. "You didn't happen to see anybody else around the ballfield that afternoon, did you?"

"People was walking through it, like they always is."

"You ever heard of a man named Bluto?"

"No, sir."

"He's very big."

"Never heard of him."

Ben took out the morgue photo and showed it to her.

Ramona studied the picture carefully. "He asleep?" she asked finally.

"Yes, he is."

Ramona's eyes dropped back toward the picture. "He look like he sick or something."

"Have you ever seen him?"

"No, sir, I ain't seen him," Ramona said, her eyes still staring curiously at the photograph. "He kin to Doreen?"

"No," Ben said. He slipped the picture from her fingers.

Ramona looked at him quizzically. "Who he is?"

"Just a man," Ben said as he tucked the photograph back into his pocket.

"He hurt Doreen?"

"He might have," Ben said. He got to his feet, then stood a moment, poking the tip of his shoe into a ridge of dusty earth. "You got any idea if somebody else might have seen Doreen after you did?"

Ramona shook her head. "None as I know of." Her eyes drifted over to the far edge of the field. " 'Cept maybe for them police boys and that fellow they was writing a ticket to."

Twenty-eight

Knots of firemen still lingered outside Police Headquarters as Ben pulled over to the curb, got out and headed slowly up the stairs. Some were still dressed in their black slicks as they stood alone, or huddled together, talking quietly as the air darkened steadily around them.

Lamar Beacham slumped against the front of the building, his long, slender body propped like a bamboo fishing pole against its granite façade.

"What happened today?" Ben asked as he reached the top of the stairs.

Beacham smiled thinly. "Where you been—Mars?"

"Working a case."

Beacham dropped his cigarette to the steps and crushed it with the tip of his boot. "They brought us into it, the Fire Department."

"How?"

"Just lined us up across the street," Beacham said. "And the Chief says, 'Turn on the hoses.' " He shrugged helplessly. "So we did."

"You sprayed the demonstrators?"

"Yeah, we sprayed them," Beacham said. His face twisted with disgust. "We sprayed them good." He shook his head. "Shit, Ben, that water comes out of them hoses at a pressure of a hundred pounds per square inch. You got any idea what that does when it hits somebody?" His eyes darted away, and he lit another cigarette. "It makes me sick, what the Chief made us do."

"Is that how the rest of them feel?"

Beacham looked at him. "A lot of us." His eyes turned back toward the avenue. A single red fire engine could be seen in the evening light. "The Chief, he better watch what he asks the firemen to do. We're not like the cops. Lingo's men, either. We're not like them. It's different with us."

"How long did this go on?"

"Seemed like forever," Beacham said. "I was holding the nozzle. That fucking thing is heavy. After a while I felt like I was holding up a car or something. And the way the water was shooting through it, it was like wrestling a bull." He laughed. "You know Jim Pointer, don't you, Ben? Little guy with a mustache?"

"Yeah."

"Well, he was my backup, you know, holding up the hose," Beacham said. "Finally he just let go of it. Said, 'No more, Lamar. They can get me to go in a burning building, but this ain't my job and I'm through with it.' " Beacham stared at Ben wonderingly. "And he just walked off. Just took off his helmet and walked right off. Can you beat that?"

Ben did not answer.

Beacham's voice took on a grim note of warning. "Chief better watch it. He's pushing too hard, and he's going to find hisself with nobody but the trash around him. Lingo's men. Shit, half of them ought to be in the pen themselves." He shook his head despairingly, then eased himself from the side of the building. "Well, take it easy, Ben," he said as he moved down the stairs. "I got to go home, but Lord knows I dread it. My wife's going to kill me for this."

The inside of Police Headquarters was less crowded than Ben had seen it in weeks. The lines of makeshift cots were empty, and only a few stragglers remained in the detective bullpen. The Chief's office was dark, and the only light in the corridor came from under Luther's tightly closed door. It was as if a strange emptiness had overtaken everything, an eerie vacancy that could be felt in the nearly deserted hallways, the unoccupied meeting rooms, even the thickening night beyond the windows. There was an odd, unworldly quiet in the air, and as Ben moved from one room to the next, he could sense that some part of the raging tumult which had been swirling in the city for so long had finally run its course, become exhausted, and simply slumped away, like a wounded beast into the enveloping brush. He did not know what part it was, but as he headed toward the dark office door of Property and Records, he sensed that it was somehow vital to the rest, a fire guttering out, one that left in its wake only the faintly acrid smell of defeated anger.

"What are you doing up here?"

Ben turned and saw a tall figure, backlit in the doorway at the opposite end of the corridor.

Ben stared in his direction. "Who's that?"

The man stepped out of the shadows, his face now half-illuminated by a slant of light.

It was Breedlove, and his body seemed taut and catlike, poised to leap.

"Most everybody's gone home," he said.

"Yeah," Ben said. "It looks that way."

Breedlove smiled coolly. "You weren't with us today, were you, Ben?"

"No."

"How come?"

"I'm still working on a case."

"That little girl, right?"

"Yes."

Breedlove stared intently into Ben's eyes. "You got some kind of special interest in that?"

"Maybe."

Breedlove took a single step toward him, his whole body now plainly visible in the hall light. "Why is that, Ben? Why are you so interested in that case?"

"She was a little girl," Ben said flatly, "I don't like what happened to her."

Breedlove smiled. "Course, it happens all the time, don't it?"

"Too much, yeah."

"You always work them this hard?"

"Always," Ben said bluntly.

Breedlove laughed thinly. "I admire your dedication," he said, suddenly forcing some lightness into his voice. "I really do." The edge was now entirely gone from his speech. It had been replaced by something else, a strained friendliness. "Well, good for you, old buddy," he said, his body relaxing visibly. "Nothing like a good cop to straighten out the world, ain't that right?"

"I guess so," Ben replied curtly.

Breedlove scratched the back of his neck casually. "Well, I got to get home like everybody else. You coming?"

"No. I want to check a few things."

Breedlove's face clinched slightly, then relaxed again. "All right then," he said. "See you tomorrow."

Ben stood silently in the corridor until Breedlove had disappeared down the stairs. Then he turned quickly, walked into the Records and Property Room and switched on the light.

Rows of gray metal filing cabinets lined the back wall of the room, and Ben walked over to the group marked "Traffic Citations." The citations were arranged by the date the summonses had been written, and Ben immediately began flipping through them, edging backward, closer and closer to the Sunday of Doreen Ballinger's disappearance.

It was a slender stack, held together by a single rubber band, and it did not take long for Ben to find the few summonses that had been issued by either Tod or Teddy Langley. One had been given in the downtown area at around two in the afternoon. A second had been issued to an illegally parked car just inside the borders of Bearmatch. A third had been issued to a speeding car at about three in the afternoon. The fourth had also been issued as a speeding violation. The time was recorded at a quarter after five, and the location was 21st Street and Second Avenue, the southwest corner of the old ballfield. It had been issued to a man named Norman Siegel, whose address was listed as 2347 Williams Street, Mountain Brook.

It was nearly eight at night by the time Ben turned onto Williams Street. He drove slowly, craning his neck to see the addresses as he passed one modest wood-frame house after another. He finally spotted the one he was looking for. It was a light-blue wood-frame house with an enclosed garage, and as Ben pulled into the driveway, he noticed the large assortment of toys which dotted the recently mowed lawn.

The door opened after the second knock, and Ben could see a short, middle-aged woman through the silvery screen mesh.

"Is this the Siegel residence?" he asked.

The woman nodded. "Yes."

"Does Norman Siegel live here?"

"Yes, he does," the woman said.

Ben took out his police identification. "It's nothing serious, ma'am," he said, "but I'd like to talk to Mr. Siegel if he can spare the time."

The woman looked at him worriedly. "All right," she said, her voice somewhat strained. "Come in, please."

The screen door swung open, and Ben stepped into the house.

"Just have a seat anywhere," the woman said as she disappeared into the back of the house.

Ben remained standing. His eyes drifted over the room. It had an exposed brick fireplace, its plain wooden mantel decked with family photographs in pink plastic frames. The carpet was reddish, with white flecks, and it was strewn with toys that looked as if they been scattered about haphazardly and then entirely forgotten. There was a brown naugahyde recliner, and opposite it, a plain tan sofa with bright red cushions.

"I'm Norman Siegel."

He was a small man in thick glasses, and he was dressed in khaki trousers and white, open-collared shirt. "I was just mowing the back forty," he said with a slight smile. "Night's about the only time I have for it." He offered Ben his hand. "Sarah said you were from the police."

Ben shook his hand quickly. "That's right."

Siegel laughed nervously. "Gee, I can't imagine being in any trouble." He shifted quickly from one foot to the next. "You want to sit down? You want a glass of tea, maybe something stronger?"

"No, thanks."

"Okay," Siegel said. He thrust his hands deep into his trouser pockets. "So what's this all about?"

"You were give a traffic ticket last Sunday, is that right?" Ben asked.

"Yeah," Siegel said. "I've already put the check in the mail."

"It's not about the ticket," Ben said.

Siegel looked at him, puzzled. "What is it then?"

"Well, not long after you were given the ticket, a little girl was seen walking in the ballfield, and not longer after that, somebody killed her."

Siegel drew in a long, slow breath. "A little girl? Well, that neighborhood's—"

"A colored girl," Ben said. "Twelve years old."

Siegel's eyes grew tense. "My God, you don't think I had anything to do with that?"

"Not at all," Ben told him quickly. "But I was wondering if you might have seen anything."

"When?"

"While the ticket was being written."

Siegel thought about it for a moment. "I usually keep my eyes right on the road when I go through that part of town," he said. "Normally, I wouldn't go through it at all, but I have a toy factory on the other side of that neighborhood, and so if I'm in a hurry I sometimes take a shortcut down Collins Avenue. It ends up taking me through there."

"Is that what you were doing on Sunday afternoon?"

"That's right."

"You were headed for your factory?"

"Yes," Siegel said. "I got to it at around five-thirty. Lots of people can vouch for that."

"Were you speeding?"

Siegel shrugged. "I guess. Lots of people speed in that neighborhood."

"Do you know about what time you were pulled over?"

"It was five-fifteen on the dot," Siegel said. "I know, because I glanced at my watch as soon as I stopped. I was hoping to get it over with as quickly as possible and then head on over to the factory."

Ben nodded.

"And I know exactly when I left, too," Siegel said. "Because I looked at my watch again." He smiled sheepishly. "I'm sort of time-conscious, if you know what I mean."

"What time did you leave?"

"Five twenty-two," Siegel told him. "Which means that the whole thing just took seven minutes."

"Did you see a little girl around the ballfield while you were parked?" Ben asked.

Siegel shook his head. "No, I don't—" He stopped himself. "Wait a minute, now. Well, yeah, I think I did. Way across the field. In a swing."

"How about in the ballfield?" Ben asked insistently, realizing that the girl in the swing was Ramona Davies. "Maybe walking toward the swing?"

"No, just the girl in the swing," Siegel said. "That's the only little girl I saw."

Ben pulled out the picture of Bluto. "How about this man," he said as he handed the photograph to Siegel. "Does he look familiar?"

Siegel stared at the picture for a moment, then shook his head. "No."

"He's a real big guy," Ben said. "Did you see a real big guy standing off somewhere? Maybe in the distance?"

Siegel handed the picture back to Ben. "No."

"Just the girl then?" Ben asked. "The one in the swing?"

"That's all," Siegel said. He smiled. "Except for those two cops." He laughed lightly. "They seemed like two real by-the-book types. One comes around one side of the car, one comes around the other, just like on *Highway Patrol.*"

Ben nodded silently. "Well, that's just following regulations."

"Oh, yeah," Siegel said. "Then why'd they just do it to me?"

"What?"

"Yeah. The next guy they pulled over, they didn't do any of that stuff."

"Next guy?"

"Right after me."

"They pulled over someone else?"

"Oh, yeah," Siegel said loudly. "Right as I pulled away, they went after another car. I was still putting all my papers back in my wallet and they were after another one."

"You saw this?" Ben asked.

"I wasn't more than a few yards away," Siegel said. "It was just at the other end of that old ballfield."

"What'd you see?"

"I saw them pull this big car over, and the two of them get out," Siegel said. "I was going real slow, sort of feeling burned, you know, and I was just heading on toward the factory, and these same two guys had pulled over another car."

"What were they doing?"

"They were going up to it," Siegel said. "To the driver, I mean. Only it was different this time. I guess they decided to forget the by-the-book stuff."

Ben nodded.

"Anyway, they were both heading toward the driver's side of the car, and when the tall one got to it, he just leaned right in."

"He leaned in?"

Siegel chuckled. "He couldn't have leaned in any further if he'd been a guy trying to kiss a girl."

"The driver—did you see him?"

"No, he was turned toward the cop," Siegel said. "I could just see the back of his head. All I can say is that he had gray hair."

"What about the car?"

"Oh, it was a nice one," Siegel said. "A Lincoln. Dark blue. A real slick deal. It didn't look like it belonged in that neighborhood."

"Did you see the car drive away?" Ben asked.

"No."

"Did you see anyone else in the car?"

"No."

"Did you see anybody get out?"

"No, not a soul," Siegel told him. He wiped his forehead. "You sure you don't want something to drink?"

"No, thanks," Ben said.

"This car, the Lincoln," Ben said. "Did you see a little girl in it?"

"No."

"She would have been in the backseat."

Siegel thought for a moment, then shook his head. "I didn't see anybody but the cops."

"And the driver," Ben reminded him.

"Well, sort of," Siegel replied. "But the ones who really got a good look were those two cops. They saw him face to face."

Twenty-nine

The day's heat felt as if it had dissipated very little during the first few hours of the night, and before walking up the broad semicircular stairs to the Davenport house, Ben took out his handkerchief and wiped his face and neck. He could feel his shirt, wet and sticky, at the back, and as he took off his hat, he noticed that a dark line of perspiration had already risen above the dark band. Not far away, a small pond glimmered motionlessly in the moonlight. A ghostly cloud of steam hung heavily over the water. A tired old mallard could be seen drifting through it, its dark beak lifted slightly, as if it were drinking from the air.

A maid opened the door, short and stocky, her body draped in a white apron. "Yes, sir?" she asked.

Ben took out his identification. "I spoke to Mr. Davenport once before. He said it'd be all right for me to come by if I had any more questions."

The woman stepped back quickly and flung open the door. "Come on in," she said.

"Thank you," Ben said as he stepped into the house.

"Just wait here," the maid said. "I'll get Mr. Davenport."

Davenport appeared almost immediately. He looked far less formal than at his office. He wore a plaid sports shirt and large, baggy trousers, pleated at the front. A golf club dangled from his right hand.

"I was just doing some indoor putting," he said as he offered Ben his hand. "Would you like some refreshment?"

"No, thanks," Ben said.

"Well, let's go talk then," Davenport said. "Come on in here. We can have some privacy."

Ben followed him into a small, wood-paneled office. Its walls were covered with fox-hunting scenes and animal heads.

"The place makes me look like the great white hunter, doesn't it?" Davenport asked jokingly.

Ben said nothing.

"Truth is, I didn't bring down a one of them," Davenport added. "Not the bobcat or the leopard, and certainly not that ugly wildebeest." He laughed again. "They all belonged to my brother-in-law, and when he died, they ended up here. My wife didn't want to part with them, so this room is the result." He strode over to a dark-red leather sofa and sat down. "Please have a seat," he said, pointing to a matching chair. "You must be pretty tired if you're still up working this late in the day."

Ben sat down.

"Have you learned anything about what happened to Doreen?" Davenport asked immediately.

"A little," Ben said.

"Well, how can I help you?"

Ben leaned forward slightly. "When I talked to you in your office, you said that you drove Doreen all the way to the ballfield."

"That's right," Davenport said casually.

"And that you let her out because she saw another little girl playing, and she wanted to go play with her."

Davenport nodded.

Ben stared at him intently. "Is that the only reason you stopped, Mr. Davenport?"

Davenport's eyes grew taut. "What do you mean?"

"Well, I'm having a little trouble with that idea."

"What idea?"

"That you only stopped to let her out," Ben said flatly.

"Why else would I stop before I got her back home?" Davenport asked.

"Maybe you got pulled over," Ben said.

Davenport lifted his head slightly. "Go on."

"By a police car."

Davenport drew in a long, slow breath.

Ben looked at him piercingly. "We got a couple of guys who work Bearmatch—you ever heard of them?"

Davenport did not answer.

"They ride around in a prowl car made up to look like a big black cat."

Davenport remained silent.

"It's even got a cat painted on the front," Ben went on. "Have you ever seen a car like that, Mr. Davenport?"

For a moment Davenport seemed to resist the question, draw away from it. "Yes," he said finally. "I've seen it. They pulled me over, just like you said. But I had already let Doreen out."

"Why did they pull you over?"

"For speeding," Davenport said. "At least that's what they said."

"Were you speeding?"

"I may have been," Davenport said. "Like I said before, I was in a hurry to get back home. I had a very important meeting."

"They didn't give you a ticket," Ben said.

"How do you know that?"

"I checked their summonses. They gave one speeding ticket out in Bearmatch that day. But it wasn't to you."

"Then how did you know that they stopped me at all?" Davenport asked.

"Someone saw them pull over a dark-blue Lincoln," Ben said.

"And you assumed that it was mine?"

"Yes."

"What else do you know?" he asked finally.

"It might be better if it came from you," Ben said.

Davenport looked at him almost sadly. "It can't."

"It has to," Ben told him.

Davenport stared at him mutely, his eyes fixed, stony and yet oddly rocked by agitation, squeezing and unsqueezing like two white fists.

"A little girl is dead," Ben added after a moment, "and everybody wants me to get to the bottom of it."

"Maybe not everybody," Davenport said. "There may be people who don't want you to get to the bottom of it at all."

"Like the Langley brothers?" Ben asked tensely, a steely edge creeping into his voice.

Davenport said nothing.

"All of you were together when she disappeared," Ben said.

"There's no law against that."

"There's a law against lying about it in a criminal investigation," Ben reminded him. "You're a lawyer, you must know that. We're talking about murder."

"We're talking about a colored girl," Davenport said hotly. "And

I might add that you would be very wise not to forget that, Sergeant Wellman."

Ben could feel a wave of heat shoot up his back. "Mr. Davenport, I was raised by people who believed in manners. I don't want to lose control of mine."

"Are you threatening me?"

"Yes," Ben said icily, surprising himself. "I surely am."

Davenport laughed. "Don't make me insult you, Mr. Wellman," he said.

"I'm going to find out what happened to Doreen Ballinger," Ben told him resolutely. "And whatever I find out, everybody's going to know it."

Davenport shook his head. "Do you honestly believe that I had something to do with Doreen's murder?"

"All I know is that you've told a few lies."

"Maybe I had reasons for doing that."

"What reasons?"

"Reasons that are my own," Davenport replied stiffly.

"Not anymore they're not."

Davenport turned away slightly.

Ben stood up, and as he did so, Davenport's eyes flashed back to him.

"Where do you think you're going?" he snapped.

Ben shrugged casually. "I thought I might head on back to the station. The Langleys ought to be coming back on duty pretty soon. I figured I might have a little talk with them about all this."

Davenport jumped to his feet. "You will do no such thing," he said firmly. "You don't know what's going on, and you're better off not knowing."

Ben turned toward the door, slowly raising his hat to his head.

Davenport grabbed his arm. "Sit down, Wellman."

Ben spun around, grasped Davenport by the collar and pushed him backward in his seat.

"Don't ever put a hand on me," he said coldly.

Davenport stared up at him, thunderstruck. "You are one of those old stubborn boys, aren't you? You think you know everything. Well, this time you don't. Believe me, you haven't even scratched the surface."

Ben said nothing.

"The water's rising," Davenport added darkly. "All around you."

Ben stared at him lethally. "I'm not going to rest until I find out what happened to Doreen Ballinger."

Davenport watched Ben's face intently for a moment, as if trying to find a way into his mind. Then his face suddenly relaxed, his eyes softening very subtly. "Let someone else do it," he said.

"What?"

"Not you," Davenport said, almost in a whisper. "Someone else." His eyes took on a strange intensity, as if he were trying to speak through them.

"What are you talking about?"

"Lives are at stake."

"What do you mean?"

Davenport started to answer, then closed his lips tightly.

Ben watched him closely. "What are you talking about?" he repeated.

Davenport said nothing. Instead, he rose slowly, walked out of the room, then to the front door of the house. "Good evening, Sergeant," he said as he opened it.

Ben stepped out into the night, and Davenport followed him, closing the door behind him.

For a moment the two of them stood together on the curved white stairs, the moonlight pouring over them, the lake shining mutely out of the summer darkness.

"No one will ever know who the real heroes were," Davenport said quietly.

Ben stared at him quizzically. "What heroes?"

Davenport's eyes drifted toward the lake. "It doesn't matter," he said, as if he were talking to some distant presence, a vision in the trees. For a moment he simply continued to stare out across the lush wet grass. Then he turned to Ben. "I can tell you this, and it's the last thing I'll ever tell you." For a moment he considered his words carefully, then he leaned forward slightly, his voice taking on a conspiratorial intensity. "Whatever it is you're thinking," he said, "you're completely wrong."

The second floor of Police Headquarters had the look of a fortress that had been vigorously defended for a while, then abandoned altogether. The cots remained empty and unmade, sheets and bedding spilling out onto the unmopped tile floors. Everywhere, desks and shelves and windowsills were littered with soda cans and plastic cups and greasy sandwich wrappers. Only his own desk remained more or less clean of such disarray, but as Ben slumped down in the chair behind it, he realized that this was only because he hardly ever used it, preferring instead the rushing forward movement of his car or the drum of his feet across the cement walkways of the city. "A deskman is a dead man," his father had once told him, speaking with a sudden, amazing clarity out of the final haze of his senility.

But now, as he leaned back in his seat and drew his long slender legs up onto the top of the desk, he was not so sure. Somewhere, he knew, people did clean things, worked at nice, clean jobs, studied questions whose answers were oddly innocent, harmless, whose solutions hurt no one at all. Police work was entirely different from that. It had a cruel edge that seemed to slice in all directions, wounding randomly the good and the bad, turning everyone into some kind of helpless victim.

He thought of Doreen Ballinger and tried to figure out exactly what kind of victim she was. Maybe Bluto had killed her for sex. Of all the dangerous things any female had to watch out for, the most dangerous was male desire, and it seemed possible that Doreen's life had ended because a strong, childlike man, in a single unbearable instant, had lost control of himself.

For a time Ben lingered on the possibility of such an action, but with each pass, it seemed to grow more faint, while Davenport's final words grew louder and more insistent.

Whatever it is you're thinking, you're completely wrong.

So he headed back along the lines that had brought him to Davenport in the first place. Perhaps it was Siegel who was lying. Maybe he was trying to shift the blame to Davenport. Maybe all those toys scattered everywhere, dolls lying faceup in the grass, maybe the answer was somewhere deep in all of that, hiding like a serpent in some secret corner of Norman Siegel's unknowable mind.

Whatever it is you're thinking, you're completely wrong.

It could even be Jacob, the driver. After all, the first place you look for a murderer is in the face of a bitter, resentful employee. He already knew of a great many cases in which the rage of such people had caused them to bomb buildings, set fire to factories, pump one shotgun blast after another into the boss's bedroom window. He had seen it more than once. Like everything else, it was at least possible.

Whatever it is you're thinking, you're completely wrong.

He took out a cigarette and lit it, allowing his mind to continue backward, flowing slowly, like a tidal stream. Names and faces swept by him. Kelly, Breedlove, Daniels, the Langleys. It caught for a moment on the two brothers. There was no doubt that they operated as laws entirely unto themselves while they prowled the depths of Bearmatch. "After me," Kelly had said, "they wanted something different in Bearmatch." They had certainly got it, but sometimes Ben wondered if they had shot beyond the mark when they had turned it all over to Black Cat 13. Or maybe the Langleys continued to be exactly what was wanted. He could remember what Luther had said the day he'd asked about them: "Who do you think controls them, Ben? Is that what you want to know? Well, who do you think? Who does all the hiring and firing 'round here?" The Chief controlled them, and only the Chief.

Whatever it is you're thinking, you're completely wrong.

The cigarette burned down to his fingertips, and he quickly crushed it into the small tin ashtray on his desk, then lit another. Two mounted fans were whirring softly in the hot evening air, and he leaned back slowly, loosened his tie and let the breeze waft over him. The silence of the bullpen settled over him, and for a time, he simply sat, watching the blades in the gray half-light, until they seemed to watch him back, two dull eyes peering at him from either corner of the room. Then he sat up, blinked rapidly and shifted his vision over to the flat unshuttered windows which fronted the street from the high vantage point of the fourth floor. He stood up, walked over to the window and peered down at the city. It seemed darker than it had ever been before, wrapped in the thick musty heat, smothering like a child beneath a heavy black quilt. He wasn't sure when he'd stopped loving it, or if he'd ever really loved it, or the South, or anything at all outside the few people who had been drawn to him by blood alone, and who were now gone far beyond recall, almost beyond remembrance, silent as their unbeating hearts.

He was back at his desk, going over everything once again, when McCorkindale came in. He sat up and stared at him, amazed.

"What are you doing here this time of night?"

McCorkindale stopped dead in the dull light, then turned and flipped on the switch, flooding the room with a hard, bright light. "What do you like to sit in the dark for, Ben?" he asked as he moved forward once again, heading for his desk in the corner of the room.

"I'm surprised to see you here, Sammy."

"Well, I don't live here like you do," McCorkindale said casually. "I got a family, and all kinds of shit like that."

"What are you doing here?"

"Ah, my wife's been sick and I had a prescription filled and left it at work," McCorkindale told him as he made it to his desk, snapped up a small paper bag and headed back for the door. "I figured she might be able to get through the night without it, but no such luck." He was now halfway to the door, still moving ponderously among the desks, the paper bag tucked under his right arm. "Thanks for getting that pistol back to Property," he said as he made it back to the light switch. "You want me to turn these things off again?"

Ben sat up slightly. "What pistol?"

"The one you turned back into Property," McCorkindale said impatiently. "They'd marked it wrong, though."

"Who had?"

"Morgue."

"Are you talking about a twenty-two pistol?"

"That's right. Cute little thing."

"It was used in a murder."

McCorkindale laughed. "No way, Ben."

"Why not?"

"Because it was missing from Property," McCorkindale said. "That's where it came from. Same serial numbers. It was the only weapon that was missing when I was logging everything in a few days ago."

Ben felt his body rise almost involuntarily. "Missing? You mean it had once been in Property?"

"That's right," McCorkindale said. "Confiscated in a holdup."

"Who made the arrest?"

"Breedlove," McCorkindale said casually. "Good old Charlie Breedlove." Then he flipped off the lights.

Thirty

The heat was still hanging like a thick web in the air as Ben pulled up just across the street from Breedlove's house. It was dark, with the shades drawn tightly down over the windows, and not so much as a lone porch light to relieve the surrounding night. The plain gravel driveway was empty, and because of that, Ben knew that Breedlove was not at home. Like almost everyone else in the city, he lived by his car, and when it wasn't at home, neither was its owner. He looked at his watch. It was almost midnight. He leaned forward slightly, wrapping his arms loosely around the steering wheel. The windows of Breedlove's house were tightly closed, despite the heat, and Ben wondered if it was possible that Breedlove's family, his wife and young son, were also gone.

For a long time he simply sat in his car and watched the house. Slowly, the long day's weariness began to overtake him, a heaviness in his legs and arms that seemed to press him down in the seat. To relieve it, he stepped out of the car, lit a cigarette and walked for a while down the narrow, tree-lined street. All the houses were dark, their windows staring toward him like bruised eyes. The world was asleep, it seemed to him, but only fitfully. The tension in the city had not been washed away by the water hoses, and as he continued down the winding, cracked sidewalk, Ben tried to imagine what the next step might be. He could see the Chief's white tank as it circled Kelly Ingram Park, and Black Cat 13 as it prowled the back streets of the Negro district like a marauding beast, slow, sullen, sniffing the air for prey. It was as if something had gone so deeply wrong in the past that it was no longer recoverable, and so the old weight only grew heavier with each day, sinking the city with it, drawing it down forever.

He made a right, walking silently, then another and another until he found himself back at the car. He pulled himself in behind the wheel, sighing heavily with the heat and his own still unrelieved exhaustion, and fixed his eyes on the house until the first hint of early morning light began to gather around it, betraying its flecked paint and torn screens, its pitted driveway and bleak, untended yard.

The light was still barely visible in the air when the first car came up the street only a few minutes later. Ben sat up, rubbed his eyes quickly and watched as it nosed around the far corner, moved slowly up the street, then halted in front of Breedlove's house.

Ben leaned forward and rubbed the dewy mist which had gathered on the inside of the windshield with the sleeve of his jacket.

The car was black and dusty, like so many others, and Ben didn't recognize it at all until he saw Luther pull himself out from behind the wheel, then walk hurriedly up the walkway, linger for a moment on the porch, his shoulders hunched over, his back to the street. He knocked several times, but the door remained closed.

Ben checked his watch. It was five-fifteen. He rolled the ache out of his shoulders, rubbed his slightly burning eyes again and glanced back at the house. The door was still closed and the windowshades remained securely drawn.

For a while Luther remained on the porch. Then he turned back toward the street, glanced left and right and finally stepped off the porch and headed hurriedly toward his car. He had already opened the door when he saw Ben coming toward him. For an instant he froze, his eyes fixed intently on Ben's face.

"What are you doing here?" he asked sternly.

Ben stepped up onto the walkway beside him. "I was waiting for Breedlove."

"Why?"

"That gun, the one that killed the little girl," Ben told him. "It came out of the Property Room. It was taken in a robbery. Breedlove's case. I thought he might know whose gun it was."

"How do you know it was missing from Property?"

"McCorkindale did some kind of inventory a few days ago," Ben told him. "He logged everything. It was the only gun that was missing."

Luther continued to stare at Ben expressionlessly. "Is that all?"

It seemed an odd question, but Ben answered it anyway. "Yes."

"And you've been waiting here all night?"

"Most of it."

Luther thought for a moment. He took a deep breath. "All right, Ben. Since you're here, you might as well come with me."

"What are you talking about?"

Luther nodded toward the car. "Get in," he said softly. "I have to go look at something."

Ben got into the car and sat silently as Luther headed down the street, turned left, then continued northward until the short, brick skyline of Birmingham was miles behind them.

"We're going out of our jurisdiction, Ben," Luther told him. "But I guess you have to say that things like that have gotten sort of blurry lately."

There was a strained quality in Luther's face, a determined stiffness, as if he were trying to keep himself under control. Sometimes it looked like fear, sometimes anger, but whatever it was, Ben realized that it was different from anything he'd ever seen in Luther before.

"I was born up here," Luther went on. He smiled gently as he looked at the landscape which surrounded them. The morning light had now brightened enough to reveal the thick green woods which spread out to the north of the city. Lines of gently rolling mountains rose on either side of the road, and the sound of crows and hawks could be heard occasionally over the rattle of the engine and the whir of the wind that poured through the open windows.

"Where are we going?" Ben asked.

"Used to fish and swim," Luther went on obliviously. "Met my wife up here. She was a mountain girl."

"Where are we going?" Ben repeated.

Luther cleared his throat roughly. His eyes shifted over to the left, out the side window, then returned almost immediately to the road. "I got a call this morning. The sheriff up here, he's an old friend of mine." He smiled briefly. "He had the sweets for my wife way back when, a million years ago, when everybody still had a little piss and vinegar in their goddamn veins."

Ben leaned toward him slightly, his eyes watching him closely. "What were you doing at Breedlove's this morning?" he asked.

"I got a call, just like I said," Luther replied.

"About what?"

"About Breedlove," Luther said. He turned back to the road, slowing the car more and more until they came to a narrow unpaved road. Then he made a hard right turn and headed down it until they reached a clearing to the right. He pulled far over to the side, vines and low-slung tree limbs brushing across the side of the car.

"Get out," he said as he brought the car to a stop.

Ben suddenly felt himself trapped in some sort of net he had not seen.

"Get out?" he asked.

Luther nodded. "That's right."

Ben stared about. "Where are we?"

"Jackson County," Luther said. "Like I told you, my old stomping ground."

Ben pushed the door against the thick brush that pressed in against it and got out of the car.

"It's just a little walk from here," Luther told him. "Just follow me."

Luther headed briskly down the narrowing dirt path until they came to a second car. It was painted light blue and it bore the letters SHERIFF'S OFFICE in large white letters. The man who got out of it was dressed in plain khaki pants and a white short-sleeved shirt with a silver star hanging loosely from the pocket.

"Hey, Luther," the man said.

"How you doing, Fred?"

"Not good, but I guess you already know that."

"Where is it?" Luther asked.

"Up top the hill," the sheriff said. "Nobody tried to hide it, that's for sure."

Luther patted the sheriff on the shoulder. "Thanks for letting me know, Fred. We'll go on up by ourselves if that's okay with you."

"Sure enough. Just let me know what you want to do."

"Okay," Luther said. Then he turned and headed up the hill, waving Ben along to follow him.

The air grew cooler as they continued through the deep wet grass. Luther was silent, his eyes fixed on the curved hill which rose above him. He walked slowly, determinedly, but from time to time he would glance back toward Ben as if trying to study his face or the loose sway of his body.

Ben could feel his body tightening. "Somebody called Leon Patterson yesterday," he said.

Luther said nothing.

"They wanted to know how long you could tell what race a person was after they'd been buried," Ben added significantly.

Luther continued forward, now breathing heavily after the long pull up the hill, his forehead beaded with sweat.

"Leon thought that maybe whoever it was that called, that he might be planning something."

"To murder somebody," Luther said casually, as if only partly interested. "To murder a colored guy."

"That's right," Ben said.

Luther continued to drive himself forward, his heavy legs staggering through the lengthening grass. His trousers were wet with dew, and Ben could see them clinging to his thighs and backside.

"So," Ben added, "if what you've got up here is a—"

Luther stopped just as he crested the hill. A long flat field spread out before them, and near the middle of it, a tall elm stood, its large green leaves fluttering slightly in the breeze.

"There it is," Luther said as he pointed to the tree. His eyes glistened slightly in the light, and for a moment he seemed lost for words.

Ben stared at the tree. It was only a few yards away, and it was easy to see the body hanging from its large trunk. The head was slumped downward, the feet together, the arms flung out and, as Ben could see clearly after a moment, strapped to two large branches.

"Breedlove," Ben whispered.

"Fred said he looked like Jesus," Luther said. "Like Jesus on the cross."

Neither of them moved toward him. For a moment they simply stood together and stared at the body. A thin early morning haze surrounded them, as if to cover the harsh details which Ben began to see as he continued to look at the body. It had been tied at the wrists, the feet roped together.

Luther shook his head. "Sometimes I think there must be a curse on us." He looked at Ben. "Like voodoo or something. Some of the colored believe in that stuff, don't they?"

Ben said nothing.

Luther stepped forward slightly, his eyes squinting hard as he peered toward the body. "I didn't know him very well, did you?"

"No."

Luther looked at Ben. "You got any idea where his family is?"

"No."

"You didn't see them at all last night?"

"No."

"Got any idea what he was doing out here?"

Ben shook his head.

Luther wheeled around to face him, his eyes red-rimmed, his body trembling. "Don't hide nothing from me, Ben," he cried. "Don't be that stupid."

"I don't know anything."

"Bullshit," Luther snapped. "What the hell were you doing parked outside his house?"

"I was just waiting for him," Ben said.

"Because of that gun thing?"

"That's right, Captain," Ben said firmly.

Luther stared at him intently. "I don't know whether to believe you or not," he said. "That's why I wouldn't tell you anything on the way up here. I wanted to keep an eye on you, maybe shake something out of you."

Ben's eyes shifted over to Breedlove's body. "I didn't have anything to do with this." He turned back to Luther. "And I don't have any idea who did."

"What about his family?" Luther asked. "You know where they are?"

"No."

"You got any idea how long they been gone?"

"No," Ben repeated.

Luther continued to watch him doubtfully. "Don't hold anything back on me, Ben," he warned. "If you do, I'll bust you down. You'll be lucky to have a foot post in a cemetery."

"I don't know anything, Captain."

"All right," Luther said weakly. "I don't have any choice but to believe you." He looked back toward the center of the field. "Let's go see what we can find out."

Ben followed along at Luther's side, stepping quietly through the tall grass until the two of them stood beside the body. Breedlove's shirt had been ripped open, and the word INFORMER had been crudely cut into his chest.

"Oh, God," Luther whispered as he stared at the hanging body. "Who would do something like this?"

Ben's eyes drifted up from the chest until they reached Breedlove's stricken face. One eye was open, the other half-closed. Blood ran from both ears and trickled down to the neck and shoulders. It had gushed from the nose in a torrent, running down into the shattered mouth. The mouth itself was wide open, and Ben could see a small wink of light come through it from the cluttered hole at the back of Breedlove's head.

"They put the pistol in his mouth and pulled the trigger," Luther said.

Ben nodded.

"It's just like Fred described it," Luther added. "They strung him up like a goddamn pig."

"It took more than one," Ben said matter-of-factly.

"Course it did," Luther said. He took out his camera, then stepped back and took a picture. "Two at least," he added. "Maybe three."

"Yeah."

Luther nosed the tip of his shoe into the soft black earth. "They could have buried him," he said contemptuously. "In this ground it would have been easy."

"They didn't want to," Ben said. "They wanted to make an example of him."

"Example of what?"

"I don't know," Ben said. He looked down at the ground around the tree. It was splattered with blood, and from the look of the way the tall grass had been beaten to the ground, it looked as if Breedlove had put up a fierce but ultimately hopeless fight before they'd killed him.

Ben pulled one of the long green reeds which had been trampled down and stared at the small dot of dried blood which clung to it. "Why do you think they brought him way up here?" he asked.

"I don't know," Luther said. "I'm not even sure they did."

Ben looked at him. "Well, why would he have come up here on his own?"

Luther shrugged. "I don't know that either," he said. "But I do know that Fred found his car right down the road back there. His police ID was on the dashboard. That's why Fred called me."

"But you don't have any idea what he was doing up here?"

Luther shook his head firmly. "No, I don't."

A siren could be heard suddenly, growing louder with each passing second.

"They're coming from Birmingham," Luther explained. "Fred

said it was okay to take Breedlove back." His eyes lifted toward the terribly torn and violated face. "I told him that he was one of ours, and that we'd find out who did this to him." He looked at Ben pointedly. "But I'm not sure we can," he said. Then he turned away quickly, plowing through the deep grass until he reached the road.

Thirty-one

At eight in the morning, the Chief marched to the front of the detective bullpen and made the announcement. He bowed his head slightly before beginning, then glared fiercely out into the assembled detectives.

"We've lost one of our own," he declared, his small blue eyes narrowing tightly. "We don't know how it happened, but, by Jesus, gentlemen, we're going to find out." His large, bulldog face squeezed together determinedly. "Nobody does something like this to one of our boys and gets away with it."

The detectives exchanged puzzled glances. Across the room, Ben could see Daniels standing alone, while a few yards away, near the opposite corner, the Langleys stood shoulder to shoulder, their eyes fixed on the Chief.

"Gentlemen," the Chief said slowly, his voice suddenly low and mournful, "Charlie Breedlove is no longer with us."

A confused murmur rose in the room, muffled and indecipherable.

The Chief waited for it to die away, then continued. "I'd like to be able to say—well, I wouldn't like it—but it would be better if I could say that Detective Breedlove had died of natural causes, or in a car wreck, or something like that." He paused, his face growing tense and angry. "But, gentlemen, that is not the case here. The case is, gentlemen, that a person or persons did this thing to Detective Breedlove. What I mean to say is, they murdered him in cold blood."

A wave of noise and shifting about swept the room, and again the Chief waited for it to fade to silence.

"Now we don't know much about what happened yet," he said, "but one of our brothers is dead by a violent hand. Captain Starnes will fill you in on the details, and I want to assure you that he'll be very frank in what he tells you about this tragedy. So all I need to add is this." He drew in a deep dramatic breath. "Gentlemen, despite the fact that we have our hands full these days, we are going to find out who killed Charlie Breedlove, and we're going to see to it that that person is severely punished for doing it."

Again a wave of noise swept the room, lingering for so long this time that the Chief lifted his hands to bring it to an end. "Now I'm telling you all this because it's going to be in the papers anyway," he said. "And there are probably a lot of people in Birmingham who will try to use this to embarrass us, or make us look stupid. Now don't any of you let that happen. Just go on with your duties, and let the officers who have been assigned to this case do theirs." He stopped, stared at the group of detectives that were gathered before him for a moment, then nodded briskly. "That is all."

Luther took the Chief's place immediately, described what he and Ben had seen earlier in the morning, and then darted away as quickly as the Chief.

Ben turned from the front of the room just as Luther disappeared behind the rear doors. He could see Daniels slumped down in the chair behind his desk. Several detectives had gathered around him, and he was talking quietly to them. The Langleys stood alone in the opposite corner, talking so intently to one another that they did not see Ben until he was almost on them.

"Hey, Teddy," Ben said. He looked at Tod. "How you doing?"

The two brothers stared at Ben expressionlessly.

"Terrible about Breedlove," Ben said.

Tod nodded, but Teddy stared rigidly at Ben.

"I didn't know him very well," Ben said. "Did you?"

Teddy watched Ben intently. "Is this your case, Wellman?"

"What?"

"They must have assigned it to somebody," Teddy said, "and it wasn't to me."

Ben shrugged. "They didn't give it to me either."

Teddy stared at him knowingly. "Bullshit."

"Why would they give it to me, Teddy?" Ben asked.

"Because Daniels is too close to it, and everybody else is too busy."

"I'm busy, myself," Ben said. "I got that little girl thing."

Teddy laughed. "That's a nigger case," he said. "You could drop that and nobody would give a shit."

"But I haven't dropped it," Ben said.

"Maybe you better."

"You know something I don't, Teddy?" Ben asked.

"That nobody gets ahead in this department by working a nigger case," Teddy said.

Daniels suddenly appeared at Ben's side. "How does a person get ahead around here, then?" he asked in a voice that was mildly accusatory.

Teddy glared at him. "Well, you ought to know, Harry, you've been greasing the pole for a few years now."

Daniels' body tightened. "What the fuck are you talking about?"

Langley laughed mockingly. "Oh, come on, Harry. Everybody notices the way you're always brownnosing the Chief."

Daniels moved toward him slightly. "You better shut your mouth, Teddy."

"There was a time when the Chief come to me for things," Teddy went on resentfully. "Now he goes to people like you. Young guys. People who are ready to make a deal with the niggers, give them what they want."

Daniels took another step toward him, glaring fiercely, his body clenched.

Teddy grinned coldly. "What do you want to be, Daniels? You want to take the Chief's place, or do you want to be mayor, or what?" His eyes narrowed. "You talk a good game, you and Breedlove, and most of the rest of the new people around here. But you're just in it for yourselves. You don't have no feeling for what you do." He shook his head. "You think I don't notice how you're always having little huddles with the Chief, or following the Captain around? You think I don't notice that?" He shrugged. "Well, one of these days you may have Birmingham all to yourself, but it'll be a mongrelized, no-account place with nothing but white trash and niggers in it."

Daniels cocked his head slightly, mocking him. "And you're going to stop all that, right, Teddy? You're going to save the whole goddamn white race."

"I'll do my goddamn best," Teddy said determinedly. "But don't think that I don't already know that if the Communists and race-mixers get desperate enough, they'll set somebody up, somebody like me, like Tod, like anybody they want out of the way."

"You think you're going to be set up, Teddy?" Ben asked seriously.

"Maybe."

"Who would do that?"

"I don't know."

"Do you have any idea who killed Breedlove?"

"No."

"Or why?"

"The only thing I know is that they didn't give me the case," Teddy said. "And that don't seem right to me." He laughed derisively. "But nothing seems right about this thing. I mean, tying him to a tree like that. Calling it in to the local sheriff." He grimaced. "That's the sort of thing you do when you want to get attention or set somebody up. Any other way, it don't make no sense."

Daniels glanced over to Tod. "You feel that way, too?"

Tod started to speak but Teddy interrupted. "My brother agrees with everything I say."

"Stay together pretty much, is that right?" Daniels asked.

"That's right."

"Well, you boys better be careful," Daniels said sneeringly. "People might get the idea that you're closer than nature ought to allow."

Langley's body tensed but he did not move.

"Were you two patrolling Bearmatch last Sunday?" Ben asked quickly.

Teddy nodded.

"Around that old ballfield?" Ben added pointedly. "Maybe at about five in the afternoon?"

Teddy smiled. "This about that little girl?"

"Why did you pull Horace Davenport over?" Ben asked bluntly.

Daniels' lips parted. "You pulled Horace Davenport over?" he asked, astonished.

"That's right."

Daniels laughed. "You know who he is, Teddy? He could be the next mayor of this town."

"He was speeding," Teddy said sternly. "And I don't allow no speeding in Bearmatch."

Daniels laughed again. "My God, you are an idiot."

Teddy stared at him coldly. "Why don't you go find out who killed your partner," he snapped. "That'd really get you in tight with the big wheels."

"Davenport lied to me," Ben said to Teddy. "He told me that he let that little girl out because she saw a friend of hers playing in the field."

"Maybe he did."

"He said that was the only reason he stopped in Bearmatch."

Teddy said nothing.

"But you pulled him over," Ben said. "You and Tod."

The two brothers looked at each other nervously.

"Why did you pull him over?" Ben demanded.

"We pull over a lot of people in Bearmatch," Teddy said harshly. "We like to keep a close eye on things. Shit, Wellman, we pulled over a guy just before Davenport."

"Norman Siegel," Ben said. "I know. I talked to him."

Teddy looked surprised. "You really are working the shit out of this case, ain't you?" He looked at his brother and sneered. "Maybe Ben's going to try to pin this little nigger cunt on us, too."

Before he could stop himself, Ben saw his own hand fly out and slap Teddy Langley's face, then fly back and slap it again, back-handed. Langley tumbled backward, stumbled over a chair and sprawled onto the floor.

Tod Langley's body stiffened, but he did not move forward. Instead, he pressed his back reflexively against the wall behind him and stared at Ben, thunderstruck. Daniels seemed almost equally astonished, his eyes wide and staring, but a thin, satisfied smile growing on his face.

For an instant the room was completely silent. The few detectives who had remained after the Chief's speech looked on in motionless disbelief as Langley pulled himself to a sitting position on the floor, but did not rise. He was still resting, half-dazed on the floor, as Ben slammed through the doors of the detective bullpen and headed for his car.

Thirty-two

Ben had already tromped down the stairs and pulled himself in behind the wheel before he realized that he had no place to go. It was almost two hours before King was scheduled to speak, and he had been assigned no duties in the meantime except to continue looking, in whatever way he could, for the man who'd killed Doreen Ballinger.

Everyone else was very busy, as Ben could easily see as he glanced about. The firemen were mustering on the steps again, surrounded by scores of uniformed policemen and Alabama Highway Patrol. They stood in ranks, or gathered together in small knots, but always separate from each other, the firemen looking oddly sad and disengaged, while they warily watched the police swagger up and down the stairs, their thumbs notched in their thick black gunbelts. For a moment Ben remembered how often he'd seen Breedlove do exactly that, his shoulders hunched, his long shadow cutting jaggedly at the steps as he moved toward the glass door. Now he tried to imagine what Breedlove must have thought as he laughed with the Langleys, or joked with his partner, or slammed Coggins against the wall of the detective bullpen with such pretended fury that even Daniels had been fooled by it, and had finally moved in to stop him. But it had all been an act, and it seemed to Ben that to create an atmosphere in which such acting could be called for, in which decency had to wear a grim disguise, was itself a grave and desperate wrong. He wished that he'd known about Breedlove before it was too late, because he realized now that he would have behaved differently toward him, perhaps touched his arm from time to time, or offered him a subtly pointed look, anything that might have let him know that even within the ranks of his fellow detectives, he was not entirely alone.

Ben looked at his watch and tried to imagine some way to kill the next two hours. For an instant he saw Doreen's face in his mind, then Esther's, then Ramona's as she swung beneath the tree, watching Doreen saunter toward her from the other side of the field. After that it was a stream—Kelly Ryan swaying in summer heat, then Bluto's body swelling with decay, and after him, Breedlove, his arms stretched out like broken wings, his shattered head drooping toward his chest. It was as if some dark angel had descended upon the city, randomly swinging its sword, slicing whoever stood within its path.

He glanced back up toward City Hall. The Chief had just stepped out of the building, casting his short, stubby shadow across the stairs. The men on the steps stiffened immediately, and they were still standing at attention when Ben hit the ignition and fled down the avenue and away.

"You got anything for me?" Ben asked as he walked up to Patterson's desk.

"The girl's in the ground, Ben," Patterson said resignedly, "and it's going to be just like it would have been with any other little girl from Bearmatch." He shrugged. "I knew it would. I said so from the beginning."

"I mean on Breedlove," Ben told him.

Patterson straightened up from the paperwork on his desk. "You working that case, too?"

"Just a little," Ben said. "Sort of unofficial."

"Unofficial? I never heard of that."

"I don't know who they'll finally turn it over to," Ben told him. "But for now I'm just checking up on it. You know, on the side."

Patterson stared at him suspiciously. "Which means what, exactly?"

Ben did not answer.

Patterson smiled slyly. "They don't have anybody else they can trust, do they?"

Ben remained silent.

Patterson shook his head. "Is it really that bad?"

Ben shook his head. "It's complicated, Leon," he said.

"Like everything else lately."

"I guess so."

Patterson stood up. "Well, what do you want to know?"

"I'd like to take a look at the body."

"Okay," Patterson said. He led Ben back into the freezer room, opened the vault and pulled back the cover. Breedlove's body lay naked on the stainless steel carriage.

"He was shot in the mouth," Patterson said. "Then they cut him up and tied him to the tree. He was dead when they did that."

"Has he been officially identified?"

"By his wife," Patterson said.

"His wife? She came down here?"

"Yeah."

"When?"

"About an hour ago," Patterson said. "And she was real upset. And not just about her husband. Other stuff."

"Like what?"

"Well, when the body came in, the wedding ring was missing," Leon said. "She made a big stink about that. I even made sure that he'd worn a ring." He lifted Breedlove's left hand and held it up to the light. "He'd had a ring all right," he said as he pointed to the faintly pale circle around Breedlove's finger. "But I never saw it."

"Where do you think it is?"

"Could have fallen off during all that was happening to him," Patterson said. He returned the hand to the carriage. "Who knows?"

"I'll call the sheriff up there," Ben said. "Maybe they found it in the field or in his car or something."

"Were you up there?" Patterson asked as he pushed the carriage back into the wall.

"Yeah."

"Pretty soggy, I guess."

Ben looked at him. "Soggy?"

"Well, from the look of Breedlove's shoes."

"It was a grassy field," Ben said. "It wasn't soggy."

Patterson's eyes took on a sudden intensity. "Well, Breedlove's shoes were covered with some kind of thick, pasty clay. White clay."

"Then he picked it up somewhere else," Ben said. "Did you run any tests on it?"

Patterson shook his head. "No."

"Find out what it is," Ben said quickly, "and let me know as soon as you can."

. . .

Susan Breedlove answered the door almost immediately. She was a small, but slightly overweight woman, with reddish hair and pale complexion. Her son stood at her side, staring silently into Ben's eyes.

"I'm sorry to bother you, Mrs. Breedlove," Ben said as he took off his hat.

"Who are you?"

Ben took out his identification. "Ben Wellman," he said.

Mrs. Breedlove stared at him suspiciously. "Did you know Charlie?"

"Yes."

"I never seen you with him."

"We weren't exactly friends," Ben said. "Not like Daniels."

The woman's eyes continued to watch Ben apprehensively. "Well, thank you for coming," she said at last. Then she stepped back and began to close the door.

Ben caught it in his hand. "I'd like to talk to you for a minute."

"What about?"

"I understand that Charlie's wedding ring was missing."

Mrs. Breedlove's body grew taut. "Somebody stole it."

"It might have fallen off."

She scowled bitterly. "They stole it. The people that killed him." She shook her head resentfully. "There's no way that ring fell off. It was too tight for that. Somebody pulled it off Charlie, that's what happened."

"He had twenty dollars in his wallet," Ben said, "Nobody took that."

For a moment Mrs. Breedlove considered Ben's remark. "I don't know how to explain it," she said finally. "I just know that it didn't fall off my Charlie's finger. Somebody pulled it off." She glanced down at her son, then ran her short fingers through his light-brown hair. "Go on out in the back, Billy," she said.

The child backed away reluctantly, his eyes still on Ben.

Mrs. Breedlove waited until he had disappeared into the back of the house. "Are you looking into all this?" she asked, once the screen door had sounded and she knew the boy had made it to the backyard.

"Yes."

"How come it ain't Harry?"

"They figure he's too close to it, I guess," Ben told her.

She looked at him quizzically. "Wouldn't that be a good thing, though?"

"It might be," Ben said.

She opened the door slightly. "Well, come on in, anyway," she said with a small shrug.

Ben followed her into the small living room. There was a short square television in the corner and a brown, hooked rug on the plain wooden floor.

"The ring, it looked just like this," Mrs. Breedlove said as she placed her hand flat beneath a table lamp. "It had one of them little blue stones, just like this." She smiled to herself, her voice softening as she spoke. "Sapphire they call it. Pretty. It stays that same blue forever. At least that's what the man at the jewelry store said."

Ben stared at the ring. "Did it have anything written on it?"

" 'For Charlie. Love Susan,' " Mrs. Breedlove said. She shrugged. "That's all." Her eyes swept the empty house. "I don't have no family," she said as she lowered herself into a small, plastic-covered chair. "Charlie didn't have none either. That's why it's like this, empty. Nobody to come and comfort us like family people do." She shook her head. "Course, there's been a few dropped by. Harry come over, that was one. And the Chief come. And Mr. Starnes. Some of the neighbors come over for a few minutes this morning. But that ain't the same. Besides them, it's just been me and Billy setting around the house."

Ben took a seat on a small green sofa. "I'm real sorry about Charlie," he said. He waited a moment, watching her face, trying to determine what to ask next. "May I ask you, ma'am, if you knew what Charlie was doing?"

"What do you mean, 'doing'?"

"What he was investigating."

"No, he didn't never talk about it."

"And last night," Ben continued gently. "You were away."

"Charlie told us to leave for the night," Mrs. Breedlove said.

"Why did he want you to do that?"

"Said it was the colored people," Mrs. Breedlove told him. "Said it was because of all the trouble."

"That's all he said?"

"He didn't give no other reason," Mrs. Breedlove said. "He just came home, said he had to take us to the bus station early, picked up our old garden shovel and took us to the station."

"He picked up a shovel?"

"That's right."

"Did he say why?"

"No. He just put it in the backseat of the car and off we went."

"To the bus station?"

"Uh huh."

"And he said he was taking you early because he had someplace he needed to go."

"Someplace to go, right, and that he had to get on over to wherever it was."

"Did he mention where he was going?"

"No," Mrs. Breedlove said. "But he never mentioned things like that. He always kept me in the dark about what he was up to. Charlie was like that. Maybe I knew him a little, but I don't think nobody else did."

"What time did he leave that afternoon?"

"He took us to the bus station at around six, I reckon," Mrs. Breedlove said. "He told me to call him from Huntsville when I got there."

"To call him at home?"

"Yes."

"Which meant that he expected to be back at around eight?"

Mrs. Breedlove nodded. "It's about two hours to Huntsville."

"When did you call him?"

"A little after eight," Mrs. Breedlove said. "But nobody answered. I kept calling every thirty minutes till it was almost morning. By then I was getting real worried. So that's when I called the police back here in Birmingham."

"Who'd you speak to?"

"Captain Starnes," Mrs. Breedlove said. "He sounded funny."

"In what way?"

"Just jumpy-like."

"What did he say?"

"To come on back home to Birmingham," Mrs. Breedlove said. She shrugged. "I guess he already knew about Charlie by then."

Ben looked at her sincerely. "I'm sorry about all these questions," he said.

Mrs. Breedlove watched him intently for another moment, then her eyes drifted toward the back of the house. Through a long narrow hallway, the boy could be seen running back and forth, firing a cap pistol. Mrs. Breedlove smiled slightly. "It's funny how things work. I never had a daddy, now Billy won't have one neither." She looked at Ben. "Did you have a daddy?"

"Yes, ma'am."

Mrs. Breedlove's eyes glistened. "Was he nice?"

"Yes, he was."

She looked away, swallowed hard, then turned back to him. "I sure would like that ring, Mr. Wellman," she said almost pleadingly. "You reckon you might be able to find it for me?"

Ben could feel something harden with him, grow almost murderous in its furious resolve. "Mrs. Breedlove," he said, "I can tell you this: nobody will try any harder."

Thirty-three

Ben had just walked back into the detective bullpen when he heard a voice from behind him.

"What are you doing here, Ben?"

Ben turned toward him. "Working a case."

"What case?" Luther asked as he stepped up to him.

"Same one as before," Ben lied. "That little girl in the ballfield."

Luther shook his head. "Trail's too cold on that one, Ben," he said. "I want you to concentrate on King. He's made two speeches since this morning, and you weren't there for either one of them."

"Plenty of people were," Ben said.

"That's not the point," Luther snapped. "We're two men down since all this shit got started. First Ryan, now Breedlove. We got to tighten our belts."

"How you plan to do that?"

"By dropping the dead-end stuff right now," Luther said emphatically. "Fact is, you haven't brought anything back to the barn on that little girl killing, and the way I figure it, that whole thing is dead in the water."

Ben said nothing. Luther was right, it was dead in the water. A little girl had gotten out of a car, walked out into a littered ballfield and simply disappeared. It was as if she'd been lifted up into the clouds, murdered and raped, then set down again only a few yards from where Ramona Davies had last seen her.

"Am I right, Ben?" Luther asked pointedly.

"I guess so."

"I'm glad you can admit it," Luther said. He glanced at his watch.

"King's giving a final pep talk at Sixteenth Street in half an hour. Be there."

For a moment Ben stood in place and watched as Luther spun around and rushed away, his body plunging loudly through the double doors. Then, reluctantly, he felt himself slowly begin to cave in under the weight of the Captain's authority. But he also recognized that it was a weight which had become more burdensome to him during the last few days, and even as he strode out of the bullpen and headed for his car, he could feel it bearing down upon him in a way that seemed different than it ever had before, heavy, but also willfully malicious, like something chewing at his flesh while it rested on his shoulders.

The mood in and around the Sixteenth Street Baptist Church had changed considerably since the last time Ben had stood outside and listened as King's voice swept out over the wildly jubilant crowd. The dogs and water hoses had not broken the spirit of the young people who now gathered on the steps and along the cement walkways, but it had changed it visibly. Faces had darkened and grown sullen, eyes more set and watchful. The murmur of the crowd seemed more tense, and the strange, transcending joy he remembered from the day before had been transformed into a grim and bitter determination, one that seemed poised for explosive action.

Not far away, the Langley brothers slouched against Black Cat 13, their eyes scanning the crowd suspiciously. Tod sat on the front fender, his legs dangling toward the ground. Teddy stood beside him, straight and tall, as if at attention before the continually shifting crowd. For an instant he stared rigidly at Ben, his eyes squinting in the light. Then he turned away briskly and walked to the rear of the car. His brother followed him instantly, sliding off the fender, his body plowing through the thick layer of dust that had gathered on the hood. For a time they talked together, huddled closely, their faces nearly touching. Then they parted, Tod going in one direction and Teddy in the other.

The sound of the church choir began almost immediately, and Ben glanced up at the loudspeakers which had been installed outside the building. It was a rousing version of "Leaning on the Everlasting Arm," but the people on the streets and sidewalks only listened silently, without joining in, their bodies held rigidly erect, rather than swaying to the beat of the old hymn as Ben had seen them do in the days before.

One hymn followed another, and as the singing continued, Ben let his eyes sweep over the crowd once again. He began to see faces he recognized from the streets of Bearmatch. They were the people who'd passed his car while he parked beside the old ballfield, or whom he'd seen along the way, faces that had glanced at him from bus stops, alleyways or tumbled-down porches, always dark with large brown eyes, lost in a blur until his own familiarity had suddenly made them identifiable, faces he'd seen now more than once, faces that had repeatedly marched down Fourth Avenue, confronted the dogs and water hoses, watched him from behind the bars of holding cells or peered at him from the dusty windows of countless school buses. For a little while it was as if he knew everyone around him, had struggled through some common experience with them, shared something fierce, grave, intense, and because of that, now had some small investment in the outcome of their lives.

"I know you're tired," King's voice rang out suddenly over the steadily more animated crowd.

"I know you're weary."

A few shouts of "Amen" rose from the crowd, followed by scattered applause.

"But we must go forward in Birmingham."

There were a few more shouts of "Amen," and the smattering of applause increased by a barely audible degree.

"And I know there are some people that want us to move on."

"Yes, Lord," someone shouted, and the crowd applauded again, this time with a slightly increased force.

"But we're staying right here in Birmingham until justice comes," King cried.

Ben took out his notebook and flipped through it to the first blank page.

"Governor Wallace may not want us here," King shouted. "But there is a higher authority than he is."

The "amens" now began to burst steadily from the crowd.

"And Mayor Hanes may not want us here," King cried, his lean metallic voice recharging the previously exhausted air. "But there is a higher authority than he is. For God is in His Heaven, and He is watching over His own."

Ben pressed his pen down on the paper.

"How long will we stay in Birmingham?" King demanded. "Not long. Because no lie can live forever."

The applause now rose over the isolated shouts of "Amen" and "Yes, Lord." It swept along the streets in a tidal flow, building more fiercely as it moved.

"How long? Not long, because truth crushed to earth will rise again."

Now the applause took on bursts of wild cheering which seemed to break like fireworks over the heads of the crowd.

"How long? Not long, because although the moral arc of the universe is wide, it still bends toward justice."

Now the cheers and applause mingled in a single sustained roar which moved back and forth from the church to the streets and back to the church again, building with each pass, feeding on itself, growing stronger with each sustaining wave.

Ben looked up from his notebook, his fingers loosening halfheartedly around the pen, his eyes now focused on the church, his ears attentive to the voice.

"How long? Not long. Because God is tramping through the vineyard where the grapes of wrath are stored."

The crowd began to jump and shout, sing and dance, hundreds of long brown arms swaying in the sweltering air.

"How long? Not long? For His truth is marching on!"

The roar of the crowd seemed to rise in one long, mighty chorus, and as Ben stood beside the tree and listened to its fierce, rebellious glory, he found himself suddenly caught up and inexplicably lifted by its amazing grace.

"What are you doing?"

Ben turned toward the voice. It was Coggins. He was staring at him lethally.

"What are you doing?" he repeated as he nodded toward the still open notebook.

Ben felt his mouth open speechlessly.

Coggins' eyes filled with a strange disappointment as they returned to the notebook, then lifted up again and settled on Ben's face. "My God," he said despairingly. He shook his head. "My God."

For a moment Luther simply stared at the small notebook which Ben had placed on his desk. Then he picked it up and flipped through the blank pages. "There's nothing written in here," he said finally.

"He didn't say much," Ben said with a slight shrug.

"Looks to me like he didn't say anything at all," Luther replied. Once again he flipped through the empty notebook. "I didn't tell you to write down whatever you wanted to, Ben," he said. "I told you to write down everything King said."

Ben glanced away, his eyes on the window to the right of Luther's desk. He did not speak.

Luther stared at him accusingly. "Did you go to the church?"

"Yes."

"Did King make a speech?"

"Yes."

Luther lifted the notebook and waved it in the air. "Well, where is it? There's nothing but a bunch of blank pages in this thing."

"I didn't take anything down," Ben said.

"Nothing?" Luther said, astonished. "Not one goddamn word?"

"No."

Luther slapped the notebook down on his desk. "Then what are you giving me this thing for?"

"I'm turning it in," Ben said suddenly, before he could catch himself.

"Turning it in?"

"Yeah," Ben said, this time more firmly. "I don't want that assignment anymore."

Luther's eyes narrowed into two small slits. "Since when do you decide what your assignments are, Sergeant?" he asked angrily.

Ben said nothing.

"You realize how shorthanded we are?" Luther asked.

Ben remained silent.

Luther stood up. "You have an official assignment," he said sternly. "I expect you to carry it out."

Ben stared at him evenly. "No."

"I order you to carry it out."

Ben shook his head.

Luther's body tightened. "Turn in your badge, Sergeant Wellman."

For a moment Ben hesitated. He had never faced anything more sweeping in its cause or transforming in its result, and for an instant he tried to find a way around it. But he felt his hand around the pen again, stark and inanimate, and he knew that he could never make it move across the page.

"Your badge, Sergeant," Luther repeated.

Ben slowly pulled the badge and identification folder from his jacket pocket. It felt heavy, as if everything he had were attached to it. Once again he hesitated. Then he lowered it to the table and let it go.

Luther glanced at it quickly, then looked at Ben. "Don't expect a good recommendation from this department," he said coldly. "As far as I'm concerned, you've deserted under fire."

Thirty-four

Esther was sitting quietly on her porch when Ben pulled the car up in front of her house and got out. Several hours had passed since he'd left Luther's office, and during that time, he'd simply driven around the city, trying to come to terms with what he'd done. At first it had been a relief, a sudden throwing off of the worries which had been accumulating during the preceding days. He had walked out of the headquarters with his head in the air, driven the streets of Birmingham in a spirit of exhilarating liberation, and then, as evening fell, found himself once again in Bearmatch.

Esther sat up slightly as Ben edged his way past the little wire fence and stood at the bottom of the stairs, his hat in his hand, his eyes fixed on the dark, silent woman who watched him warily from her chair.

"You don't have to worry about me showing up at your door again," Ben assured her quickly. "I'm not on Doreen's case anymore." He smiled. "Fact is, I'm not on any kind of case."

Esther continued to stare at him mutely, her dark eyes trained on his face.

"I sort of quit, I guess," Ben said. "Or got fired."

"From the police?" Esther asked.

"Yes."

"How come?"

"They had me doing things that I didn't want to do."

Esther shook her head. "Lord, if everybody did that, there wouldn't be a soul left working in Birmingham."

"I guess so," Ben said with a slight smile. "Anyway, I just wanted to tell you that I was off her case, and that's all I came to say." He started to turn back toward the car, but her voice drew him around to her again.

"Who's looking into it, then?"

"I don't know."

"Probably nobody."

Ben nodded. "You could be right about that."

"So it's all over then," Esther said. She fanned her face with a white handkerchief. "I didn't think it'd come to much."

"I tried, Miss Ballinger," Ben said. "I surely tried."

"You think Bluto did it?" Esther asked him pointedly. "You think he had the sense for it?"

Ben looked at her evenly. "Maybe the sense to do it," he said. "But not the meanness."

"So you don't think he killed Doreen?"

"I don't know who killed her," Ben admitted. "I don't have any idea at all." He shook his head mournfully. "I don't guess you believe that," he said softly. "I don't guess there's any way to make you believe it."

For the first time, her eyes seemed to embrace him gently, almost lovingly, as if to do the work her arms could never do.

Ben had been back in his house for several hours before he finally stopped trying to figure out all the things he wouldn't have to do anymore. He wouldn't have to fill out arrest sheets, sit for hours outside some courtroom, listen to the Chief's speeches or drink coffee from the machine in the detectives' lounge. He could hardly have been more willing to give up such things. But there were other parts of his job, as well, and there were a few he didn't want to give up. He would not be able to search through Bearmatch anymore, or follow Bluto's zigzag trail during the hours before he died, or pace the bare worn path which led from the torn storm fence to the cement drain where Doreen Ballinger had died. These things needed to be done, but they had been lost in the instant his badge had come to rest on Luther's desk, lost with the coffee and the courtroom boredom. His badge was gone, and because of that, he seemed to weigh less now than before he removed it, to float from room to room, anchorless and without direction. The badge, his job, had served to hold him in place, guide him through the world's confusion with a reliable set of duties and obligations. He had thought that it had only provided him with a living, but slowly, as the night wore on, he realized that it had also provided him with a reason to live, and that without it, he would have to improvise a certain part of his life until he could work out a new set of guidelines, hammer out a wholly different badge. He was making the first attempts at doing exactly that when, around midnight, Lamar Beacham knocked at the screen door.

"I'm glad I found you awake," Lamar said, his face strangely gray and spectral behind the wire screen.

Ben smiled slightly and waved him inside. "Come on in, Lamar. What are you doing out so late?"

Lamar walked into the living room and stood awkwardly, his hands thrust deep down in his trouser pockets. He had the look of a misplaced farmboy, lank and slender, with blondish, windblown hair and skin that looked as if it had been toasted lightly by the fire.

"I heard you quit the police today," he said.

Ben nodded.

"How come?"

"They had me doing stuff I didn't want to do."

"Like what?"

"Following King around, writing down what he said," Ben told him. He shook his head in mild disgust. "That's not decent work for a man, Lamar."

"Well, spraying people with water hoses ain't much better," Lamar said wearily. He walked over to the chair opposite Ben and sat down.

"Want some ice tea?" Ben asked, lifting his half-empty glass.

"Tea? No. But I wouldn't say no to a beer."

"All gone."

"Mine, too," Lamar said. "I went out to get another six-pack, but the package store was closed." He smiled. "So I just kept on driving around. Finally I ended up over here."

"Something on your mind?"

"I'm thinking about quitting, too," Lamar said flatly. "You know, the same thing you did."

Ben smiled. "Well, good for you," he said. "I hope everybody quits."

"I don't think the landlords would feel that way."

"You'd get another job."

"I guess so," Lamar said. "What about you?"

"I guess I'll get another one too."

"You got much money to live on till then?"

Ben smiled. "Three hundred and seventeen dollars is what I've got in the bank."

Lamar laughed. "Four dollars more than me," he said. Then, suddenly, the smile disappeared. "Charlie Breedlove was my cousin, did you know that, Ben?"

"No."

"Did he ever talk to you much?"

Ben shook his head, his eyes suddenly focusing more closely on Lamar's face.

"You got any idea who killed him?" Lamar asked bluntly.

"No, I don't," Ben said.

For a moment Lamar watched Ben intently. "You got any idea what he was up to?" he asked at last.

Ben straightened himself slightly. "What are you getting at, Lamar?"

"He wasn't what he looked to be," Lamar said, his voice suddenly taking on a strange softness. "He was a lot better than he looked to be."

"Meaning what?"

"He couldn't trust anybody in the department," Lamar went on. "He couldn't even trust you. At least not for sure." He stared at Ben warily. "Hell, Ben, I'm not even sure I can trust you, but when I found out you'd quit over this King thing, I figured I'd have to take a chance, and you were the only guy I felt like I could take it with."

"A chance on what?"

"Telling a few things," Lamar said. "About Charlie."

"What things?"

Lamar hesitated.

"You've gone too far to go back, Lamar," Ben said. He shrugged. "Besides, I'm just a regular citizen now."

Lamar shook his head assuredly. "No, you're not. If I thought that, I wouldn't be here." He took a long slow breath, inhaling deeply, then holding it in for what seemed an impossibly long time while his eyes stared piercingly into Ben's face.

"Okay," he said finally. "I'll let it fly. Once I'm done, it's up to you."

"Go ahead," Ben said without hesitation.

"I don't know if it has anything to do with his death or not," Lamar began, "but whoever killed him got it right."

"Got what right?"

"Well, that he was an informer."

"Are you sure?"

"Yes."

"Who'd he work for?"

"I don't know," Lamar said. "But he was gathering stuff on people, and he was going to let it all out some way."

"What kind of stuff?"

"Racial stuff," Lamar said. "You know, about the situation here."

"You mean things about the Klan, things like that?"

"Things in the department," Lamar said. "Police things. He was keeping an eye on what was going on in the department."

"But you don't know who he was reporting to?"

"No, I don't, Ben," Lamar said. "I really don't. But the way I see it, somebody could have found out about Charlie, and that's why they did what they did to him."

"How do you know about this?" Ben asked.

"Charlie told me."

"Why?"

" 'Cause he was getting scared," Lamar said. "Real scared. But I'm not sure it was for himself, you know?"

"What do you mean?"

"He was close to something," Lamar said, "and it was scaring him to death."

"When did you talk to him last?"

"The night he died," Lamar said. "He called me up and said he'd sent Susan and Billy out of town for a while. He said he was checking up on a few things."

"But he didn't say what?"

"No, he didn't," Lamar said. "But that night, the one he died, he was really on edge, and he did something he'd never done before. He called me up, he said, 'Lamar, do you remember when we used to go caving together?' " Lamar's face softened. "We used to go caving up in De Kalb County. You know, just boys looking for danger."

Ben nodded.

"Anyway," Lamar said, returning to the subject, "Charlie said, 'Well, you know how we used to let somebody know where we was going, just in case we got stuck?' I said yeah, I remembered that, and he said, 'Well, this is where I'm going tonight,' and he gave me an address."

Ben felt his bones grow hard within his flesh, stiffen, turn to steel. "What address?"

"I wrote it down," Lamar said. He reached into his pants pocket and handed Ben a folded piece of lined paper. "Here it is."

Ben opened the paper and looked at the address. "Have you taken a look at this place?"

Lamar shook his head. "No, I haven't," he said quickly. "I'm not like Charlie was. I'm an ordinary-type guy. But Charlie, he was brave." He smiled quietly. "You'd have to be to think the things he did."

"What things?"

"Against the Chief," Lamar explained. "Against the way things are."

"So you don't think he was doing it for money?" Ben asked.

"Informing, you mean?" Lamar asked. "For money?" He waved his hand. "Oh, hell, no, Ben," he said. "Not Charlie. Whatever he was doing, he was doing it for his own self."

"Are you sure?"

"Let me tell you something," Lamar replied. "When Charlie was just a boy, he lived in a small town in the Black Belt. It was one of those one-horse towns—you know, the kind with one main street, unpaved."

Ben nodded.

"When it rained, the place turned to mud," Lamar went on. "And there was only one narrow sidewalk on each side of the street. And one time, after a rain, Charlie was walking down one of those sidewalks. An old colored woman was walking on it to, walking toward him, an old woman, with her arms full of groceries. And she stepped off into the mud and let Charlie pass by. Without a thought, she stepped right off that sidewalk and went down ankle deep in mud. Charlie never forgot that. So when this whole business started with the colored, he decided to do what he could for them."

Ben watched Lamar silently while he thought about Breedlove again, about the things he said, the way he joked with the Langleys or slammed Leroy Coggins up against the wall.

Lamar's right eye narrowed somewhat. "Did you see him, Ben?" he asked after a moment. "His body, I mean."

"Yes."

"I heard it was real bad."

"It was."

"I hope something can be done about it," Lamar added, as if in conclusion. "It shouldn't be left to rest."

For a moment Ben saw Charlie Breedlove's ravaged body as it hung lifelessly from the tree, the head slumped forward, concealing the blasted face. "It won't be," he said.

Thirty-five

Ben glanced down at the address Lamar had given him, matching it carefully with the small frame house which faced him from across the street. The house itself looked bleak and untended, and the yard which stretched out in front of it was bare except for occasional clusters of wild onions or crabgrass. A stand of poke salad rose along the sides of the tiny cement porch, but there were no flowers or green shrubbery to relieve the overall feeling of abandonment.

The driveway was little more than two parallel ruts in the muddy ground, but even from his position across the street, Ben could see recently made tire tracks. For a moment he stared at them, as if the pattern of the tread marks might suddenly form itself into a written message. Then, slowly, he settled his eyes once again upon the house.

Despite the heat its windows remained tightly closed with wooden shutters, as if someone were trying to seal off the interior, protect it from prying eyes. For a long time Ben watched the shutters, trying to peer through their bleak, unpainted slats. He was looking for movement, a passing shadow, anything that might signal someone's presence in the house. Finally he gave up, drew in a long slow breath and got out of his car.

He circled the house once, then again, concentrating on the windows. Shutters had been put up over most of them, but a few had simply had their glass panes covered over with a thick, impenetrable black paint on the inside.

The back door was nailed shut, and the front was secured by what Ben assumed to be a dead bolt. He knew that he would have to batter the door down, that it would not simply spring open if he slammed into it. Once again he circled the house, his eyes searching for some less daunting entrance. But the house had been converted into a wooden fortress, impregnable to the usual means.

He circled the house once again, then shrugged helplessly. He couldn't simply take the fireman's ax from the trunk of his car and splinter the door. For a moment he stood silently in the still, dark air and stared at the house, his eyes moving along the tiny porch, then up the front door, and finally over the drooping metal drains to where a short brick chimney sat firmly at the crest of the roof. A dark, smudgy layer surrounded the chimney vents, and Ben realized instantly that the chimney had once been used to draw up the thick, black smoke of a coal stove. Because of that, the house had to have a coal chute somewhere along its foundation.

It took him only a few minutes to find it, a small square which had been cut out of the cement foundation and covered over with a flimsy wooden door. Ben glanced around, hoping that he had not been seen, then crawled quickly through the hole.

In the dank, musty darkness, he could see a square made of thin lines of light. He lowered himself onto his belly and slowly pulled himself across the ground until he was directly beneath the light. Then he turned over and pressed upward, his hand flat against the underfloor. The tiny metal hinges of the trapdoor creaked very slightly as it opened, flooding the crawlspace with light.

For a moment he waited, his back pressed against the ground, and listened. Then he pulled himself up slowly, opening the trapdoor further and further until it fell backward and slammed onto the floor.

He got to his feet quickly, hoisted himself up into the house, then closed the trapdoor. A single lamp was burning in the room, and in its faded yellow glow Ben could see a huge blue circle painted on the opposite wall. Inside the circle two black zigzag lines ran parallel to one another and vertically from the lower curve of the circle. Two words had been painted in white, their full letters pressing out against the dark lines. They spelled out the words PURE BLOOD. Two grainy photographs had been taped to the wall on either side of the blue circle. They showed a young white girl being kissed passionately by an old Negro man who stared wickedly at the camera.

Ben turned slowly, allowing his eyes to search the room item by item. Several high-powered hunting rifles leaned together in one corner, along with a scattering of automatic pistols. Boxes of ammunition were stacked beside the guns, arranged by caliber, their tops already opened for immediate access.

A single wooden cot rested just to the left, and beyond it, a small metal desk whose sides were covered with slogans. There was a mail-order catalogue open on the desk. It was from a weapons importer, and it displayed two full-color ads for various foreign-made automatic rifles.

Ben stepped over immediately, picked up the catalogue and looked at the mailing address. It had been sent to Teddy Langley.

The desk's top drawer was not locked, and Ben opened it. There were pencils, pens, sheets of paper and a stack of twenty or thirty copies of the same picture that hung on the wall. Someone had scrawled a sentence above each photograph: **Is this what you want for your children????**

The second drawer was also open, and as Ben quickly riffled through it, he found more catalogues of weapons and paramilitary materials, along with messages and memos which appeared to have been written by Teddy Langley to himself or to his brother. They were mostly filled with racial slurs and rabid exhortations to violent action. Ben made a brief effort to comprehend Langley's mind, so clogged with hatred that it seemed hardly capable of light or air or the simplest of life's humanities, its small acts of mercy, kindness and generosity. He tried to imagine how Langley, or anyone else, could become so addicted to his own poison that it became his life's blood. And yet, as Ben continued through the desk, it was clear that this was exactly what had happened to Langley. Without his hatred, he was nothing. It was what gave his life a meaning, a purpose.

The third and final drawer was cluttered with an assortment of unconnected items. A police badge, a belt buckle, several packs of matches, a pair of scissors, tape, paper clips. There was a twenty-two pistol and a half-empty box of shells, a small pocket knife and a bottle of aspirin. A roll of electrical tape was nestled in the left-hand corner of the drawer, and as Ben picked it up, he noticed a small circular ridge on its surface. He peeled the tape back slowly, spooking it over his hands as he unraveled it. The ridge grew more visible until the last strand of tape was peeled from its surface. It was a gold wedding band, and as Ben turned it slowly in his fingers, he could read the inscription plainly: For Charlie. Love Susan.

"Charlie Breedlove's ring," Ben said as he tossed it onto Luther's desk.

Luther picked it up and stared at it unbelievingly. "How do you know?"

"His wife told Patterson it was missing," Ben said. "When I talked to her about it, she told me the inscription."

Luther continued to roll the ring between his fingers. "Where'd you find it?"

"It was wrapped up in a roll of electrical tape," Ben said. "I found it in a little house over on Courtland."

"Courtland?"

"That's right."

"Whose house?"

"There was some mail in a desk. It was all addressed to Teddy Langley."

Luther's face grew rigid, and his light-blue eyes seemed to go pure white. "Langley?"

"It's full of racial stuff," Ben said. He handed Luther one of the pictures he'd found in Langley's desk.

"Oh, sweet Jesus," Luther groaned as he stared at it.

"Did you know Langley was caught up in stuff like that?" Ben asked.

Luther shook his head. "I knew he wasn't liked over in Bear-match, that he was always busting up their shothouses and roughing people up." His eyes shot up to Ben. "But no, I didn't know he was into trash like this." He leaned back in his chair. His eyes settled onto the picture once again, held there a moment, then lifted toward Ben. "Do you think he killed Charlie Breedlove?"

Ben nodded. "Maybe."

"Why?" Luther asked. "Because he thought Breedlove was an informer?"

"Yes."

Luther eased himself forward and placed his elbows on his desk. "But if Breedlove really was an informer," he said, "then who in hell was he reporting to?"

"I don't know."

Luther stared at him accusingly. "Bullshit."

"I don't know, Captain," Ben said firmly.

"Well, how'd you know about this house on Courtland Street?"

"I got a tip."

Luther's face turned sour. "A tip?" he demanded. "What kind of tip?"

Ben didn't answer.

Luther glared at him irritably. "Are you telling me that you've got your own little nest of informers in the Police Department?"

"Not in the Police Department," Ben said. "That's all I can tell you."

Luther did not seem to know what to do. His eyes appeared to grow large and menacing, but with an anger which he could not direct toward anything or anyone. "All right," he said finally. "We'll do it this way. You're back on the force, Ben."

Ben said nothing.

"Do you want to be back on the force?"

"I guess so."

"Good," Luther said. "I'm glad to hear it. Because I've already got your first assignment for you."

Ben waited, half-expecting it to have something to do with Martin Luther King.

"The first assignment, Ben," Luther said, almost tauntingly, "is to find Teddy Langley and bring his ass to me."

Thirty-six

It took Ben several hours finally to spot Black Cat 13. It was parked under a shade tree in the heart of Bearmatch, and Langley was resting leisurely on the hood, a cigarette dangling from his mouth and a bottle of Double Cola in his hand.

"I wouldn't mess with me if I were you," Langley said as Ben approached him. "That shit at headquarters, that was a free one. It's the only one you're ever going to get." He took a hard pull on the bottle, then wiped his forehead with his fist.

"I been trying to find you all morning," Ben said.

Langley laughed sneeringly, the cigarette bobbing up and down from the right corner of his mouth. "Well, maybe you got me so scared of you I was hiding out." He smiled grimly. "I guess that's what ever-body in the department thinks, anyway." He plucked the cigarette from his mouth and tossed it out into the street. "But they don't know everything. Not by a long shot, by God."

"Where've you been all morning?" Ben asked crisply.

"Here and there."

"Don't you ever report in to headquarters?"

"When I want to."

"Everybody else has to it whether they want to or not."

"Everybody else works something besides Bearmatch," Langley said. This time the smile had an edge of bitterness. "Niggers got their own time, and that's what I got to keep track of."

Ben leaned against the tree, nudging his shoulder up hard against it. "Where do you live, Teddy?"

"Right in town."

"I mean the address."

Langley eyed him cautiously. "What do you care where I live? You ain't invited to supper."

"I looked your address up in the personnel file," Ben said. "It said you lived in a trailer park on the south side."

"So what?"

"Do you still live there?"

"What's it to you where I live?" Langley asked resentfully.

"Scottish Glen Trailer Park, is that right?"

Langley watched him irritably. "You doing the census?"

Ben let it pass. "What'd you know about Charlie Breedlove?" he asked bluntly.

"Nothing."

"Did you like him?"

"Nothing special."

Ben stared at him evenly. "You glad he's dead?"

Langley shrugged halfheartedly. "It didn't mean much to me one way or the other."

"Some people might think that's a strange attitude," Ben said cautiously.

"What do I care what some people think?" Langley said irritably. "Some people think we should eat and go to school and have babies with niggers."

"Is that what Breedlove thought?"

A short, edgy laugh suddenly broke out of Langley. "Well, I'll be shit, Ben, you must have figured Breedlove out." He slapped his knee and laughed again, this time more freely. "Hell, boy, you're better than I thought."

"What are you talking about? Figured out what?"

"That Breedlove was an informer."

"What makes you think that?" Ben asked, astonished at Langley's bluntness.

"Hell, I'm no fool," Langley said. "It was easy to spot. He was always overdoing it. Nigger this and nigger that. Always yelling at them, pushing them around. He was always doing that kind of shit."

"So do you."

"Yeah, but with some people, when they do it, it's for real. You can tell. They got blood in their eye, you might say."

"And Breedlove didn't?"

"Hell, no," Langley said. "With Breedlove it was all an act." He waved his hand. "I always knew that. It was just for show. There was nothing to it. He was just doing it to cover up for something."

"And because of that, you fingered him for an informer?"

"Well, you figure it this way: Maybe it's an act because he wants to be like the rest of us, a real tough guy, something like that. So, to look good, he slaps a dumb burrhead up against the wall once in a while. Or maybe it's something else. Maybe he's acting this way because these ain't his real feelings at all. Matter of fact, his real feelings is just the opposite." He took an idle swig from the bottle. "That's how I figured it with Breedlove."

Ben nodded. "But did you have any proof?"

"Proof?" Langley asked. "That he was an informer? No, I never had no proof. I just knew it, that's all." His eyes slid up toward the overhanging limbs, then dropped back to Ben. "Just like I know you for a nigger lover, Ben," he said. Then he smiled. "Course, you don't make much a secret of that, do you?"

"I guess not."

Langley drained the last of the cola, then tossed the bottle into the yard beyond the cracked sidewalk. "They decide to put you on the case?" he asked.

"Which one?"

"The Breedlove thing."

"You might say that," Ben told him.

"Why you?"

"Maybe because I'm a nigger lover."

Langley laughed. "You know why I didn't beat the shit of you back at headquarters?"

Ben did not answer.

" 'Cause that's exactly what the niggers would want," Langley said. "A full-scale fight between two white cops would have got us both fired." He shook his head. "And then I wouldn't be busting heads in Bearmatch anymore, breaking up their crap games, raiding their stinking shothouses, smashing their little basement stills and chasing their whores out of town." He smiled cunningly. "That's why I didn't whop your ass, Ben," he said with a sudden coldness. "But I can't always be depended upon to control myself."

Again, Ben kept silent. He could see the sort of rage that swept back and forth like a hot wind in Langley's mind, and he wanted to cool it slightly, coax more talk out of him.

"Where's Tod?" he asked finally.

"Sick," Langley answered dully. "He's got a fever, so he didn't come in." He glanced up and down the street, his face grim and oddly bitter. "If you worked this shithole," he said at last, "you'd get just like me."

"I thought you liked it."

"I do," Langley said, lifting his face proudly. "You know why? 'Cause I can do some good here. For my own damn race." He eased himself off the hood of the car, leaving a wide swath across its dusty, unwashed surface. "Well, that's about all I got to say to you. I mean, you know how it is, a cop's got to be on the street."

Ben touched his arm. "Not yet," he said.

Langley stopped abruptly and turned toward him. "I meant what I said just now," he said grimly. "Don't you ever make a move on me again."

"I took a look inside a little house this morning," Ben began.

"What house?"

"Little wood-frame thing, over on Courtland."

Langley's face turned rigid but he didn't speak.

"You know the one I'm talking about?"

Langley did not answer.

"Sort of let go, the house," Ben went on. "No paint. A lot of crabgrass."

Langley shifted nervously on his feet. "What about it?"

"You don't live there, do you?"

"No."

"Why do you keep it?"

"That's my business."

"It's some sort of headquarters, right?" Ben asked.

"I can think whatever I want to," Langley said bitterly. "I don't have to account for it. And I'll tell you something else. The niggers, they got some sympathy right now, but deep in every white man's heart they's just one truth. You know it, and I know it, and they's not a white man on earth that don't know it."

"What's that, Teddy?"

"A nigger is lower than a white man," Langley said authoritatively. "He's closer to the monkeys. Nothing's ever going to change that fact. Not Martin Luther King, or the Kennedy brothers, or you or Breedlove, or anybody else. Race is race, and that's the end of it." He started for his car again, but this time Ben grasped his upper arm firmly.

"I have to bring you back to headquarters, Teddy," he said.

Langley looked at him astonished. "Headquarters?"

"That's right."

"Why?"

"Some people want to talk to you."

"What people?"

"Captain Starnes," Ben said. "Me."

Langley started to laugh, then abruptly stopped himself. "Because of that house?" he asked with a laugh. "Shit, I don't make no secret about how I feel. I know people don't like some of the things I got in that house. Those pictures. I know that. But they'll get used to seeing them. You know why? Because they like the ideas behind them. They know it's the truth."

"I found a ring in your desk," Ben told him quietly. "Third drawer down."

"What desk?"

"The one you have in that little house on Courtland."

Langley looked at him quizzically. "Who told you about that place, anyway?" he asked.

"Breedlove told someone where he was going the night he was killed. He gave the Courtland address."

Langley stared at Ben wonderingly. "He told somebody he was going over there?"

"Yes."

"Was it you he told?"

"No."

"But somebody told you, and you went over there to have a look around."

"That's right."

Langley laughed bitterly. "Shit, Ben, you do more than love niggers, you pimp for them."

Ben felt his fingers draw more tightly around Langley's arm. "I found a ring," he repeated. "It was wrapped up in a spool of electrical tape." He watched Langley's eyes as he delivered the last line. "It belonged to Charlie Breedlove. He wore it the night he was killed."

Langley's face paled in a sudden realization. "So that's it, then," he said quietly. "They're going to pin it on me."

"Where were you the last night?" Ben asked.

Langley looked at him mockingly. "What difference does it make?"

"We're talking about a murder," Ben said.

"And so you want me to come up with some alibi?"

"I want to know where you were."

Langley shook his head. "It don't matter. The niggers want me strung up. The big wheels want that, too. I embarrass them."

"Where were you?" Ben repeated.

"I was with Tod," Langley said determinedly. "He was sick last night, just like I told you. Had a fever. I tended to him all night."

"Did anybody else see you?"

"No," Langley replied. "It was just me and Tod in his house. All alone. By ourselves. Just me and Tod. You figure anybody'll believe that?"

Ben did not answer.

"Hell, no," Langley said firmly. "Not a soul." He shook his head. "I'm already gone. They've already stuck me in the pen. Locked up tight." He smiled haughtily. "But I'll tell you one thing, by God: when the people come back to their senses, I'll be a goddamn hero. They'll bring me out of jail on their shoulders."

Ben tugged him forward toward his car. "Maybe so, Teddy," he said. "But not yet."

Thirty-seven

Luther pounded his fist on the desk. "Goddammit, Teddy!" he cried. "What is this about a house and crazy pictures on the walls and shit like that?"

Langley sat calmly in a chair across from Luther's desk, his eyes shifting slowly from one face to the next.

Ben stood in the left corner by the window. Daniels leaned on the wall opposite him, his eyes watching Langley steadily.

"What's in that house, Teddy?" Luther demanded.

"You already know," Langley replied almost offhandedly. "Wellman's already told you. You've already found everything you need."

Luther leaned toward him menacingly. "Crazy shit, right?"

Langley said nothing.

"Goddammit, Teddy, you know what this makes us look like?" Luther demanded. "Like a bunch of idiots, morons!"

Daniels straightened himself from the wall. "I don't give a shit about that house," he said. "But if you laid one goddamn finger on Charlie Breedlove, I'll—"

Langley shook his head despairingly. "They'll do it for you, Harry," he said. "They already have."

Daniels stared at Langley threateningly. "Did you kill Charlie?"

"No."

Daniels stepped away from the wall. "Don't you lie to me, Teddy. Charlie Breedlove was my partner."

"I didn't lay a hand on Charlie Breedlove," Langley said coldly. "I figure the FBI did it. They been after all of us, sniffing around, trying to pin things on us."

"FBI, my ass," Daniels hissed. He scooped the ring from the top of Luther's desk and pressed to within a few inches of Langley's face.

"You see this, Teddy? This was Charlie's wedding ring. You know where Ben found it?"

Langley didn't bother to answer.

Suddenly, Daniels stepped over and slapped his face. "Do you know where he found it, you little shit!"

Luther jumped to his feet. "Stop it, Harry," he shouted. "Give me that goddamn ring." He snapped it from Daniels' fingers. "Where'd you get this?" he demanded, his eyes bearing down on Langley.

"I never seen it before," Langley said sullenly.

"Harry already took it over to Mrs. Breedlove," Luther said. "She identified it. She said it was definitely Charlie's."

Langley remained silent.

"Where'd you get it, Teddy?" Luther repeated.

Langley shook his head. "I never seen it before."

Luther picked up the roll of electrical tape and held it in the air. "How about this? You ever seen this tape before?"

"No."

"You didn't buy it?" Luther continued insistently. "It didn't belong to you?"

"No."

"It looks like the same kind of tape that was wrapped about Breedlove's hands," Luther said.

Langley's eyes shifted slowly to the right, settling on Ben's. "I never saw that tape. I never saw that ring. The niggers are doing this. Them and their big-wheel friends."

"Niggers?" Luther cried. "You think they killed Breedlove?" He laughed. "You're up to your neck in bullshit, Teddy. You're spilling over with it."

Langley drew his eyes away from Ben, then let them drift back to Luther. "You going to arrest me?"

"You got a reason I shouldn't?"

"I was with my brother."

"That may be true, Teddy," Luther replied icily. "But the question is, where were the two of you?"

"We was in our trailer, that's where we was."

"It probably took two people to hang Breedlove up the way he was," Luther said accusingly.

"Me and Tod, right?" Langley said with a snide laugh. "That's the way you figure it?"

"It's beginning to look that way."

Langley tightened his lips. His eyes returned to Ben, but he did not speak.

"Where's Tod now?" Luther demanded.

"At home."

"Home, or that little dump you got over on Courtland?"

"Home," Langley said. "You know, the trailer."

"And I guess he'll say you two were together all night?"

Langley nodded.

"And that you were in the trailer?"

"That's right," Langley said. "He was sick. He had a fever. He's my brother, and so it's my job to see after him when he's feeling bad."

Daniels stepped over to face Langley. "Let me tell you something, Teddy," he said. "If you hurt Charlie, I'm going to deal with you myself."

Langley stared coldly into Daniels' face. "I didn't lay a finger on your asshole buddy," he spat, "but Breedlove was a goddamn informer, and it don't surprise me a bit that he ended up dead."

Instantly, Daniels raised his hand to strike Langley, but Luther grabbed his hand. "You want your job, Harry, you let me handle this."

Daniels' hand trembled in place for a moment, then lowered slowly. "Okay," he said. "You're right, Captain."

Luther let go of Daniels' hand, then turned to Ben. "Go over and check on Tod," he said. "See what he has to say."

Ben nodded quickly, then stepped toward the door.

"Oh, by the way," Luther said, "you forgot this when you left this morning."

Ben turned around in time to see Luther toss his badge toward him from across the room.

The Langleys' trailer sat on plain gray cinderblocks at the back corner of the lot. Other trailers were scattered across the bare ground, their doors and windows flung open against the baking heat. A few work shirts and tattered bedsheets hung from the communal clothesline at the opposite end of the field, and beyond it, Ben could see a rusty set of swings and a crude seesaw.

Tod Langley opened the door slightly, and Ben could see a single eye peering at him from the darkness behind it.

"I need to talk to you, Tod," he said.

"Me?" Tod asked surprised. "Where's Teddy?"

"He's still on duty," Ben told him.

Tod still did not open the door. "Well, I don't know," he said, hesitant, an edgy fear in his voice. "I mean, after the way you done with Teddy, I—"

"It's not about that," Ben assured him.

"Well, what is it then?"

"It's about Charlie Breedlove."

"What about him?"

"I'm checking on a few things."

"It ain't got nothing to do with me."

Ben could feel himself growing increasingly impatient as he continued to stand in the steamy summer air. "Let me in, Tod," he said finally. "This is department business and I don't have time to argue about it." He pressed his hand against the door and felt it give way as Tod drew back.

Tod had already dropped into the small chair a few feet from the door, and for a moment Ben simply stood, his body framed in the doorway, and let his eyes adjust to the darkened room.

"Me and Teddy keeps everything closed up," Tod explained. "On account of being cops, you know?"

Ben stared at him quizzically.

"Grudges, I mean," Tod explained. "People out to get us."

Large sheets of tinfoil had been taped to all the windows, and they gave the room an eerie look of utter isolation, of something cut off from the outside world.

"It's for pictures," Tod said. "All this tinfoil, I mean."

"Pictures?" Ben asked. "You take pictures?"

"It's against pictures," Tod explained. "Against getting them taken of you. You put tinfoil on your windows, can't nobody see inside, can't nobody take no pictures." He leaned forward conspiratorially. "Like the federal boys, you know? I mean, the FBI." He laughed idiotically. "They'd take a picture of a man on his shitter if they thought they could use it against him."

Ben leaned against the doorframe. "Why would the FBI be interested in taking pictures of you, Tod?"

"Some things I believe," Tod said. "It makes them mad."

"What things?"

"About the niggers, mostly," Tod said with a sudden casualness.

He leaned forward. "I mean, you know how it is with the niggers, they all got—"

Ben waved his hand quickly to silence him. "Look, Tod, we have a serious problem in the department. It has to do with Breedlove, with his murder."

Tod sat back slightly but he didn't speak.

"Do you know about this little house on Courtland?" Ben asked.

Tod glanced away fearfully.

"I was in there," Ben went on. "I found a few things that could cause some people a lot of trouble."

"You mean Teddy? Cause Teddy trouble?"

"Yeah."

"Me, too?"

Ben nodded.

"Well, I don't see how," Tod said in a tightly drawn voice. "I mean, we got a right to our beliefs, right?"

"Your beliefs don't matter," Ben said.

"Well, what are you talking about then?" Tod asked quickly. "Them pictures." He laughed nervously. "Ain't they funny?"

Ben didn't answer.

Tod's voice took on a desperate edginess. "Listen, Ben—I wouldn't say this in front of Teddy, but with me it's just sort of a game, you know?"

"A game?"

"Like playing army, you know, like when we was boys."

Ben let him go on.

"Like playing," Tod sputtered. "I mean, it's nothing for anybody in the department to worry about. I just got them pictures and stuff—and sometimes I play with the guns a little." He shook his head vigorously. "But it ain't real. It's just for fun, that's all."

"Where were you last night, Tod?" Ben asked sternly.

Tod looked at him, puzzled. "Last night?"

"That's right."

Tod continued to stare at Ben, questioning. "Well, I was right here in the trailer," he said. "I was sick. I was running a fever."

"Where was Teddy?"

"He stayed with me. We're family. We all that's left of our family."

"Did either one of you leave the trailer?"

Tod shook his head.

"Did anybody come to visit you?"

Again Tod shook his head.

"Did anybody see the two of you in here?" Ben asked.

Tod laughed fearfully. "Well, nobody could do that, right? I mean, I got all this tinfoil on the windows."

Ben watched him gravely, his eyes bearing down. "Think, Tod," he said. "Did anybody at all see you and Teddy last night?"

Tod did not answer. He leaned forward again, this time running his fingers through his hair. "What is all this, Ben? What's last night got to do with anything? Was some other little nigger killed or something?"

"No," Ben said. "But Charlie Breedlove was."

Tod's lips parted silently.

"I found Breedlove's ring in that little house on Courtland," Ben said. "The one you and Teddy play your little games in."

Tod's eyes widened. "You think it was us?"

"Where'd that ring come from?" Ben asked coldly.

Tod stared at Ben, dumbstruck.

"You better come up with some answers, Tod," Ben warned him.

Tod shook his head. "Oh, God Almighty," he breathed. "They ain't no way I had anything to do with that. I been too sick. I been practically flat on my back for two days." He started to whimper. "I told Teddy we shouldn't have hung them flags and stuff. I told him it was too much for the average person to deal with."

Ben remained silent, watching Tod crumble slowly before him.

"I been puking all over myself," Tod bawled. "Got the runs too." He glared at Ben resentfully. "You pick up stuff when you work Bearmatch. You pick up things they brought with them from the jungle—diseases and stuff like that."

Ben leaned against the doorjamb, his eyes trained on Tod.

"Soaking wet with fever," Tod went on. "And I been that way for a long time."

Ben straightened himself. "You got a thermometer, Tod?"

Todd stared at him, baffled by the question. "Thermometer?"

"That's right."

"Yeah, I got one in the medicine cabinet."

Ben walked back through the narrow corridor, retrieved the thermometer and handed it to Tod.

"Put it in your mouth," he said stiffly.

"What for?"

"Just do it," Ben commanded.

Reluctantly, his eyes filled with confusion, Tod placed the thermometer in his mouth and waited nervously until Ben finally plucked it out.

"What is it?" he asked excitedly. "What's my temperature?"

"A hundred and two," Ben said quietly.

"See, see!" Tod cried jubilantly. "And I been like that for two whole days."

Thirty-eight

Tod and Teddy Langley were both relieved of duty and Teddy was arrested a few hours later. For the rest of the afternoon Ben and Luther made their way through the three tiny rooms of the house on Courtland Street.

"I gave McCorkindale your old job," Luther said as he slit open the mattress beside the window. "I didn't figure you'd go back to watching King anyway." He shook his head. "And if Sammy goes to sleep in his car, Daniels'll be there for backup."

Ben checked the rooms for hidden compartments, tapping lightly and listening for any hollow spaces which might have been dug out, then covered over, within the solid plaster walls.

Luther pulled a huge wad of stuffing from the mattress and felt through it for solid objects. "If they kept Breedlove's ring," he said, "they could have kept anything. The pistol they used on him, anything. Once people start doing stupid things, they's no limit to it." He stopped and stared at Ben pointedly. "And killing a brother officer, that's real goddamn stupid."

Ben continued to move along the walls, monotonously tapping them with the knuckles of his hand. In his mind, he could still see the thin red line of the thermometer as it inched up to one hundred and two. It was the sort of fact that argued against almost all the other facts that could be arrayed against it, a grudging, insistent detail that clung to him like a small note pinned to his suit.

"If you ask me," Luther said as he tossed a handful of ragged stuffing onto the floor, "they set Breedlove up. They lured him out here, killed him, then took him out in the country."

Ben said nothing. He bent down and ran his fingers along the floor, searching for loose boards. As he worked, he tried to move back through what he knew of Breedlove's death. Once again, he saw the body hanging limply from the tree, the bloody letters carved in his chest, his shattered face, the small dot of light that peeped through from the hole in the back of his skull.

Luther shook his head. "That's the way it is when you get too hot on something. It makes you crazy. Shit, Ben, there're times when I think it makes the Chief himself crazy."

Ben straightened himself, then moved on to the next wall, his mind still working the case, methodically moving through each sketchy detail. He could feel a steadily increasing unease. Too many questions were still rising from places where they should have normally been put to rest. He decided to ask one of them to someone other than himself.

"Why do you think they called it in?"

Luther continued to tear at the mattress. "Called what in?"

"Breedlove's body."

"You mean, to the sheriff?"

"Yeah."

Luther stopped, thought a moment, then went back to the mattress, sinking his hands deep inside. " 'Cause they were proud of it," he said sullenly. "They wanted somebody to see it."

"They pinned his badge to his shirt," Ben added.

"Yeah."

"Why?"

"Hell, Ben, how do I know?" Luther said. "For God's sake, they hung him up like a trophy. They're out of their goddamn minds. You don't deal with reasons for things when you deal with people like them." He threw the last of the stuffing onto the floor, then stood up and stretched. "I guess all hell's breaking loose in the park by now." He looked at his watch. "Demonstration was supposed to start at three sharp." He ran a few calculations through his mind. "I figure by now they're just about at the park."

Ben looked at him. "You can time it that close?"

"Got to," Luther said. "Time is everything in a situation like this." He nodded toward the far wall. "You done that one yet?"

"No."

"Well, I'll give it the once-over," Luther said. He walked over to the wall and began tapping at it. "You ask me, Teddy's not smart enough to think of a hiding place." He thought for a moment, his hand suddenly holding motionlessly in the thick hot air. "Course, that ring was pretty well hid."

"Why'd he take it?" Ben asked.

Luther resumed his search. "I don't know. Maybe for a souvenir. Something to remind himself of what a big tough guy he was." He shook his head disgustedly. "But he should have just kept his attention on Bearmatch. It don't take much to be a tough guy with the colored people. They're already beat down too much. But when you start screwing around with a brother officer, you better be ready to pay the price." He stopped his tapping again and looked pointedly at Ben. "If the Langleys did kill Charlie Breedlove, they're going to the electric chair for damn sure."

Ben nodded slowly, then went back to his search. He inspected each room in turn, emptied drawers, checked closets, opened the few cardboard boxes that were stacked here and there, heavy with undistributed books and pamphlets. Finally he went over the floors, probing for loose wooden slats. He found nothing but the trapdoor to the crawlspace beneath the house. He shined his flashlight into its darkness, then lowered himself down onto the dusty ground. The yellow beam swept left and right, lighting the most distant corners, but there was nothing at all beneath the house but the bare red clay, which, from all that he could tell, had rested entirely undisturbed for at least a hundred years.

He pulled himself up out of the crawlspace, then bent forward to slap the reddish-orange dust from his pants. The trapdoor was still open, its underside clearly visible in the light that poured in from the open shutters. He could see his own handprint clearly etched across its smooth surface, a dusty pattern of palm and outstretched finger. A few inches to the left, there was another handprint, dustier, less clearly visible, but unmistakably there, and which had been left when another, entirely different hand had pushed upward from the crawlspace. It was slightly larger than his own, the fingers longer and more slender, and for an instant it seemed to reach toward him, thrust out violently, as if desperately to cover his eyes.

The holding cells on the third floor of City Hall were packed with demonstrators, and they were singing loudly as Ben made his way down the corridor to the last cell on the right. It was quiet, and almost entirely empty, and as he looked in, his eyes staring between the bars, he could feel the sullen isolation that came from it, powerful as an odor, raw and resentful.

Teddy Langley sat upright on the edge of the upper bunk, his back curled forward, his eyes glaring at the seatless toilet bowl which rested near the center of the room. He looked oddly lifeless and shrunken, as if some vital force had been drained from him. He did not seem to hear the joyous singing which rocked the cellblocks all around him or feel the sweltering heat. He still wore his police uniform, the top button of his shirt still tightly snapped, the tie pulled snugly against his throat.

"What are you doing here?" he asked snidely as Ben let himself into the cell and closed the door behind him.

A burst of cheers followed the end of the song, then a long, sustained clapping of hands. Ben waited until it had all died away into the next rollicking hymn. Then he walked over to Langley and offered him a cigarette.

Langley glanced at the cigarettes but didn't take one. "Is this where you're supposed to come in and sweet-talk me into a confession?"

"Not unless you have something to confess," Ben told him.

"Well, I don't," Langley snapped. "So why don't you just go on home."

Ben said nothing.

" 'Bout time for the evening shift anyway, right?" Langley asked.

"More or less."

"What is it, five or six, something like that?"

"About five-thirty."

Langley nodded. "Yeah, that's what I figured." He slid backward on his bunk, pressing his back against the hard cement wall. "What you doing here, Wellman?"

"I thought I might talk to you a minute or two," Ben said.

"What about? You figure I killed Breedlove, right?"

"Maybe."

" 'Cause he was an informer," Langley said. "That's what they'll use for motive."

"Could be," Ben admitted.

"Did they arrest Tod yet?"

"No."

"Why not?"

"We're keeping an eye on him," Ben said. "But the mail we found in the house, it was all addressed to you."

"So there's nothing to connect him to the killing."

"Nothing yet."

"Except that he's my alibi," Langley said. "Of course, he could be telling a lie on that, right?"

"He'll go in on a perjury charge if he swears to it," Ben said. "He could be hit with an accessory if he knew about Breedlove before or after."

"You think I don't know that?"

"No, I think you do."

"Tod didn't know shit," Langley said exasperatedly. "Hell, I don't know shit as far as the killing's concerned."

Ben pressed the package of cigarettes toward him, shaking it slightly. "Sure you don't want one?"

"Ah, hell," Langley said. "I'll take one." He pulled a cigarette from the pack, then leaned forward and let Ben light it.

"I was over at the house most of the afternoon," Ben said as he waved out the match.

"I figured you would be," Langley said. "Find anything else? A pair of Breedlove's underwear, something like that? With his initials on it?" He shook his head. "It wouldn't surprise me what you found in that house. They could have planted anything."

"Trouble is," Ben said, "how'd they get in?"

Langley shrugged and took a pull on the cigarette.

"The windows were all nailed shut," Ben said. "And the doors hadn't been messed with."

Langley said nothing.

"Any other way in that house?" Ben asked pointedly.

"I don't know," Langley said. "I ain't been renting it but a few weeks. I didn't hardly ever go there." He laughed bitterly. "Maybe somebody came down the chimney. You know, like Santa Claus."

"The chimney's cemented over," Ben said. "Got any other ideas?"

Langley took another pull on the cigarette, then glanced to the right. "Them niggers sure can keep themselves stirred up, can't they?"

"You could go to the chair, Teddy," Ben said grimly. "We're taking about a cop. Informer or no informer, we're talking about cop."

Langley's eyes swept over to him. "Who wants me dead, Ben?" he asked almost gently. "I can't figure it out."

Ben stood silently, staring upward slightly, concentrating on Langley's face.

"Put up your right hand," he said finally.

Langley looked at him, puzzled. "What?"

"Put up your right hand."

Hesitantly, Langley lifted his hand, palm outward. "Like this?"

"Yeah," Ben said as he placed his own hand over it.

Langley's was smaller, the tips of his fingers barely reaching beyond the second joint of Ben's.

"What's this for?" Langley asked. "They already got my prints."

Ben drew his hand away, then stepped back over to the cell door, opened it and walked back into the corridor.

Langley continued to sit rigidly on the bunk, his hand still hovering in the air, fingers outstretched, as if reaching for an invisible bird. "I would die for my beliefs," he said fiercely. "But like a man, Wellman. Like a man. Not led down some hallway like an animal. Not with my legs in chains."

Ben nodded slowly.

"Not in the chair," Langley added determinedly. "Not in chains."

Ben closed the cell door and locked it.

"Not in chains, goddammit!" Langley yelled to him once again as he turned and walked away.

Several yellow Jefferson County school buses were lined up in the garage, and as Ben headed for his car he could see hundreds of faces behind their windows. Scores of state troopers in full riot gear ringed the buses. Inside the ring, McCorkindale paced back and forth along the side of one of the buses, slapping his nightstick rhythmically against his leg. From time to time he would stop abruptly, wheel around and smack the tip of his nightstick against the window. The faces behind the glass would jerk back reflexively, then stare sullenly as McCorkindale's enormous belly shook with mocking laughter.

Ben turned away, once again moving in the direction of his car. He was still a few yards away from it when he saw Patterson coming toward him from the other side of the garage.

"What are you doing over here?" he asked as they approached each other.

"I got the lab work on the Breedlove case," Patterson said.

"Where are you taking it?"

"Directly to Captain Starnes."

"Captain Starnes?"

Patterson nodded. "He'll probably take it straight to the Chief."

"What'd you find out?"

Patterson hesitated.

Ben stared at him accusingly. "What's going on, Leon?"

Patterson glanced left and right suspiciously. "All I know is that Captain Starnes wants me to report directly to him."

Ben looked down at the small yellow envelope that was nestled beneath Patterson's arm. "What's in the report, Leon?" he demanded.

Again, Patterson hesitated, but only briefly. "Nothing much, if you want to know the truth. The cause of death was pretty obvious. Like it always is."

"Is there anything that wasn't obvious?"

"Just that Breedlove must have been on the move a little bit that night."

"How do you know?"

"From what I scraped off his shoes," Leon said. "He had two different kinds of soil on them. One was a regular loose-grained loam. The kind you find in the fields to the north."

"Like the one we found the body in," Ben said.

"That's right," Patterson said. "It was stuck to another layer of something else, though. Some kind of whitish clay, very acidic. Those two kinds of ground, they don't exactly end up side by side." He smiled helplessly. "I know that's not much help."

"Is there anything else?" Ben asked immediately.

"As far as the . . . well . . . the mutilation, that was done after he was dead," Patterson told him.

"Anything on the knife that was used?"

"It had a serrated edge," Patterson said unenthusiastically. "And the blade was about an inch and a half wide at the hilt." He shrugged. "That's about all the help I can give you. Not much, is it?"

"No."

"You making any headway?"

Ben shook his head.

Patterson leaned toward Ben, lowering his voice as he spoke. "Is it true he was an informer?"

"I don't know," Ben said. "A lot of people think so."

"For the federal boys, you think?"

"I don't know."

"Well, it must have been somebody," Patterson said emphatically. "I mean, what's an informer do if he doesn't report to somebody?"

Suddenly Ben felt a strange night breeze envelop him, saw a dark lake glimmering in his mind.

Thirty-nine

The lights of the city blinked brightly behind the large office window, and as Davenport stood before it, they seemed to wrap around him like a shimmering cape.

"Has there been some break in the case?" he asked as he shook Ben's hand.

"Which case?"

Davenport looked at him, puzzled. "Doreen's case. Isn't that why you're here?"

"No."

"I don't understand," Davenport said. "I thought you probably came over to report on some new development."

"Are you used to that?" Ben asked pointedly.

"Used to what?"

"Getting reports from the Police Department."

"No," Davenport said. "Should I be?"

Ben thought a moment, then decided to go at it from another direction, drawing Davenport in slowly, entangling him in enough information so that finally he would not be able to squirm out of the net.

"Do you remember the last time we talked?" he began.

"Yes," Davenport answered. "It wasn't very pleasant. But then, you were accusing me of something. I'm not sure what. But it seemed to me that you thought I had something to do with Doreen's murder."

"Did you?" Ben asked flatly.

Davenport stared at him coldly. "Of course not."

Ben watched him silently.

"Why would I hurt a little girl?" Davenport asked. "What would I have to gain?"

Ben did not answer. "You said something about lives being at stake."

A fleeting look of sorrow passed over Davenport's face. It came and went so quickly that it appeared to have escaped from some deeply guarded quarter of his mind. For an instant it fluttered in his eyes, then vanished into the stern lines and set jaw which now watched Ben coolly from behind the polished desk.

"What lives?" Ben asked.

"It doesn't matter," Davenport said.

"Why?"

"It doesn't matter," Davenport repeated. "Let it go at that."

"Why doesn't it matter?"

Davenport said nothing. He stared at Ben unflinchingly.

"Because it's too late now," Ben said. He paused, waiting for Davenport to respond.

Davenport continued to sit stiffly in his chair.

"When you warned me not to keep at this case," Ben said, "you told me that I should let someone else do it. Do what?"

"I don't know what I meant by that," Davenport said, his voice weak, unconvincing, "I'm not even sure I said it."

"Let someone else do the looking," Ben replied insistently. "That's what you said."

Davenport nodded. "Maybe."

"Who was that someone else?"

Davenport's body grew tense. He did not answer.

"It was someone else in the Police Department," Ben told him. "Someone who was reporting to you."

Davenport remained silent.

"Charlie Breedlove," Ben said flatly.

Davenport drew in a long, slow breath. "And so I told you the truth, didn't I? There was a life at stake."

"How long had he been reporting to you?" Ben asked immediately.

"For several weeks."

"What about?"

"The FBI was concerned that there might be some kind of Death Squad in the Birmingham Police Department. They were worried about their agents, and a few other targets. One federal judge in particular, and a few other people. They mentioned a few names. There was a prominent businessman who's been actively trying to work with the Negroes. They thought he might be ripe for assassination." He shook his head. "Breedlove never really developed anything. He came up with the idea that Doreen's death might have been done to provoke the Negroes, cause them to riot. He thought the Death Squad might be behind it."

"Did he find any evidence of that?"

Davenport shook his head. "No. He told me that he got desperate one night and went after you."

"Me?"

"In your house," Davenport said. "He told me that he thought he scared you pretty well, but that you didn't tell him anything."

"I didn't know anything," Ben said.

"That's what Breedlove figured," Davenport told him with a slight smile. Then he stood up. "I could use a drink. Want one?"

"No."

Davenport walked to a small bar at the opposite end of the room and made himself a drink. For a moment he simply stared at the amber liquid he'd poured into the glass. Then he downed it quickly and returned to the desk. "I don't have to tell you how important it is for you to keep your mouth shut about all this. I mean, that Death Squad—it may still be out there." He shrugged. "Or it may be nothing. It may be purely imaginary, something they dreamed up in Washington."

"Well, somebody killed Charlie Breedlove," Ben said.

"Yes, somebody did," Davenport said. "Teddy Langley."

"How do you know that?"

"I don't know it for sure," Davenport said. "But Charlie was afraid of Langley. He thought that Teddy suspected him, and that if anybody had the making of a Death Squad type, it was Langley. I mean, for God's sake, he's been going after Bearmatch like some kind of avenging angel. And according to Charlie, he's really gotten brutal since the demonstrations began, talking even meaner than before." He hesitated, glanced at the window, then back at Ben. "There are times when I think he killed Doreen," he said. "Maybe he found out about me, too, and just decided to get even in some way."

"Would killing Doreen make it even?" Ben asked doubtfully.

"We're not talking reason here, Sergeant Wellman," Davenport said. "We're not talking high intelligence." He shook his head. "We're talking about something in the guts, like a fire in the guts. Who knows what that could lead to?"

"Did Charlie ever mention Langley's house?"

"House?" Davenport asked. "What house? I thought they lived in a trailer."

"They do," Ben said. "But Teddy Langley had a house, too."

"What kind of house?"

"It doesn't matter," Ben said, "if Charlie never mentioned it."

"Yes, but—"

"Did Charlie suspect anybody else?" Ben asked quickly.

"Of what?"

"Of knowing that he was an informer."

"I don't think so," Davenport answered.

"Starnes? Daniels? McCorkindale? Even the Chief?"

Davenport shook his head.

"Anybody outside the department?"

Davenport's lips curled downward. "I don't think Charlie knew many people outside the department."

"So you don't have any idea who fingered him?"

Davenport shook his head. "I'm afraid not." He turned toward the window. Beyond it, the city glowed in the summer darkness. "It could have been anybody," he whispered. "Anybody at all." He looked back at Ben. "That's the trouble with a situation like this," he said. "You just don't know who's who."

Forty

Outside his bedroom window, Ben could hear the agitated sounds of the crickets and the katydids. The soft whir of the single rotating fan served as a gentle background, but did nothing to relieve the heat. He lay on his back, a single sheet beneath him, his underwear clinging to his chest and thighs. Inside the room, the darkness was nearly total except for the small gray rays that came through the window, a sure sign that Mr. Jeffries was up and about, incessantly roaming the dingy corridors of the house across the street. From time to time a single car would whiz down the narrow street, some teenage hot rodder on his way to the late-night drag strips which dotted the rural counties that surrounded Birmingham and whose fabled ability to strip city boys of their hard-earned money had been legend since his youth.

He turned onto his side, closing his eyes tightly, drawing himself into a perfect darkness. He tried to think of nothing at all, shut down his mind entirely. But as the minutes passed, he found that his thoughts couldn't be marched into some separate room, locked up for the night and then released again in the morning. They were insistent, nagging, sleepless, and they plagued him like small animals gnawing at his flesh.

He saw Esther in his imagination as he had never seen her in his real life, stretched out on the iron bed he'd glimpsed briefly the day he'd come inside her house. She lay like him, sweaty, sleepless, her body shifting left and right, her eyes closed at first, then peering out into the darkness, peeling it back as she stared at the opposite wall, lingering first on the scattering of pictures her niece had taped to the unpainted walls, then on the single black and white photograph of Doreen, herself, a little girl in a worn, checkered skirt and black, buckled shoes who posed motionlessly on the steps of the Sixteenth Street Baptist Church.

He made a full turn, resting on his stomach, his face pressed into the pillow. Now the darkness was complete, and for a moment he almost slipped into its comforting oblivion. But his mind continued to resist, and so he squeezed his eyes together even more tightly, turned back onto his back, drew in a deep breath, waited a few minutes and then, finally giving up on sleep, opened them widely.

The soft gray rays which had penetrated the room a few moments before had disappeared, and so he assumed that Mr. Jeffries had returned to bed. He stood up and peered out the window, his eyes watching the gentle rise and fall of the slender branches of the small mimosa that stood beside his house. For a long time he remained at his window, trying to pull some of the night's determined quiet into his own mind. But the restlessness continued, and so he pulled himself to his feet, put on his trousers, walked into his living room and sat down in the old wooden rocker that rested near the center of the room.

The heat was thick and stifling, but rocking back and forth in the chair relieved it slightly, and Ben remembered how he'd slept in his father's arms, his small white face pressed into the old man's gray flannel workshirt. It was a gentle memory, but in his present frame of mind it became a disturbing one, mocking innocence, full of a strange despair, and to escape it, he got to his feet again, walked out onto the porch and sat down in the rickety, unpainted swing.

For a long time he sat quietly, his mind still moving from Doreen to Breedlove, pausing here and there to concentrate on some point in one case, then move on to some detail of the other. Slowly, his exhaustion began to overtake him, coax him back into the house. He walked into the living room, his head bent forward slightly as he headed back toward the bedroom.

The floor had not been swept in days, and a small rounded ball of dust and grit rolled silently across its wooden surface. He stopped, glanced about the floor, gearing himself up for the quick cleaning it already needed. Everything needed it. A layer of light dust and pollen lay on everything. The chairs, the small telephone stand, the coffee table. But the floor was worse than anything. A whitish dust had gathered in one corner of the room, layering there like a light, gritty snow. Other things had come from the yard, bits of leaves, grime, small slivers of sunbaked grass. But the dull white dust which had accumulated in the corner, blown there by the breezes that swept over the room each time he'd opened the front door, that was different, and as his eyes lingered on it, he realized that it had come from somewhere else.

Patterson's voice was thick with interrupted sleep. "What, what?" he stammered. "Who is this?"

"It's Wellman."

"Ben?" Patterson said, wonderingly. "What time is it?"

"Around three in the morning," Ben answered quickly. "Leon, listen, I'm sorry to wake you up, but I got a question for you."

"If it's about that ring, the news is bad," Patterson said. "Breedlove's ring was completely clean. No prints of any kind."

"It's not about his ring."

"What then?"

"His shoes."

"Shoes? Breedlove's shoes? What about them?"

"You said there were two different kinds of dirt on them."

"That's right."

"One was a sort of white clay?"

"That's right."

"What was it?"

"What do you mean?" Patterson asked faintly irritably. "I told you—a white clay."

"Where would you find that?"

"Not up in the northern counties, that's for sure."

"Whereabouts, then?"

"Well, it's the sort of stuff they use on road crews," Patterson said. "They mix it with plain granite gravel. That's the kind of clay it is."

"So where would you find it?"

Patterson answered immediately. "Gravel pits, probably. They'd be your best bet."

"Thanks, Leon," Ben said. He started to hang up.

Patterson stopped him with a question. "What's this all about Ben?"

"Nothing I'm really sure of."

"A hunch?"

"Maybe a little more than that," Ben said. "I'll let you know when I get back."

"Get back? From where?"

Even as he hung up the phone and headed for his car, he was not sure he had an answer.

Ben dropped his identification on the counter. "I was hoping you boys might be able to help me a little," he said.

The uniformed desk sergeant glanced at the badge. "Birmingham police, huh? What you doing out here?"

"Checking on a murder."

"In our jurisdiction?"

"No, mine."

The officer looked back toward the nearly empty office. "Well, this early in the morning, things thin out a little."

"I just need some information."

The man smiled, relieved. "Well, I'd be happy to give you what I can. Who you looking for?"

"Nobody in particular," Ben said. "A place."

"Well, we got a map of the whole area right on the wall," the man said happily. "Shoot."

"A gravel pit of some kind," Ben said. "You know, where they make chert."

"You mean in the whole county?" the man asked.

Ben thought for a moment, trying to remember. He could see Kelly Ryan's body swaying gently in the moist air and hear the rain falling across the tarpaper roof of his house. Over the rain, he could hear voices talking about Kelly, about the crazy things he said, the crazy accusations about an old Negro buried in a chert pit in Irondale.

"Just here in Irondale," Ben said, his eyes focusing on the officer once again.

"Well, we got one, all right," the man said, "but they wouldn't be nobody there until later in the morning."

"That doesn't matter," Ben assured him.

"Okay," the man said with a shrug. He stepped over to the map which had been spread across the wall and pointed to a tiny gray square. "It's right here," he said. "Dawkins Road goes right by it."

Ben found Dawkins Road only a few minutes later. It was long and narrow, and it spiraled its way up a hillside thick with the full summer growth of brush and forest. About halfway up the hill, the black pavement ended in a sudden jagged line. After that, the road narrowed even further, finally becoming little more than two clay ruts cut out of the undergrowth. The twin yellow beams of the headlights jerked violently up and down as the car plunged forward along the pitted road, and in his rearview mirror, Ben could see swirls of yellow dust rising in the hazy dawn light.

The gate to the gravel pit was fully open, and after pausing a moment at the entrance, Ben guided the car inside. A second narrow road led through the trees to a flat, unpaved parking area which had been blasted out of the side of the hill. A wall of jagged rock rose at the far end of the parking area, and Ben could see a small shed at its base. A large red sign warned that explosives were housed inside the shed, and that any unauthorized meddling with them was a federal offense.

Ben got out of the car quickly. For a moment he stared out over the edge of the hill. A few lights could be seen twinkling in the darkness, and far down below, the whistle of a freight train blew long and lean as it chugged toward Birmingham.

The whistle had entirely died away before Ben headed out across the parking lot. He kept his eyes on the wall of solid rock which rose above the small tin shed, but he'd already found what he was looking for. A wide swath of whitish-clay ground spread out from the base of the stone wall, and when he reached it, he bent down, scraped some of the clay onto his fingers and looked at it carefully.

The voice, when he heard it, seemed to slice him like a cleaver.

"What you doing here, mister?"

Ben turned instantly, his breath locked in his throat.

The man was dressed in bib overalls and a shortsleeve plaid shirt. He cradled a twelve-gauge shotgun in his naked arms, its long black barrel nosed slightly upward, toward the top of Ben's head.

"This ain't no lovers' lane," the man added threateningly.

"I know," Ben said softly.

"So what are you doing here?"

"I'm with the Birmingham police."

"You got any proof of that?"

"Yes, I do."

"Well, let's see it then," the man said coldly.

Ben lifted one hand into the air while the other crawled slowly beneath his jacket pocket and pulled out his identification.

"Just hold it up," the man commanded.

Ben lifted it toward him and watched as the man peered at it for a moment, then stepped back.

"You may be with the police," the man said, "but it still don't tell me what business you got up here."

"I'm looking into a murder," Ben said. "It might have started here."

"In the chert pit?" the man asked unbelievingly.

"Yes," Ben said. "Are you here every night?"

The man shook his head. "Naw," he said. "Company just put me on. It's my first night."

"Was anybody guarding the place before tonight?"

"No. They just decided to put a guy on because they's been a few little robberies."

"Robberies?"

The man laughed. "Yeah. It don't look like they's much to steal but rocks and dirt."

"What was stolen?"

"Oh, this and that," the man said. "Nothing much. But the company gets real jumpy about it. You know how it is, they got to keep track of things."

Ben forced a smile. "Yeah."

The man shook his head. "But murder—I ain't heard nothing about that."

"You wouldn't have heard anything about it," Ben told him.

"Who got killed?"

"A policeman."

"From Birmingham?"

"Yeah."

The man shook his head despairingly. "Well, don't that beat all." He smiled again, lowered the barrel of the shotgun to the ground and tapped the pouch of his overalls. "You want a drank?"

"No, thanks."

" 'Cause you're on duty?"

"No, because I don't want one," Ben said. He stepped away slightly. "I got to get back to Birmingham."

"Okay," the man said cheerfully. "Just wheel your car all the way around. You start backing up, you'll hit them ruts on the side of the hill."

"Thanks," Ben told him.

The man was still standing in the middle of the lot as Ben began the wide turn out of the lot. He circled slowly, waving at him as he passed, then guided the car up near the face of the stone. He could hear the spray of the white clay slapping up underneath the car as he pressed down on the accelerator and made his way back toward Birmingham.

Forty-one

The short gravel driveway in front of the Langleys' trailer was empty, and because of that, Ben was surprised when Tod Langley opened the door, rubbing his red-rimmed eyes with his fists, his body clothed only in a pair of tattered Boxer shorts.

"You come to get me?" he asked groggily.

"No."

"Ever-time I hear somebody knocking, I figure they've come to get me."

"Where's your car?" Ben asked.

"Which one?"

"Didn't you drive a Chevy, a '59?"

"Yeah."

"Where is it?"

"In the shop," Tod said. "Busted radiator. I guess it overheated."

"Which shop is it in?"

"Gallager's."

"How long's it been there?"

"Three days," Tod said. "Why, was you gonna take it?"

"Take it?"

"Like they did the Black Cat," Tod said. "They already took it away from us."

"When?"

"Yesterday," Tod said. "They sent McCorkindale over here for it. He said Captain Starnes told him that since me and Teddy was both suspended, we didn't have no right to ride around in it no more, and he wanted it back."

"Where'd McCorkindale take it?"

Tod shrugged. "I don't know. To the police garage, I guess. They'll probably scrape the paint off and make it look like a regular patrol car."

"Have you talked to Teddy?"

Tod shook his head, then looked at Ben worriedly. "They going to arrest me, too, Ben?"

"I don't know."

"They ain't got nothing on me, have they?"

"Not that I know of," Ben said.

"It's to please the niggers," Tod said emphatically. "That's what Teddy says." He opened the rust-stained door of the trailer slightly. "You want to come in?"

Ben could smell the mingled odors of unwashed clothes and dirty dishes from inside the trailer. "No, thanks, Tod," he said quickly.

Tod looked at him almost pleadingly. "It ain't right, Ben," he said. "Trying to pin that killing on us. We done what we was supposed to do in Bearmatch. We busted ass."

Tod went on for a while after that, almost playfully relating the crap games he and Teddy had broken up, the shothouses they'd raided. There was an eerie delight in his eyes as he spoke of throwing men downstairs, or tossing them through windows, and as Ben listened, his mind drifted toward the other Bearmatch which must have helplessly stood by and watched all this from behind its hundreds of cracked windows.

"We stirred them up," Tod concluded with a laugh. Then his face soured. "Maybe a little too much." He looked at Ben questioningly, his large, dull eyes blinking painfully against the harsh late-morning light. "That's what Teddy says. He says they're blaming us for stirring up the niggers."

"Who's blaming you?"

"The people downtown," Tod said. "The big wheels. Teddy says they're mad at me and him for bringing this whole shit-storm down on them. He says that if we hadn't kicked so much ass in Bearmatch, then the niggers would of stayed quiet." He looked at Ben intently. "You don't believe that, do you, Ben?"

As if from some great height that he had only lately reached, Ben saw the dark sprawl of Bearmatch as it swept out from the rusting railyards like a pool of oily water. He saw the unpainted clapboard houses, the muddy alleyways, the squat chicken-wire fences that cut across its face, dividing it into tiny grassless plots.

"No," he said softly, shaking his head. "No, I don't think they would have stayed quiet, Tod." He could feel his eyes grow narrow as he glared at him. "I think that sooner or later, they'd have come after you and Teddy with every goddamn thing they've got."

Gallager's Auto Repair was little more than a tin shed with a single hydraulic lift surrounded by an oil-stained assortment of parts and tools. A large faded sign proclaimed the lowest repair rates in Birmingham.

The Langleys' '59 Chevy was on the lift when Ben walked into the garage. A short man in coveralls worked beneath it, pulling strenuously at a long steel wrench.

Ben pulled out his badge, and the man stopped immediately.

"This car belongs to Teddy Langley, right?" Ben asked.

The man seemed to draw back slightly, as if afraid to answer. "Yeah, it does," he said hesitantly.

"How long's it been here?"

"Three days."

"You sure?"

"That's when it come in," the man said assuredly. "And it sure ain't in no condition to go out."

Ben's eyes drifted upward toward the side of the car. It was dusty and unwashed, but there were none of the whitish flecks which had been blown across the sides of his own car as he'd left the chert pit.

"I towed it in," the man said as he stepped out from beneath the car. "Teddy called me and had me pick it up."

Ben nodded. "They didn't have another car, did they?"

The man shook his head. "Not that I ever seen." He grinned broadly. "Except for the Black Cat," he added. "And they used that for most everything."

McCorkindale looked up from the piles of paper that lay scattered across his desk.

"Morning, Ben," he said.

"I was over at Tod Langley's this morning," Ben told him.

McCorkindale stared at him lazily.

"He said you picked up their patrol car yesterday."

"That's right."

"Who told you to do that?"

"Captain Starnes," McCorkindale said with a slight shrug.

"There wasn't much to it. Tod give me the keys without a fuss. He's scared shitless if you ask me."

"Where'd you take it?"

"Right downstairs," McCorkindale said. "You probably passed it coming in."

"I parked out front."

"Well, it's down there with all the other cars," McCorkindale said. "They're getting ready to fix it up again. You know, repaint it. Word is, the Langleys got way out of line—I mean, even before this Breedlove thing—and they're going to retire the Black Cat and forget it just as soon as they can."

"But they haven't done it yet?" Ben asked quickly.

"Far as I know, it's still down in the garage."

It was sitting in an isolated corner of the garage, but Ben saw it immediately, a gray blur which seemed to lunge toward him from the corner of his eyes. As he approached it, the cat took on the shape that he remembered, brutal, snarling, its reddish eyes glaring hatefully back at him as he walked toward it through the thick gray air of the garage.

The car had not been washed, and as Ben circled it slowly, he noted what appeared to be months of accumulated dirt, dust and grime. It was as if the Langleys had purposefully made the car look as battered as possible. At the back, he bent down and looked for signs of white clay on the sides of the fenders and the rims of the tires. They were both entirely free of the white flecks which had been spewed across his own car as he drove out of the chert pit. He bent lower and carefully checked the treads of the tire itself. Nothing.

He was already back on his feet when he heard footsteps moving toward him from the entrance of the garage. He turned immediately and saw Luther walking toward his own car.

Luther slowed when he saw Ben, nodded quickly, then walked over.

"What are you doing down here?" he asked.

"Checking a few things out."

"On the Black Cat?"

"Yeah."

"What things?"

"This business with Breedlove and the Langleys," Ben said. "Some of it doesn't fit together very well."

"Like what?"

"Well, that second handprint on the trapdoor, for one," Ben told him. "It wasn't mine."

"So what?" Luther asked. He shook his head dismissively. "That could have been anybody's. It could be one of the Langleys'."

"Why would they come in their own house through a dirty crawl-space?"

"Maybe because they got shit for brains, Ben," Luther said irritably. "Those two never did have much sense, you know."

Ben looked at him doubtfully.

"Or it could have been a burglar," Luther added. "Somebody trying to break in."

Ben said nothing.

"You don't think so?" Luther asked crisply.

"No."

"Why not? You know something I don't?"

"Well, I think I know where Breedlove went the night he died," Ben said.

Luther took a small step toward him. "You do? Where?"

"A gravel pit over in Irondale."

"What was he doing over there?"

"Looking for a body."

"A body?" Luther asked unbelievingly. "Whose body?"

"I don't know," Ben told him.

"What do you know?" Luther demanded. "I mean, for sure."

"Nothing."

"Well, where'd you come up with this bullshit about Irondale and a body?"

"From the Langleys."

Luther chuckled. "And you believed them?"

"The day Kelly Ryan died," Ben began slowly, his mind suddenly drawing back to the dank room, the sound of the rain, the gentle sway of the body, "Daniels was talking about how Ryan had always thought that Teddy and his brother had killed a colored man and buried him in a chert pit in Irondale." He started to continue, then stopped.

Luther watched Ben silently, his face almost motionless. "Well, go ahead," he said impatiently.

Ben remained silent, still trying to bring the entire scene back into his mind.

"What are you getting at, Ben?" Luther demanded.

Ben did not answer. Over the patter of the rain, he struggled to hear again all the voices he'd heard that day in Kelly's room. He heard phrases, muttered words, strained laughter. All of it tumbled chaotically in his mind.

"This whole business with Kelly Ryan sounds like bullshit to me," Luther said sternly. "And we don't have time to go on wild-goose chases."

Ben nodded, his eyes staring straight ahead, focused on the dark-green car which was parked only a few feet away. It was the same car he'd seen only a few days ago as it sat parked next to the edge of Kelly Ingram Park, but it looked different now. Before it had been dusty, and Ben remembered the track which Langley had left in the dust on its hood when he'd slid off it. But now it gleamed softly, despite the dark air which surrounded it, and in the sheen which spread across it, he could tell that it had not only been recently washed, but carefully and meticulously waxed as well.

"Whose car is that?" Ben asked as he nodded toward it.

Luther turned to look. "That green one?"

"Yeah."

"That's Daniels' car," Luther said.

Ben's mind raced back to Kelly Ryan's dreary bedroom. He saw it frozen before him, each man in a place that now seemed oddly destined for him, some of them in the open, full of their belief, while others waited in the wings, silently holding to the curtain.

"Daniels," he whispered.

"That's right, Daniels," Luther repeated loudly. "Looks like he's finally give it a wash."

Ben nodded. "I wonder why," he said almost to himself.

"Probably for Breedlove's funeral," Luther said matter-of-factly. "They were partners, after all."

Forty-two

Charlie Breedlove's funeral was held late in the afternoon at a small graveyard outside Birmingham. Several neighbors gathered beside the grave, but only Daniels and Ben came from the department, and they stood side by side, perched beneath a maple tree, and watched as Mrs. Breedlove and her son wept softly in the fading light.

"Nobody's safe," Daniels said mournfully after the service had ended. "Maybe it's true, you know."

"What?"

"About how the good die young."

Ben did not answer. He could see Breedlove's wife and son as they stood peering down into the grave. He wondered how much Breedlove had told them, how much they knew of what he really was.

"You know what really bothers me about all the trouble we're having down here now?" Daniels asked suddenly.

Ben shook his head.

"The fact that so many innocent people get drawn into it," Daniels said. "White and colored. I mean, you take all these little kids they got locked up downtown. Shit, Ben, the most of them don't have the slightest idea what they're doing." He bowed his head slightly and dug the toe of his shoe into the ground. "And as far as Charlie's concerned, we may not ever know what he did, or if he did anything at all."

"Well," Ben said tentatively, "we do know what happened to him, though."

"But we don't know why," Daniels said. "At least not for sure."

Ben added nothing else, and for the rest of the service the two of them stood together, watching silently until the last prayer had been said. Then they walked over to Mrs. Breedlove.

"I'm real sorry, Susan," Daniels said quietly as he shook her hand. "And I just want you to know that we're going to find out who hurt Charlie, and we're going to make them pay."

Daniels stepped aside quickly and allowed Ben to shake Mrs. Breedlove's hand. Then the two of them made their way across the cemetery to the plain dirt road that wound its way through it.

Daniels shook his head regretfully as he walked slowly at Ben's side. "They sure did get him in the ground in a hurry," he said.

Ben nodded.

"I hear the department made them," Daniels added.

"How could it make them?"

"Otherwise it wouldn't pay for the funeral," Daniels said matter-of-factly. "And you know how it is, nobody has any money. They wanted a rush job, and so they put the pressure on."

"Why would they want a rush job?"

"Well, any way you look at it, Ben, Charlie was sort of embarrassing to the department." He shrugged. "I mean, on one side you got an informer, and on the other, you got a victim, right?"

"Victim? Of what?"

"The people who wanted him dead."

"You mean the Langleys?"

"Whoever didn't want to be informed on," Daniels said. "It could been have been anybody."

They stopped at Daniels' car, pausing for a moment to look back toward the city. Its stunted skyline was barely visible through the summer haze.

Daniels's eyes drifted back toward Breedlove's still-open grave. "Do you think Charlie really was an informer?" he asked.

"Somebody thought so."

"You got any leads?"

Ben shrugged. "Everybody seems to figure it must have been the Langleys."

"Do you?"

"I guess."

"You got any evidence?"

"Well, Breedlove's ring had to have come from somewhere."

"Yeah," Daniels said sadly, as if mourning the fate of his fellow officer. "Yeah, I guess you're right."

"Unless it was a plant," Ben added casually. "Like a throwdown, something like that."

"Is that possible?"

"Anything's possible."

Daniels laughed bitterly. "Yeah, in this kinda work, that's the truth." He grasped the door handle of the car. "Well, I got to get on back to town."

"You on duty tonight?"

"Naw," Daniels said, waving his hand. "Since I was Charlie's partner, they're giving me the day off. What about you?"

"I'm still looking into a few things," Ben told him.

Daniels opened the door and slid in behind the wheel. He leaned out the window, loosening his tie, and took in a long breath. "I'm going to be looking for a new partner," he said. "You interested?"

"Maybe."

"Course nobody could replace Charlie."

Ben smiled quietly and stepped back. "I guess not." He drew his eyes along the body of the car. Daniels had done a thorough job. If there had ever been any tiny white flecks on the car, they'd long ago been washed off with a power nozzle and a buffing brush. "Looks like you gave it a good polishing," he said lightly.

Daniels chuckled slightly. "Yeah, and it needed it. The funny thing is, Charlie was always complaining about that. He said I shouldn't let it look so dirty and beatup."

In his mind, Ben saw Breedlove's own car, battered, caked with an oily city grime. "He didn't exactly practice what he preached, did he?"

Daniels' eyes flashed over to him. "What?"

"Well, he never kept that old Ford of his looking very sharp."

"No, he didn't," Daniels said. "That's funny, I never thought about that." He smiled quietly. "I'll miss him, though. We didn't get together much after work, but on the job, Charlie was a good old boy."

Ben nodded silently.

Daniels hit the ignition. "Well, take it easy, Ben."

"Yeah," Ben said. He stepped back once again, edging himself onto the grassy shoulder of the road.

Daniels revved the engine slightly, then threw the car into gear and pulled away.

Ben watched as the car moved forward. A cloud of red dust swam out from behind it, and he could hear the sounds of tiny bits of gravel as the rear tires threw them up against the bottom of the car. It was the same sound he'd heard the night he'd pulled out of the chert pit, and he realized that what he'd heard was the sound of hundreds of bits of moist white clay as they collided with the bottom frame of the car. Still wet from the drenching rains of the day before, they must have clung to the complex steel underbelly of the car as they struck it with tremendous speed. Only the most thorough washing could have gotten rid of them entirely, and a wax job would have done no good at all.

Patterson answered the phone immediately.

"Leon," Ben said urgently, "I've been trying to get you all night."

"I was at a VFW meeting," Patterson said. "You're a veteran, aren't you, Ben?"

"Yeah."

"You ought to think about joining."

"Listen, Leon," Ben said. "I want you to do something for me."

Patterson did not answer.

"It's important," Ben added.

"Is this official business?"

"Yes."

"About what?"

"Breedlove."

"Well, I don't know, Ben," Patterson said, his reluctance still in his voice. "What is it?"

"I want you to call up Harry Daniels. Tell him you have something on Breedlove that he might be interested in."

"Like what?"

"I want you to tell him that you've come up with something that you don't know what to do with. Tell him it's about Breedlove, and that you don't trust me with it, and so, since he was Breedlove's partner, you've decided to come to him. Then you pick him up at his house. Make sure he goes with you. I want him to leave his car at his house."

"What if he won't do that?"

"Make sure he does."

"Just a second, Ben," Patterson said. "This is beginning to be a lot more than I think I'm up for."

"I don't have anybody else, Leon," Ben said.

"How about the Captain?"

"Leon," Ben said pointedly, "I am talking about trust."

"You don't trust the Captain?"

"No."

There was silence, and through the line, Ben could almost hear Patterson's mind running through its accounts.

"I'd really appreciate it, Leon."

"All right," Patterson said. "So I call Daniels up. What do I tell him? I need some kind of bullshit story."

"Tell him about the gun we found in the storm drain," Ben said. "Tell him that you've found out it was Breedlove's."

"Is that true?" Patterson asked unbelievingly.

"Yes," Ben said. "But it doesn't matter. It's just something to tell Daniels."

"Okay," Patterson said. "But what do I do when I'm finished with the story?"

"Then you drive him back home," Ben said. "But be sure you stop off somewhere first and call me at Daniels' house."

"You got his number?"

"Yeah," Ben said. Then he gave it to him. "When you call," he added, "I won't say anything. I'll just pick up the receiver. You tell me where you are, then hang up."

"All right," Patterson said. "I got it."

"Good," Ben said quickly. "Now, before you pick him up, I'll be parked near Daniels' house. After that I'll be in the house until you call me. Be sure you get there at eight o'clock. And keep him out for at least half an hour. You understand?"

Patterson did not reply.

"Leon, do you understand what to do?"

"Ben, am I in danger doing this?"

"No."

"You sure?"

"I'm sure."

Patterson took a shaky breath. "All right," he said finally. "I'll be there at eight."

Patterson was right on time, and from his car only a block away, Ben could see Daniels as he walked across his small lawn, nodded quickly to Patterson, then got in the car.

Ben waited until the car had disappeared over a small hill before he headed slowly down the cement sidewalk, made a quick left at the fence and moved as casually as possible down the driveway to Daniels' garage. He opened the door immediately and went inside. For a moment, he stood motionlessly in the darkness, waiting for his eyes to adjust. Slowly, the interior of the garage revealed itself, and Ben made his way through a snare of tangled water hoses and lawn chairs to the rear side of Daniels' car. He didn't bother to inspect the tires or fenders, but instead pulled himself immediately underneath, took a small flashlight from his jacket pocket and turned it on. In the yellow light beneath the car, he could see hundreds of flecks of white clay, and he quickly scraped a few samples into his hand, then brushed them into a plain paper bag.

A single door led from the garage into the house, and Ben had no trouble picking the lock. He stepped into the kitchen, closed the door and then walked into the living room.

Daniels had left a single lamp burning in the room. The telephone rested beside the lamp, and Ben tried to decide where to start looking first before Patterson's call. He let his eyes wander about the room. There were pictures of Daniels in his World War II khakis, and several old photographs of what Ben took to be his mother and father. An ancient upright piano stood at one corner of the room and a small writing desk at the other. Everything looked ordinary, and more than anything, it reminded Ben of his own living room, the worn rug and Salvation Army furniture, all of it arranged haphazardly.

He was still glancing idly about the room when the phone rang. He snapped up the receiver and waited. For a brief moment there was no sound. Then, suddenly, he heard a deep, resonate voice, thick with the rhythms of Bearmatch. "Okay. Midnight, like we planned. Same p-place. Collins Avenue. After that, before dawn, GM, Thirty."

Then there was nothing but a sharp click, followed by the dim buzz of the severed connection. Ben sat back in his chair, the voice still echoing in his mind.

The phone rang again a few minutes later, and again Ben picked it up.

"I'm at Smith's Cafe," Patterson said. "We're leaving now."

Ben said nothing.

"I'm hanging up now," Patterson said nervously. "Smith's Cafe. Downtown. I'm leaving right now. It should take about ten minutes."

Forty·three

Ben had already been sitting in his car for several minutes when he saw Patterson pull up to the curb in front of Daniels' house.

Daniels got out immediately, then stood in the yard, waving quietly, as Patterson drove away. For a time he lingered outside, his tall, thin body clearly visible in the light from the streetlamp a few yards away. He looked up and down the street as if expecting another car to come for him, then he turned abruptly and walked back into the house.

Ben eased his car into gear and silently drifted a short distance down the low, sloping hill. When he had coasted far enough to see the edge of Daniels' driveway, he stopped, pulled out a cigarette and waited. During the next hour one cigarette followed another, until he finally snuffed out the last one from the pack. The air inside the car was a thick, tumbling blue, despite the open windows, and from time to time he had to lean forward slightly and wave it away in order to keep Daniels' house in clear view.

While he waited, Ben continually repeated the message he'd heard earlier in the evening: Collins Avenue. Midnight. After that, before dawn, GM, Thirty.

Collins Avenue was a stretch of sparsely populated road which ran in a winding path from one side of the city to the other, from the railyards beyond Bearmatch to the spacious lawns of Mountain Brook. It was sometimes used by people who were in a hurry to get across town and who wanted to avoid the more commercial boulevards that crisscrossed the city in the same general direction. Other than that, it remained more or less unused, a stretch of broken road which had long ago been replaced by the carefully tended avenues which funneled people rapidly into the central business district. Ben tried to reconstruct every inch of Collins Avenue, moving first along the shaded lanes of Mountain Brook and down the mountain through nearly deserted forest lands, then into the sprawling shanties of Bearmatch, where it finally came to a dead end at the railyard fences.

Then he edged his mind over to the second part of the message, trying to decipher where the next meeting place might be. GM, before dawn. He knew that there was a General Motors plant on the outskirts of Birmingham, and it seemed at least possible that this was the place Daniels was supposed to go. But who was he going to meet there, and why?

Ben was still going over the possibilities when the taillights of Daniels' car flashed on suddenly. He leaned forward quickly, peering toward the tiny red lights of Daniels' car and waited until it had backed out into the road. It headed north, then rounded a small curve and disappeared.

Ben glanced at his watch. It was eleven forty-five. He hit the ignition quickly and pulled away. He could see Daniels' car again as he made the turn at the end of the street. It was moving slowly, as if Daniels were simply out for an evening drive.

The car continued west until it reached Collins Avenue. Then it turned north and headed toward Mountain Brook. Traffic was sparse, as it always was on Collins Avenue, and Ben had no trouble keeping up with Daniels' car. "Like we planned." The phone call had just been confirmation. Daniels expected the meeting. He followed it at some distance, keeping his headlights on dim, until the lights of the city fell away and Collins Avenue turned into a narrow, badly kept and generally abandoned road which meandered through the most heavily wooded section of the city.

Daniels slowed his pace considerably as the forest thickened around him, and Ben eased back too, trying to stay as far away as possible without losing track of Daniels' car altogether. Still further on, he saw the brake lights go on and watched as Daniels' car pulled off the road and stopped beside an isolated picnic table.

A deep trench stretched across the road just where Daniels had pulled over, and Ben slowed down slightly before moving over it. Then he drove a few hundred yards further, pulled off onto a narrow dirt road and got out. He walked a few yards into the woods, far enough that he could not be seen by any other passing cars, and headed toward the picnic table.

Daniels was sitting quietly at the table, smoking a cigarette, one leg crossed over the other. The darkness was very thick, but the orange glow of the cigarette faintly illuminated Daniels' face. For a while there was no other light, but after a few minutes another car appeared, moving slowly down the avenue from downtown. It slowed as it neared the trench, passed over it and nosed in just behind Daniels' car, bathing it for a moment in a thin, silvery light.

Daniels did not stand up. He simply watched the car, still smoking idly.

A tall man got out of the other car and walked over to Daniels. He was very large, and when he spoke, Ben recognized the voice. It was the same one that had delivered the message on Daniels' telephone only an hour or so before.

"Everything went g-good, I guess," the man said.

"No problems at all," Daniels told him. "Teddy'll take the rap for Breedlove."

"You used the ring?"

"Yeah," Daniels said. "But I didn't have to tip anybody. Someone else stumbled onto Langley's place."

"Who d-done that?"

"That's not your business," Daniels said sharply. "You got your own work to do. Is it set?"

"We thought it was f-fucked-up."

"Because of the girl?"

"Uh huh," the man said. He chuckled softly. "B-but we handled that."

Daniels spit on the ground. "Yeah, you handled it," he scoffed. "And it was a real sloppy job if you ask me."

"Well, we didn't have much t-time now, did we?" the man asked coldly.

"Just the same," Daniels told him, "too many goddamn bodies have been piling up on this thing." He crushed the cigarette onto the cement table. "It was supposed to be just two, remember? One for one, to seal the relationship." He shook his head. "When we do business from now on, it's got to go smooth. I got places to go, and I can't be cleaning up messes like this all the time."

"You getting scared?"

"Do I looked scared to you?"

"Way you're t-talking," the man said, " 'bout that girl and all."

Daniels waved his hand, already tired of the conversation. "The girl's not my business anyway," he said. "It wasn't my doing and I don't want to get into it." He glanced about nervously, and Ben lowered himself into the dense undergrowth. He could smell the honeysuckle in the air, and somewhere in the distance he could hear water falling gently, as if over a small falls.

"The thing is, I did my half," Daniels added crisply. "Now you do yours. The rest of it's up to you, like I said. I don't want to get into it."

The man took an envelope from his jacket pocket. "I guess *this* is your b-business, though," he said playfully. He waved it back and forth tauntingly. "I b-bet you'd like to get into this."

Daniels nodded.

"Here you are, then," the man said as he handed the envelope to Daniels.

Daniels snapped the envelope quickly from the other man's hand. "This is just the beginning," he said. "We're going to run Birmingham without the kind of shit we've been having lately."

"On both sides of the f-fence," the man said.

"That's right."

"B-by the way," the man said, "where's them Black Cat boys? I got to keep up with them." He laughed softly. "Least till dawn, right?"

"Teddy's in jail," Daniels said. "And that where he'll stay for a long time."

"Yeah, you fixed him good, d-didn't you now?"

"The other one's off the force," Daniels replied curtly.

"We d-don't care about the other one," the man said. "We didn't n-never care about him. He just a little n-nothing, like the man say. He ain't got much sense."

"Well, Teddy's finished," Daniels said. "You don't have to worry about him anymore." He smiled tauntingly. "I delivered, didn't I?"

"You d-done what you said," the man told him dryly.

"But your half of the bargain," Daniels added, "that's still not finished with."

"Don't you worry n-none," the man assured him. "It will b-be."

"It'd better be," Daniels warned. "When it happens, the Chief'll be finished. There's no way he'll be able to hold on to the department after all that shit breaks loose. The new mayor'll go in without a hitch, and he'll be looking for somebody new to run the department."

"And you'll be r-right there waiting for him," the man said.

"That's right," Daniels told him. "You'll be rid of your problem, and I'll be the new Chief." He glanced down at the envelope and smiled. "With a little campaign war chest all my own."

"You real smart," the other man said. "You maybe the smartest white m-man I ever seen."

Daniels continued to go through the envelope. Then his head suddenly snapped up.

"You're five short," he said. There was an edge in his voice.

"We had expenses, like you know."

Daniels stood up. "And like I said, that's not my problem."

"You picked the p-place," the man said sternly. "That's what f-fucked us up."

"Bullshit," Daniels blurted. "Look around. It's perfect. I can't help it if that little bitch came right out of the blue."

"We c-could of done it down south a little, the Black Belt."

Daniels laughed derisively. "Yeah, and wouldn't that have looked funny? You and me pretty as you please, sitting on a park bench having a nice little talk, with all the old farts whittling together."

"That ain't what m-matters," the man said. "We had expenses."

Daniels' leg began to shake nervously. "I made a deal with you. You need somebody out of the way. So do I. It was supposed to be a fair exchange."

The man said nothing.

"The way it stands right now," Daniels said, "your problem's settled. But mine's still hanging around."

"B-but not for long," the man said. "Before the sun comes up, just like I say."

Daniels stood up. "Look, I did everything I was supposed to. I did more. Shit, I even picked up what you needed to take care of the girl. I didn't have to. But it was there, so I got it for you." He drew in a deep breath. "Now I want my money."

For a long, icy moment, the two men stared at each other. Then suddenly the large man laughed heartily.

"Sure, you d-do," he said, still laughing. "Gimme the envelope, I'll get it for you. I was just kidding you a little. I'll put it in, give it right back."

Daniels reluctantly handed him the envelope, then watched warily as the man walked back to his car and got in.

"Here it is," the man said after a moment.

Ben looked toward the car. He could see a slender white envelope waving in the dark air.

Daniels walked over to the car. "You do business the right way, this whole town'll be ours one day." He laughed coldly. "You must have learned by now that you could use a friend in high places."

"Sure enough," the man said happily. "Sounds g-good to me."

Daniels leaned forward and reached for the envelope. Suddenly a short hiss broke the air. It sounded like a quick spurt of water. Then Daniels' body staggered backward, his hands grabbing for his chest. Another hiss, this time with a short, stubby flash of orange, and Daniels' face jerked upward, white in the moonlight, a jet of blood spurting from his forehead.

For one frozen instant Ben stood in place, unable to move. Then suddenly his body returned to him, and he sprang up out of the brush, grabbed his pistol and plunged through the undergrowth. The lights of the car shot through the deep green woods as it raced backward through the gravel, its rear tires churning up dusty arcs of loose dirt. As it sped away, the sound of its wheels peeling across the pavement were almost as thin and wrenching as Daniels' final cry.

Forty-four

"What did you hear exactly?" Luther demanded.

Ben shook his head. "I already told you."

Luther stared at him lethally. "I got two cops murdered in about as many days, Ben. Now I want some goddamn answers."

"They talked about a deal," Ben said wearily. He glanced at the clock over Luther's desk. It was nearly three in the morning, and in the last two hours he'd sat in Luther's cramped office and meticulously repeated his story at least twenty times.

"But you couldn't make out what it was?" Luther asked.

"It sounded like somebody had paid Daniels to set Langley up."

"For Breedlove's murder?"

"I think so."

"And that's all?"

"The Breedlove murder was only Daniels' part of some deal," Ben told him. "The other man hadn't done his part yet."

"And you have no idea what that part was?"

"Only that it's going off sometime before morning," Ben said. "Maybe over at the GM plant."

"We got that whole place surrounded," Luther told him.

"But it may not be the GM plant," Ben said. "He just said, 'GM. Before dawn.' "

The Chief slouched in the far corner, chewing a cigar, his eyes staring accusingly at Ben. His eyes were puffy with lack of sleep, but when he moved, it was in quick jerks, as if only his eyes were tired. "And you say this other fellow, he was a Nigra?"

"Yes."

"How you know that for sure, Sergeant?"

"By his voice."

"A lot of people stutter," Luther said.

"It wasn't the stuttering."

"Was it some kind of Nigra talk you heard?"

Ben shook his head. "Just his voice."

"So it might not a been a Nigra at all, is that right?" the Chief said. "I mean, what about his face?"

"I couldn't tell in the dark."

"Course not," the Chief said. He thought a moment, then looked quickly at Luther. "Has the FBI got any colored agents?" he asked.

Luther shrugged. "I don't know."

" 'Cause this right here could be a set-up job all the way around," the Chief said. He looked at Ben. "Maybe Daniels was the real informer. Maybe he killed Breedlove to cover for hisself."

Ben said nothing.

The Chief's eyes drifted slowly toward the ceiling. "Maybe he was working for the FBI the whole time. Maybe the Justice Department. It wouldn't matter. They all want us to look like a bunch of murdering animals down here." He took out what was left of his cigar and blew a column of thick smoke into the already stiffling air. "And God knows they all want to get rid of me." He smiled at his own cleverness. "They could get two birds with one stone, you know?" he said. "Get rid of me and Langley. Lord, that'd be paradise for them." He looked at Luther. "What do you think about that idea, Captain?"

"It's possible," Luther said.

The Chief chomped down on his cigar, popping the ashy tip up slightly. "What about you, Sergeant?" he said to Ben.

Ben shrugged. "I don't know."

"Well, I'll tell you this," the Chief said. "If they try to drive me out of office, they'll have a hell of a fight on their hands." He considered it a moment longer, then crushed his cigar into the small ashtray on Luther's desk. "The new mayor, he sure wants me out, too. Maybe Daniels cooked up something with him and his cronies."

Ben said nothing.

The Chief shot one stubby finger into the air. "So we got the FBI, the Justice Department and the new city government, all of them wanting to get me out of office so they can put themselves or somebody they like in my place." He grimaced at the gall of such a conspiracy. "Lord, boys, we got to watch our backs."

"Yes, sir," Luther said immediately.

The Chief walked over to Ben and put his hand gently on his shoulder. "Go home and get some sleep, Sergeant," he said. "Nothing more to do tonight." He laughed. "Even the Nigra leadership's over at Gaston's, all tucked in, nice and peaceful." He laughed. "They're getting their beauty sleep so they'll be all rested up for the mess they'll be making tomorrow."

Ben nodded.

"And try not to think about all this shit too much," the Chief added in a deep, paternal voice. "Just remember, you're like everybody else that's still on two feet in this business. You're lucky to be alive."

But Ben did not feel lucky, and as he slumped down in the swing on his front porch, loosening his collar in the thick summer night, he could sense, however vaguely, that his days were numbered in the department. For a long time he tried to imagine some other work that might suit him. Men had left the force before, but what had happened to them after that could hardly be thought encouraging. Some ended up as pot-bellied security guards at the local hotels and country clubs. Others, already addicted to the ceaseless movement of the streets, took jobs as cross-country truckers, endlessly hauling tons of steel or food or diapers from one coast to the next. There had to be a better way to make your daily bread.

He slapped at a mosquito, then lit a cigarette. He knew that the smoke would drive them away, and so he took several deep draws, letting the smoke out in a steady stream as he turned his head slowly, seeding the humid air with tumbling clouds. It reminded him of the spray of tear gas he'd seen rising over the heads of the marchers the day before. That was all part of what he had not bargained for in 1949, when he'd come on with the department. He'd not bargained for the violence of recent days, whether it was on the streets or in the countryside, or simply in someone's hate-filled mind. But more than anything, he realized suddenly, he had not bargained for doing wrong, being asked, being ordered, to do what he knew was wrong. He thought of that first young boy he'd pushed across the park, then shoved through the open doors of the school bus. He had not bargained ever to be looked at like that boy had looked at him.

He stood up restlessly, walked to the edge of the porch and leaned against the old wooden pillar that supported it. It creaked with the weight of his body, but he continued to press against it anyway, his eyes peering off across the street, then over Mr. Jeffries' house, to where he could see the blinking lights at the top of the Tutweiler Hotel. There were only a few of them. Everyone else was sleeping. The whole city was sleeping, it seemed to him, even the Negro leaders, as the Chief had said, tucked securely in their beds, deep in the heart of the Negro district. It seemed to him that they could probably sleep more soundly than anyone else in Birmingham. They were doing what they had to do. Their souls were full of purpose. And even at the practical level they were safe. At the Gaston Motel, they were at the dead center of the colored district, protected even from the white communities that encircled them. Only other Negros could get close to them, and because of that, at least until morning, they were . . .

He felt his fingers tighten around the slender wooden post as his mind flew back to the dark ground off Collins Avenue, the deep Negro voice of the man who spoke to Daniels, promising to deliver on his half of the bargain: GM, before morning, Thirty. He felt a slender rod of steel go through him, hard and cold.

GM.

Gaston Motel.

He rushed back into the house and dialed the Gaston Motel.

The desk clerk answered sleepily.

"What room is King in?" Ben demanded.

"What?"

"What room is King in?" Ben repeated.

The man did not answer.

"Tell me, goddammit!" Ben yelled.

Silence.

Ben realized that his own voice was a white voice, a wild white voice. He softened it immediately. "Please," he began. "It's important. I got to know."

The clerk hung up.

Ben hit the button on the cradle, raised another dial tone, then called headquarters. It was on the second ring that he realized there was no one there he could trust, no one he could rely upon. He slammed the phone down and rushed from the house, leaving his front door wide open behind him.

At the car, he hit the ignition, then drove his foot down hard against the accelerator. The rear tires spun wildly, and the car lunged forward, peeling loudly on the smooth black pavement. He continued to press down on the accelerator. The dark lines of houses whisked by him in a blur. He could feel the wind ripping through the car, blowing back his hair, flapping loudly in his shirtsleeves.

The pale neon sign of the Gaston Motel shone dully ahead as he raced toward it, then pulled over to the curb. Sammy McCorkindale was snoozing in a patrol car only a few yards from the driveway. A lone young man stood in the driveway itself, his hands toying with a two-way radio.

It was Leroy Coggins, and he stared quizzically as Ben's car thundered toward him, then screeched to a halt.

"What room is King in?" Ben yelled as he got out of the car.

Coggins stared at him, astonished. "What are you doing here?"

Ben grabbed him by the shirt collar. "Is he in Room 30?"

Coggins' eyes narrowed angrily. "You think I'd tell you?"

Ben shook him hard, jerking his head violently. "Is King in Room 30?" he screamed.

The anger drained from Coggins' eyes. "Look, man, I can't just . . ."

Ben ripped the radio from Coggins' hand and pressed the transmitter button. "Get King out!" he cried. "Get everybody out of Room 30!"

He handed the radio back to Coggins. "Go make sure they're getting out of there, Leroy," he demanded frantically.

Coggins backed away, his hand grappling with the radio, bringing it to his mouth. "Get everybody out!" he yelled as he ran toward the motel.

Ben backed into the street, staring at the plain, cement-block façade of the motel. He could see figures moving on the second landing, and even from the distance, he could hear their fists knocking on doors, their voices crying desperately.

He glanced toward the patrol car. McCorkindale was still snoozing obliviously.

When he looked back toward the motel, the second landing was clear, and he could see several people making their way quickly down the stairs and out into the parking lot.

The explosion came in a sudden flash of white light. The men in the parking lot dove onto the pavement, some of them scrambling under cars to escape the falling glass and cement that showered down upon them from the blast on the second floor. The door of Room 30 had been blown from its hinges and now tumbled over the metal railing and smashed through the windshield of the car parked beneath it.

The parking lot filled with people almost instantly. They stood, staring thunderstruck, as the first white light of the explosion spread out in a wave of orange flames. For a moment, an odd, unworldly silence descended upon everything, and there was nothing but the sound of the crackling flames. Then, suddenly, the cries of the people began to break the air, and along with them, the distant wail of scores of sirens. Within minutes police cars began screeching up the streets, and behind them, the fire engines.

Ben stepped back across the street and watched as the people around the motel began to mass themselves, shouting angrily and tossing rocks and bottles at the police and firemen. It was as if this small motel, burning in the night, had become their final redoubt, the place where they intended to make their ultimate stand. The police moved forward under a hail of debris, their nightsticks drawn. Behind them, waves of state troopers stood in tight ranks, waiting for their signal.

It came almost immediately, and Ben stood, staring in disbelief, as the troopers drove fiercely into the crowd, firing tear gas before them. But the crowd continued to resist, retreating slowly, but fighting as it retreated, pausing to scream curses and hurl bricks, bottles and pieces of shattered wood at the charging troopers. Steadily, the troopers themselves picked up their pace, driving the crowd toward the flaming wall of the motel. They fell upon the stragglers with a terrible vengeance, beating them to the ground, then dragging them unconscious to the waiting police vans. Wave after wave of troopers charged across the littered parking lot, seizing people already dazed by the gas or stunned by nightsticks and finishing them off with a final blow to the head or kick to the belly.

Ben stood silently, half-hidden behind a tree, his face flickering in the light from the fire, his mind desperately returning to where it had all begun, his ears tuned to the voice of the man who had met Daniels in the darkness, listening to every word, the deal, one for one, King for Langley. King was an obvious target. But Langley?

Coggins came up a moment later, his clothes torn and dirty, his whole body limp with exhaustion.

"Look at that," he said as he nodded toward the smoldering ruin of the motel.

"They'll rebuild it," Ben said.

"The whole city's going under," Coggins said. "Everybody's hurting. Negro business. White business. Everybody." He shook his head. "Even the shothouses are empty."

Ben felt something in his mind open up suddenly like a small, long-buried chest. "Yes," he whispered.

Coggins looked at him. "Yes, what?" he asked.

But Ben was already gone.

Forty-five

The early morning darkness had only begun to lift as Ben drew his car over to the curb not far from the house. He got out quietly and tucked the envelope he'd picked up at an all-night drugstore into his trouser pocket. Then he walked to the back of the car and opened the trunk. The short black tire iron was nestled in a bed of oily rags, so he wiped it carefully before tucking it securely into the back of his trousers. Then he took off his jacket, tossed it into the trunk and closed the door.

The man on the porch got to his feet quickly as Ben made his way up the cement sidewalk. He stood, his legs spread, and peered down at him, waiting.

"I was expecting Gaylord," Ben said lightly.

The man did not speak.

"Doesn't Gaylord usually keep guard around here?"

"Gaylord d-don't keep nothing," the man said in a voice that was deep, faintly musical, and which Ben recognized instantly even without the stammer.

"Who are you?" Ben asked.

"Name's D-douglas."

"Mine's Wellman," Ben told him. "I came to see Mr. Jolly."

" 'B-bout what?"

"Business."

"Well, he don't usually see n-nobody this time of night."

Ben smiled coolly. "He might want to see me," he said.

The man laughed. "Why's that?"

"Because I'm replacing Teddy Langley here in Bearmatch," Ben said in a lean, vaguely threatening voice. "And I figured it would be a good idea if I met the man that everybody says runs this part of Birmingham."

"So you is with the p-police, that right?" the man asked.

"That's right," Ben said. He patted his shoulder holster. "That's why I've got this." He smiled. "I'm supposed to wear it, on duty or off."

"Well, the thing is, Mr. Jolly d-don't allow no guns 'round him."

Ben shrugged. "I can understand that," he said. He lifted his arms. "Take it."

The man stepped forward and snatched the pistol from Ben's holster. He lifted it lightly up and down in his hand. "Got good balance."

"I'm pretty good with it, too," Ben said lightly. "But I don't think I'll be needing to use it very much in Bearmatch."

The man smiled happily. "Well, now, that's go-good to hear. Mr. Jolly, he gon' be glad to know that. 'Cause them Black Cat boys, they been giving him a lot of shit."

"Yeah, I know," Ben said. "That's a shame, too. But they're not around anymore."

"Mr. Jolly, he be glad to know that, too."

"I figured he would be," Ben said. "And I reckon I can understand that, too." He shifted slightly on his feet. "Course we need to have a little talk first." He stared around casually. "And I sort of figured this time of day was better than broad daylight."

"Yeah, you right 'b-bout that," the man agreed. He smiled broadly, his white teeth gleaming in the porch light. "Well, you stay right here. I'll tell Mr. Jolly you waiting on him."

Ben stepped up to the porch as the man disappeared into the house. Quickly, he checked for the tire iron, keeping his fingers wrapped loosely around it until the man returned.

"Okay," the man said as he came back through the screen door. "Mr. Jolly say he see you now."

"Thanks," Ben said.

The man stepped to the side, waiting for Ben to pass in front of him.

"After you," Ben said politely.

The man nodded quickly and turned toward the house.

The tire iron hit him exactly where Ben had intended, and he went down hard, his body slamming against the plain wooden floor, a wave of blood spreading down his neck, soaking his shirt collar. Ben straddled him immediately, then cuffed him. The man groaned slightly, but remained unconscious. His breathing was shallow but rhythmic, and as he stepped over him and headed toward Jolly's office in the back of the house, Ben half-hoped that there'd be no breath left in him at all when he came back.

Roy Jolly was sitting behind his desk when Ben entered. He was dressed in a bright-red smoking jacket that looked two sizes too big. An enormous gilded mirror hung on the wall behind him, and as he stepped up to the desk, Ben caught his own reflection in it, worn, bedraggled, a face that suddenly seemed so old and broken that he could hardly recognize it.

"Douglas tell me you come in place of the Black Cat boys," Jolly said.

Ben nodded.

"They been pushed aside, that right?"

"Yes."

Jolly did not smile. His voice remained almost expressionless, a dry wind blowing through dry reeds. "How come you wants to see me?"

"I hear you run Bearmatch."

"I in business," Jolly said modestly. "A businessman, he got to keep his ear to the ground." One eyelid drooped slightly. "Got to keep his eye on the sparrow, ain't that right?"

Ben said nothing.

"Ain't nothing took from nobody that they ain't let it go," he said. "That's the truth, ain't it?"

"Except life," Ben said. "I'm not sure Daniels wanted to let his go."

Jolly's head tilted to the right slightly. "What you want, Mr. White Man?" he asked.

Ben stared at him silently.

"People do for me, I do for them," Jolly said. "That's the way it is in this world. Ain't no paradise." He laughed softly. "More like Hell, you wants to know the truth of it. More like Hell." He leaned forward slightly, his small brown eyes bearing down on Ben. "How come you got Bearmatch?"

"I wanted it," Ben said.

"So did them Black Cat boys," Jolly said. "They come in here, starts messing around. I say, 'Okay, I lets you mess. I don't fuck with you.' " He waved his finger at Ben menacingly. "For a time, I do it. For a little time, I lets you get it out of your system. Least till you figures it out. Then we makes a deal."

"What kind of deal?" Ben asked.

Jolly grinned boyishly. "One thing for another."

"But the Langleys wouldn't make any deals."

"No, them boys wouldn't make no deal," Jolly said. "You know why? 'Cause nigger money, they wouldn't have none of it." He laughed at their stupidity. "Now money, it's jes' one color. It ain't white. It ain't black. It jes' green, that's all." He waved Ben forward gently. "Step over to the light," he said. "I seen you before."

Ben stepped toward him, his face now bathed in the red-tinted lamplight that came from Jolly's desk.

"Oh yeah," Jolly said lightly. "You come in here before. You come looking in on that little gal."

"That's right."

"You settle that one?"

"I think so," Ben said. He waited a moment, then added, "Collins Avenue."

Jolly stared at him, unmoved. "You was there tonight."

"Yeah."

"Was you in it with Daniels?"

"No."

"What you there for, then?"

"I was looking into something else," Ben said.

Jolly shrugged. "It don't matter to me what you seen," he said. "You come to me like you should have done. I ain't going to let you go away mad."

Ben stared at him silently.

Jolly leaned back slightly. "What you wants from Roy-Joy, huh? You wants a little gal for yourself? I got plenty of them. Sweet as candy."

Ben did not answer.

"Money, maybe," Jolly said. "Got plenty of that, too."

"When I was here last time," Ben said, "you told me how you like to see a man face to face when you make a deal with him. Do you remember that?"

"Don't have to remember nothing," Jolly said. "The whole world already in my head."

"That's what you did late one Sunday afternoon," Ben told him. "You met Harry Daniels on Collins Avenue."

Jolly stared at Ben calmly.

"You met face to face with him, like you always do," Ben went on. "You thought you'd be alone. But a car came by. It was a dark-blue Lincoln. There was a deep rut in the road, so it had to slow down quite a bit as it passed. There was a little girl in that car. You saw her, but what mattered is that she saw you. She was from Bearmatch, so she must have recognized you."

"She wave at me," Jolly said almost tenderly. "Sweet little thing. Big smile on her face." His eyes shifted over toward the door, as if looking for Douglas. "It surprise you, don't it? It surprise you that I come right out and say it?" He laughed. "But it don't matter now. 'Cause you come to me, and ain't nobody going to go home mad."

Ben watched him icily.

"Daniels was a fool," Jolly said. "He say he just want this and that. But in his eyes, he want everything." He smiled. "You look different to me. You look like I could do my business with you."

Ben remained silent.

"That's right," Jolly went on. "Your eyes, they tell me we going do business, you and me. And when you do business with somebody, you got to come clean about things. You can't have no secrets. In Bearmatch, we don't have no lies. Ever-body know ever-thing. Ain't a living soul don't know how ever-thing work." His hand lifted up gracefully. "They all know who bring in the whiskey and the whores. They wants them." He laughed. "Daniels, he want to be a big shot. He want to be Chief of something. But the old Chief, he still around." He shook his head, chuckling to himself. "Can't kill him. That wouldn't do no good. Got to get rid of him in some other way. Got to embarrass him."

"By killing Martin Luther King," Ben said.

Jolly released a high, piercing cackle. "They be a terrible uproar over that, now," he said. "Ain't no Chief going to still be around when the smoke clear on that one." He shook his head. "And that little shit Daniels, he think he going be Chief after that." His face curled into a snarl. "He ain't got enough sense for that. He don't even know how to show respect. He like them Black Cat boys. He hate Bearmatch." He lifted his head grandly. "But I loves Bearmatch. I knows what it need the most."

Ben said nothing.

"Relief," Jolly said loudly. "A little relief that a man can get from a drink of whiskey and a gal."

"You killed Doreen," Ben said.

Jolly smiled. "Done for me."

"Did Douglas rape her, too?"

Jolly scowled. "The ole fat boy done that," he said, "not Douglas. He don't need no little girl. He got a good-looking woman for his own self." He waved his hand. " 'Sides, Doreen already dead when Bluto climbed on her. Douglas say, 'She want you, boy. She your wife. Go 'head.' " He shrugged. "That Bluto, he never was worth nothing to me till right then."

Ben said nothing. He could see it all as if it were a film unrolling in his head. He saw Doreen's small body shudder as Bluto ravaged her, then Bluto's own body slump forward as Douglas fired the pistol a few inches from his head.

Jolly smiled coolly. "We took off that ole ugly ring and stuck it in the girl's dress," he said. He leaned back slightly. "Now see what I mean, I didn't have to tell you that. But I wants you to know that I ain't kept nothing back. You and me, we works together." He drew a single envelope from some papers on his desk and slid it toward Ben. "This for you," he said. "I ain't greedy." He smiled knowingly. "This be nothing to you down the line." He shoved the envelope a little further across the desk. "But you can take it anyway."

Ben did not move. "Langley was only half the deal," he said, "The other half was King." His hand crawled toward the tire iron. "Are you going to try again?"

Jolly smiled. "The folks in Bearmatch, they think he can give them what I do," he said. "But they wrong 'bout that. He come in and whoop them up, then he fly off to the next place. But me, I here forever."

Ben could feel his fingers as they touched the steel rod at his back. "Are you going to try again?" he repeated.

Jolly said nothing.

"You missed him this time," Ben said.

Jolly grinned. "But they's always another one. And the Chief, he ain't out yet."

Ben drew the tire iron from behind his back and slapped it loudly in his hand. "Leave King alone," he said resolutely.

Jolly smiled cheerfully. "Why? You gon' do it your own self?"

Ben lifted the tire iron and heaved it toward the mirror. It crashed into it only a few inches above Jolly's head, sending a shower of glass over him, filling his lap, gathering on the shoulders of his smoking jacket like a thin layer of sparkling snow.

"I don't know how all this is going to turn out," Ben said in a hard, utterly determined voice, "but I've come to tell you this. Whatever happens to King, happens to you."

Jolly's body jerked left and right as he slapped the glass from his jacket. "Douglas!" he screamed. "Douglas!"

Ben reached across the desk, grabbed the wide lapels of the smoking jacket and pulled Jolly forward. "Whatever happens to King, happens to you," he repeated. Then he dragged him over the desk and tossed him sprawling onto the floor. "I don't have time to argue with you," he said in a voice that had suddenly grown strangely calm in its iron resolution. "I just have time to stop you."

Forty-six

The first bluish light of dawn was only beginning to filter into the air when Ben made his way back downtown. He passed the old ballfield where he'd first glimpsed Doreen Ballinger's tiny hand, and then on along the littered road which bordered the Gaston Motel. Part of the motel itself was still smoldering, and in the morning light, Ben could make out the remains of Room 30, its charred interior and blasted walls. State troopers stood in ranks before the ruins, their rifles slung over their shoulders like dead animals, their shoulders hunched wearily as they stared about, their eyes nervously combing the trees and neighboring buildings for snipers. All around them the metal frames of burned-out cars rested in a strange silence which was broken only by the first awakening birds.

Once at headquarters, he placed the envelope on Luther's desk, then told him all he knew.

"I don't know if all this is enough to arrest Jolly and his people," he said, "but whoever takes over Bearmatch should be told about it."

Luther sat exhausted behind his desk, has face still soiled from the battle at the motel.

"Maybe you should take it over, Ben," he said. "Maybe the people over there'll trust you."

Ben shook his head, then took out his badge and laid it down on Luther's desk.

Luther stood up quickly. "I know how you feel, Ben," he said. "But we could use you for a few more days."

"No."

"But they're planning a big demonstration this morning, and . . ."

"No," Ben repeated. "No more."

. . .

As he left headquarters for the last time, Ben realized that he had one more duty still left to him. He got in his car and drove toward Bearmatch. Long lines of Negroes were moving down the broken sidewalks toward the Sixteenth Street Baptist Church, but they seemed hardly to notice him as he sped by them, moving steadily but slowly toward the heart of Bearmatch.

Mr. Ballinger was sitting quietly on his front porch when Ben got to the house. He did not move as Ben got out of his car, then walked through the tiny gate and up the rickety front steps.

"I was wondering if I could talk to your daughter for a few minutes," Ben said.

"She ain't here," Mr. Ballinger said.

"I drove by the place she works," Ben said. "I didn't see her around there."

"She ain't at work. She's with the rest of them. They all going downtown."

"You mean for the demonstration?" Ben asked.

Mr. Ballinger nodded. "She gone for that, yes, sir. She probably at the church by now."

"Thank you," Ben said as he turned and walked back to his car.

Scores of people were already flowing down the steps of the church when Ben got there. He stood where he had stood so often before, but now he was almost alone, except for the state troopers. The Langleys were gone and Daniels and Breedlove were dead. Only McCorkindale remained, lazily leaning against a telephone pole as he watched the procession pass him slowly on its way to Fourth Avenue.

Several minutes passed before Ben spotted Esther coming down the stairs. He moved toward her quickly, joining the crowd as it surged down the street, the people singing now and clapping hands.

"I wanted to tell you a few things," he said quickly as he stepped up to her.

She turned to him, surprised. "You better go off, now," she whispered vehemently. "You shouldn't be around here."

"I know what happened to Doreen," Ben said.

Esther's eyes widened.

"It was Roy Jolly," Ben said. "He made a deal with some people in the Police Department. Doreen saw him make it."

Esther's eyes glistened in the bright sunlight. Her body trembled slightly, then stiffened. "All right," she said, "you told me. Now you better be gone from here."

He did as she asked, melted away from her, but continued forward with the crowd, keeping pace with the line of march until they flowed over the hill at Fourth Avenue. He could see ranks of state troopers and firemen as they stood in a thick line at the bottom of the hill, blocking off the business district of the city. For an instant he stepped out further from the crowd and let it flow on without him. Then, suddenly, he began walking again, slowly, steadily, only a few feet from the great moving bulk of the march. He could see the Chief as he stood at the bottom of the hill, his small eyes peering at the approaching crowd. When they were near enough, he lifted his megaphone and shouted to them.

"This march will not continue," he cried.

But the people proceeded anyway, and Ben walked along at a distance beside them, his eyes straight ahead, his heart pounding wildly as he came nearer and nearer to where the firemen and troopers waited.

The march stopped only a few feet from the Chief's position, and for a moment the two groups stared silently at each other. Then the Chief shouted into the megaphone again, warning them to go back to their churches and neighborhoods, that the march would have to end.

Suddenly a man stepped out in front of the crowd and addressed the men behind the Chief, addressed them personally, almost intimately, as if speaking in a quiet, persuasive voice to each man individually.

"We have done nothing wrong," he declared, "and we only want the freedom that is supposed to be for every American in this country."

The Chief stepped back slightly, then turned on his heels and headed back toward his men.

The other man did not seem to notice him. He continued to speak to the ranks of policemen and firemen.

"We have a right to be treated like human beings," the man cried. "We're just people, like you. We want the things you want."

His voice rang over them, and Ben could see some of the firemen's hoses begin to droop limply in their hands as they listened to him. He could see them glancing at one another, their lips moving softly.

"We have the right to pray," the man declared. "And we are